Bernice Rubens was born in  at the University of Wales, of

Her writing career began when she was thirty and around the same time she started work in the film industry. For some time, Bernice alternated between writing novels and making films. For the last ten years she has concentrated solely on writing. Her sixteen novels to date include the Booker Prize Winner *The Elected Member* and *Five Year Sentence* which was shortlisted for the Booker Prize. In 1987, Bernice was on the Booker Prize jury and she has also won the Welsh City Council Prize for *Our Father*. Two of her books have been successfully transferred to film; *I Sent A Letter To My Love* and most recently *Madame Sousatzka*, directed by John Schlesinger and starring Shirley Maclaine. *Kingdom Come* is her latest novel.

Bernice's other love, apart from writing, is playing the cello. She has two daughters.

BERNICE RUBENS

Kingdom Come

An ABACUS Book

First published in Great Britain by Hamish Hamilton Ltd 1990
Published in Abacus by Sphere Books Ltd 1991
Reprinted 1991

ISBN 0 3491 0043 8

Printed and bound in Great Britain
by Cox & Wyman Ltd, Reading

Sphere Books Ltd
A Division of
Macdonald & Co (Publishers) Ltd
165 Great Dover Street
London SE1 4YA
A member of Maxwell Macmillan Publishing Corporation

In memory of my mother

Prologue

At the time I was staying a while in Istanbul with the excuse of brushing up my Turkish. I was already reasonably fluent, but with that fluency of an academic nature. In other words, though I could read and translate with ease, and carry on a reasoned argument, I could make little headway with the man in the street. And such was my purpose as I wandered through the market-places of the city, eavesdropping on the stall-holders' chatter, and understanding barely a word.

On one such evening, a Friday it was, I chanced by a mosque. The muezzin was moaning across the courtyard, and having nothing else to do, I thought I might enter and watch the faithful at prayer. Hitherto, I had hesitated at entering a mosque, because orthodox believers, of whatever creed, tend to be rather picky about their places of worship, but that evening I considered it my right as a tourist to satisfy my curiosity in whatever came my way. I passed through the huge portal and left my shoes at the door. They were of the native kind, a shuffling sandal, and looked at home amongst the clusters of footwear that lined the threshold. On entering I noticed the remarkable dome, a mosaic of stained glass that filtered the waning sunlight into a rainbow. It was an awesome sight, and for a moment threatened my comfortable and long-acquired agnosticism. I hurried to the prayer-mats and knelt alongside the others and was relieved to find that, after a few moments, my homely scepticism had returned. From time to time I looked up and around

3

the small congregation. At one of these peeking moments I caught the eye of a worshipper who was doing likewise and quickly I lowered my head. But when I dared look up again, he was still staring at me. I made to pray yet again but could not resist checking on him, only to find each time that he was doing the same with me. I became nervous; he had singled me out as a trespasser. I would have left, had not my exit been barred by a further row of worshippers who knelt behind me. I was forced to kneel it out until the end of the service. My knees were hurting me and part of the pain was fear.

At last everybody rose. Nobody was in a hurry, and haste in that company would have looked undignified as well as guilty. So I took my time as I manoeuvred my trembling exit. But he was already at the door, his shoes only a few feet away from mine. I shod myself quickly and shuffled off, and almost immediately I heard his sandalled steps behind me. Soon he was alongside and I dared to look at him. Again I found him staring at me but his manner was shy and I was no longer afraid. It seemed that he wished to talk to me, so I smiled to give him encouragement.

'Did you enjoy our service?' he said.

I nodded, not wishing to offend him.

'But you are not a Moslem,' he said.

'No,' I came clean. But not all that clean. I am a Jew, but in the courtyard of a mosque, Jews are rarely the flavour of the month.

He said no more until we were in the street and well clear of his place of worship.

'Are you a Jew?' he asked.

'Yes.'

'They have much in common, your religion and mine.'

They don't, I thought to myself, except on the periphery, but I was not going to argue with him.

'What is your business in Istanbul?' he asked. 'Are you a tourist?'

4

'No, I am a writer,' I said, 'and I'm interested in Turkish literature.'

He touched my shoulder. 'I would be honoured if you would come to my home for supper,' he said.

I heard pleading in his voice, a certain urgency, as if he needed someone to confide in. I was doing nothing that evening and I had never been invited into a Turkish home. I was happy to accept his invitation.

He lived not far from the mosque, and he was silent as he led the way. His house was in an avenue set back amongst trees. The area seemed comfortable without being rich. I was surprised that he had no key for he knocked on his own front door. After a while a woman answered. She looked uncommonly like my own mother, with that same nervousness in her fingers as she picked at her apron.

'We have a guest, Leyla,' my host said.

I noticed how she glanced at her husband with an undeniable question in her eye.

'It's all right,' he said.

Then, with her husband's sanction, she welcomed me and led me into the dining-room. I was not prepared for what I saw. Indeed I was astonished and not a little confused, for the sight of that dining-table shipped me right back into my childhood. I saw the three-fingered candelabra, the candles flickering as my mother waved them thrice into her blessing, and at the head of the table stood my father, the silver wine-cup in his hand. I heard him singing his welcome to the Sabbath, breaking the plaited loaf at his side. I recalled how, in the street, my host had remarked on the similarities of our faiths, but there was nothing Moslem about that table. I noticed how, at that moment, he was drawing the curtains of the dining-room, taking meticulous care that not a chink of light was visible. When he was satisfied, he groped in the half-light for the lamp-switch and motioned me to a seat at the table. I watched how his wife lit the candles, blessing them one by one. 'Good Sabbath,' she said as she took off her apron. Then she

5

sat down as her husband raised the cup and blessed the table.

'My name is Osman,' he said. 'And my wife is Leyla.'

I gave them my name in return, but refrained from uttering my thoughts. I could not help feeling that it was up to him to offer some kind of explanation as to why, with the smell of the mosque so lately upon him, he was now holding a Kiddush cup in his hand. I wasn't sure who was taking whom for a ride: Allah or Yahweh.

'You are bewildered,' he said.

'Yes,' I answered. 'I don't begin to understand it.'

'We are Dönmeh,' he said.

I shrugged, for the label meant nothing. With all my academic training, the word was unknown to me. I supposed it was a street word, but I doubted whether that was Osman's style.

'Have you not heard that word?' he asked.

I shook my head.

'As you see,' he said, 'we are Jews. My wife, her parents and mine, and theirs before them.'

'But you worship in a mosque,' I said.

'We are outwardly Moslem, but in secret we practise the Jewish faith.'

'But why?' I asked, wondering whether it was any of my business.

'We are simply following the example of our Messiah Sabbatai Zvi, the Holy One, blessed be his name. We follow in his path and worship according to his teachings. We are known as the Dönmeh. That is the Turkish word for "turning", used in a derogatory sense. Renegade, turncoat.'

I detected an undeniably evangelical zeal, and I was wary. I hold religions of any kind to be of little value. Each one of them implies a 'chosenness', an 'élitism', and such implication leads to belligerence. I, for my part, am happy with the faith I was saddled with at birth, and give it as little regard as I would any other. Yet my curiosity was aroused. I have always been attracted to the clandestine.

6

'Who was this Sabbatai Zvi?' I asked.

Osman was happy to embark on his story. But he gave it to me swiftly, and in digest fashion, throwing out the odd tit-bit here and there, enough to tease me into further research, for it was clear, even from his highly condensed version, that there was far more to Sabbatai's story than his follower was prepared to reveal. I plied him with questions, which he parried. He wanted to ascertain my genuine interest. It was clear that Sabbatai's story was no fireside tale. It was the story of one man's disturbing faith, and faith of any kind is not lightly told. I asked Osman if I might return and record his story with a view perhaps to translating it for a wider audience. This possibility fired his evangelical zeal, and he readily agreed.

Thus I heard the story of Sabbatai Zvi.

Over the next months I spent many evenings at Osman's and Leyla's home, the blinds carefully drawn against our subversive exchange. The story-telling took almost a year to complete. The tale itself was simple enough, but it relied heavily on interpretations of the Kabala, in which book Osman was fairly learned. At the end of it, I think I had won Osman's trust, as he certainly had mine.

'Will you write the story?' he asked. 'It needs to be told.'

'I will write it,' I said, 'but for my own needs. I'm not interested in spreading gospel.'

He smiled. 'Then I shall give you something as a precious loan,' he said.

He unlocked his bureau and handed me a sheaf of parchment. 'These are very dear to me,' he said. 'They have been handed down in my family for many generations. But Leyla and I have no children. After our deaths, they are doomed to an unopened cupboard in a library. I would like them to be read and their thoughts published. They are an intrinsic part of Sabbatai's tale. They are fragments of a journal, and now you know enough of the story to piece it all

7

together. Let us say that they are the Gospel According to Saul.'

'One of his disciples?' I said.

'Yes. But he was more than that. Much more.'

It was a generous offer and I thanked him. And, though Osman had not meant it so himself, I regarded the loan as a form of gentle blackmail, that it was now incumbent upon me to commit to paper the story of Sabbatai Zvi. And this I give to you, reader, guided by Osman's telling and his precious sheaf of fragments.

1

An odour of something or other

In Poland, in the small town of Homel, Saul's birthplace, Rabbi Vlonski had a dream. God came to him and told him that the birth of the Messiah was at hand. He awoke with joy and cradled his new-born son in his arms.

'Saul,' he whispered. 'You will live to be redeemed.'

That was in the year of 1626.

In that same year, in the coastal town of Smyrna, nowadays called Ismir, halfway down the western shores of Turkey, Sabbatai Zvi was born. The date, according to the Jewish calendar, was the Ninth of Av. An auspicious day, for it marks the anniversary of the destruction of the Second Temple. A day of mourning and, according to Jewish tradition, the day on which the Messiah would be born. On that day, Mordecai Zvi was preparing to go to the synagogue. His wife Clara, big with child, was folding his prayer-shawl.

'I shall pray for your safe delivery,' he said, although his first-born was not due to enter this world for at least three weeks. He kissed her forehead. 'Eat something,' he said. 'You need not fast today.'

He threaded his way out of their cluttered living-room. The room also served for sleeping. The bed stood in one corner and, opposite, a wardrobe. For Mordecai, the wardrobe was a memory of his father's home in Patras. When he had left Greece as a young man, his father had insisted that he take the wardrobe so that he would have something ready to establish a home. But it was more than that. He meant it

11

as a link between them, a constant reminder of his parents' love, both for each other and for himself. So, together with his friend Nissim Arditti, they filled the wardrobe with all their worldly goods, and between them they carried it like a coffin to Smyrna. Mordecai had never seen his parents again, and each time he passed that piece of furniture, he touched it in their memory.

He went down the rickety steps into the shop below. The marble slab which, on a weekday, was laid end to end with plucked chickens, was bare and wiped clean. A few chicken feathers floated up from the floor as he opened the back door of the shop and went into the yard and through the chicken-run, scattering the birds to each side. Clara followed him, throwing seeds across the yard. The hens clucked and nibbled and she counted them as she did every morning. Fifty-two in all. Those birds, together with the little shop and the single room above, were the sum total of the Zvi estate. She went upstairs again and waited for the bread to rise.

In the synagogue Mordecai prayed. He mourned the destruction of the Temple and, like all the other worshippers, pleaded for the coming of the Messiah.

'O proclaim,' he prayed, 'and reveal the day of redemption that is locked up in Thy heart.' Towards the end of the service, a sudden flash of light streaked across the cupboard that held the scrolls of the Law. It was blinding in its radiance.

'There'll be a storm,' his neighbour said and they waited for the roll of thunder. But none came.

'It must be a long way away,' someone said.

But Mordecai knew there was no storm and that the flash of lightning was no lightning. He saw it as a sign and it struck fear in him. He folded his prayer-shawl and hurried home.

From the end of his street he heard the chickens clucking, an unusual din, that shrill of mortality when the slaughterer came amongst them. He hurried, fearful. Outside his house a gaggle of women stood gossiping and laughing, but when they saw his approach they were hushed and seemed embarrassed. He rushed towards them.

'Clara?' he whispered.

'She's well,' one of them said. 'You have a fine first-born boy.'

'But . . . it's not ready,' Mordecai muttered as his heart throbbed with joy.

'He was in a hurry,' one of the women laughed.

But Mordecai, not knowing the ways of women's flesh, could not understand it. He was bewildered as he was so very often to be, by the antics of his first-born. For even in the hour of his birth, Sabbatai had his eye on the Messiah's crown. He made sure he came on time, on the day of the Ninth of Av, even though that time was against nature. Moreover he was to arrange his death fifty years later in the same manner, on yet another auspicious day, the great Day of Atonement. Whatever errors he made in his life, and there were many, Sabbatai Zvi had a superb sense of timing.

Shyly Mordecai entered the bedroom. Clara lay on their bed holding a shawled bundle to her breast. The two women who tended her withdrew when Mordecai entered, and sidled past him out of the room. Mordecai approached the bed and looked down on his first born.

'Can you smell him?' Clara said. 'He smells as an angel must smell.'

Mordecai sniffed. He had never smelt a baby before, nor for that matter had he ever sniffed at an angel, but Clara was always right about everything. He touched the child gently. He could not connect it with himself and it troubled him a little.

'Hold him,' Clara said.

He picked it up gently, fearful of its fragility, and the baby, robbed of its mother's warmth, started to cry. And with a cry of such piercing protest that Mordecai was pleased to hand it back.

'He's a mother's boy,' he said, with prophetic clarity. Then when the child was once more settled, he said, 'Today is a sabbath, and a holy one. We will call him Sabbatai and he shall dedicate his life to the Holy Writ.'

In Mordecai's poor circumstances, it was an act of extravagance, to say the least, to donate his son to divine instruction. Such was the privilege of the rich, and those with sons to spare. For a Biblical scholar could earn little in the way of his own living, leave alone supplement that of his family. But it seemed to Mordecai Zvi that, since his child had been born on that most holy of days, he had a duty to acknowledge the honour to the Lord.

'Sabbatai will be a scholar,' he said, and he left the house.

He had much to do. It was a good hour of the day to walk the streets and spread information. The men were on their way home from worship and they would tell their wives, and the good news would telegraph with joy and speed throughout the Jewish quarter. And with whomsoever he talked, Mordecai did not omit to mention the new-born's effluvience. That of an angel.

By the time he reached the Rabbi's house, he was aware of a following. Not by the noise of the people, rather by their shuffling silence. It unnerved him a little, but he told himself they were celebrating his son. He decided to take joy in it.

Rabbi Joseph Eskapa was the most esteemed scholar of Smyrna. It was he who would take the boy as a pupil, and he, too, who would celebrate his circumcision. It was for the purpose of arranging this ceremony that Mordecai had visited the Rabbi's house.

'Mazeltov, mazeltov,' Rabbi Eskapa said, his already red face flushed with pleasure. 'A first-born son, and on Tisha B'Av,' he said, or sang almost, in a paean of praise and thanksgiving.

It's only another baby, Mordecai wanted to say to offset all this exaggerated fuss. He decided that this time he would not mention the boy's angel odour.

When the arrangements had been made, Mordecai took his leave, bowing his way out of the Rabbi's presence. But it was the Rabbi who did reverence, blessing the Lord who had appointed him to carry out this solemn covenant.

A crowd had gathered outside the Rabbi's house, and the people parted to give Mordecai way. Then they followed him back through the mean streets. This time their women joined them, walking some paces behind, and all murmuring with wonder. When he reached his dwelling, the courtyard was full of people, the chickens scattered in their coops. Again they fell silent as he approached and made way for him. He went up the stairs and sat at Clara's side.

'I went to the Rabbi,' he said.

'There are people outside,' Clara whispered. 'So many. I can hear them.'

'They've come to see the boy,' Mordecai said.

Then he knew what he must do. He knew what was expected of him. He took the child and carried him to the door of the house, then held him aloft for the crowd to see. Thus Sabbatai Zvi made his public debut and, had his eyes been open, he would have seen a sea of hundreds of faces, as he would so often in his life, staring at him in awe and adoration.

'He smells like an angel,' someone said, having heard it from the midwife who had heard it from Clara.

Mordecai cradled his son and returned to Clara, but the crowd lingered.

Inside the room, Mordecai listened to their murmurings. He had had greatness thrust upon his house and he was not sure that it pleased him. For he knew why they lingered there and he felt the fervour that spread amongst them. He knew what they hoped for. He knew their fearful expectations. For they were suffering from Messianic fever, and there is no fever more contagious. Indeed at that time it was spreading all over Europe. It was not a fatal disease. Except perhaps to the spirit. The body would weather it, and offensively so, despite all setbacks. It would weather it out of simple need, out of an implacable yearning. The Messianic hope had never been entirely absent from Jewish history. In prosperous times, the notion of a Redeemer was faintly resistible; indeed it was a relief not to be nagged by the possibility of His coming and thereby rocking the thriving boat. Hope in His appearance was a last resort, and occurred only when the scattered people were victims of oppression and tyranny. But amongst the poor and the faithful, the Messianic hope was perennial. At the time of Sabbatai's birth in Turkey, there were poor and faithful in plenty, and it seemed that all of those in Smyrna were gathered in Mordecai's back yard. He listened to their prayers of thanksgiving, and wished them and their contagion far from his house. For his new son might catch their fever, and the thought occurred to him that he could possibly die of it too. He went to the door and urged them to go away. Clara wished to sleep he said. Slowly they dispersed. The chickens clucked and clattered, but muted now, as if they were aware of the suddenly sanctified ground on which they pecked.

Over the next few days word spread among the whole Jewish population of Smyrna about the coming of the poor poulterer's son. Not so much word as whisper, and less whisper than wonder, and each day they came in awesome curiosity, Sabbath-dressed for the occasion, to view the site of his coming. They did not enter the courtyard, but hovered on the fringes, for the yard had assumed the untreadability of an altar, and the chickens tiptoed from grain to grain, their shrivelled necks for once erect, in the sure certainty of immortality. Untouchable now, for the hallowed ground on which they stood.

The myth of the new Messiah generated itself through rumour, hyperbole and downright invention, and not to believe in it was heresy.

All over Smyrna that week, the Jewish women prepared sweetmeats for the ceremony of circumcision. It was a

16

token of their acknowledgment of redemption. It was all too much for poor Mordecai. He stayed indoors as much as his affairs allowed, for to venture into the streets was to invite isolation. People paused when they saw him, and kept their distance and bowed. Business in his little shop had become one of muted exchange. Gone were the friendly gossip and trivia. His customers collected their chickens and took care to avoid his hands as he passed the birds over the counter. Then they walked backwards out of his shop.

He dreaded the coming ceremony. He dreaded the adoration. But what terrified him more than these were his own thoughts. For he could not deny to himself that he was beginning to dislike his son. One night in the still small hours, when it was no longer dark, yet the day refused to break, in that uneasy limbo of time, he rose from his bed and went over to Sabbatai's cot and prayed him dead under the Rabbi's knife. Then, horrified at such a thought, he prayed to his son for forgiveness, then quickly emended to God, the addressee of his prayer, in fear of falling into the trap the whole of Smyrna had laid for him. And with rare cunning, he prayed for more children, so that Sabbatai would be but the eldest son, for Messiahs, by tradition, had no siblings. Brothers and sisters would reduce the concept of Mcssiah to a banality. Then he picked up his first-born and cradled him. But Mordecai smelt no smell of angels. No frankincense, no myrrh. Nothing offensive. But there *was* a smell. Undeniable. And untellable too. He shivered.

If you were wandering on the streets of Smyrna on the Day of the Covenant, you would have noticed the threads of a procession. It began early in the morning, almost before sunrise, and snowballed itself in the alleys and by-ways of the city. By the time it reached the shore-line, it had accumulated and swollen, like huge waves that threaten but fail to break, evening themselves out in yet another wave that follows close behind, a swelling full of promise, yet with fulfilment withdrawn. So it was with the procession, its rear bringing up yet another rear, bloated with expectation. The people could have been travelling to Lourdes, bent on a similar swindle. Men, women and children, Sabbath-dressed, all wanted to be included in the miracle. So that in later years, when the Kingdom of God was established on earth, they could say to their grand- and great-grandchildren, 'I was there'.

Rabbi Eskapa walked alone. All night he had prayed, mindful of the magnitude of his calling, and of the weighty duty that had been thrust upon him. Between the lines of his prayers, and even during the prayer itself, he was not unaware of the honour of his mission. It could only enhance his standing, not only amongst the Jews of Smyrna where it was already high enough, but with luck, if Sabbatai Zvi proved to be genuine, then throughout the Jewish world. And even beyond, he dared to hope, for what living soul, no matter how rich or wretched his life, did not crave a Messiah? Then quickly he humbled himself to God, pricked by his vanity.

The path of the procession turned inland and climbed the rise to where Rabbi Eskapa stood, musing once more on his mantle of greatness with repeated and futile attempts to push his vanity aside. As he viewed the procession, he was mindful of his own isolation. He tried not to see himself as Moses, though it was an obvious comparison. Had Moses not assumed the leadership, even though it meant that he would never live to see the Promised Land? Yet, was not Moses more revered than Aaron? He waited for them, that band of straggling sinners, their golden calves put aside for a rainy day. What more guarantee did they need for salvation, for God's sake, than the miracle on which their steps were now bent?

If one is standing on the brow of a hill, and a vast procession is making its undeniable way in one's direction, it is very difficult not to entertain vainglorious thoughts. 'I'm only human,' Rabbi Eskapa comforted himself. And, with this self-sanction, he allowed himself, and could be forgiven for, a small gesture of weighing the tablets of the Law in his mighty hand.

He waited till the crowd drew near, then smiled, though sternly, and turned, assuming their leadership, in the direction of Mordecai Zvi's house.

Meanwhile, in the house yard, even the chickens had vanished. That short spell of intimations of immortality, when they had strutted the yard with necks erect, was now gone for ever. The myth was shattered. For now they lay on the tables in the shop, tables bedecked with cloths and flowers for the ceremony, and they themselves, carved, sliced, stuffed and garnished for the pleasure of the redemption of others. Clara, her new-born son on her arm, busied herself with the laying-out of wines and sweetmeats, which, during that week, had arrived from all parts of Smyrna, as tokens of respect. Mordecai, from his corner, watched her, and felt like an outsider. It seemed to him that, ever since Sabbatai had been born, he had never left his mother's arm, save for some small hours when she laid him in his cot. Even then she would keep her hands about him, pressing him gently into the crook of her embrace, indelibly printing him with her motherhood. It was an impression as unique and as permanent as a fingerprint, and Sabbatai glowed in its caress for the whole of his life. Even as an old man, his hopes stubbornly refusing to shatter, he would often fold his hands crosswise over his shoulders, stroking himself in recollection of the only presence in his life that he had truly loved.

Mordecai and Clara had been up since dawn, raised prematurely by Sabbatai who seemed to summon them to prepare for what was to be his day. Mordecai was already awake, having slept fitfully, and Clara stirred by his side.

'The baby's hungry,' Mordecai said. Even by the eighth day he still could not call his son by name. Perhaps he hoped that if he maintained its anonymity the child, for loss of an identity, would simply evaporate.

'That's not a hungry cry,' Clara said, who knew Sabbatai as if she were inside him, as if at his birth, baby and mother had swapped lodgings.

'Then why is it crying?' Mordecai dared to ask, for the baby had reasons beyond any human understanding.

'Perhaps he needs comfort,' Clara said.

Love blinds us to a reality that might shock or disturb. Comfort was benign. Any baby was entitled to that. No strings attached to comfort. In Clara's ear, Sabbatai's early cry was for a fundamental human need. But Mordecai's ear was more finely tuned, unstuffed as yet by the fuzz of loving, and he heard the cry as pure and simple blackmail. He had it in mind to go straight to the cot and smother the child. But Sabbatai was already on Clara's arm, and at her breast where he nestled, unfeeding, but victorious.

Shortly afterwards, Nissim and Perla Arditti arrived. They were the Zvis' closest friends. Nissim was a tailor. Like Mordecai, he scraped together a kind of living. Though, unlike Mordecai's, his trade was seasonal. Prior to the Holy Days, his workshop was cluttered with bolts of cloth, trimmings, buttons and chalks. Over the last week, after the Ninth of Av, and with no specific Holy Day in the calendar, he had barely slept, so overwhelmed had he been by orders for new clothes for the unexpected event which he now attended. When he told Mordecai of this sudden unexpected turn in his fortunes, thanking him for his partial responsibility, he wondered why his friend did not seem to share his pleasure, and he ascribed it to the anxieties of novel fatherhood. He knew about such things, for he himself, six months before, had become father to a first-born son, David, who now straddled Perla's arm.

The two men wandered into the empty courtyard, leaving the women to their preparations. Occasionally they heard one of the children cry.

'Which one is that?' Nissim asked.

'That's mine,' Mordecai said.

The boy had a cry that was not of this earth's children. It lay somewhere between a curse and a prayer, between a wail of grief and a paean of joy. But wherever it lay, it grated on Mordecai's ear, like an alarm bell of terrible forebodings.

'It's Sabbatai,' Mordecai said, dredging his son's name out of the lump in his throat. 'It's Sabbatai,' he said again, hoping that by naming him, his son's spirit would be soothed.

Six months before, when Nissim's and Perla's son had been circumcised, it was Mordecai who had acted as godfather. It was he who had been honoured to hold the child and offer its manhood to the Covenant. Now Mordecai would return that honour to his friend, who would do likewise for Sabbatai. The two men had known each other from childhood. The parents of both had come from Patras in Greece. Their fathers in their own time had been close friends, and both had come from a long line of poverty. It seemed that their sons would fare no better, but poverty was of little account. What mattered to their parents was that their sons should be educated, for knowledge was the only wealth that secured peace on earth. The notion that ignorance was bliss, especially amongst the poor, would have appalled them. Thus, though Mordecai was a poor poulterer, hardly scraping a living from his fowls, and Nissim an even poorer tailor, craving the Holy Days for a living, both men were learned scholars in the Torah and the Talmud and were held in respect by Smyrna's Jewish community.

Mordecai now cursed that knowledge that all his life he had so eagerly sought, for had he been an ignorant and heathen peasant, no-one would have saddled him with the terrible potential of siring that nameless thing, which, at this very moment, the whole of Smyrna was bent on worshipping. He returned to the house and waited.

Sabbatai must have been the first to hear the crowd, for he let out a warning cry. This was taken up by David. Thus was established between the two children the semaphore that would orchestrate their whole lives. For as Sabbatai grew in power and glory, he would give out his signals, and David, as his first and forever faithful disciple, would spread his master's word abroad. Soon both children were crying, Sabbatai almost melodiously, and David with pale and devoted descant.

Only some minutes later did Mordecai hear the tread of the faithful as they rounded the corner of his street, and then, as he waited in fear and trembling, the tremendous roar of their trusting feet.

He dared not look outside. Now begins my penance, he thought. The idea shocked him for he had no notion of any act of his that called for such manic atonement. He thought of his father and the sins thereof, but it was a risible equation, for his father had been gentle and unaccusable to the point of others' fury. Mordecai clapped his hands over his ears to shut out the obscene roar of faith on its oh-so-certain warpath to his erstwhile humble door. Rabbi Eskapa, burdened as Moses, reached the courtyard and raised his hand and bade the multitude rest. Then he went alone to Mordecai Zvi and the two men exchanged bewildered words. Although there was enough food for the faithful, there was clearly not enough room, but they could fill the courtyard in turn and bide their worshipping time. This decision Rabbi Eskapa conveyed to his flock, though those bringing up the rear barely heard a word. Mordecai conveyed the state of the proceedings to Clara, who seemed nothing daunted by his dire presentation. Indeed, it was almost as if she expected it, a feeling no doubt shared by her offspring who, at that moment, chose to donate to the world his first smile, either of wind or cunning. Either way, in his father's eyes, it augured ill.

The courtyard was already crowded but there was no pushing or jostling for place. Simply to be in the aura of the child, an aura which no doubt haloed the whole of Smyrna, was enough, indeed more than enough to quench many lifetimes of Messianic craving.

Those who were first to fill the courtyard saw the back of Rabbi Eskapa as he disappeared into the poulterer's shop to perform his sacred duty. And they feared for him, for to how many is it given to touch, nay to sanctify such holy flesh?

There were few people privileged to be invited to the ceremony proper. Intimate friends, the Ardittis, Leah Mizrachi, the spinster and time-honoured midwife of Smyrna, who had eased Sabbatai's passage into this world, and who would later live to regret it. Isak, the Smyrna 'shnorrer', whose presence was obligatory on every festive occasion, the alms-receiver who helped assuage the guilt of pleasure. In one corner sat two women. Clara's mother, Beki, and her elder daughter, Sarah. Beki would have loved to join in the magic circle of the child and its parents and the Rabbi. Sabbatai was after all her first grandchild, first of her only fruit that could bear. For Sarah, her eldest, was now beyond child-bearing, and it was she herself, her mother, who had shrivelled her. For Beki had kept Sarah by her side when her own husband had died, as an insurance for her old helpless age. She could not look her in the eye, though Sarah dared her often enough.

Now Beki longed to join the others, or even to breathe the free air of the courtyard as an unfettered outsider, but she was bound to her daughter's side in a conspiracy of isolation. And Sarah pinned her there, as her mother had pinned her when her father had died. A price must be paid, Sarah consoled herself as she stared into her mother's face. But that face that once had all the answers was now vacant, and Sarah waited for its tenancy of regret. For that was all she wanted. An apology. I'm sorry, she wanted to hear her mother say, but that was unsayable, for it would have acknowledged the hurt she had done her. But her mother owed, and Sarah would stay by her side until that debt

23

was paid, and if necessary force it from her dying lips for she herself could not survive such an unacknowledged infliction of pain. Yes, one day her mother would say she was sorry. Sarah shivered at the prospect, for after that, what should she wait for? Her life's purpose had been an attendance on apology. What then, after such a purpose had been fulfilled? With luck, she thought, she might die before her mother, as an involuntary act of punishment. She kept staring at her mother's vacant face, that stared in every direction but her own.

'Why don't you go into the courtyard, Sarah?' the face said. 'The fresh air will do you good.' Meaningless, moonshine words, for Beki knew that her daughter's pain was beyond the solace of fresh air, nor would pollution have touched her, Sarah in her barrenness had become untouchable.

In any case, even if she had been willing to let her mother off the hook, Sarah would not have ventured outside. For somewhere in the courtyard, or in the straggling procession behind, was Nahum. Nahum, who had grown tired of waiting, or rather whose mother had grown tired, and had transferred her nagging fatigue to her son; Nahum, whose mother had found Lusi, as a willing daughter-in-law. Lusi would be in the procession as well, a few steps behind Sarah's erstwhile intended on whom her mother had had no intentions at all. No, Sarah could not face Nahum any more than he could face her, for between them still lay those longings that time and absence had only served to strengthen. So Sarah remained at her mother's side, and watched Clara, that younger sister who had once been so close, and who had slowly, after her wedding, achieved a wife's distance and now, as a mother, a remoteness forever beyond her reach.

Rabbi Eskapa was draping his prayer-shawl around his shoulders. Then he opened his long black box. The knife glinted on the blue velvet pad. By its side lay a roll of lint. This he opened carefully, then stood erect. He was

24

ready. Clara kissed her son. She was glad that his eyes were closed. She hoped that he was sleeping. Mordecai moistened Sabbatai's lips with brandy, but the baby twisted his mouth away. He tried again, but to no avail.

'Leave him,' Rabbi Eskapa said. 'It's his wish.'

Mordecai shivered. Rabbi Eskapa was well on the way to idolatry.

Mordecai felt suddenly very alone, and in his isolation, treacherous. For out of all that mighty throng, in the courtyard and far beyond, it seemed that it was only he who refused his first-born's glory. For a moment he thought of snatching the child away, of denying him the Covenant, a denial that would disqualify him once and for all from the role that they would thrust upon him. But Clara was already handing the baby into Nissim's arms. Mordecai looked at his wife's face and it seemed suffused with beatitude. He turned away, defeated. He did not watch as Nissim offered his son to the knife. He waited until he would hear Sabbatai's cry, then he'd know that it was over and done with. In time the cry was heard, but Mordecai knew it was not his son's. He looked around and saw how David was writhing and whimpering on his mother's arm as if he had taken on Sabbatai's pain for his own. Sabbatai, for his part, lay calm on Nissim's arm, a small trickle of blood smudging his groin. He's dead, Mordecai hoped, then prayed for forgiveness. Then he saw his son stir and his heart melted with love. He went forward to take him from Nissim's arms and he held him gently as Clara linted the wound.

Wine was brought and each celebrant drank a toast. Again Mordecai moistened his son's lips with brandy, and this time it was not refused. Relished even, as if it was his new-found manhood that Sabbatai had chosen to anaesthetise.

Outside, the crowds waited. They knew the ceremony must be over, for out of their own silence they heard laughter within. And a rumbling which did not come from inside

25

the shop. A rumbling which turned to a roar, a roar familiar to them and to every Jew in Smyrna, the roar of the idiot, Raphael. Those grown-ups amongst the crowd remembered him as children, when he himself toddled in the market-place, clinging to his mother's skirts. He had been a beautiful boy, so lovely indeed that all had remarked on his beauty, remarks unaccompanied by the traditional blessing that would ward off the evil eye. Thus that eye had had free rein, so all the elders said, and had punished his brain for his beauty. Filled his belly with the roar of a lion, tucked him in with nightmares of future visions and, in pity, fed him on a diet of rainbows, so that occasionally his dreams might be beautiful. The grown-ups did not fear him, but they used him as threats to their own children. 'If you're naughty, you'll end up like Raphael.' Now those children clung to their own mothers' skirts as they heard his mighty roar.

Raphael had been at the very back of the procession. Straggling was his style of movement. Then slowly a fever had come over him and he had weaved his way between the lines. He had little difficulty in reaching the courtyard, for people made way for him out of either pity or fear. Not one of them would oppose the idiot for, though he was a fool, some said he was a holy one. As he reached the courtyard, he let out a final feverish bellow, then he lingered amongst the crowd, biding his time. Those around him patted his head, hoping to calm him. But Raphael was quiet enough. His fever mounted in silence as he gathered his strength.

It was at this point that the laughter ceased in the shop, and a clinking of glasses could be heard. They waited, and then Rabbi Eskapa appeared in the doorway, Sabbatai cradled in his arms.

'L'Chaim,' he shouted to the crowd. 'To life!' and he raised Sabbatai on his arms, presenting the miracle child to the throng.

For a moment there was silence, followed by a monumental and unison sigh of faith and wonder as if the promise of paradise had been proven. Then another silence which was Raphael's cue.

'Beware of false prophets,' he thundered, 'which come to you in sheep's clothing, but inwardly they are ravening wolves.'

Rabbi Eskapa trembled, and he lowered the child, holding it close to shield its ears from such blasphemy. But Sabbatai had heard well enough, and he let out a long and windy sigh. Rabbi Eskapa's nostrils were seen to flare in horror, and a grimace of distaste spread over his face. Quickly he returned to the shop and handed the baby over to its mother. Then, stammering, he hastily took his leave. The crowd in the courtyard was surprised at his sudden leave-taking. And surprised, too, at his look of despair.

One of the women touched his sleeve.

'Does he not smell like an angel, Rabbi?' she asked.

'Does he not smell of myrrh?' another woman said.

'Or frankincense?' asked another.

'How art thou fallen from heaven, O Lucifer, son of the morning,' Rabbi Eskapa whispered. But softly, so that no one but his own sore self should hear. He wondered whether he should speak. Whether his thoughts could bear the telling. But he had to pronounce them. He owed it to God.

'He smells of sulphur,' he whispered.

2

The occasional trance

Rabbi Eskapa's verdict was only a whisper. The smell of frankincense and myrrh was irresistible, and its rumour louder. Over the years of Sabbatai's childhood, the rumour rumbled without let-up. Even the birth of two more children, brothers for Sabbatai, did nothing to subdue it. In Sabbatai, the first-born, he who was delivered on Tisha B'Av, he who smelt like an angel, in that child rested the hopes and cravings of all the Jews of Smyrna.

With the birth of his two younger sons, Joseph and Elijah, Mordecai felt released from the Messiah hook. Whatever the Jews of Smyrna might think, in Mordecai's eye, Sabbatai was merely his first-born and the date of his birth and his effluvium, however one interpreted it, were factors incidental. In this new light, Mordecai grew to love his eldest son and favoured him above the others. But Sabbatai was not a responsive child. He shuddered at the touch of any hand save that of his mother. Mordecai wooed him from a distance, occasionally eliciting a smile, and then his father's heart would falter and he longed to hold him in his arms. But the boy had declared himself untouchable.

Day by day Mordecai loved him more and more, and day by day he feared for him. Not on account of others' Messianic hopes, but for Sabbatai himself. For he was indeed a singularly strange child. There were his dreams, for instance, and what he called his visions. Mordecai attempted Biblical interpretations, and his findings were far from comfortable. His son's sleep was nightmarish. Often he would creep into his parents' bed full of words and terror, and into the warmth of his mother's arms he would stammer out the nightmare that assailed him. Almost always it was the same.

'It was the fire,' he whispered, 'the same fire in the sky. And it came down and burned my . . .' At this point he would shield his manhood with his tiny fist.

'I know, I know,' Clara sang to him, sparing him the word which modesty forbade her to pronounce.

'It burned, it burned,' he cried, 'and they were beating me, beating me all the time.'

'Who? *Who?*' Mordecai tried not to shout, for his fear for his son threatened anger.

'Sh . . .' Clara said.

'I need to know,' Mordecai screamed. Sometimes he disliked his wife a little.

'They're visions,' she whispered. She even smiled, and Mordecai could have struck her.

'Visions,' he spat. He hated the word. It was loaded with Messianic pretension. Sabbatai was his eldest son, no more, no less. And like many children, he was prone to nightmares. That didn't make him a Messiah. But there were other things. Not necessarily Messianic, but there was little comfort in that. For those other things were against nature. For whoever heard of a child of seven beating himself for pleasure? Not once, but several times, Mordecai had caught him at it. There was a stick they used in the chicken-yard for shooing the birds into their coops. Sabbatai's job, and had been ever since he had been able to walk. Whatever the weather, he never shirked the task. Indeed he seemed to enjoy it, and one day Mordecai understood why. For he saw him shooing the birds with one hand, and using the stick to beat his own thigh. The sight of such self-flagellation was disturbing enough, but what offended Mordecai even more was the spectacle of his son's perfect rhythm. Shoo, beat, shoo, beat, it went,

32

with an increasing tempo and fervour until all the birds were cooped. Then Sabbatai would lean against the shed and, as the stick dropped from his little hand, he would close his eyes in what looked disturbingly like ecstasy.

'What are you doing?' Mordecai tried not to shout at him.

'Putting the fowls away,' Sabbatai said. He seemed in no way disconcerted by a witness. 'Why do you ask?' he said, and the very question proclaimed his innocence.

What else were you doing? Mordecai ached to ask him, but he feared putting ideas into his son's head.

Thereafter Mordecai watched his son at his daily task, and each time the routine was the same. The thought crossed his mind to tell Clara, to bring her to the courtyard door and have her witness as he had done. But he feared her interpretation. Whips, scorpions and scourges littered every Bible page, and she was bound to find some Messianic justification for such behaviour. So Mordecai was alone in his fears for his son and his love for him grew with his fears.

Only when Sabbatai was playing with David Arditti did his fears abate. For then they seemed like a pair of ordinary, playful and mischievous children. They were inseparable and, though David was the elder, he seemed to be in Sabbatai's thrall, willingly and joyfully taking Sabbatai's orders, fulfilling his every demand. Mordecai took care not to watch them too closely, lest keen observation would feed further fear.

It was about that time that Mordecai's livelihood underwent a radical change. Smyrna, which hitherto had been a sleepy little town by the sea, now suddenly buzzed with commerce. The Turkish government was unstable. Sultan toppled sultan and all were ineffectual. In 1640, Sultan Ibrahim ascended unsteadily to the throne. Unsteadily, because he had recently emerged from an eight-year prison sentence imposed on him by a rival sultan. While he was languishing behind his bars, all the male heirs to the throne had been slain in battle or murdered by adversaries, and Ibrahim was released as the sole legitimate claimant. 'Mad Ibrahim' as he was known, and with good reason. It is possible that his long confinement had impaired his intelligence – certainly it had done little good to his health, for he was prone to convulsions – but at the same time it had seemingly nurtured his imagination. For he wore pearls in his beard and gave money to fish urging them to go out and enjoy themselves.

Ibrahim knew that to maintain his throne he must exhibit some irrefutable authority. He must do something positive. To this end, and with little thought of its consequence, he declared war on the Republic of Venice, his country's time-honoured enemy. It was as good a way as any to be taken seriously. The object of the war was to capture Crete. At that time all the Eastern Mediterranean stretch was part of the Ottoman Empire. All, that is, except that small island with its enviable strategic position. But Venice coveted Crete, too. It was sufficient reason to go to war. As a result, Constantinople and Salonika, the traditional centres of commerce in the Empire, were in chaos, and European traders were forced to re-route their caravans to the East.

The natural centre of this route was Smyrna. This diversion wrought a great change in the seaside town, that town where Nissim the tailor plied his spasmodic needle and thread, and Mordecai scraped a living from his fowls. And the lives of both were changed. For Nissim and Mordecai were well-versed not only in the Turkish tongue but also in Greek, and, through their religious scholarship, in Hebrew and Arabic as well. Both found employment as agents and interpreters. Counting-houses and caravanserai mushroomed all over Smyrna. Even Mordecai's poultry-shop and chicken-run were taken over, and the family moved to a larger home in a prospering district.

Being Jewish was no impediment to prosperity. The Ottoman Empire was tolerant to its Jews. Stretching from the Balkans to Syria and Palestine, it welcomed to its dominions all those who sought shelter from oppression. After the expulsion of the Jews from Spain in 1492, the Sultan encouraged their immigration to Turkey where they adapted successfully, even to the extent of becoming members and servants of the court. Both Mordecai and Nissim were to benefit from this tolerance.

When the children were told of the move and their sudden good fortune, Elijah and Joseph rejoiced. But Sabbatai was heart-broken. 'We can't leave the chickens,' he said.

Clara was moved by her son's solicitousness and, like everything else he thought and did, it was for her yet another confirmation of his special sainthood. She ascribed the change in their fortunes to the glory that surrounded her eldest born, and when Mordecai discouraged such thoughts, she looked at him with undisguised pity.

A week before moving day, as darkness fell, Sabbatai shut himself with the chickens inside the coop. He put a plank of wood against the door and allowed no one inside. He knew that the slaughterer would come that day and leave not a single bird behind. The family gathered in the courtyard, pleading with him to come outside. Clara pleaded with soothing words, while Joseph and Elijah clung to her skirts. Mordecai hammered at the chicken-coop door with violence in his eyes?

'God knows what he's doing in there,' Clara said.

But Mordecai knew. For he could hear the faint lashings of Sabbatai's herding-stick. Then a scream, short and staccato, shortly followed by another, again and again, and Mordecai shivered in the echo of its ghastly rhythm. He listened for a while, trembling. Then he felt tears on his face, and his fear was compounded with shame. Yet he did not stem his tears. He let them flow, and he sobbed, too, and cared not to stifle his weeping. But there was no blackmail in his sobbing, nor threat in his tears. He was simply weeping for the ominous shadow that stalked his son's future.

Elijah, the youngest son, loosened his hand from his mother's skirt and all of his seven years gasped with horror at the sight of a grown-up's tears. And rage too. He sprang to the door of the chicken-coop and banged his little fist on the wooden slats.

'You made Papa cry,' he screamed. 'Come out or I'll kill you!' Then he ran to his father and held his hand, stroking the hair on the backs of his fingers with whispered gentleness. Mordecai embraced him. His youngest worshipped Sabbatai as a hero, but that moment unmasked the feet of clay. And in its stead was anger and shame that he had been so hoodwinked.

The slaughterer came into the yard, carrying his tools in a fabric bag. In his despair, Mordecai had forgotten the arrangement he had made for the killing and he was embarrassed by his predicament. He did his best to explain.

'Sabbatai's so fond of the chickens,' he said. 'They're playmates almost. It'll break his heart.' He tried to paint his son as the eleven-year-old he truly was, loving, trustful and easily reduced to tears. As he talked about him, he knew he was describing a perfect stranger, that Sabbatai was no child, but an old man with a head full of cunning.

'I understand,' the slaughterer said. Whatever Sabbatai Zvi, that holy child, thought and felt, had to be understood and respected. He began to walk backwards out of the yard. 'I'll come the day that you've moved to the big house. He shall see nothing of it.' He bowed to Clara and ruffled Elijah's hair. That child, at least, was touchable. Then he shook Mordecai's hand and took a respectful leave.

'Let's go inside,' Clara said when he had gone. 'Sabbatai will come out when he's ready.' She started to go towards the house, and Mordecai started after her in wonder. Had it been Joseph or Elijah who had locked themselves up in the coop, she would have torn down the door with her bare hands in fear for their health and welfare. But she seemed not to extend those natural maternal anxieties towards her eldest born. All she gave him was her boundless love, confident that his divinity would take care of his other needs. Joseph strode after her, sharing her certainty.

'We can't leave him here,' Elijah said. 'He'll be cold and he'll be hungry.'

'Mama's right,' Mordecai said. 'He'll come out when he's hungry.' Then he picked up the boy and made for the house.

'We're going,' Elijah shouted out over his shoulder. 'We're leaving you alone,' he yelled. 'We don't care,' he screamed, and he smudged his tears on his father's jacket.

Inside the house Clara was preparing supper. She was actually singing at her work. Mordecai would have liked to talk with her, to discuss with her some strategy to retrieve their son, but he knew that such discussion was pointless, for it would spring from two diametrically opposed premises: one that their son was a saint, and the other that he was a lunatic. So there was silence in the house. Although it was cold, Mordecai insisted on keeping the door open, so that he could keep an eye on his son's chosen prison. Not that he could see very much for the moon was barely crescent and there were no stars in the sky.

'There are no stars tonight,' he said, for he had to say something, something to break the silence, something benign, for the alternative was violence.

'The stars will come out with Sabbatai,' Clara said, and started to sing again. Mordecai stepped into the courtyard because he didn't trust his hands. 'He'll be hungry,' he heard Elijah say. 'He's bound to come out for supper. Papa,' he called, 'tell him it's pancakes for supper. He'll come out for pancakes.'

'That's not true, Elijah,' Clara said. 'I'm not making pancakes. It's barley soup.'

'It's pancakes, Sabbatai,' Elijah yelled into the yard. He would commit any sin, no matter how heinous, for his brother's release.

Clara interrupted her singing to slap him hard on his bare legs. 'You must not tell lies, Elijah,' she said.

Mordecai was enraged and he rushed over to the chicken-coop door. 'It's pancakes,' he whispered, and there he stayed until Joseph came to bring him to supper. But he could not eat and he marvelled at his wife's appetite.

'Don't worry,' she said to him. 'Sabbatai will come out when he's hungry.'

After supper, she put the two boys to bed. Elijah begged to wait up for his brother, but anxiety had sharpened his fatigue and he fell asleep while pleading. When the children were in bed it was Mordecai's habit to fetch down the Bible or its commentaries and to read aloud while Clara pottered at the sink. But this night he couldn't concentrate, and he sat at the table staring through the open door. But he could see nothing. The crescent moon was half-covered in cloud and it had begun to rain. He sat there staring till midnight. 'He must be starving,' he whispered. Then he ran quickly into the courtyard and listened at the barn door.

'Sabbatai,' he whispered, 'Sabbatai, my son, let me carry you to bed.' But from inside he heard nothing.

'Shut the door and let's go to bed,' Clara called.

Sometimes she astonished him. 'You go,' he said. 'I'll wait a while.' He returned to the house. All night he sat at the table. From time to time he dozed, then woke with a fearful start and he would run to the chicken-house door and listen. But only to silence. He was sure Sabbatai was asleep. There was no chink in the door which would serve as a peep-hole. The door was solid.

It was fortunate that Mordecai could not see his son. For had he seen him, he would have panicked. Far from being asleep, Sabbatai was wide awake, his eyes shining like hot coals in the darkness. Around him the chickens slept, and the cockerels clung to their perches, their heads curved in the coxcomb pillow. Sabbatai had nested in their midst, his head upright, his legs crossed in perfect symmetry, his hands resting gently on his knees, in Buddha-like meditation. He was starving and he relished it. That self-imprisonment was his first lesson in abstinence and he learned it with joy. Thus he sat the whole night through and by morning he had achieved the euphoria of hunger. He did not wait for the cocks to crow. He smelt the growing light outside the door sooner than they, and quietly he slid the bolt and shooed the fowls into the yard, beating his legs with the herd-stick as he did so. As they saw the light, the cocks began to crow and Sabbatai once more bolted the door and sat in contemplation.

The cockerels startled Mordecai who was slouched on the table. He registered that they were in the courtyard and knew that only Sabbatai could have released them. And relief that his son was still alive overcame him. He rushed to the coop-door. 'Sabbatai,' he shouted, 'it's time you came out. You must be starving.' He listened to the infuriating silence behind the door. 'Sabbatai,' he pleaded, 'answer me.'

But Sabbatai barely heard him, neither his words nor his tone of supplication. For his mind was soaring. He had begun to count, convinced that he could reach infinity. His hunger would be a spur. He counted slowly, savouring each digit, and when he reached eleven, he stopped, and was silent for a while in deference to his own achievement of years. Then he counted further, his fists beating his knees the while in digital rhythm. All day he spent counting, until his knees were sore. He did not hear the chickens clucking in the yard nor the insistent supplication of his father outside the door. His whole mind and body were devoted to the achievement of infinity, that single number that would cause the sun to set and the sea to cover the land, and the gates of heaven and hell to open, and mankind to be no more. And he, Sabbatai Zvi, from a humble chicken-coop, would have engineered it all. He was laughing now with the joy of expectation, the numbers dropping from his lips like pebbles. Soon he began to sing them, ornamenting them with trills and turns. This took longer of course, but Sabbatai had time; he had eternity. His hymn of numbers was endless. He would wait for God to orchestrate the final chord.

Outside the barn-door Mordecai listened. He feared now not only for his son's health but for his sanity. And he began to hate all those who encouraged his Messianic pretensions. For the boy was surely influenced by them, by the silent deference of others. Why, even the children at school had caught that worship from their parents. It was natural that his son should play the role that they had cast for him. This must all have a stop, he said to himself, though he wondered now whether it had gone too far.

'Sabbatai,' he whispered, 'it's getting dark. The chickens must go to bed in the coop.' He waited for a pause in his son's hymn in case he had not been heard, but no pause was allowed. It seemed to Mordecai that his son was in a trance and he shivered. Then in his desolation he began to bang his head on the chicken-coop door. Although he banged with all his strength, he felt no pain. His despair overwhelmed him and left room for no other sensation. He noticed after a while how his banging rhythm had involuntarily attuned itself to his son's hymn, like a ghostly descant to Sabbatai's lamentations. Suddenly he stopped, his head throbbing. This is collusion, he thought, and he fled from the barn-door through the yard and into the house. Then he shut the door. He no longer wanted to hear the chanting. He wanted to sleep and wake up to find that it was all a bad dream.

Clara was pottering in the kitchen. 'Tonight it really is pancakes,' she said.

'Do you know your son hasn't eaten for twenty-four hours?' Mordecai said. Her imperturbability angered him. 'D'you know he could die of starvation?' He heard the futility of his argument, the inappropriateness of his words. For in Clara's ears the vocabulary of death and starvation

40

did not apply to her eldest son. Mordecai suddenly felt very isolated. He reached out for Elijah who was playing with a wooden box on the floor, and he drew him to him like a natural ally. Then in the silence that followed, a door creaked. Elijah rushed into the courtyard and watched the barn-door open. Sabbatai stood there, his herd-stick in his hand. Then, as if nothing untoward had happened, he started shooing the chickens back into the coop, beating his legs with the stick awhile.

'He must have become hungry,' Clara said, confirming her prophecy of the day before.

Mordecai wondered what had prompted his son's sortie. What magic number had he reached that had unbarred his door? He watched him as he herded the last chicken inside, then went out to bring him into the house.

Elijah hovered in the courtyard. He was glad and relieved to see his brother again, but he would not show it. Let his father, who hadn't threatened to kill him, welcome him back into the family.

Mordecai tried to assume Sabbatai's nonchalance. He took him by the hand.

'There's pancakes for supper,' he said.

Sabbatai smiled right through him. 'I'm not hungry,' he said. He let himself be led into the kitchen. Clara had already set a plate of steaming pancakes at his place. 'Eat my son,' she said.

'I don't want them,' he whispered. He was high on hunger, and no succulent pancakes were going to bring him down. So he sat in his place and passed the plate to Joseph. 'You have them,' he said.

And at last Clara was roused. Mordecai noted her anger with some relief. Her rage was wondrous to view. She strode across to where Sabbatai sat, and gripped him by the shoulder. 'You're lying,' she said. 'You must be starving. Now you just eat those pancakes!' She even slapped him across the ear. It was the first time she'd laid hands on him in anger. But Sabbatai caught her hand as it fell to

41

her side, and he kissed it. 'Don't worry, Mama,' he said. 'I'm not going to die.' Mordecai watched as his wife turned quickly away. She slouched towards the sink, shrivelled. 'Forgive me,' she whispered without turning her head. Then Joseph reached over to Sabbatai and kissed him and even little Elijah, crumpled in confusion, went over and held Sabbatai's hand. Only Mordecai stayed aloof, and viewed the dire collusion.

'Enough!' he shouted, standing up and heedless of consequence. 'If Sabbatai isn't eating, he must go to bed.'

Sabbatai stood up and smiled at him. But it was no smile of affection. Rather of victory, as well as one of pity for one who was undeniably on the losing side. Then he turned and walked slowly from the room, or rather took his leave in adult ceremonial.

Neither Clara nor Mordecai ate that evening. But for different reasons: Clara out of pure and displayed penitence, and Mordecai from fearful loss of appetite.

A few days later, they left the site of their poverty. On top of their cart, serving as a weight to their few belongings, lay Mordecai's wardrobe, a travelling memory. Once they were out of earshot, the slaughterer came with his fabric bag of tools. Had Sabbatai looked around, he would have seen the courtyard bloodied and feather-strewn.

The new house stood above the sea-shore, within easy running-distance of the waves. It was a large house and allowed a single room for each of the children. Joseph and Elijah regretted their separation, and after a few lonely nights, ignored the privilege and crept into each other's beds. But Sabbatai was delighted with the privacy and more so when he discovered that his brothers had rejected it. Now he was the only person in the house who kept to his own quarters. It set him apart from the others and it seemed to him that that was how it should be. Whether the feeling was due to the deferential behaviour of the people around him, he never questioned. To him it was

42

a *natural* feeling, that he was in some way special and apart.

When he was not at school, he spent most of his time in his own room savouring his privacy. He paced the floor, measuring his aloofness. Above all, he delighted in his cupboard which he opened and shut with rhythmic pleasure. In the old house, such clothes as he had were placed in a neat pile at the foot of his bed, except for his synagogue suit, which, alongside his brothers', hung behind the door. Now his wardrobe was increased and there was space to house it. His joy was an embroidered shirt, ruffled at the neck. The night of the pancake episode, his mother had taken her needle and coloured threads, a length of soft cheesecloth, and had begun her penance. Her design was geometrical and Sabbatai would lay the blouse flat on the floor and stare at it with alternate eyes until the kaleidoscope patterns sent him into a trance.

Thus he would enjoy his privacy in spells of trance-inducing games, meditation, and counting his numbers to unreachable infinity, and each and every one of these pursuits conducted in his own rigid rhythm. But above all he studied. The study of the Torah and its commentaries. He read the Prophets as other children of his age would read adventure tales, and found in them the same sense of urgency. At school he astonished his teachers. Even Rabbi Eskapa, renowned for his scholarship not only in Smyrna but in the whole of Turkey, had to admit that, despite his sulphuric odour, the boy was a genius. And something of a hero-figure in his class. In the little Jewish school, there was no envy of scholarship. On the contrary, learning commanded respect. And more. For Sabbatai's schoolmates revered him to the point of idolatry. They had heard from their parents of the legends that attended his birth and it seemed to them right and proper that he should be a master scholar and they his disciples. Of these, the most devoted and loyal was David Arditti. David and Sabbatai were inseparable. David's father, too, had bettered himself in the wake of Smyrna's prosperity. Mordecai had secured him a position similar to his own, with a French merchant trader, and Nissim had put away his needle and thread.

But despite the change in the family fortunes, they still maintained the ghetto mores. Indeed they strengthened them, reinforcing their sense of community isolation, as if their sudden wealth might seduce them into assimilation.

In the evenings, Mordecai and Clara would sit on their porch as hitherto they had sat in the chicken-run, then on cushions, but now on rocking-chairs, listening to the sounds of the sea. Now, as then, Clara embroidered or kneaded the dough and Mordecai engrossed himself in the Bible. At such times Clara liked to talk about their children, and especially to envisage their future. Mordecai was wary of such discussion and he tried to confine it to Joseph and Elijah. For they were safe and predictable. They would follow in their father's footsteps and become agents like himself. But as for Sabbatai, his future was unimaginable, and Mordecai needed a world of courage to give it even a thought. But Clara was happy to envisage it, and with prophet-like foresight. 'He will lead his people,' she kept saying. 'He will redeem them.' Mordecai shivered at the word. Such a word belonged to the Holy Book and should never, never leave it. Because whilst it lay in its sacred pages, it remained a vision, a dream. And that was the only way his belief could accommodate it. When he read the Bible, he took care never to speak aloud the word redemption, lest it escape from its true element. For on the page, it was safe. On the page, it would live for ever. It would give rise to no crippling expectation, only to hope and blessed fantasy. And now his wife was airing it, as if it were public domain, using it to clothe her son, and under his very nose in his own house. Yet he dared not deny her for he feared her mockery.

One evening she broached the subject of Sabbatai's barmitzvah. 'It's less than six months away,' she said. 'We should make preparations.'

'What preparations?' Mordecai asked. 'Sabbatai is more than ready.'

'I know that,' she laughed. 'He was ready before he was born.' Mordecai didn't want to go into that, so he remained silent. 'I mean proper preparations,' Clara said, and he was bound to ask her to clarify.

'I want the barmitzvah in Jerusalem,' she said.

Now it was Mordecai's turn to laugh. He didn't care any more and he laughed long and loud. It wasn't that her suggestion was funny. His laughter was one of despair, for it was the subtitle of her suggestion that worried him, the innuendo, the unspoken arrogance and expectation.

Clara ignored his reaction. 'It's the right and proper place for him,' she said. 'Sabbatai, above all people.'

'Sabbatai is no different from anybody else.' He stood up. It was out at last, that heartfelt assertion that he had for so long and so painfully stifled.

She stared at him in horror as if he had spoken the name of God aloud. But her look could not silence him. Her disgust fed his courage. 'Sabbatai will have his barmitzvah here. Here in Smyrna,' he dictated, 'and there will be a small party afterwards. Here, in this house,' he added. He thumped his hand on the table. 'I want no more talk about Jerusalem,' he said. He went to sit down again, but thought better of it. He felt that at last he had assumed some measure of control over his wife, and sitting down would have immediately diminished it. So he stood for a while in her silence, relishing it, then dared again to take his seat. He fully expected a further explosion but her continued silence indicated that his message had been received. Jerusalem was never mentioned again, but from that time Mordecai noticed a distinct cooling-off in his wife's affections.

A few months before his thirteenth birthday, Sabbatai climbed to the top landing of the house, took a deep breath, and over the stairs he shouted, 'Fuck!' The obscenity echoed down the stairwell and throughout the house. The family was gathered in the kitchen awaiting supper. Clara's soup-ladle hovered mid-air and trembled. Joseph and Elijah were too shocked even to giggle, and Mordecai raised his head enquiringly, needing a repeat, for he could not for one moment believe what he had heard.

And Sabbatai obliged. 'Fuck!' he shouted again, and waited for the echo to recede. 'Fucked three times,' he said. Then, after a pause, 'An abomination'. That word took a little longer to land its five accusing syllables, bouncing down each stair.

There was a silence then as the kitchen quaked with the full impact of the message, and the soup dripped from the ladle with the rhythm of a metronome. Mordecai rose from his seat, his knees trembling. He went to the foot of the stairs. He did not expect to find Sabbatai. He surely must have retreated into some black hole to hide from his shame. He hoped so, for he had no idea of how to confront him. But he saw him skipping down the stairs, between one landing and another, his face wreathed in smiles of achievement. 'Isn't that right, Papa?' he shouted from the second landing. Mordecai hung on to the banister for support, and dreaded his arrival. For what could he say to this boy of his, who seemed not to know right from wrong, who turned sin into pious joy. Sabbatai reached the bottom stair, his shining face expectant, awaiting his father's praise. And all Mordecai could do was to hold him and his embrace was helpless, despairing and suffocated with love. And as he held him, his son's body felt like a wall of heat, and Mordecai touched his forehead under the black fringe and it oozed sweat.

'You're not well, Sabbatai,' he said, and there was a surge of relief in his voice, for illness could account for everything, including blasphemy. 'Come, I'll take you to bed,' he said.

He practically carried him up the stairs, then undressed him and put him to bed. He tried not to notice the smell

46

of brimstone that steamed off his son's body, and he had to turn away, for he was overcome with nausea. 'Sleep,' he said. 'I'll be back soon.' Then he hurried downstairs to report his findings.

In the kitchen, Clara still stood at the stove, the ladle in exactly the same angle of her hand as if transfixed in trauma. Joseph and Elijah sat protectively close to one another, waiting for the clap of thunder.

'He's not well,' Mordecai said. 'Joseph, go and fetch Doctor Bensiyon.'

'Can I go with him?' Elijah said, and ran after his brother without waiting for a reply. Because he didn't want to stay with those grown-ups who seemed to him now to be so old, so very old, and so burningly accused. And he had fled with an instinctive fear of contagion, for he had not forgotten his threat to kill his brother.

When they had gone, Clara returned the ladle to the pan. 'What's the matter with him?' she asked.

'He has a fever.'

Then Clara crossed over to Mordecai and took his hand. 'Come,' she said, 'let's go to him.' She put her arm around him as they climbed the stairs, sensing his frailty.

'Don't worry,' she kept telling him. 'He'll be all right.'

'But he's just an ordinary little boy,' Mordecai said, and said it again and again until they reached Sabbatai's door. It was his only defence against her fantasy.

They opened the door and found Sabbatai sitting bolt upright in bed. Although they were directly in his line of vision, he seemed not to see them. One arm was folded backwards on to his shoulders and he was rocking himself, humming faintly all the while. It was his retreat into infancy, recalling with his folded arm that imprint of his mother's nursing care. And he rocked himself as she had rocked him, humming. Inside that love-print he was safe, and all that had affected him since, that great wall of awe from the community, with its paralysing expectations, now dissolved as if it had never been.

Clara sat on his bed and took him in her arms, rocking him in his own rhythm. Sabbatai laid his head on her breast, smiling.

Doctor Bensiyon came shortly afterwards. He was puzzled and tried not to show it. While he was considering his verdict, he tried all manner of examination to give himself time.

'There's nothing the matter with our Sabbatai,' he finally said, chucking him under the chin. Then to his parents, 'Children often run high fevers for no reason at all. Excitement I suppose,' he said helplessly. He listened to his own words and he didn't know what he was talking about. He made his way out of the room with as much haste as decorum would allow. He said that he would come again in the morning, and the thought crossed his mind that during the night the boy might well turn into an angel and fly away.

But Sabbatai was there in the morning, asleep and healed in his mother's arms. Clara had insisted on sleeping with him, and Mordecai did nothing to dissuade her. Indeed, he was relieved that night to sleep alone, unencumbered by his wife's fretful faith, to know himself in the dark and the silence and to understand with absolute certainty that his eldest son was not whole.

The preparations for Sabbatai's barmitzvah were against the background of the same frenzied faith as had attended his circumcision. For two weeks before the ceremony people came with their offerings. Although the tables were groaning, to refuse them would be tantamount to denying a blessing. By dawn the synagogue was already full and those who could not find places crowded outside in the courtyard. When Sabbatai and his family arrived, a great way was cleared for them, the crowds falling back on each other to give space not only to the family but to the troop of angels that attended them. Some claimed to see them and to hear the fluttering of their wings. The doors of the synagogue remained open so that those outside could celebrate, together with all the Jews of Smyrna, that day on which Sabbatai Zvi became a man.

They listened to the prayers that preceded the initiation. Then they heard the silence that followed, broken only by the steps of the young Sabbatai as he mounted the platform to read his portion of the Law.

Sabbatai's performance was as much visual as it was aural, and those outside were deprived of half the occasion. For when he took his stand before the Scrolls of the Law, he lowered his head as if ordering a further silence. He was clearly in no hurry to begin. After a while he placed his hands on the table, one on each side of the Scroll, then he raised his head, now utterly in command. And not only of himself, but of the whole congregation. He looked at them. And those who believed in him, or harboured the need to believe, saw in that look a blessing. Even some of those blind outside saw it.

But a few, a very few, amongst them Rabbi Eskapa and Mordecai, saw in that look a thirst for power. Mordecai stared at his feet, unable to bear it. Then he heard his son's voice and its beauty pierced him like a pain. 'Thus saith the Lord,' Sabbatai sang. 'The Heaven is my throne and the earth is my foothold. Where is the house that ye build unto me, and where is the place of my rest?' He sang as if asking each member of the congregation a personal question and in that level of intimacy he proclaimed himself as God. The tone was not lost on Mordecai and he looked around at the people and saw how they accepted it without judgment, and he shuddered at their craven trust. He heard how his son's voice gradually mellowed and sang, as if a lullaby, 'As one whom his mother comforteth, so will I comfort you, and you shall be comforted in Jerusalem.' The congregation heaved a unison sigh, and the walls of the synagogue trembled. Outside they had begun to weep. Mordecai dared to look at his son. On his face he saw that same trance-like air that Sabbatai had worn when emerging from his chicken-coop prison, that same look that had steamed on his face in his bed of fever, and Mordecai dreaded its manic consequences. Please God, he prayed to himself, Sabbatai is only Thy servant.

He realised that he had stopped listening, at least to the words, for they were threatening, but that angelic voice had never ceased to sting his ear. Then he heard how, towards the end, it grew louder, angry and menacing. 'And they shall go forth,' his son promised. 'And they shall go forth and look upon the carcases of men that have transgressed against me, for their worm shall not die, neither shall their fire be quenched and they shall be an abhorring unto all flesh.' This last he thundered into the pit of the synagogue and the sounds reverberated to heaven.

Once more Mordecai prayed to God to forgive his son. He's only an ordinary boy, he pleaded. But as he looked at his son, he knew that there was nothing ordinary about him. God would not be fooled by that presumption. He went forward to meet him as he descended from the platform, and he was not surprised at Sabbatai's lack of personal recognition. For his look embraced the whole congregation as if he were about to walk amongst them. Which he clearly intended, and not only through the aisle of the synagogue itself, but out into the courtyard where he knew they were waiting for him. Now it was the turn of those inside to strain their ears, and Mordecai was glad he could no longer see his son, for that look on his face presaged the smell of sulphur.

Then suddenly out of the courtyard came a great roar, not of the crowd, but of a single voice, that lion's roar of Raphael, the idiot, that prefaced each and every one of the judgments that he bellowed through the streets of Smyrna like a prophet in fury. Inside the synagogue, Mordecai feared for his son, but he was alone in that fear, for most of the members of the congregation were smiling, some even laughing aloud in anticipated contempt for what the idiot was about to say. And when it came, they laughed even louder, almost drowning the words. But Mordecai heard them almost as acutely as his son. And heard them before they were said, for he knew their matter. He had heard them before at Sabbatai's circumcision, and would hear them, he feared, again and again, as a knowing descant to his own surmise.

'Beware of false prophets,' he heard, 'which come to you in sheep's clothing but inwardly they are ravening wolves.'

Let Sabbatai stay outside, Mordecai prayed, so that the sulphur would disperse, unknown, into the air.

Outside, those nearest Raphael took his arm to comfort him, for they pitied him for his blindness. Sabbatai, from the look on his face, that distant almost smiling look, seemed not to have heard. He walked a little amongst them, then turned back into the synagogue, taking his place beside his father in the front pew, and nodding as if as a signal for the service to continue. Mordecai wanted to put his arm around his son, to whisper some words of praise into his ear, but he felt him as a stranger, untouchable. And when Clara reached out to touch his son with love and approval, he feared for the outcome. But Sabbatai simply took his mother's hand and squeezed it, for he well knew who his disciples were. At his mother's cue, Joseph stretched across and held his brother's hand, but little Elijah, Mordecai noticed, withheld his greeting. Perhaps he, too, like his father, was pre-empting rejection.

When the service was over, Sabbatai was surrounded by respectful well-wishers. First the Rabbis, led by Rabbi Eskapa. He would congratulate the boy, he decided, but only on the attainment of his manhood. Such formal good wishes would be expected of him. But they would be laced with no reverence, and he would make a point of their lack of adornment. For he knew that, even if the boy himself were not a charlatan, then his unthinking worshippers would make him so, and it was his duty, as the leader of the community, to inject some reason into their Messianic yearning. Other Rabbis followed him, and their opinions were divided. Some of them, those without envy, had little difficulty with the disciple role, others were angry to the point of considering excommunication. But not on this day. So some shook Sabbatai's hand, some touched him, and Sabbatai knew who of them were his friends.

Because of all the congratulations, both inside and outside the synagogue, it took some time for Sabbatai and his family to leave the precincts and make their way back to the festive house. Again a procession formed, for all the congregation were invited if only for a cup of celebration wine. The house was not far from the synagogue, but Clara hurried to make final preparations. And she was there at the house to welcome her family and friends with Sabbatai at her side. Many of the congregants gathered in the courtyard, one of much larger dimension that the annexe to Sabbatai's circumcision. Even so it was crowded. Then Isak, the beggar, made his way to the door and took his time-honoured position just outside it. Raphael, the idiot, was there too. His presence at all community occasions was considered right and proper. Although he was never invited, he was never turned away.

Inside the house, the family had gathered in the same groups as at Sabbatai's circumcision. Only an outsider would have noticed how they had aged, for amongst themselves they were blind to the wrinkles, the stoops and the sagging flesh that time had served to each one of them. There were Nissim and Perla Arditti, who only a few months before had celebrated the barmitzvah of their own son David. Clara's mother, Beki, sat soldered to Sarah, each of them loaded with a further thirteen years of guilt and resentment. While outside in the courtyard, Nahum, Sarah's old love, stood apart from Lusi, the wife who had been thrust upon him.

And like the guest list of those years ago, the menu was the same. For the same people had brought those same dishes that they had been honoured to bring to bless the Covenant. Rabbi Eskapa was tortured by the same doubts, and Mordecai Zvi by the same terror. In the midst of it all, Sabbatai played with David, and for a moment, as he watched them, Mordecai believed that his son was whole. Until he overheard a guest call attention to the boys' play, remarking that Sabbatai was really just an ordinary boy. Or could be when he wished. Then Mordecai feared again, for he could not share his hope of normality with those who thought his son so special. But he could not take his eyes off Sabbatai and David. It *was* normal, what they were doing, picking the cherries off cakes, pulling girls' pigtails, and darting between the tables in a game of tag. Mordecai watched them with joy. Until Sabbatai caught David in his arms and guided him behind the side-board, where, half-hidden, he kissed his friend with an adult passion. And as Mordecai watched, his joy soured. He would not believe it. He willed it to be a nightmare so that he could wake and shiver it away. He wanted to call on all the guests to view the spectacle at the side-board, to have their illusions finally dispelled, for in no way could their Messianic hopes be centred on such a monster. No status on earth could excuse such a perversion. But no one seemed to have noticed.

He watched Sabbatai relax his hold and as he turned he saw the trance across his features. Mordecai looked away. He would never want Sabbatai to know that he had seen what he had seen. In his heart he knew that, in Sabbatai's terms, that kiss marked his true and only initiation into manhood.

3

Another brother

The first fragment of Saul's journal appears to have been written about this time. Its language is Polish, its handwriting that of an adolescent.

'. . . and I have not kept up with this journal. The preparations for my barmitzvah have taken up so much of my time, but now it is over. I am a man now, Papa tells me, and old enough to understand many things. So he told me about Chmielnicki and his attacks on the Jews. I know that he worries, but I can't imagine that Chmielnicki will ever come to our little town . . . In his sermon yesterday, Papa spoke again about the coming of the Messiah. I suppose it's because he's so worried about the pogroms. He spoke of someone called Sabbatai Zvi who lives in Turkey. There have been rumours about him for many years. Everyone knows his name. They say that he has fire in his eyes, and that God lives in his ear. Papa spoke of him in whispers, smiling. After the sermon he told me that Sabbatai Zvi was my age. I felt faint suddenly. I couldn't explain it. But now I think of him all the time . . . Perhaps he will kill Chmielnicki with a miracle . . . Papa is very quiet nowadays. Mama too. They are worried, I think.'

There are many years between this fragment and the next entry in Saul's journal. The handwriting has lost its childish curls. There are no flowers in its lettering. Its calligraphy is stiff with anger. Was Saul too preoccupied in the business of survival to give time to the luxury of keeping a journal? Perhaps there is nothing missing after all. The language, too, is different. It is written in Ladino, a form of Jewish/Spanish, a language current at the time in the Balkans.

'I am weary of my journey and sometimes I long for an end to my days. But I must survive until my repentance is done. I must atone to my father for my sins, to my mother too, and my sisters. How many lifetimes will I need for such a repentance? I betrayed them. I must not shrink from that word, for it was nothing less than that, and my green years at the time will not excuse such an act. I ran away like a coward. I loosened my little sister's trusting hand but the print of that tiny hand still sears my own . . . I am tired and hungry. I beg in the streets. There are many like me, fleeing from the fire . . .

Today in the market place I heard talk of Sabbatai Zvi. Everywhere in my travels I hear his name, and always it is spoken in a whisper. He will redeem us, they say, and always at his name I feel faint as I did the first time when Papa spoke of him. I faint with a kind of longing I cannot explain. I know where my steps are taking me, but it's a very very long way to Smyrna.'

Again there is a gap in the journal, either from lethargy or loss. But Ladino persists as Saul's mode of expression.

'. . . and when I reached the outskirts of this great city, I felt that my wanderings were coming to an end. More and more they talk about him. They whisper his name. They say that he has never been here, has never left Smyrna. But there are rumours that soon he will come to Constantinople. Perhaps I should wait for him here . . . I am hungry and there are too many beggars in this great city.'

The years of Sabbatai's puberty were spent in intensive study of the Talmud and the Torah. And something more. For during those years, young Sabbatai discovered the forbidden book. Its reading was not uniformly forbidden, but it was certainly discouraged amongst those of tender years. The Kabala, with its exotic mysticism, was considered dangerous temptation for the young susceptible mind. Its study was strictly confined to those mature scholars who had achieved perspective and powers of reasoning. But seemingly Sabbatai had tired of the dull commentaries of the Bible and had sought its inner meaning, its paradoxical interpretations, and where else but in the Kabala, the Book of Enlightenment, could one find that which one discovered at one's own raving peril? For besides its alluring mysticism, it embraced the possibility of clairvoyance as well, through the reading of the Tarot, and all these new avenues of Biblical interpretation seduced Sabbatai like a drug.

He studied the Kabala secretly, and then, at the age of eighteen, when no one in Rabbinical authority could deny him his Kabalistic rights, he revealed himself as its most learned exponent. The Rabbis were astonished, and after much consultation, for the honour which they proposed to mete out to Sabbatai had never been conferred on one so young, they gave him the title of 'Chacham' or 'the wise one'.

The adulation that surrounded Sabbatai did not ebb through his growing years. Indeed it flourished, as it embraced Sabbatai's extraordinary scholarship. Moreover, his appearance had taken on an extremely saintly aura. Most of the time he looked as if in a dream and on the verge of discovery. This was not a fantasy image endowed him by his followers for it is clear from portraits of the time that Sabbatai had the face of an angel. His brothers grew in his shadow, yet they adored him. Joseph, the elder, followed him blindly; Elijah, though faithful, was plagued at times by doubts that he shared with no one, having great difficulty in acknowledging them himself. Clara attended to Sabbatai's every need in an attitude of obeisance and adoration, and as her worship intensified, so did Mordecai's bewilderment. And fear. For when the title of Chacham was conferred upon his son, he was filled with pride, but a pride slightly soured by the innuendoes it carried in the minds of those of the faithful. For now they flocked to him, the old and the young, to learn from him and to ask his advice.

For Sabbatai, it was his first recognition of his separateness. Hitherto it had been based on rumour and surmise. But now that it was ratified, and by the highest authority, he felt entitled to consider himself as one apart. As a leader. And as a corollary of this position, he was entitled to followers. Out of those who came to seek his teachings, he selected a group of young disciples and promised to reveal to them the secrets and mysteries of life itself. Previously, others had endowed him with the Messianic role, and he had never been able wholly to trust their casting. But slowly he shed his doubts and by his eighteenth birthday he was well on the way to believing in his heart, and with absolute certainty, that he was the true Messiah.

Mordecai's business affairs took him to Constantinople and, as a reward for his son's diligence, he offered to take Sabbatai with him to visit the big metropolis. Sabbatai was delighted. He had never ventured beyond Smyrna. Part of his excitement was the thought of enlarging his parish. Even as he thought of it, he viewed himself passively and in the third person, as if he were an object of his own thinking. This process fascinated him, that he could stand outside himself and view the sanctity of his own being. It was a breach in his identity which, as he grew older, would deepen and grow raw, and forever wound his spirit. Mordecai already had an inkling of this rift in his son, and though he had no words for it, or even understanding, it disturbed him profoundly. He was wary of this visit to the capital for he was never at ease with Sabbatai. He would not take him on his business visits, he decided. He would point out to him the centres of interest and leave him to his own devices. He dared not consider what those devices might be.

They arrived at the capital late at night and put up at a hostelry. After the long and tiring journey, Mordecai was ready to retire, but Sabbatai was anxious to wander around the city. 'But you won't know your way,' Mordecai tried to dissuade him. 'I shall find it,' he said. 'It will be shown to me.'

Mordecai panicked. He shivered at the phraseology. For him, it was an indication that his son actually believed in others' certainty. Even the kiss Sabbatai placed on his forehead did not seem to him a filial one. Perhaps Sabbatai had meant it as a blessing, but Mordecai wondered at the assumption of such rights.

'Sleep well, Father,' Sabbatai said and he went out into the night.

In his growing-up years, Sabbatai had become a nocturnal creature. His best studying hours were after midnight and, when he closed his books, he would often walk along the seashore. The movement of the waves mesmerised him and finely tuned his spirit to contemplate the nature of God and the universe. As he walked along the shore, he prayed – a prayer was rarely from his lips – and sometimes he sang, tuning his voice to the winds and sounds of the sea. But here in Constantinople he wandered through streets and into dark alleys where shadows loomed suddenly and as suddenly disappeared. He felt no fear, rather a yearning to be part of those shadows, and to know their turnings and destinations. He heard noises and paused to identify them. Hammers on wood, and the scurrying of feet. He walked in the direction of the sounds and, as they grew louder, he found himself on the side of a large square, lit by the occasional lamp and the shadows of workmen at its centre. He went towards them. They were hammering stakes into the ground, sectioning the area into small squares, open-sided booths of a sort. The square was used on market-day, Sabbatai surmised, for the sale of livestock and farm produce.

'When is market-day?' Sabbatai asked one of the workmen.

'Tomorrow,' he said, and drove the hammer firmly into the wood.

Sabbatai walked slowly around the square. There was a raised platform in the centre and he wondered as to its purpose. The cattle market in Smyrna had no such platform. Indeed it had no booths. The stock was led around a ring in the centre of the square, auctioned and delivered to the highest bidder.

'Why the platform?' he asked the workman standing next to him.

'For the parade,' he said.

'Will there be a band?' Sabbatai asked, excited.

'No, no band,' the workman smiled. 'It's just for the stock.'

'But cattle and sheep don't like climbing stairs,' Sabbatai said, noting the steps to the raised area.

'Who said anything about cattle?'

'Then what kind of market is it?' Sabbatai asked.

'Slaves,' the workman said shortly. 'Men, women and children.' He hammered in rhythm with his words.

'Slaves?' Sabbatai had never seen a slave-market. Such things did not happen in Smyrna. Slaves were the stuff of capital cities. He grew excited. 'Where are they from?'

'Poland, of course. Haven't you heard? They're *your* people.' His hammer was getting impatient.

There had been rumours. Sabbatai had heard them in Smyrna. But they were too monstrous to credit. In his house they spoke of it behind closed doors, his mother, his father, the Ardittis, his aunt and grandmother. David, too, was kept out of earshot.

'I've heard rumours,' Sabbatai said. 'D'you know any more about it than that?'

62

'It's more than rumours,' the workman said. 'Go and ask Ahmet over there. The one in the grey apron. He knows about it.'

'Thanks,' Sabbatai said, and eagerly crossed the square to where Ahmet stood, fashioning a gate out of planks of wood. 'Ahmet?' Sabbatai asked as he approached him.

'The same,' the man said. He stood upright, his muscles bulging through the shoulders of his smock.

'They said you could tell me about Poland. What's happening there?' Sabbatai asked.

'Massacres. That's what happening there,' Ahmet said. 'They're killing the Jews again. It's a Polish hobby.'

So it was true, that whisper of hearsay and rumour that rumbled about Smyrna.

'Chmielnicki. He's the leader,' Ahmet said. 'Oh, I've heard some stories about him,' he said with undisguised relish, and he put down his tools, glad of an ear to listen to his tales.

'Who told you?' Sabbatai asked. He was unwilling to show an interest, yet he was curious.

'I got them from the horses' mouths,' Ahmet laughed. 'The refugees. They're streaming into Constantinople. They're up for sale in the market tomorrow.'

'But why? Why?' Sabbatai asked. He wanted to shake the man as if he personally were responsible.

'Have the Poles, the Ukrainians ever needed a reason?' the man asked. 'Hate,' he shouted, 'that's all you need. Hate. Someone to blame. Who better than the Jews?' Ahmet paused and touched Sabbatai's arm. 'You know your history better than I,' he said.

'Tell me what you know,' Sabbatai said, and he sat himself down on a block of wood, feeling that he might need some support. For he was troubled by his appetite for the tales of horror Ahmet clearly wanted to share. Ahmet sat down, too, making himself comfortable on an improvised stool.

'Unbelievable,' he whispered to himself, setting the tone. 'In Nemirov,' he said slowly, 'in Tuleyn, in Podolia, twenty-one thousand Jews were killed because they would not convert to Christianity. Imagine,' he said, 'twenty-one thousand. They were killed as they prayed.' This for openers. Ahmet was intent on painting the scene. 'The Cossacks are the worst,' he said, warming to his theme. 'They flay the Jews alive and throw their flesh to the dogs.'

Sabbatai shivered and Ahmet leaned closer. 'I heard tell of a very popular torture,' he whispered.

How do people invent such things? Sabbatai wondered. Ahmet was teasing now, baiting his listener with sundry pauses in his speech. But Sabbatai did not respond. His horror at the story already told had blunted his curiosity. So Ahmet hurried on, anxious to rekindle his interest.

'One of the women told me,' he said. 'It happened to her uncle. Among many others. She actually witnessed it. They ripped open his belly and sewed a live cat inside him. Then they held his arms above his head and watched him die in helpless agony.'

Sabbatai rose. He needed to get away from the man for, despite Ahmet's relish, it was clear he was telling the truth. 'I must go,' he said. 'It's almost morning.' He rocked unsteadily as he took his first few steps, then slowly and feverishly, he made his way back to the hostelry. For the rest of that night he slept fitfully and dreamed of cats. Screaming.

And awoke in pain. He clutched his stomach, and was horrified at the texture of the skin beneath his hand. He dared to look at himself. Descending from his navel in a straight line, was an undulating ramp of scabs, biscuit-dry and ripe for falling. Yet he dared not touch them. They were holy, and to pick at them would have been to desecrate a shrine. He wrapped his prayer-shawl around him.

'Lord,' he whispered. 'I have become unclean.'

He felt the fever creep upon him and he welcomed it, for he knew it as a springboard for his visions. He closed his eyes and let the pain and fever overwhelm him. In his darkness, he saw a field, fallow and desolate. And in its centre, a red heifer. Then he knew the meaning of his scabs and the source of his pain. For did not the Zohar declaim that the Messiah was as a red heifer, who purifies the unclean but, in the process, becomes himself impure? He dwelt on the vision a long while, until his pain subsided and, touching his body, he caressed the smoothness of his skin. He offered up a prayer of thanksgiving. And of love, too. He felt it in his loins, and God was the sole target of his passion. And with the love came the shuddering fear of loss. 'Never, never desert me,' he pleaded. 'I am lost without You.'

In the morning he joined his father for breakfast. As he caught sight of him at the long table, surrounded by others, though very much alone, he was pierced by an overwhelming love for him. It was sudden and he could find no reason for it. It was as if his father, long assumed dead, had come to life again, a symbol of survival. Heedless of the company, Sabbatai rushed towards him and embraced him with joy.

Mordecai was afraid. Such a spontaneous display of affection from his first-born was unknown to him, and he was not schooled to accept it. From Joseph or Elijah it would appear normal, but from this one, this outsider, this untouchable, it appeared as a prelude to disaster. He responded as calmly as he could, his shoulders stiffening in the embrace. But Sabbatai seemed not to notice, for it was a gesture made solely on his own behalf. Mordecai scratched in his mind for a topic of conversation. 'How did you find the nocturnal city?' he asked.

'There's a slave-market today,' Sabbatai said in flat announcement.

'Refugees?' Mordecai asked.

'You knew, didn't you?' Sabbatai said. 'Thousands are dead. There are terrible stories.'

'I've heard them too.' Mordecai touched his son's arm and noted how it trembled.

'It's a sign,' Sabbatai said.

Mordecai would let that pass, but his son pressed on.

'It's a sign that redemption is at hand.'

Mordecai's heart curled in fear. 'Eat your breakfast,' he said, gruffly. He wanted to reduce their exchange to banality, but after his son's prophecy it sounded more like blasphemy.

'I'm not hungry,' Sabbatai said. He sipped at his coffee.

'What will you do today?' Mordecai asked, though he knew that his son was bound for the market.

'I shall go to the square,' Sabbatai said.

'It will upset you.'

'I need to know and to see everything.' He looked at his father and his eyes were steel.

Mordecai turned his face away. It was impossible to reconcile this man with the son who had so lately embraced him with such love. For a moment he considered offering to take Sabbatai on his business rounds, but he feared his coldness that so quickly could turn to wrath. 'Take care of yourself,' was all he could say.

Sabbatai made his way to the square. He already felt at home in the city and he knew that he could come back to it again and again. He passed the same alleys that in daylight assumed an air of innocence. Children were playing where hooligans had lain in wait, and women, their baskets over their arms, stopped to chatter where their nocturnal sisters had plied their trade. The streets were crowded with people, all of them moving in one direction. To the square. For the slave-market was a spectacle. Children were amongst the crowd, hanging on to their mothers' skirts. They were the same crowd that would flock to a public hanging. Sabbatai was ashamed to join them, yet he followed in their jostling path.

The sundry booths around the raised platform were already occupied. The crowds were milling around the barrier, but Sabbatai was tall and had a fine view of the traders as they passed from booth to booth examining the goods. Those on sale were young, both men and women. Sabbatai noticed that some of the women clutched babies in their arms, and these goods the traders passed quickly by. Most of the booths were occupied by young boys who flexed their frail muscles as the traders passed by. Already weakened by their flight from terror, emaciated, listless and without hope, they were bargains for nobody. But they could be got cheap and fattened up for service.

Sabbatai threaded his way through the crowds and entered the arena as if he were a trader. He felt ashamed of his curiosity, of the voyeur he saw himself to be. He wished he had money in his pocket to prove, at least to others, that he was genuine. He passed quickly by the women's cages, which held no interest for him. Only pity, and pity is not a voyeur's tool. The auctioneer released some of the men from the booths and marshalled them on to the platform. Then Sabbatai watched the traders inspecting the goods on offer. Taking off their gloves, they climbed the steps. Sabbatai followed them. But he kept his hands covered. Men and boys on sale were lined up on the platform. Sabbatai watched as the dealers passed in front of them, pausing occasionally to run hands over chests and arms, testing possible strength, suitability for service, and if they were satisfied, they would nod their interest to the auctioneer, who, in his turn, would shout to them the number of the lot in the bidding. Sabbatai dawdled along the line, his hands firmly clenched behind his back. Then he saw him. And froze. The trader behind him tripped as he suddenly stopped, then cursed and bypassed him in haste. As did the others who followed. For Sabbatai's feet were rooted. His eyes were fixed on the boy at the end of the second row. He stood but a few feet distant but he feared further approach, for it seemed to him that to take one step forward would have shattered the mirror of his own reflection. And, with no trace of vanity, he found it beautiful. The boy stared back at him, heedless of the traders who fingered and passed him by. Each was mesmerised by the other. Then the boy stepped out of line and timidly went to where Sabbatai stood.

'Buy me,' he pleaded. 'All my family are dead. I am alone. I shall work hard for you. Please,' he begged. 'Touch me. Feel my muscle.'

But Sabbatai dared not lay a hand on him. Instead he signalled to the auctioneer, who in his turn shouted out the number of his chosen lot.

The boy smiled. 'Thank you, sir,' he said. 'I shall be your willing slave.'

'You shall be my brother,' Sabbatai said. Then he hurried away.

He had no money. He went quickly to the auctioneer and arranged with him to hold his lot until his return and, as a pledge, he left the gold chain that his father had given him when he had received the title of Chacham. Then he rushed back to the hostelry.

His father was entertaining a client from England, but at Sabbatai's request, fearful of denying him, he excused himself and went with his son to an outer room.

Sabbatai poured out his story. 'We have to take him, Papa. We have to save him.'

'Calm down, my son,' Mordecai said softly. 'Of course we'll save him, if that is your wish. But why this boy? This particular boy?'

'He is the same as me, Papa. He looks the same. He could be my twin. You'll see. I must have him. I simply must have him.'

He was talking about the boy as if he were a bright toy, and Mordecai feared what he wanted with this toy and how he would use or abuse it. 'Here,' he said, handing him his purse. 'And buy him some clothes for the journey. We leave for home early in the morning.'

When he had gone, rushing out of the door, Mordecai wondered what he had done. Within the space of a few moments and with no consultation with Clara or his sons, he had adopted an unknown into his family. And all on the whim of his first-born. And a wave of resentment swept over him that he had been so neatly colonised. And, if he dared to think about it, that was exactly what Sabbatai was doing with the whole family and possibly even with his friends. He had never heard one of them gainsay him. His son had everybody in thrall. Clara, a willing victim, would have been proud, but he, his father, found such power a source of shame. He returned to his business with little appetite, then waited for his son and his so-called twin to return.

Sabbatai hurried to the square. The market was in full spate, the auctioneer's voice rang over the crowd in the tone of profit. Sabbatai had little difficulty in securing his lot, and cheaply too, for no one else had bid for him. He redeemed his gold chain and handed over the selling-price. Then he went to collect his prize.

The boy was waiting on the platform and in the same spot where Sabbatai had left him. Now Sabbatai had no difficulty in approach, nor even in touching him. He laid his hand on the boy's threadbare sleeve.

'You are mine,' he said. 'What's your name?'

'Saul. Saul Vlonski.'

'And I am Sabbatai. Sabbatai Zvi.'

Saul stared at him in wonder.

'I know,' he said. 'They have talked of you. They know who you are.'

'Who knows?'

'In Poland they talk about you. In Bulgaria. In Hungary. You were born on Tisha B'Av, as was ordained.'

Sabbatai trembled, but he was not surprised. Many Jews in Smyrna had relations in Poland. Letters had been exchanged, and Messianic craving travels well, especially to threatened terrain.

'Are you sure,' Saul asked, 'that I should be your brother?'

'You will be more than that,' Sabbatai said. 'Come.'

Saul waited for him to lead the way, then he followed.

Sabbatai felt his person behind him and he felt suddenly as one who was followed. Not pursued in rage, or dogged with cunning, but shadowed with faith and adoration. The person of Saul who trailed his footsteps was one of thousands. Sabbatai stood still. His brow was fevered and, had his father seen his face at that time, he would have recognised the trance that crossed his son's features. For that short moment, Sabbatai Zvi knew that he was the Redeemer, and that, when the time was ripe, he must declare himself. But he would bide his time.

Sabbatai clothed Saul in garments like his own, then he took him back to the hostelry where his father was waiting.

'This is Saul,' Sabbatai said. 'Does he not look like my twin?'

Mordecai stared at the newcomer, straining to find some resemblance. The boy was fair, his hair almost golden, and continents removed from Sabbatai's black locks. The eyes were translucent blue, and spoke of a vision far-flung from the smoky brown of his own son's. Their build, too, was genes apart. The boy was short, almost stocky, while Sabbatai looked down on him from his lean height. Mordecai did not know how to respond. What was the quality of his son's vision, what distorted dreams or unnatural imaginings could fashion a mirror-image from this boy? He drew on what was left of his courage.

'I see no resemblance at all,' he said.

'Of course you don't,' Sabbatai said pityingly. 'Saul is my spirit's twin.'

Mordecai let it pass and stretched out his hand in welcome to the boy. 'You shall be one of my family,' he said.

'I must go out again,' Sabbatai said quickly.

'But where?' Mordecai said. His son's moods were completely beyond him. He noticed the sweat on Sabbatai's brow. 'Are you all right?' he whispered.

For reply, Sabbatai kissed him. He knew the value of the occasional embrace. It could buy his father's acquiescence any time. Mordecai, innocent of the blackmail, smiled. 'I'll take care of Saul,' he said. Yet he wondered why his son who so lately had declared this stranger to be a soul-brother, now left him with no explanation or apology. He decided not to question it.

'He needs to be alone,' he heard Saul say, and the boy's explanation gave Mordecai a certain peace.

Saul was right. Sabbatai desperately needed to be alone. He had to test this new soul-twin of his. He had to leave his body inside Saul's, for Saul to care for, for Saul to tend its fever, so that he could go about his own business. And that business was the role that Saul and the others had cast for him, the role of leader, the one to be followed. As he walked the streets, his brow cooled. He heard the muezzins' chants from the minarets of the city and, automatically, his steps moved in the direction of their sounds. Soon he was part of the crowd intent on prayer. At the threshold of the mosque he, with all the other penitents, stepped out of his shoes. Those about him stared, not with hostility, but rather with curiosity, for he was clearly not one of them. His apparel and appearance marked him as a Jew. His long gaberdine, his flat hat and his ringlet sidelocks spoke of a faith that no mosque could house. They chose to believe that the stranger was tasting the Koran so they did not hinder him. Sabbatai shuffled after them into the large hall and with them, in ordered lines, he knelt on the stone floor, taking part of his neighbour's prayer-mat for his ease. The act of kneeling was the first blasphemy. Jews did not kneel. That gesture was alien to their relationship with God. Prostration, yes. And out and out obeisance. But kneeling was a half-measure.

A tepid gesture. An insult almost to the All-forgiving, He who wanted all or nothing. But it did not disturb Sabbatai. Indeed he savoured its perversity.

He listened to the other's prayers, allowing their chanting to line the walls of the mosque with their known domestic tongue, then he started on his own discordant Hebraic descant. He launched into the beginning of the Sabbath morning service. 'How goodly are thy tents, O Jacob, thy tabernacles, O Israel. Lord, I love the habitation of Thy house, the place where the glory dwelleth.' He looked up at the dome of the mosque, at the mosaic patterns of glass and the gold leaf that framed it. He fully expected the dome to shatter, as if, with his Hebrew prayer, he had struck the exact timbre of its pitch. But it shivered only a little, as if offended by the intrusion. He remained kneeling and praying meanwhile, until the service was over. As he rose from the prayer-mat, his neighbour touched his arm.

'What are you doing here, brother?' he asked.

'I am about my Father's business,' Sabbatai said.

He put on his shoes and hurried back to the hostelry where he found his father and Saul in spirited conversation. But Saul fell silent when Sabbatai appeared and Sabbatai was pleased for he took it as a sign that he was now permitted to re-enter his own body.

'Saul has been telling me about his family,' Mordecai said. He wished to prolong their conversation and he was slightly irritated that it had been interrupted.

'I have been to the mosque,' Sabbatai said.

'It's a beautiful building,' Mordecai said quickly, keeping his son firmly on the outside of it in his mind's eye, gazing up at the gold-leafed dome, willing him into the attitude of tourist.

'I went inside,' Sabbatai said. 'I prayed with them.'

Mordecai did not want such a subject prolonged so he made no comment.

'I need to know everything,' Sabbatai said.

72

Again there was no reaction and Mordecai feared that his continued silence would sour into hostility. 'Of course you must,' he said, because he had to say something.

'Just this once, Father,' he said. 'I won't make a habit of it.' He laughed and Mordecai laughed with him with a measure of relief. 'Now tell me about your family, Saul. I missed your story.'

He seemed in a jovial mood, but for Saul such a mood was inappropriate to the story he had to tell. He had told it once to Mordecai, and to himself countless times, but no matter how often he re-told it, he could never succeed in burying his dead.

'I'm tired,' Saul said. 'I'll tell you another time.'

'Go to bed then,' Mordecai told him. 'We leave early in the morning.'

When Saul had gone, Mordecai made as if to retire also, but Sabbatai detained him. He needed to know Saul's story, and begged his father to tell him. Mordecai was glad of conversation even though the subject was so dire and he told his son Saul's story, exactly as he remembered it, and in Saul's tone of helplessness.

Sabbatai was deeply affected by the tale, and when it was told, he asked, 'Papa, if it was a question of saving your own life, would you convert?'

'I am not sure about myself,' Mordecai said, 'but I would not hesitate to prepare my children for baptism.'

Sabbatai was astonished, yet for some reason his father's answer pleased him. In the Kabala, much was made of redemption through sin and, in his father's response, Sabbatai began to understand its import and to be excited by it. The dark shadows of his belief, those shadows that masked the reverse face of God, where lurked the Devil and all that was forbidden, in those shadows were enticement and seduction, and Sabbatai longed to embrace them.

'What I write now I do not believe myself. Perhaps as the letters fall upon the parchment it will make it real. I am

become his brother. The brother of Sabbatai Zvi. I saw him in the crowd and I knew him at once. There was no reason for me to recognise him. I had never heard him described. But he could be no other. The light in his eyes pierced unfiltered through the crowd and though he did not smile, his face was suffused with an unearthly joy. I knew at once that not only did he love God but that he had lain with Him. He could not guard the secret of such congress for it flushed his cheeks with fire.'

During the journey back to Smyrna, Mordecai studied Saul, that inconsolable boy, no blood of his, but thrust upon him as a son. He wondered what had prompted his son's need for a shadow. It occured to him that Saul was designated to be not so much a shadow as a disciple, and the thought saddened him for it evoked Messianic disturbance. For some reason, perhaps for self-assurance, he stretched his hand out across the carriage and patted Sabbatai's knee in a gesture of affection. Sabbatai's features were undisturbed by the gesture. It was Saul who smiled.

Sabbatai was at present immune to those around him. He was experiencing once again the tremors that had shaken him in the streets of Constantinople. That thought of Saul as a mirror-image he considered a divine inspiration. In his manic moments, and he knew them now to be more and more frequent, he could bequeath his fevered body to his new-found brother, and go off alone to deal with his spirit, for that spirit was the fire of the Messiah. He had no doubt of it, and he longed for the release of proclaiming it. He would return to Smyrna and devote all his energies to creating his ministry. Bethlehem, after all, was no special location. It simply meant the House of Bread, and Smyrna would do just as well.

4

Maybe a miracle

'I love him. I loved my parents. My sisters too. But it is not that kind of loving. I cannot declare this love. Sabbatai has need of me, and such a declaration might impair his trust. For I see what no one else sees and I hold his secrets. We are often alone. He teaches me the hidden meanings of the Kabala and as he does so, he is often in a trance. Yesterday he fell into a state of melancholy that he could not understand. And then suddenly and with no reason, he felt joy. He began to sing. I could make no sense of the words. He had invented a lexicon to clothe his ecstasy. When he was finished, he touched my face with his hand. "Saul," he said. "I have seen God." Then he fell into a fit and foamed at the mouth. I tended him and when the fit had subsided, he begged me to speak of it to no one. It is hard to guard others' secrets and one's own love at the same time.'

It's unlikely that Sabbatai Zvi would have made his mark as a possible Messiah were it not for the thriving age of communications. For he had no special message. No new sermon. Other claimants had preceded him with equal qualifications, equal zeal, and equal mania, but for want of the means of report, neither their fever nor their fame had spread. But in Sabbatai's day, letters crossed by mail throughout Europe, and word of mouth and rumour travelled happily by caravan. The Polish massacres, now known throughout Europe, had fuelled Messianic hope and the time was ripe for the appearance of a Redeemer. But Sabbatai was not yet ready. His certainty in his role was subject all the while to fluctuation, depending on the height of his fevers. Often he was in doubt and terror. Yet, amongst his disciples, he fostered belief in himself as leader.

His followers were a small group, fanatical and devoted. His brother Joseph worshipped him as a fraternal hero-figure, and Saul took his prompted place alongside. David, his life-long friend, was a loyal devotee. There were six other disciples, all from the seminary, and together they studied the mysteries of the Zohar and Kabala. The practice of the rituals was aesthetic and strict and involved prolonged fasting, penitential exercises and mortification of the flesh. Thus the spirit would become finely tuned into a sensitivity that would embrace all that was transcendental and supernatural. Indeed, into a state that would render the soul fit to converse with God. Although such ritual was practised daily in some small measure, it was not until Friday that it was translated into a veritable orgy of self-denial. Friday was the day that heralded the onset of the Sabbath, and on that day, the Zvi household was alive with preparation.

The Friday night celebration was always a family affair. Grandma Beki and Aunt Sarah were wont to arrive early on the Friday morning, laden with their offerings for the Sabbath. The presence of Beki and Sarah in the Zvi household invariably accentuated the tension between them. Clara spent most of the day keeping them apart, but she noticed how quickly they countered each other, at whatever distance, as if out of habit or sheer need. The two of them thrived on abrasion. On this particular Friday, they were near to breaking-point, but not close enough for Clara, in whose eyes a total explosion between them might have been beneficial. Almost involuntarily she stirred the ferment between them. Both Beki and Sarah knew the perils of explosion. They knew the threat of peace. And how could they, those two women who for years had found their only loving in blame, resentment, guilt and pity, how could they accommodate peace? So on a Friday, when Clara's children were gathered round her, and the togetherness of family shrieked its attendance, the battle between Beki and her thwarted daughter erupted into splendid flower. It ended neither in victory nor in defeat. Truce was the only possible outcome, in order to ensure its continuance.

On this particular Friday, Grandma Beki had complained of feeling unwell. Clara, who could afford credulity and concern, urged her to lie down. But Sarah, who was familiar with the 'unwell' plea, and knew it as a ploy to re-arm and gather forces, ignored it, and refused to let up on her attack. Her verbal onslaught had nothing to do with the real issue between them. To have mentioned Nahum's name, or anything to do with the frustrated love between them, would have been to break all the rules of battle. It would have been below the belt for both of them. But words there were between them, torrents of words, peripheral words that sometimes hovered dangerously close to the centre of the fire.

'I'm not well,' Beki pleaded.

'Let her lie down,' Clara said.

Sarah shrugged with contempt and went into the kitchen. Clara helped her mother up the stairs.

'You're a good daughter to me,' Beki said, and Clara felt it as an insult, for everything her mother said was sub-titled. The 'good daughter' that Clara was, was a mere translation of the pain she endured from the 'other one'. Clara would not pursue the theme. She was not clever at innuendo. The words that came out of her mouth were the words that expressed her thoughts. Without subterfuge.

'I'll leave the door open,' she said, after she had settled her mother in bed. 'Call me if you want anything. I'll send Sabbatai to see you.' In Clara's eyes, Sabbatai was the healer. Of the spirit as well as the body. Like her sister, she suspected that it was the former which ailed her mother.

Sabbatai was in his room with Saul. She knocked timidly at his door.

'Sabbatai,' she called. 'Grandma isn't well. Would you go and see her?'

He opened the door almost immediately. He touched her shoulder. Of the whole family, Clara was the only one who merited his touch. She lowered her eyes, blushing like a lover.

'I'll go at once,' he said. He returned to his desk for his prayer-book. 'Don't worry,' he said, and he glided past her across the landing. Later he came down into the kitchen and reported that she was sleeping.

It was but two hours before the first star in the sky would announce the Sabbath, and time for Sabbatai's personal preparation. He called his brothers, Joseph and Saul, and together with their hyssops, they made their way to the sea-shore. They were silent except to give the occasional greeting to one of the followers they encountered on the way. From the top of the hill they viewed the huge expanse of sea, and, with Sabbatai as their leader, all nine of them followed him down the path of the rise until they reached the shore. Here they unwrapped their prayer-shawls and set about their worship. Sabbatai led them in prayer. Sometimes he broke into song and his voice opened like a flower across the water. And with such purity of sound that the others refrained from accompaniment, the better to hear his song. When the prayers were finished, they folded their shawls and made themselves naked on the sand. Then taking their hyssops they lashed themselves, gently at first, and then with a growing frenzy, as Sabbatai, with his solo prayers, dictated the rhythm of their worship.

A witness would have turned away from the spectacle, in horror at the thing itself, and even more in terror of its consequences. But that same witness, had he had the courage to fix his eye unswervingly on the ritual, would, when it was done, have marvelled at the unmarked flesh of the penitents, a skin unblemished and as smooth as alabaster. He would have seen too how they embraced, holding each other for a long while, while Sabbatai stroked the heads of each one of them. And afterwards, how they leapt into the sea like children.

Sabbatai swam out towards a group of rocks, while the others, lesser swimmers, frolicked in the shallows. After a while, they went back to the shore, leaving Sabbatai in the sea. As they dressed, they heard someone call his name. Faintly at first and then louder and with some urgency. They scanned the brow of the hill which, in the gathering dark, was less discernible. Still they heard the cry, and now it echoed across the sea with recurrent pleading. And then they saw the voice. Little Elijah, scampering down the hillside, calling his brother's name. They looked towards the sea for Sabbatai but he was nowhere to be seen. They were in no way anxious. Sabbatai loved to swim under water, to investigate the crevices in the rocks and the fauna and flora that dwelt in that silence. It was the silence that he most loved and, holding his breath, he would listen to it, for its soundless sound was palpable. So seductive was that silence that he raged when having to leave it, to be deafened by the air and his own sudden intake of breath. Even his heart-beat offended him. He prayed for breath long enough to be embraced by that peace and finally to succumb to it, for, if God dwelt anywhere on earth, it was in that silence. So Sabbatai was deaf to Elijah as he screamed his name, and deaf to all his followers who echoed Elijah's call.

Now Elijah had reached them, his face red from running, and his breath short.

'Grandma's ill,' he panted to Joseph. 'She's calling for Sabbatai.' Even through his breathlessness it was hard to disguise the contempt in his voice that, surrounded in any case by all her family, including the doctor who had been called, she still felt the need for Sabbatai's presence. As if he could work some miracle. For Elijah had been infected with his father's doubts. He had shared his father's sighs and tears, and sometimes he hated Sabbatai for the pain he caused him. And now that hate was curdling, as Sabbatai, wallowing in silence, could not but be indifferent to his cries.

'None of us can swim that far,' Saul said.

But Elijah was already stripped.

'He's around the rock,' Joseph called after him as he plunged into the sea.

Elijah's hatred fuelled his strokes and within a short time, he'd reached the rock. Then, taking a deep breath, he dived below. He saw his brother's feet, white and still as death and his heart turned over with the pain of loss. He had to surface then for air, and he breathed awhile as the tears flowed. He knew he had to go down again, at least to touch his brother, to embrace him, to thrust his body into the air. But if Sabbatai was dead, he wondered, why did he not float to the surface? For a moment he nurtured some hope, but then he envisaged the possibility that his body had been wedged in the rock. He took a deep breath, more of sorrow than of air, and dived once more below. His brother's feet were as before.

Sabbatai was holding them still, in fear of breaking that silence that he now, like a lover, embraced. Elijah touched him, and suddenly his whole body sprang like a wounded shark and surfaced in an anger that was sublime. Elijah came up timidly beside him.

'Why did you do that?' Sabbatai screamed at him.

Elijah turned his back in disgust. He started to swim to the shore. 'Grandma's very ill,' he said, over his shoulder. 'The doctor's with her. She's calling for you.'

Sabbatai shot past him like an arrow and reached the shore with miraculous speed. Elijah took it easy. He was breathless and weary but, above all, confused. He trod water for a while as he watched his brother throw on his clothes and make for the hill, followed by Saul in close pursuit, then Joseph and the rest of them. He wished that Sabbatai would be like ordinary boys, like normal elder brothers with whom he could play and tease and sometimes worship. But with Sabbatai, only the last was permissible. Joseph found it easy, natural almost, and so did Saul, that stranger from a distant land who, out of the blue, had become a brother. He envied them their acquiescence and he wondered why he baulked at it, though in his young heart he knew that one of them had to look after their father. That appeared to be his role. But they were outnumbered, the two of them, and he wondered with fear what would be the outcome of it all. He swam slowly to the shore, then dressed and made his way home.

When he arrived, the family had gathered in the bedroom. Except for his father whom he found in the kitchen in whispered conversation with the doctor.

'How's Grandma?' he said. 'Is she going to die?'

Mordecai drew Elijah towards him. 'She's had a heart-attack,' he said. Elijah wondered whether a heart-attack was what he had had in the water looking down at Sabbatai's dead feet. 'Then she'll get better,' he said, wondering what all the fuss was about.

'We all have to die, Elijale.' His father used the diminutive by way of affection. 'And Grandma is already quite old.'

'What do people do when they are dying?' he asked. He wanted to make sure before he offered to visit her.

'She's sleeping, and sometimes she wakes. Then sleeps again. First have something to eat. Then go and sit with her.'

The Sabbath candles were lit, so prayers must have been said over the table. He broke some bread, made a blessing and crammed it into his mouth. He was starving. He turned away from his father, ashamed to be so alive and so well when death was lurking upstairs. But his father came to the table and prepared a dish of fish and beans for him and bade him sit and eat.

'I'll come first thing in the morning,' the doctor was saying and his father showed him to the door. He heard them whispering in the hallway, but he did not strain his ear, sensing that their words would not please him.

When his father had shown the doctor out, he went straight upstairs. 'Take your time,' he said to Elijah. 'Eat slowly and take some fruit when you've finished.' But Elijah hurried with his food, sensing that this was no time to dawdle and certainly not to enjoy. Besides, although he had been famished, he was now, after only a few mouthfuls, unpleasantly full. He was tired, too, and would happily have gone straight to bed, but he felt that his father needed his protection. He entered his grandmother's room and took his father's hand. She was sleeping. Elijah wondered whether she was already dead. The presence of Sabbatai, shawl-wrapped and praying fervently in the corner, could have meant life or death, and the urgency and passion of his prayer, either. His mother and Aunt Sarah sat on either side of the bed, each holding Grandma Beki's hand. His mother was weeping, but Aunt Sarah sat expressionless, not knowing what to think, and certainly not how she *should* be feeling, but aware only of a fearful future. After a while, Sabbatai interrupted his prayer and suggested that they all go to bed. Elijah dragged his father towards the door.

'Shall we not stay with you?' Saul asked.

'You should all go,' Sabbatai said. 'You too, Mama and Aunt Sarah.'

Clara released her mother's hand and got away up straightaway. She would not question Sabbatai's wishes. But Aunt Sarah, untouched by Sabbatai's glory, stayed firmly put. She had always been wary of her sister's claims for the boy. Scoffing almost. Was it not enough to have a child, she thought bitterly, did he have to be a Messiah as well?

'I'm staying, Sabbatai,' she defied him.

'Come, Sarah,' Clara urged. 'We can do nothing here.'

'I won't leave her,' Sarah said.

Suddenly the full horror of her mother's possible demise overwhelmed her. The loss of that figure in whose shadow she had lived all her life, with whom she had sparred, both winning and losing, loving and loathing. How could she live alone in an arena with no combatant in sight? Over the latter years she had become addicted to her mother, and already the thought of her death stirred the pains of withdrawal.

'I want to stay with her,' she said. Clara shrugged, kissed her mother's forehead and left the room. Sabbatai did not move from the corner. He turned his back and prayed to the wall.

The house was silent. In its sleep it gathered strength to accept the morning's loss. Even Sarah loosened her mother's hand and fell into terrible dreaming. So she did not notice Sabbatai as he crossed over to the bed and touched her mother's forehead. But later on, she was to swear to it. Simply that he touched her, stroking her mother's cheeks with his long fingers and praying all the while. And that he had seemed for a while to go into a trance, the fever vivid on his forehead. And that he had sung prayers like an angel. She swore to having seen it all, a blind eye-witness who, in her imaginings, had viewed the night's events and had seen them exactly as they were.

In the morning, when she stirred, she felt a hand clasp her own, and, opening her eyes, noticed that Sabbatai was gone and the room was prayer-less and her hand was being stroked by her mother's gentle fingers. And looking up, she saw her sitting up in bed, smiling and flushed, as if woken from a long and remedial sleep.

'Mama,' she whispered, 'how do you feel?'

'I'm well,' Beki said, her voice strong and already armed for battle. 'Why shouldn't I be well?' she said.

'You were ill last night,' Sarah said. 'Very ill.'

'It's because you give me so much aggravation.' Beki was now well and truly back in harness, and Sarah hugged her with the relief that she would go on living to torment her so.

In her joy she ran through the door and shouted through the house, 'A miracle. A miracle.'

They woke to the sound and those who walked in the street heard it too and they carried it from one ear to the other, and in time it reached the synagogue for Sabbath morning prayers. And before the day was out, it had sieved its magic through the whole of Smyrna. The doctor had arrived early in the morning, fully expecting to sign a certificate of death. And he found the old lady breakfasting at the family table.

'It's a miracle,' Clara said. 'That's the only explanation.'

The doctor was inclined to agree with her, though his profession forbade belief in anything that was not provable. Mordecai took him to one side.

'Is it possible,' he whispered, 'that the diagnosis was wrong?' He craved a natural cure. The word 'miracle' stuck in his throat. There was no room for such a word in his house, for who knew what madness would follow?

The doctor was offended. 'There is no doubt in my mind,' he said, 'it was a heart-attack. By all the laws of nature, she should not have recovered. But what happened last night was no natural law.'

Mordecai turned away. The man might just as well have pronounced the word 'miracle'. The belief was abroad, and proof would be to hand, snowballing from mouth to mouth, ornamented at every turn, and laced with wonder. It was now too late to stop the avalanche. 'Where's Sabbatai?' Mordecai shouted, as if he would find him and punish him for the trouble he had caused.

'He's already in "shul". Saul and Joseph are with him,' Clara said. 'And it's time you went too.'

Mordecai noticed how, of late, Clara had assumed a self-confidence, one that allowed her less subservience to all in the household except to Sabbatai. And as her humility to her eldest-born increased so did her authoritarian reign over her house. A passing visitor would have assumed that Clara ruled the roost. She ushered Mordecai out of the house, served the doctor breakfast, and sat quietly at the table for a while, glowing in the aftermath of her son's divine power. She knew that last night was a turning point in all their lives, that no longer could the sceptics scoff, or those several Rabbis invoke blasphemy. For there was proof for all to see. That day her mother would walk the streets new-born, and the doctor could only offer his baffled bewilderment.

In the synagogue the word passed along the pews, but now it was no longer rumour. Somehow the manner and matter of the 'miracle' had become known and it was more than one's life was worth to doubt it. In the face of its most palpable truth, Mordecai was impotent. When asked, he could only confirm what all had heard. He had no proof to deny it. He heard the Rabbis call out Sabbatai's name, honouring him to approach the Ark of the Covenant. There was a hush throughout the congregation as his son slowly climbed the steps to the Holy Sanctum. Now Mordecai knew it was too late for sanity, and he squeezed Elijah's hand as he stood by his side, and found some comfort in his alliance.

When the service was over, Mordecai noticed how Sabbatai, shadowed by the ever-faithful Saul, David and Joseph, hurried from the hall, as if loth to be approached or questioned. But no one moved towards him. He had already become untouchable. So they turned their gossip-hungry tongues to Mordecai, wanting to hear over and over again, and this time from a reliable witness, the details of Sabbatai's first miracle. For that was how they termed it, as if there were many more to follow. In their eyes was the light of Redemption and Mordecai could not bear to disabuse them. Neither did he have the words to do so, so he went along with their desperate fantasy, taking care in his mind to mock each and every one of his syllables. For he knew that he too could fall into the trap of rumour and that he alone must remain as a bulwark of sanity against the Bedlam that was Smyrna. He alone, with perhaps Elijah at his side.

Sabbatai hurried home and went straight to his room. He felt the fever upon him, and he turned to Saul who stood by the door and he held him close.

'Be Sabbatai,' he said, clinging to Saul's body as if willing it to absorb his troubled spirit. Like a scapegoat which would carry his sins. 'Take me to yourself,' he said, 'and leave me to still my fever.' Then he kissed him and turned him gently from the door.

A little later, Clara came into Sabbatai's room, and she found him, as she had so often found him before, sitting bolt upright in his bed, staring into nothing, his one arm tucked behind his back fondling that magic groove of his infancy. She sat beside him on the bed and took his other hand.

'They say it was a miracle,' she whispered.

'And what do you think, Mama?' he said.

'I think that what they say is true.'

He shook his head, then turned away as if he would have none of it. 'What shall I do, Mama?' he said helplessly.

She put her arms around him. 'Nothing,' she said. 'You just go on being yourself.'

'That's just what I cannot be,' he said.

She didn't understand him and feared to ask for an explanation. 'Is it such a terrible burden for you, Sabbatai, to be what you are?'

'What is it that I am?' he asked.

She was afraid to name him. It was not her place. She was his mother and a natural disciple. It was for others to tell him his name, then she would echo it along with the multitude. 'Shall I bring you some breakfast?' she asked. She was more at ease in the maternal role.

'I shall fast today,' Sabbatai said. Then he smiled. 'Just in case it *was* a miracle. Has Saul eaten?' he asked suddenly.

'He's waiting for you,' Clara said.

'Tell him to eat today. He must eat. I order it.' Then after a pause, 'Do you love him, Mama?'

'I love him as you love him,' she said. Then she kissed him and left the bedside.

But she did not go back to the kitchen. She went to her room. She needed to be alone. Sabbatai's self-doubts had disquieted her. In the beginning she'd had no doubts about the role her son was destined to play. As he grew into boyhood those beliefs remained. Indeed they were strengthened in the face of Mordecai's continued scepticism. Today more than ever, she believed in her son's God-given destiny. Had he not wrought a miracle to prove it? But what disturbed her was Sabbatai himself, his fear of the role, his unwillingness to accept it. Yet there were times when he longed for it, had even hinted at it himself. Now for the first time she realised the enormous responsibilities entailed in such a role and she wondered whether she should underplay her expectations, to save him from such a burden. As Mordecai did. But now she would have to counter her mother and sister too, who, since the miracle, had become fervent disciples. Only their gender prohibited more active support.

She heard a murmuring outside the window and, wary of what she would discover, she half-lifted the curtain. It was as she feared. A crowd was gathering, a quiet murmuring throng. They were assembling outside the house, as if they had a mind to stay and keep vigil. She noticed that the men were carrying their prayer-shawls, threatening supplication. For a moment she hated God and all that He had done to her. She wanted to scream to them to go away, to take their blessed curse off her home and family. But she knew it had all gone too far. It was too late now for underplay; her expectations had gone overboard, beyond hope of moderation.

She returned to Sabbatai's room and quietly opened the door. She saw his still, curved body beneath the sheets and she thanked God that he was sleeping.

For the rest of the day the crowds gathered. Their stealth and silence were remarkable. When the Sabbath was over, they did not go to the synagogue. The ground around Sabbatai's house was holy enough terrain on which to salute the Sabbath's end, and she heard their prayers and shivered.

In his room Sabbatai heard them too, and his fever was high. He dared not look out of the window, nor light the lamp. Both would have been a gesture of acknowledgment. So he dressed in the dark and crept downstairs. Even to face his family would be an ordeal, for the Sabbatai that was yesterday would be a stranger to them today. As he expected, they were all assembled in the kitchen, well away from the windows, the curtains firmly drawn. He felt he ought to apologise to them for bringing such catastrophe on the house. For that was how he viewed it. They looked at him with tenderness, and their awe struck him like stones.

'What shall I do?' he said.

'Be yourself, my darling,' said his grandmother, that new recruit, burning with the zeal of a convert. She said it with such confidence, as if she knew exactly what Sabbatai was. Of what he was made. Of the devil and the divine in him, of the evil and the good, of the aesthetic and the needling sybarite. Above all, of the sound and perilously unsound mind.

He looked to Saul.

'I am with you,' Saul said.

'And I too.' Joseph went to stand by his side.

Elijah looked to his father. 'Why can't we all go away from here?' he pleaded.

Sabbatai went towards him, clasped his shoulders, then with little effort lifted him in his arms. He smelt the fear in his youngest brother and his lack of belief and he was glad of it. Relieved that at least one of his brothers reflected the very doubts he had in himself, he prayed that Elijah and his father would have the courage to doubt for ever. They were his safety-valve and, between them, they could care for his sanity.

He turned to Saul. 'Call the followers together,' he said. 'We shall study. Joseph, go with him.' Together they would be less of a target for the pious throng outside.

'Will you eat something?' his mother asked.

'Later on, after our meeting. Then I shall go to the sea, and afterwards I shall break my fast.' He knew what would be the outcome of the meeting with his followers. He longed for it, yet he dreaded it too. It would call for a strict ritual, probably the strictest and most holy of his life. And he would do it alone. Under the rock, in that divine silence.

They waited. Sabbatai sat Elijah in a chair and crouched beside him. He held his hand. Elijah was close to tears. He recalled his many angers with his brother, his rage at the pain he caused their father, yet all his fury could not quench his love. He feared that as they both grew older, the anger and the loving would intensify and to such proportions that they might cancel each other out once and for all. One of those feelings would finally overcome, and Elijah knew that, whichever was the victor, the result would be chaos.

Eventually Saul and Joseph returned with the followers. Together with Sabbatai they went to a room at the back of the house, one that overlooked the garden. Sabbatai hoped that in that place there would be silence, away from the murmuring throng in the streets. But the rumour spread even there and, peering through the window, Sabbatai saw and heard the hum of the crowd. They covered the grass entirely, even the paths of the surrounds.

'Go and get candles,' Sabbatai said.

They sat in the darkness for a while until Joseph returned with a candelabra. Sabbatai wished he had brought a simple candle. That over-ornate three-branched stand could in no way be trivialised. Its presence proclaimed a holy urgency. Perhaps Joseph's choice had been deliberate, for he, like Sabbatai, well knew the outcome of their deliberations.

They gathered in a circle, and began the Sabbath evening prayers. When they were done and there was silence in the

91

room, they heard the echoes of the same prayers from outside the house and the garden below. They listened to the end and to the silence that followed.

Then out of that silence, a lone woman's voice. 'A miracle. A miracle,' she cried. 'The Messiah has come.'

In all his life Sabbatai had not heard that word spoken in his presence. Its meaning was often voiced, but camouflaged in synonym. 'He will redeem,' they would whisper around him, or 'He will save us', but no one within earshot had so solemnly named him. He felt the fever upon him and he went to the window and opened it wide, more for his own cool comfort than for display. The people below roared their greeting. Shocked, he waited for the noise to subside. Then, in the silence that followed, he quoted from the Zohar, his voice ringing over the crowd. 'The Messiah will not come until the tears of the gentile will be exhausted.' Then he shut the window fast as if that were his final word. But he was not prepared for the reaction of his followers. He looked at their faces and sensed that they had, each one of them, lost that acquiescent look. He even noted a hint of rebellion.

'That time will never come,' Saul ventured to say. 'The Redeemer will come, and only then will Edom cease its weeping.'

'Saul is right,' Joseph said.

'You are called, Sabbatai,' David whispered. 'You must listen to them.'

'I listen only to my followers,' Sabbatai told him, and regretted it even as he spoke.

'Then we declare you,' Saul said.

Sabbatai stared at him, at this unblood brother of his, at this figure he had chosen as scapegoat, as the leper had sacrificed a bird. Now that offering was flung in his face.

'You are ready, Sabbatai,' Saul said, taking his hand. Then they circled around him and Sabbatai felt it as a trap. Yet his heart soared in the joy of his calling, a joy that for the moment offset the terror. He nodded his head, and his followers embraced him.

Outside there was a rumbling. Sabbatai went to the window and drew the blind. There was jostling in the garden. The crowd from the front of the house now pressed into the garden which seemed to have become the more eventful venue. They were calling his name. He opened the window wide and looked down on them. Not since his infancy, since the day of his circumcision, had he attended that bird's-eye view of power, when Rabbi Eskapa had held him up to the ecstatic crowd in the chicken-run of their old home. He recalled it in a blurred eclipse, through his eight-day-old unfocused gaze, but he relived that young sensation in acute detail. And its sour aftermath. He uttered a primal scream of recollection.

And, as before, so many years ago, the crowd had parted for the outsider, to give him space and air for his protest, so now did they make room for Raphael, the idiot, and his perennial warning. The threat of it was dire, as if his dangerous prophecy had already been fulfilled.

'Beware of false prophets,' he shouted, 'which come to you in sheep's clothing, but inwardly they are ravening wolves.'

The crowd let him have his say. As an idiot, Raphael was entitled to holy licence. And taking his cue from the crowd, Sabbatai raised his arm over Raphael as if in blessing.

Thus it was that Sabbatai Zvi was declared the Messiah. That first declaration was irrevocable.

5

Two marriages of positive inconvenience

'It is generally believed that Sabbatai is the Messiah. But Sabbatai is beset by doubts. When we are together I smell his fears. "Why are you afraid, Sabbatai?" I asked him. "The devil is in my body," he said. "But that is not why I am afraid. I am afraid because of my desire. I want the devil inside me. He feeds me passions. He is a better nourisher than God. I pray to be without flesh. Then I should really be holy. A simple skeleton clothed in soul." He touched my arm. "They want to find me a bride," he said.'

On the whole, Messiahs don't get married. Perhaps it's because a less-than-celibate state would strain credulity. And this was exactly what Mordecai hoped for as he set out to arrange a marriage for his eldest son. He had doubts about his son's manhood, doubts that had often been confirmed as he'd watched the boy grow up, but he nurtured the vain hope that marriage might change his son's ways. He knew he must look for someone very special, and he found her in Constantinople, the daughter of a rich merchant. History does not recall her name, and it is possible that even Sabbatai did not know it; certainly he could not have used it, for such familiarity would have been a token of a relationship between them. It was in Constantinople, amid much ceremony and festivity, that Sabbatai took a nameless virgin for a bride and brought her back to Smyrna. A house had been prepared for them though Sabbatai had protested. He saw no reason why he should leave the family home. There was plenty of room for both of them. Now the crowds shifted their venue from the courtyard of Mordecai's house to that of their Redeemer, and each night they offered up prayers for the health and happiness of the bridal pair.

On their first night in their new house, Sabbatai had shown his bride to the bridal chamber and had retired alone. The bride knew nothing of marital procedures, but her instinct prompted her that all was not well. Yet she retired with relief for she had heard rumours that the marriage-bed was frightful. But Sabbatai could not sleep. The thought of touching that nameless creature filled him with nausea, and he longed for Saul to come and take his place. He wondered whether he could invent a Kabalistic law whereby marriage by proxy was permissible. He pondered on that for a while, but he considered it would be taking his authority too far. He himself could not touch her. His sexual aversion to women was sublime. From his Biblical and Talmudic studies, he had learned that woman was beauty, virtue and all things natural. Such things were an abomination to Sabbatai. His pleasure could be found only in what was ugly, sinful and decadent. This he knew to be his true nature and it troubled him.

He rose quickly from his bed and stole from the house. His marriage home was but a few yards from the sea-shore, its only advantage. Once on the sand, he stripped, and in the light of the moon he viewed his body. Had it translated his soul, he thought, it would have been covered with suppurating sores in which maggots fed and celebrated. But his skin was white and smooth and he marvelled at nature's deception. His unblemished body disgusted him and he dived swiftly into the sea to hide it from his eye.

He swam to the rock. The moon lit the water and filtered through to the life beneath. But he didn't need the light.

It was the silence he craved, and his hand caressed the rock-face as he dived below. He stayed there for a while, holding his breath, keeping absolutely still, and he asked God what he should do. He expected no answers. Simply to declare his helplessness was enough. Occasionally he came up for air, loth to break the silence. After a while he swam back to the shore, dressed, and dragged his reluctant steps back to his marital home.

During the daytime, Sabbatai was very kind to his wife in an attempt to offset his nocturnal neglect. But he knew he could not get away with it indefinitely. An issue would be expected of their union and nothing short of a miracle could produce it. He recalled that exactly such a miracle had occurred before, or so they said. He couldn't expect another, for that would diminish the first. Night after night he took to his celibate bed, occasionally rushing to the sea, holding his breath under the rock, and night after night his bewildered bride wondered what she had done to offend him. Two months passed in this fashion, and in her despair she sent word to Constantinople, begging her parents to visit her. They arrived post-haste. Sabbatai slunk down to the shore, while his bride stammered out their catastrophe. Her father lost little time in getting down to business. He went straightway to the Rabbinical Court and reported his son-in-law's incapacity. Rumour spread around Smyrna. In the market-place his followers prepared a rationale for his defection, and concluded that the bride was not to Sabbatai's taste. Anyone could make a mistake, even a Messiah. Indeed it enhanced his status, for it lent him human error.

His disciples knew that their leader was not the marrying type and no woman would make him so. And their hearts went out to him in his dilemma. Sabbatai never referred to it. In all their meetings since the marriage, and they had been more frequent than hitherto, in all their ceremonies and prayers, he had kept silent. He'd lingered with them long after his teachings were over, his pain visible yet unspoken. And it seemed to Saul that Sabbatai was avoiding him, and with such deliberation that he knew that a confrontation might be explosive.

The Rabbinical Court sat in closed session. Sabbatai stood accused. Outside the Court a row of women waited. The bride and her mother sat apart and alongside them, at a distance, the womenfolk of the culprit, Clara, Grandma Beki, Aunt Sarah. They assumed a belligerent front. Their rationale was clear and unanimous. The girl from Constantinople was simply not good enough for Sabbatai. She was neither clever nor attractive. A divorce would be a blessing. Their opinion, however, was not shared by Mordecai, who offered no opinion at all. To have expressed his feelings to his wife would have resulted in hurt, anger and disbelief. Elijah, young as he was, had understood, and was young enough to make his feelings clear. 'Sabbatai can never marry, Papa,' he had said, even before the ceremony. Joseph had his doubts too, and so had Saul, but they were too old to voice them.

Soon the bride's father emerged from the chamber. Sabbatai was to be questioned alone. Then the bride's family left, with an air of victory, it seemed, though what victory could signify in such a case was clear to nobody.

Inside the chamber, Sabbatai took the stand. The Rabbis were wary of questioning him. Most of them sanctioned the name that his followers had given him, and a man so named was accountable to nobody. Moreover, the matter of the bed-chamber was a very private one and not one of the judges was prepared to cross-examine.

'Tell us what happened,' their Chairman said.

'It's true what my bride reports,' Sabbatai said. He was careful to use that word. She was still a bride to him. 'Every word of it is true. But I have no defence. I can offer no explanation.'

The Rabbis had no choice but to pass judgment. They ordered Sabbatai to return to his house and offer his wife her conjugal rights or else to divorce her forthwith. With some relief he chose the latter, and he left the Court, in his terms, a free man.

He returned to his mother's house. The matter was never referred to, for Sabbatai's looks forbade it. But Clara and Mordecai discussed it together and decided, for different reasons, that a new bride must be found. Joseph was approaching marrying age, and he could not take a bride before Sabbatai. When, after some weeks had elapsed, they confronted Sabbatai with their decision, he was aghast, for there was no way in which he could tell them the truth. He submitted, but he decided to use cunning. A suitable bride was found. Again history does not record her name, in deference perhaps to Sabbatai himself, who refused for the second time to acknowledge his marital status. The new offering was the daughter of a Rabbi of Smyrna. She came with a dowry of house and handmaid. History has recorded the name of the latter, possibly because she figured far more in Sabbatai's consciousness than did his second nameless bride.

The marriage took place in Smyrna and was intended to be of a private nature. But the Smyrna community, having been deprived of the nuptials in Constantinople, were determined to make of it a festival. The streets around the synagogue were bedecked with bunting, and after the marriage the whole community followed the bridal procession. There was dancing in the streets, songs, wine and merriment and a positive will amongst the celebrants that this time the marriage would be consummated.

Sabbatai viewed it with horror, resenting the fact that they were taking it all so seriously. He turned to Saul who stood by his side. 'Would you could take my place,' he said. He took his arm and guided him from the room. 'Let's go,' he said. He excused himself from the festivities,

101

pleading that he needed to go to the sea to pray, to offer up thanks for his state of celibacy that today would come to an end. The guests nodded their approval. Clara marvelled at his piety, and Mordecai turned his face to the wall.

They ran down to the shore in silence. There was no need for words between them. Both of them knew why they had left the festivities and both throbbed with the urgency of their pursuit. And the ecstasy, too. When they reached the sand, they held each other close, then moved as one towards the shelter of a sand-dune. There they undressed each other silently, and lay together on the sand, two white virgins, fearful of what they had engendered, but impatient for the Paradise that would result. At first they fumbled, both green to that joy, and slowly and together they found a way. And Sabbatai knew it as a way of no return. Saul's body trembled beneath him. He kissed his lips and found them cold, but that did not trouble him, for he knew the blood was elsewhere. 'This is redemption through sin, beloved,' he whispered, and together, in that licence, they touched the sky.

Afterwards they bathed in the shallows, lying on the sea-bed, still soldered together, loth to part.

'This is my marriage,' Sabbatai said as they dressed. 'This is the only one I shall consummate.'

The guests noted the flush on their cheeks when they returned, and innocently attributed it to the ardent aftermath of prayer. But Mordecai dared not look at either of them.

Bride number two stuck it out longer. It took her innocence six months to suspect that something was amiss. Sabbatai was very attentive. Each night he came to her room to bless her and bid her sleep well. And each morning he was at her bedside with a greeting. She enjoyed being married. It wasn't all that trouble that her mother had hinted at. Her mother was a great hinter, and each time they met, which was frequent, for her mother was a daily visitor at her home, she would drop hints of questions as to how the 'trouble' was faring. After three months, she tired of innuendo and one day she turned her face to the wall and asked if there were any signs of a baby. The bride didn't know to what signs she referred and, unwilling to show her ignorance, she answered very positively in the negative. It now became a daily question from her mother, who didn't even bother any more to turn her face to the wall. For she was growing impatient, and impatience does not allow for modesty. Then one day, she finally lost her temper, and with prudence to the winds, she questioned her daughter as to the activities of her marriage bed. Apart from sleeping well, her daughter had no events to report. Whereupon her mother detailed the purpose of that terrible bed and the bride was dumb-founded, disgusted at the horror tales she heard. And at last she understood what her mother had meant by 'trouble'.

Within a week they were storming the Rabbinical Court, and once again the session was closed. Sabbatai's womenfolk sat in the waiting annexe and pretended that the bride and her mother were not there.

'She wasn't right for him,' Clara kept saying.

'Not good enough,' Beki echoed.

'Not even pretty,' Sarah whispered, for she had to say something.

Thus they comforted each other in fantasy, but each of them prayed that Sabbatai would not marry again. The whole business was far too humiliating.

That morning Mordecai had left early for his business. He wanted nothing of Sabbatai's problem. He had foreseen the result of this marriage, as clearly as he had seen the first, though for both he had nurtured some hope. Now he, too, decided he wanted no more of it. Sabbatai would return home and there he would stay. He would keep a stern eye on him. And on Saul too. It pained him to think of Saul. He had loved the boy when Sabbatai had first brought him to the hostelry in Constantinople. And he was grateful to him too. For since his inclusion in the family, Sabbatai had become more approachable, happier, it seemed, and less prone to those manic episodes which curdled his heart with fury and pain. But he could not forget the second wedding ceremony. He could not forget their sudden leave-taking and their flushed return. And that morning of the second sitting of the Rabbinical Court, he could not erase that image from his mind, and he feared the consequences of their dwelling under the same roof. For a moment he considered sending Saul away, to a seminary perhaps, in Constantinople, but Clara would hear none of it, and certainly Joseph and Elijah would protest his leaving. For both had grown to love him. That day he went about his business with a heavy heart, and tried not to think of his son whose manhood, at that moment, was on trial for the second time.

In the courtroom, the bride's father had given his evidence to his peers, and had left the chamber with the same triumphant air as had his predecessor. Inside, Sabbatai took his faltering stand. He was aware that the second time round was not as straightforward as the first. He could be forgiven for having made one mistake, for having chosen a bride who was unsuitable. So unsuitable, in fact, that he could not come near her. To go astray a second time was less accountable and would, among mischiefmakers, arouse suspicions of things unnatural. But suddenly he was inspired. He praised his bride for her patience and sweetness, and he owned to his continued celibacy. But in mitigation he offered a plea, a plea that in such Rabbinical company, could not be denied.

'I have been visited by the Holy Ghost,' he said, 'the Ru'ach Ha Kodesh.' He paused to give the name its due solemnity and the court breathed a holy sigh. 'He has told me that neither of my brides was destined for me by heaven.' It was a stroke of genius and only the impious would find it unacceptable. Sabbatai left the Court in triumph and even before he reached home, his real home where Saul waited, rumour had reached the market-place of this further proof of their Redeemer. He had been visited by the Ru'ach Ha Kodesh.

Mordecai heard it on his way home and it did little to lighten his heart. All he could appreciate was his son's cunning.

Sabbatai's plea of defence was masterful. Not only did it give him the right to postpone his third marriage for ever, but it made a great public impression. Now, more than ever, was he proclaimed the Messiah. And not only in the Ottoman Empire. Through avenues of commerce and trade, his name and destiny were known throughout Europe and pilgrims came from Poland and Germany to seek his blessing. In those communities where Jews were most oppressed, many families packed their belongings in readiness for the signal that would propel them towards the Promised Land. Word of these Messianic expectations reached Sabbatai's ear. It was clearly the time to act. Rumour was not enough. Neither was other people's nomination. He had to declare *himself*. He had to go into a public place and say with sure and certain conviction, 'I am the Messiah.' He craved the power and he was ripe for it.

Since the consummation of his love for Saul, he had grown in self-confidence, almost to the point of arrogance. But at the same time he was aware, more than anyone else, of the collision between his ambition and his piety, as he was so acutely aware of the cleavage in his whole person. Saul had helped to smooth the jagged edges. Saul dealt with his composure and left him to handle the fever himself. He had to own that those fevers were becoming more and more acute, and that they were related to other people's expectation. The fear of not fulfilling them, the resentment of the terrible burden they imposed, but above all the terrible question with which he plagued himself: 'Am I,

Sabbatai Zvi, seer of visions, hearer of voices, presumptive heir to godhead? Or am I out of my mind?'

When the tales came to his ears of far-flung and desperate Jewish communities preparing for the call, he imagined the practicalities of such preparations. He saw the strapped bulging suitcases on the quaysides of east European ports, sewing-machines, violin cases, gem-cutting and furrier's tools, those portable skills of people who must be forever on the run. Those people had led him on, seduced him into saviourhood, connected him with miracles. Their *will* to believe was so sublime, that it needed no proof, no hard and fast evidence. Rumour was more than enough. It was because of him that those thousands of people breathed hope in every breath, stood on quaysides, their eyes skinned for the blinding star.

He sat on the sands and let the waves lap his bare feet. And all the time I might be a fraud, he whispered to himself. He dived into the sea and swam to the rock, where he fathomed its silent secrets. Then he sprang into the air and let out a curdling scream that rang out across the water, with all the pain of his unknowing, and all the horror of his global deception, should he prove to be a fraud. 'Yet I am he,' he said to himself. 'Was I not born untimely, earmarked for delivery on Tisha B'Av, that holy day endorsed for the birth of the Messiah? Do I not have visions? Do I not hear voices? And after all my prayers and learning, after all my rituals, am I not cleansed?' He buried his head in his hands, tormented by his doubts. But his doubts also gave him hope, for only a lunatic enjoys certainty. Therefore he was not out of his mind, only *beside* it perhaps, viewing its mists of qualms and scruples and the occasional lightning shaft of faith. Then he was only a little bit mad, sufficiently sane for leadership but unhinged enough for the obsession that that leadership required. As he swam to the shore, he knew that he had solved nothing. He was faced with a choice. He must either declare himself loud and clear, and with utter conviction, so that those on the quaysides would not wait in vain, or he must confess with equal clarity and belief that he was a charlatan, and had been since the very beginning, and all false hopes could be abandoned once and for all.

He dressed and made his way to his house. He made long detours in order to avoid passing either of his former marriage homes, those futile nests built for his self-deception. When finally he reached home, he went straight to his room to study and to pray. After a while Saul knocked on his door. But he barred him. Saul was temptation and he was at his prayers.

'Supper's ready,' Saul called.

'I shall fast till tomorrow at sunset,' Sabbatai replied. 'Please let me be.'

Saul took the news to the family table.

'I think Sabbatai is troubled,' Joseph said. Joseph rarely voiced an opinion. As the middle son he had little status in the family. For a while, until Elijah was born, he had been the baby and he recalled those years as his happiest. But as he grew, he assumed the role of the middle-man, the peace-maker, the go-between. As Sabbatai's disciple, he had his elder brother's ear, and bidden or otherwise he would appraise his brother of the varying attitudes of the family. He was two years younger than Sabbatai, a twenty-year-old, and, after the seminary, he had entered his father's business. There, too, he was a go-between, a runner, a carrier of messages and opinions from one trader to another. In the family he was considered the reliable one, the dependable. He gave no trouble; he fulfilled his parents' hopes which, in his case, as the second son, were minimal, Sabbatai having borne the heavy burden of parental expectation.

It was not difficult for either Clara or Mordecai to love Joseph, for he gave little cause for concern. When he had offered the opinion that Sabbatai was troubled, he had spoken out of character. But he was changing. Since his brother's abortive marriages, when he was away from the family home, Joseph had assumed the role of elder sibling. He had been polite, but he had become more assertive and though he had now once more been relegated to the middle son, his assertiveness remained. But it was out of place now, and sometimes he longed to leave home so that his independence might flower. Besides, the presence of Saul disturbed him. In the beginning he had accepted him as a brother, filled with compassion for his desolate orphanhood. But as he watched his growing closeness to Sabbatai, he grew jealous and mistrustful. He feared for their friendship, for Saul did not have a brother's blood. Saul's own blood-kin had betrayed him by dying. Was it not possible Saul could do the same to Sabbatai?

'How do you mean, troubled?' Clara asked him.

'The rumours,' Joseph said. 'The people waiting for boats to the Holy Land. Those pilgrims who want to see him. He prays all day for guidance. He does not feel worthy.'

Mordecai had thoughts which were inexpressible, and so had young Elijah, and together they shared their silence.

'All his life he hasn't felt worthy,' Clara said. 'His humility forbids it.' Clara, Sabbatai's champion. Or so everybody thought. For in truth, Clara was even more tormented than Mordecai. As fervently as Mordecai thought Sabbatai a fraud, so devotedly did she believe in her son. Her torment, like Mordecai's, was focused on his future. For either way, charlatan or saint, the future was perilous. She feared for him. She did not fear his frequent fasting, nor his strict self-denial. Nor even his strange and mystical un-approach to womenkind. She feared primarily for his loneliness and isolation, and she feared it all the more because she knew that Sabbatai feared it too.

'Why does he have to be so different from the rest of us?' Elijah could hold his tongue no longer, and as he spoke he gripped his father's hand, assuming to speak for him too. 'We have nothing but trouble from him.' Elijah was no disciple, nor ever would be. At seventeen, he was still at seminary and next year he would follow Joseph into their father's trade. He was a good, pious and observant Jew, and he could wait for the Messiah, for ever if need be. He didn't understand why such a holy concept could cause such pain.

'He's different from us,' Clara said. 'He *is* special. Special people are never easy.'

Mordecai felt he would burst. He rose quickly from the table.

'I'll go and talk with him,' he said.

'Be gentle with him,' Clara said under her breath, for she saw the vein of anger on her husband's forehead. 'Get on with your supper,' she said to the rest. Her voice was gruff. She was angry that Mordecai had left, and fearful, too, of his mission.

Mordecai knocked on Sabbatai's door. On his way up the stairs he had tried to calm himself for he knew he must not face his son in anger.

Sabbatai's gruff reply did not help matters. 'Who is it?' he asked, impatiently.

'It's Papa.'

'Come in,' Sabbatai said, and his voice was afraid. 'Why do you knock? I'm your son.'

The familiarity was blackmail of a sort, though unintentional. Sabbatai was not at prayer as his father had presumed. He was sitting bolt upright in bed, in that position he had often found him in, a position that boded ill. It was fever position, a manic pose, with the accompanying gesture of that rocking hand on his back, that safety-net of his infancy. He knew better than to ask him what was the matter. He sat beside him on the bed and daringly took his free hand.

'I have to go to Constantinople next week,' he said. There was no reason at all for him to go to the capital, but perhaps after all it would not be such a bad idea. They could eat together, drink wine, visit the shadow-play even, and talk

109

of things that had nothing to do with faith or heresy. 'Would you like to come?' he asked timidly.

'I have things to do here, Papa,' Sabbatai said. 'I have to make decisions.' He paused, then after a while, 'I'm troubled, Papa,' he said.

He'd said it with love and Mordecai squeezed his hand. 'Don't touch me,' Sabbatai shouted, drawing his hand away. 'You want to buy me with your touch.'

How truly his son had spoken, Mordecai thought, for that indeed was what he had tried to do. But that was insight, not insanity. Perhaps his son was whole after all, or possessed a wholeness of a kind. Mordecai folded his hands on his lap. He refused to be rebuffed, but touching his son would have helped his argument.

'D'you want to talk to me about those decisions?' he asked. He was like a child begging forgiveness. 'Perhaps I could help you.'

'How can you help me if you don't believe in me?' Sabbatai whispered.

'Of course I believe in you,' Mordecai said. It was his truth. He believed in him as his son, as a scholar, as a credit to his home and his people.

'Do you believe in the name they give me?'

Now he was trapped. He wished that he could touch him in some way to soften the truth he had to tell. 'I think they are wrong,' he said, steadily. 'But they can be excused. For they *need* to think so.'

'And *you* don't have that need, Father? Are you so much better than they?'

It was the 'Father' that hurt him, that turned his heart to stone. For it made them strangers. Mordecai knew that 'Papa' was not a child's word, nor 'Father' a man's. They were words far more profound, and their differences far more painful. They were to do with loving. And its waning. 'Papa' could be shouted from the roof-tops without any shame. 'Father' was a whispered word. 'Papa' was careless of its clothing. 'Father' was Sabbath-dressed every day of the week. It was stiff, formal and distant. You could not touch with such a word. Between 'Papa' and 'Father' lay a million alien miles.

'You are no better than the idiot Raphael,' Sabbatai concluded.

Out of his heartbreak, Mordecai persevered. 'Then why are you troubled?' he asked. 'What are these decisions you have to make?'

In response, Sabbatai began to sing. His song had no words, and practically no melody. A rhythm too was non-existent. It was his mad madrigal of dismissal.

Mordecai rose to leave. When he reached the door, Sabbatai called, 'Send Saul and Joseph to me.' Then, after a pause, 'I love you, Papa.'

When his father had gone, his fever rose and he leapt out of bed, stripped himself naked and he opened the window wide. The cold air swept over his body, but did nothing to diminish its heat. And out of the wind, he heard a voice, a gentle voice that at last proclaimed his mission. 'Thou art the Saviour of Israel. I swear by my right hand and by the strength of my arm that thou art the true redeemer and that there is none that redeemeth besides thee.'

Suddenly his body cooled. He dressed, put on his prayer-shawl and prayed with a fervour that he had never known before.

On his way downstairs, Mordecai repeated to himself his son's last words. Over and over again. He had to, in order to erase the ugly words that had gone before. If a son declares his love for his father, other words don't matter. He was still saying them aloud as he entered the kitchen.

'What is it?' Clara said.

'He loves me. He said so. I love you, Papa, he said.'

She took his hand and brought him to the table. Somehow there was no joy in what he said. Just a startled realisation of his son's separateness.

He turned to Joseph and Saul. 'He wants you,' he said, listlessly.

They left the room, touching his hunched shoulders on the way. Elijah, finding himself alone with his parents, grew fearful of their confrontation. He quickly excused himself from the table, saying he had work to do. Neither Mordecai nor Clara made a move to stop him. But both envied him that he could remove himself from a grief that was inconsolable.

'What are we to do?' Mordecai asked.

'What *can* we do?' Clara knew that they would argue from two diametrically opposed assumptions and that nothing could come from such argument.

'He's ill,' Mordecai said. 'We should call a doctor. He has fevers.'

'He's always had fevers. Since he was a child. They subside. The doctor says he'll grow out of them.'

'They are not those kinds of fevers.' Mordecai was being as gentle as he could. 'Our son is not normal.'

'Of course he's not normal,' Clara screamed at him. 'He is the Redeemer.'

Outside the door Elijah listened, then tip-toed quietly away.

When Saul and Joseph entered Sabbatai's room, they found him at prayer. They waited until he was done, sensing from his fervour that they had been called to him on a special account. In his prayer, he was swaying with a momentum that suggested trance. The Zohar states that the soul of a Jew is attached to the Torah as a candle is attached to a flame. Hence the swaying, and Sabbatai looked as if his soul would be singed by his own fire.

After a while it was clear he was unaware of their presence and, during a short interval in the prayer, Saul dared to cough, but Sabbatai would not turn until he was done. At last he finished and turned to them. He put down his prayer-book but they noticed that he kept his prayer-shawl about his shoulders. He was smiling at them. 'Sit down,' he said.

They sat at his feet. From the look on his face, its gloss of purity, he seemed to dictate that position. Sabbatai remained standing and looked down on them. 'What is it you have called me?' he asked.

'You are the Redeemer,' Saul said.

'And you, Joseph?'

'*All* your followers.'

'Then tell them that I have heard a voice. Out of the wind and the darkness, but its message was as clear as a bell. It told me that I am the Saviour of Israel.'

Saul and Joseph fell on his bare feet and kissed them.

'Now you have said it, it is true,' Saul said.

'Let us go to the sea-shore. All of us,' Sabbatai said. 'We must pray and make our ablutions. We must purify ourselves for a new age.'

So together they left the house, calling on the rest of their group on their way to the shore. Once there, they made themselves naked and began their orgiastic rituals. Then, exhausted, they lay in the shallows. But Sabbatai swam out, hungry for the silence beneath the rock. Once there, he dived below and in the still, coralled deep he gave thanks for his deliverance. For deliverance it truly was, a release from his prison of doubts and uncertainties. He had been told who he was, and now he believed it. Tomorrow he would tell the world that he had come to save them. Slowly he rose to the surface and clung to the rock, his body pulsing with rapture.

6

Into exile

'He came to my room early on Sabbath morning and he stroked my cheek with his hand. "I have lain with God this night," he said, "and I mean to speak His name aloud."

"Sabbatai," I said, "it's against the Law. The name of God must never be uttered. In private and in whispers, perhaps, but never in a holy place."

"Today I shall go to the synagogue and utter His name without shame," he said.

"Do you want the people to love you?" I asked.

"Of course. But God above all."

"They will turn against you," I told him.

"But I am married to God. May I not call Him by His name? In my sleep, I stood under the bridal canopy. And the Rabbi said, 'Where is the bride?' The Torah unrolled itself from the Ark and stood beside me. I am married to the Torah," he said. "May I not call its Maker by name?"

Then he kissed me and left, to prepare for the synagogue.

I went with him, trembling. It was a full congregation. Sabbatai stood next to his father who viewed his face with horror. For it was ashen with trance. Like the death-mask of a saint. He prayed for a while, then made his move. I tried to stop him, gripping his arm as tenderly as I could, but he felt nothing. Perhaps his flesh had numbed itself according to his wishes and I was touching his untouchable soul. He made his way down the aisle, or floated rather, towards the "Almenor". All eyes were upon him. He seemed to levitate

117

towards infinity. I touched Mordecai's arm. I sensed he needed some comfort. Though of late he had turned cold towards me. I looked at the Rabbis who were conducting the service. Some of them thought Sabbatai a holy fool who, if left alone, would harm nobody. But others saw him as a downright menace to the community. Then I looked around the congregation, and what the Rabbis thought did not matter any more, for there was love and awe in every eye. I prayed that they would continue to love him. There was a pause in the prayers and I saw how Sabbatai slowly raised his hands over the congregation like a blind man seeking direction. And indeed I do not think that he knew where he was, or even what he would say, because the Devil was inside him who, that night, on the eve of the Sabbath, had pretended to be God. He opened his mouth to let out whatever word the Devil prompted.

"God," he said.

He shouted it across the synagogue. Then said it again, for the Devil wanted to make himself abundantly clear. The Rabbis tried to pretend that nothing untoward had happened, and they hurried on with the service, their words garbled in shock. The congregation was stunned, not knowing what to make of it. But all were offended, and some to the point of disgust. At the end of the service, I went to Sabbatai's side. There were tears in his eyes. The Devil, having done his work, had departed, and for the first time that day, Sabbatai heard the word that he had uttered.

"I am become as dirt," he said.

I shielded him out of the synagogue. People made way for him, but not with respect. Some even spat in his path. Sabbatai was desolate.

"Leave me," he said. "Don't touch me. I am unclean."

I have not seen him for three whole days and nights. He keeps himself to his room all the while, fasting and praying.'

Sabbatai was inconsolable. He had fully expected the congregation to rise and accept him. He needed their affirmation; he needed their approval, for once again the niggling doubts beset him. Much of the time that he spent in solitude, alone and isolated, he tortured himself with questions as to the truth of his calling. He recalled his visions and his voices, for they were safe and true and substantial proof that he was the ear and the eye of God. He had prayed and purged himself daily, and undergone the strictest ritual to purify himself for the role. All these thoughts were positive and cheered him a little, but the nagging doubts remained. Not only in the lack of public recognition, the absence of their ecstasy, though that was hurtful enough, but in the tremblings of his own heart. Sabbatai prayed for some demonstrable proof of his role, so undeniable that even he would be forced to believe it. He sank to his knees, wrapping his prayer-shawl around him. He did not care that genuflection was forbidden. He needed to entreat, to beseech, to plead, to beg even, to humble himself as painfully as any rejected lover, bargaining for a sign of that once so certain passion. 'God,' he muttered, over and over again, and with a tinge of anger, for whether God liked it or not, He had loved him once. He loved him enough to let him name Him.

'Don't leave me now,' he begged, 'or if You must, then return. I shall wait. I shall wait with patience if You promise Your return. You loved me. You sent me Your voices and Your visions. Are You ashamed now that You have over-shared with me? That You have made Yourself known to me too well? I have kept Your trust, I have told no one of Your failings, Your fears, Your jealousy, Your sheer bloody-mindedness.' Sabbatai was shouting now. 'I hate You God,' he screamed. 'I shall tell them all Your secrets!' He crumpled to the floor. 'I will not be abandoned,' he whimpered. 'Love me. Love me as You once did. Embrace me with Your fevers. Touch me with Your teasing finger of Heaven. Pierce me with Your divine sword and push and lunge into my soul, up, up, up and up, to the very gates of heaven.'

He sighed, melting into his ecstasy. And rested a while. Then he took down a hand-mirror from his tallboy. He rarely looked at himself, but now he studied his face very carefully as if he could find in its features some sign, some blemish even, of Godhead. Sabbatai was not a vain man, but he had to confess to the beauty of the reflection. His mother had often said that he looked like an angel. Such an interpretation was helpful. To be an angel was to be at least in the proper dimension. But it was not enough. He breathed heavily on to his hand, and put the scent to his nostrils. There was an odour. No doubt about it. He did it again and again with mounting excitement, trying to pinpoint the smell, but its identity was elusive. That did not worry him. For how could he name it, since he had never smelt it before. This discovery gave him new hope and faith in his singularity. But the people saw him all the time, and as he walked amongst them they must have smelt his odour. Yet they were not convinced. In the market-place, they talked openly of him as the saviour; the rumours that spread were those of the Messiah. Yet the populace did not acclaim him, so that all could hear and see. He was a rumoured Messiah, a Saviour on the grapevine, a buzz in the market-place. It was not enough for him. But the fire was in him, the fire to preach, to evangelise, to bring to the people those messages to which only he, as the ear of God, was privy. He would go amongst the poor, he decided, where the hunger for redemption was the most acute. To them he would give his word and his promises.

Smyrna, like any other rich and thriving city, had its share of poor. And that poor, since the massacres, was now augmented. Moreover, there had been a famine in Jerusalem, and they who had depended for alms on their Polish brethren were now destitute, since their donors themselves were refugees. Hundreds of Jews from Palestine had poured into Turkey seeking sustenance. What better audience for a Messiah than those who perforce had left the Promised Land? So Sabbatai took his disciples, now a number swollen to twenty, and he went into the slums of Smyrna.

And like sleuths, the Rabbis kept a keen eye on him. His audience was easily roused. Hungry people lose their resistance to reason. God finds rite of passage into an empty stomach. Here came a man amongst them, with the face and voice of an angel, and he gave them hope. It was more than they had been offered in a long while. He stood before them, his fever raging. They caught his energy that, like a benign virus, burnt its easy passage through their weakened spirits. And multiplied there in communal flowering. It was this manic fever that emanated from Sabbatai's spirit that would eventually inflame and galvanise the whole of European Jewry.

'Follow me,' he cried to them. 'And I shall lead you to the gates of the Holy City.'

And not only did they follow him, but they argued with those who doubted, and the arguments led to scuffles, and sometimes the scuffles to riots, while the Rabbis' watchful eyes grew beadier. At last a riot broke out in one of the suburb's synagogues and the Rabbis, salivating punishment, gathered in secret session. They were still divided and in the same categories. The believers held their tongues; those who excused Sabbatai on the grounds of lunacy only whispered their protest; but Rabbi Eskapa and his gang were loud and clear in their denunciation. They decided to pronounce a curse on him and to banish him from Smyrna. The curse did not mince words, and went something like this:

'By command of the angels and the judgment of the Holy One, we banish, cast out, curse and condemn Sabbatai Zvi. Cursed be he by day and cursed by night, cursed when he goeth out and cursed when he cometh in. For the anger and the fury of God shall be kindled against him and bring down upon his head all the curses that are written in the Law.'

121

And so on and so forth. As the curse continued, their bodies shook as if in climax. Only a sentence of death would have given them greater pleasure. But the curse was enough, for in that curse and its consequence, they gave birth to the greatest Messianic movement in Jewish history, with the cursed one who presumably could not lie down, get up, go out or come in, as its revered and sacred leader.

The news spread around the city and was received with a mixture of horror, relief and pity. Mordecai was shamefacedly relieved.

Joseph wanted to go with his brother, but Mordecai forbade it.

'I cannot lose two sons,' he shouted. He was close to tears. 'Let Saul go with him.'

He wished he had not said it. Saul had been a son to him once, that night in Constantinople when, to Mordecai alone, he had offered up his desolate orphanhood. But after Sabbatai's second hopeless marriage, he had, against his will, turned away from the boy. He deeply regretted what he'd said. But Saul came to him and embraced him. 'You are still my father,' he said, 'and I will go with Sabbatai as a brother.'

Elijah made no offer. He would miss Sabbatai terribly, but he would be relieved that he was gone. Clara simply mourned, more for Sabbatai's lack of recognition than for his future absence. Mordecai tried to comfort her.

'He may not come to you,' he said, 'but you may go to him.'

The order of banishment was to be carried out forthwith, but since the day was a Friday, a day in which travel was forbidden in case it ran into the Sabbath, Sabbatai was given leave to wait until the following evening before he began his exile.

It was a mournful day in the Zvi household. Grandma Beki and Aunt Sarah came to say their farewells.

'It's not for ever,' Sabbatai told them. 'One day they will beg me to return.'

The women were preparing the Sabbath table. The house thronged with visitors, family friends who had come to commiserate and say goodbye. Amongst them, Nissim and Perla Arditti and David, Sabbatai's first and most loyal disciple. He sat apart from his parents and his face was ashen with anger.

Nissim approached Mordecai and Mordecai knew from his friend's look of despair that David had chosen to join his son, to accompany him into voluntary exile. He loved the boy for it, but he was moved by his father's pain. He touched Nissim's shoulder. 'We are both bereaved,' he said. 'We must comfort each other.'

There was a cry from the corner of the room. 'I hate you,' Elijah screamed to no one in particular, though his target was clear. Then he broke down into sobbing. He bore the burden of the whole family's sorrow; he was the scapegoat, not for their sins but for their tears; he was the leper's bird, not for his sores, but for his weeping.

Sabbatai acknowledged his hate. 'What can I do?' he said. 'I am what I am.' Then he went to his room, not to emerge until the first star in the morrow's sky would light his way into exile. In his room he prayed, swaying like a sapling in a storm. But no tumult would uproot him. His mission was fixed, his piety unshakable. Downstairs there was no regret that he had withdrawn. Clara preferred to grieve in his absence for his presence only served to aggravate her grief. To view him and his gaunt unearthly beauty was to rive her heart.

'You will take great care of him, David,' she said. 'And you, too, Saul.' Then, with a smile, 'Elijah and Mordecai will take care of me.'

The men went to the synagogue and left the women to make the final preparations for a last family Sabbath. Grandma Beki took no care to hide her grief. She moaned in her corner. There was no one at hand to comfort her, for

123

each dwelt silently in their own sorrow. Clara had gone into the kitchen, needing to be alone. Her mind was in torment. To lose Sabbatai was grievous enough. What aggravated that grief was the fact that he would be alone, without family. She did not argue with Mordecai when he forbade Joseph's going. She was glad Saul was going, but Saul was not family. And never had been in her heart. She loved him because he had loved Sabbatai, but it was a love one gives to a stranger. When the verdict of banishment was given, she had been tempted to go with him into the wilderness. But she knew it would be impossible.

There was an alternative, and this she pondered as she scraped the carrots and re-diced the pimento. There was Sarah. Since Grandma Beki's miraculous recovery, Sarah had become a disciple. In principle she would willingly go with Sabbatai, and Sarah was family, close family, and her companionship in exile would ease the hearts of those at home. But in her heart, could she leave her mother? Clara was wary of asking her sister, for an enforced refusal would ruffle her spirit for ever. No, she would not ask her. She would not present her with a choice that would strain her loyalties on all sides.

In the kitchen, Sarah was setting the table, leaving Perla to comfort Beki. She was taking her time for she had much to think about. She would not miss Sabbatai as her sister would, but she would worry herself about his welfare. For although she believed in him, she did not think him immortal. He was as prone to sickness as any other. His specialness would not shield him from his continuous fasting and self-inflicted punishment. She wanted desperately to go with him, but the pull from her mother was as strong. Yet she knew that for her own sake she must sever that cord, that in doing so she would have forgiven her mother. So that when Grandma Beki died, there would be no unfinished business. But could she live without the hate that had curdled her heart, that hate that had for so long sustained her vitality? She noticed how frail her mother looked and she marvelled that such frail packaging could encompass such power. Impulsively she went over to her and dared to touch her.

'He will be all right, Mama,' she said. And in that moment she made her decision. She went straightway to the kitchen. 'You are not to worry about him, Clara,' she said. 'I am going with him, and I shall look after him.'

Clara turned from the carrots that by now were scraped almost to nothingness, and she flung her arms around her sister. 'I love you, Sarah,' she said. 'I will tell Sabbatai,' and they almost laughed together in their common relief.

But Clara's next question sobered them both. 'Have you told Mama?'

Sarah shook her head.

'Then we must both tell her. And now.'

Clara went straight to the dining-room and Sarah followed fearfully. She was glad that Perla was there. The presence of a third party would subdue the offended reaction that they feared. The sisters looked at each other. It was clear to Clara that she would have to be the spokeswoman.

'Mama,' she said, 'now that Sabbatai will be gone, it would be a great comfort to me if you come to live with us.'

Sarah gasped at her sister's cunning. Never had she associated such a trait with her sister. Suddenly she understood Sabbatai a little more.

'Will it be a comfort to you?' Beki said. She was not one to be caught doing anything for her *own* pleasure. 'What do you think, Sarah?' Beki asked.

'I think it would help Clara,' Sarah said. She knew her mother's talent for sacrifice and she laboured on. 'You would be doing her a "mitzvah",' she said. She would have gone on in that vein had not Perla interrupted.

'You must do it, Beki,' she said, 'for the sake of all of them.'

Thus the sacrifice was reinforced. Grandma Beki was almost beaming in the reflection of her own virtue. Clara had the instinct then to change the subject. The news of Sarah's defection could come later.

'Come,' she said, 'let's wash our hands. The men will return soon.'

'Perhaps Sarah should go with Sabbatai,' Beki said. She, too, since the order of banishment, had had her private thoughts. Parents need their freedom from their children even as much as their children need release, for children are gaolers even as their parents. Sending Sarah with Sabbatai would in many ways deliver her from her guilt of her daughter's thwarted love. It would be a way, tardy perhaps, of forgiving herself.

'Yes,' she said, resolved. 'Sarah must go with him.'

Thus the matter was resolved. God is occasionally good.

In a while the men returned from their prayers and prepared themselves to welcome the Sabbath.

'Shall I call Sabbatai?' Saul said.

Mordecai hesitated. He was not sure he wanted a last supper, for that event had had the most ominous consequences. It was the first tolling bell of the crucifixion. He looked to Clara for guidance.

'Tell him that supper is ready,' she said.

Saul went upstairs to Sabbatai's room and delivered the message as Clara had spoken.

'I'm fasting,' came the reply. 'Tell my mother to come to me after supper.'

Saul went downstairs and he decided that he would not deliver that message until the meal was over. For he dreaded that particular farewell. A parting between mother and son, and one that was perhaps for ever, was no event to be promoted or to call for rehearsal. It was as if a last act had opened a play without any preamble. He himself knew nothing of farewells. He had fearfully deprived himself of their finality, and in the light of this present sadness, he was grateful for it. His parents had left him without knowledge of parting, for in their minds, wherever they were going, it was to be a journey en famille. Only Saul knew that he was not with them, and to have said farewell would have added to the betrayal. He wished that Sabbatai would go, like himself, without a word.

'He's fasting,' he said to the supper-table.

'Then we shall begin,' Clara said.

After prayers, the supper was silent. The confirmation of Sarah's departure and Grandma Beki's change of address were the only items that broke the silence and neither was commented on. After supper the women cleared the dishes, while Mordecai and Nissim continued their weekly game of chess. Saul and David took themselves to another room, each of them withdrawing in their own way from the eye of sorrow. It was not until Clara distributed her goodnights to her family that Saul gave her Sabbatai's message. He noticed how she flushed when she heard it, both with fear and pleasure. 'I'll go to him,' she said.

She went to his door, and for a while she listened outside to his praying. She heard the creak of the floorboards as he leaned his flame towards the Torah, and she knew that his one hand was cradled on his back, rocking him into that warm cocoon of his swaddling years, and into that safety-net that catches the pain of salad days. She waited a while before she knocked. Sabbatai did not respond. It was possible that he did not hear, so enrapt was he in his prayers. So she opened the door quietly and went inside. She sat on his bed, in his line of vision and waited patiently until he was done. He continued for a while, as if unaware of her. She watched him, heedless of the tears that rinsed her cheeks. Her heart would burst, she thought, not with sorrow, but with a loving that no heart had ever known. That no heart had ever understood, that no heart had ever been called upon to accommodate. Then he turned to her and came quickly and knelt at her feet, laying his head on her lap. Quickly she put her arm where his own had lain, and cradled his fevered back into his first joy. So they sat for a while in a loving, beyond earth, beyond time.

'It's not farewell, Mama,' he said at last. 'I shall return. The people will call me.'

She cradled him in affirmation.

'D'you remember, Mama,' he said, 'when I had my first vision? God came to me and gave me numbers. He gave them to me as a gift, He said, for numbers were a passport to eternity.'

Now her rocking was desperate. Her son was already outside himself. He had already gone into exile, and left her with but the body of his infancy. She shuddered. For the first time since Sabbatai had been born, she was assailed by a piercing doubt. She looked at his cradled head on her breast, and she could not help but wonder whether this grown child, trembling with his uncertainties, fearful as a young bird, racked with terror of his future – was it possible that this child of hers was God's chosen one? That this frightened powerless boy, in all his craven innocence, would lead his people into paradise? She eased him from her lap and clung to him, sobbing. And the child in him broke with her, smothering her in tears.

'Sleep, Mama,' he said at last, as if she were a child. 'Hold me in your eyes,' he said, 'as I shall hold your face in mine for ever.'

He took her gently to her room and bade her goodnight. Once back in his own, Sabbatai noted that his fever had abated. He felt strangely as other men must feel; in his father's words, he felt normal. He felt whole. The feeling was good and he yearned for its permanence. But he knew that in the nature of his own destiny, such permanence was impossible. Such wholeness was a rare bonus in a nature that was so essentially disposed to schism. He knew that in himself. He knew, too, that he was more at home in the fevers, but only in his haleness could his heart be broken.

Sabbatai stayed in his room for the whole of the following day, dwelling in his own Sabbath. In the evening when the first star threatened, Mordecai pressed money into

Saul's hand, enough to sustain them all in their exile. As the first star shone, Sabbatai left his room and said his final farewells. Elijah, though as tall as he, clung to his coat, unwilling to release him. 'Send for me, Sabbatai,' he whispered.

'But you are not a disciple.'

'I love you. Isn't that enough?'

'It's too much,' Sabbatai said. 'It leaves no room for worship.'

'I shall come in any case.'

'I shall be back,' Sabbatai said to them all. 'They will beg my return.'

Mordecai held him close, insinuating the flesh of his own body into the gaunt armature of his son's, as if needing to affirm their kinship, more for Sabbatai's sake than his own. For father and son were beyond words.

The family gathered in the courtyard. Nissim and Perla, their arms around David's shoulders, waited there. All of them knew that this was not a farewell to be prolonged. None of them dared say goodbye.

'God bless you all,' Mordecai said. 'And be safe.'

He spoke for all of them. They watched as the small group disappeared into the darkness and waited till the echo of their exiled footsteps faded away. Then all returned to the house and each in their corner entered the land of grief and sorrow.

The following day the Zvi family woke to a Redeemer-less morning, and Grandma Beki got up and died.

The astonished wailing of the mourners crept through the streets of Smyrna, and the Rabbis trembled, for the inference was clear. As clear as it was to the mob that gathered outside the Rabbinical Courthouse and demanded the recall of Sabbatai Zvi. Inside, the Rabbis were adamant. Uncertain now of their cause, their intransigence was bull-like. Those who had been on Sabbatai's side refrained from saying, 'I told you so'.

'It will pass,' Rabbi Eskapa said. 'It's a nine-day wonder.' Myopia is often the handmaid to piety, and most agreed with him. But they stayed in the courtroom, fearful of exit, until the crowd dribbled away, withdrawing not from lack of fervour, but simply to strengthen their forces.

The doctor stood at Grandma Beki's bedside. He tried to underplay the auspicious timing of her death. 'She had a bad heart,' he was saying. 'It could have happened any time.'

'Her talisman was sent away,' Clara insisted between her tears.

The funeral was arranged for the following day, and Mordecai knew it would be something more than a simple interment.

They started gathering outside the house at dawn. Hundreds of them. Those refugees from the Holy Land, Sabbatai's preaching still ringing in their ears, had traipsed the length of the city from their hovels on the other side of the shore. Others came too, those who had always believed, but who had been afraid to speak out. Now they whispered in chorus and in the safety of their numbers. 'Bring Sabbatai home.'

They waited in the courtyard until the funeral procession left the house, winding its slow way through the streets to the cemetery. They followed. On the way they were joined by others, whispering their Sabbatai call, and the sound was that of a thousand ghosts seeking recompense. The crowd was swelling dangerously, so that by the time the cortège had reached the burial ground, its tail still lingered inside the city, and scuffles broke out in a stampede to reach the graveyard in time. But it soon became clear to the crowd that there was no possibility of that, and those remaining disciples, in whose hands Sabbatai had left his Smyrna following, seized on the situation to hold burial services wherever they found themselves to be. Thus the town of Smyrna became a charnel-house, God's acre in prayer. The city's commerce came to a standstill, simply because it could not move. There was anger amongst traders. Nothing in life, not even death, could be permitted to postpone profit. The situation looked ugly. Jews at prayer are rather more ostentatious than most. Their supplications are loud, their movements zealous and untiring. Anti-semitism, it is said, is a very light sleeper, and needs only the slightest nudge to stir it into action. The traders, helped by the local keepers of the peace, lost no time in making the city a fit place for business transactions. Many worshippers lay injured in the streets, still mouthing their prayers. Then the cry went up for Sabbatai, fitfully at first, then strengthened in chorus as it stretched along what was left of the line. Finally it was picked up in the burial ground where Grandma Beki was just about to go to her final resting-place. The grass might well have withereth, and the flower fadeth, but it was Sabbatai's name, that rhythmic passing-bell, that orchestrated her final obsequies. And there was nothing the Rabbis could do about it. As the coffin was lowered, Clara was seen to smile. The chanting of her son's name promised his swift return.

But the Rabbis dug in their heels. The impostor's name was never to be spoken aloud, on pain of excommunication. So along the streets of Smyrna and in the market-place, the name was whispered in a murmuring hum that has more power than a scream. For a scream is quickly exhausted; a whisper gathers momentum and grows until it is a whirlwind. For that was what the Rabbis had reaped.

131

7

To Smyrna in disguise

On the first stage of his exile, Sabbatai Zvi settled in Salonika, which at that time housed the largest Jewish community in the Ottoman Empire, and was the centre of Kabalistic study. The Rabbis of Salonika had heard of him of course, and of his great scholarship. Rumours of his questionable state of mind they dismissed with impatience. Idle gossip attended all men who were public figures. They welcomed him into their circle of scholarship and learned to marvel at his teachings. At first, Sabbatai kept quiet about his Messianic claims. For a while the fevers had left him and he felt no compulsion to proclaim himself. Or perhaps he was simply being politic. But for whatever reason, he was lying low. The Rabbis found him a simple house in the city, close to the synagogue, and there he lived with Saul and David, and Aunt Sarah who cared for them all.

'. . . Today we had news of Grandma Beki's death. Poor Aunt Sarah. I feel so close to her now. For so many years I have dwelt in that very special grief, that sorrow of unfinished business that is the natural legacy of orphanhood. She keens in her corner. Sabbatai too is desolate. He blames himself. "She died of my banishment," he shouted at me and I saw hatred in his eye. When the mourning ended, his fever rose. "I will go amongst the poor," he said. We followed him. I saw how he aimed his gaunt black-robed figure like a calm spear through the market-place. His black ringlets trembled

135

on his cheeks like quivering arrows. His outstretched arms were swords of peace. The people flocked before, behind and alongside him. Soon he found a stand and they gathered about him. The light from his eye sparked a current through the crowd, and fused them to his message. "Follow me," he said. His voice was a whisper, but a deaf man would have heard its holy ring. "Cleanse yourselves of all sin," he said, "for redemption is at hand. God sees that the poor have the power of angels, that their songs are the sweetest, that their repentance is honey in His mouth. For it is the poor who will lead the Redeemer. The poor will show him the way to the gates of the holy city. For only to them will God reveal His path." Amongst the crowd I saw a man in trance, and then another. Women threw themselves at Sabbatai's feet and offered him their babes for his blessing. They stretched out their hands to touch him but drew back from the fire of his flesh. There was loving in their eyes, both the men's and the women's, carnal almost, and I shivered. In time they will call him the Redeemer. Every day they wait for him and every day he gives them his glory. When he prays, his voice sometimes flowers into song and its angelic tones water the crowd's ears, and open their gates to heaven . . . Today they proclaimed him.

". . . Moses was with me today," Sabbatai told me. "He came with a sackful of shattered stones. He emptied them on to my floor. 'At last the Commandments are broken,' he said. 'It is the beginning of redemption.' Then he picked up the fractured Law, piece by piece. 'This one,' he said, 'is for the worship of idols. Promote it. It will anger God. Call Him by name. It will offend His vanity.' Another stone was the broken Sabbath, but the most shattered piece of all was fidelity. 'Adulterate,' Moses said. 'Fornicate. Dwell in the sewers. Descend into hell, for the ladder to paradise is rooted in Gehenna, and only from that nether place can one ascend to heaven.'" He was in ecstasy, and when I touched his flesh, my hand was on fire. Then he lay with me and called me God. For a while I did not think about my father.'

On the following Sabbath, he went to the synagogue of Qehal Shalom and, mounting the pulpit, he declared that the Passover, The Feast of Weeks and the Sukkot, all these festivals of pilgrimage, should be celebrated in the course of one week so as to atone for all the sins ever committed. 'Then God' – again the ineffable Name – 'will give us a new Law and new Commandments to repair all the world. Blessed is He,' he shouted, 'who permits that which is forbidden.'

But it was too much for the Rabbis. The generous diagnosis of madness was no longer acceptable. For there was a strange Kabalistic logic in Sabbatai's declaration, and the Rabbis feared that, in the ears of the unlearned, such a sermon could unleash chaos. No, Sabbatai Zvi was not mad. He was a blasphemer and an impostor, and must at once be banished. But the Rabbis of Salonika were more generous than their brothers in Smyrna, for they gave Sabbatai a week to prepare for his departure. And that week was a godsend, for had he left forthwith, he would not have received the news from Smyrna. Letters from home were regular and frequent, and always in his mother's hand. She would give him news of the Smyrna community, stressing their continual call for his return. The letters were punctuated with worship and love. Sometimes there was a scribbled postscript from Joseph recording the progress of their conversions and occasionally Elijah contributed a drawing with some tart caption that veiled his brotherly love. His father wrote rarely but always in haste. His main concern was for Sabbatai's health, but that too was choked with love.

But this missive that Saul handed to him was different. There were no signs of his mother's hand. It was his father's writing on the wrapping, an ominous sign. His stomach heaved a warning. He asked Saul to leave him, embracing him first, as if the need to touch life had been urgently dictated by the letter in his hand. Then, alone, he held it for a long while. He knew instinctively that all was not well, and that the area of unease circled his mother. He began to mourn. The tears flowed as he entertained the possibility of never seeing her again, and, already orphaned, he at last opened the letter.

His father's hand seemed infirm, trembling with the news he had to impart. His mother was very ill, his father had written. Her disease was unmentionable and the doctor did not expect her to live for very much longer. She sent her boundless love to him and all her blessings. As for himself, he hoped Sabbatai was in good health, his usual greeting, and he signed 'Papa' with screaming sadness.

At once Sabbatai summoned his followers. He told them in his own words the import of the message from Smyrna for he could not bear to read his father's letter aloud. Its coldness might have frozen in a public airing, and its ardent love turned to conflagration. They must take the caravan to Constantinople, he told them, where in a few weeks he would join them. But he himself would make straightway for Smyrna.

'I have to see her just once more,' he whispered.

'But you are banished from there,' Saul said.

'I shall return in disguise.'

'But how? You will be recogniscd.'

'I shall find a way,' Sabbatai said.

'Then I shall come with you. It will be easier with two of us,' Saul said.

'No. Aunt Sarah needs you both in Constantinople.'

Later that evening, David came to Sabbatai's room. 'Let me come with you,' he said.

'I've told you,' Sabbatai answered him. 'It will be easier for me alone.' He looked at David's crestfallen face and realised that David's visit had little to do with his request. Rather he was asking for acknowledgment, of which, since Saul's arrival, he had felt bereft. He knew of Sabbatai's love for Saul, and of the special quality of that love, and, in plain and simple terms, he was jealous. With all his piety and devotion, he still suffered the mundane pangs of rejection.

Sabbatai embraced him tenderly and, bypassing preamble, he said, 'We have a different kind of love, you and I.'

'But it was not always so,' David said. 'Not when we were younger.'

'It was right for both of us at that time,' Sabbatai said. 'I love you as well as I love Saul. More, perhaps, because I sense its permanence. Saul will betray me. I know it. Go with him to Constantinople and be my torch-bearer. Aunt Sarah loves you like a son. Look after her. Leave me now.'

When David had gone, Sabbatai took out his father's letter and read it once more. And as he read, he slipped his arm into the crook of his back and let it solder there. It would hold forever his mother's imprint; it would give her life. It would sentence her to cradle him until he died.

The next morning all was prepared for their departure. Aunt Sarah was tearful. She was close to Clara and she was free to return. The thought had crossed her mind to go at once to Smyrna, but she was still mourning her mother and would do so for the rest of her days because that unfinished business was now and forever beyond completion. Besides, she had grown attached to David, in whose company all her thwarted maternity blossomed. And Sabbatai's movement drew her too, the frenzy of it, the acclamation of the throng. Even the punishment of the Rabbis thrilled her, for she was acquiring a martyr's appetites. So she had not offered to travel with Sabbatai, and she knew that Sabbatai understood. Yet she felt nervous of travelling to Constantinople without him, leaderless and without direction. As did the others. But they were at pains to hide it as they took their leave. They each begged Sabbatai to take care to avoid discovery. Aunt Sarah added that he should look to his health, for she already saw the signs of fever.

Sabbatai accompanied them to the caravan depot which lay in the poor quarter of the city. It served too as a begging-centre, for travellers are often to be caught in a generous mood. Many of Sabbatai's followers were there for that purpose, and they hailed him.

'Are you leaving us now?' one said. His voice was accusing.

'You know I am being sent away,' Sabbatai said. 'And I leave tomorrow. But I shall return. I shall answer your call.'

The crowd waited until the caravan set off, then they followed their leader at a distance, chanting his name.

Sabbatai hurried home and quickly packed his meagre possessions. He had made his plans. In the Salonika ghetto, where his followers were legion, he had made the acquaintance of a woman who had never left his side. Once she had told him her story. It was similar to Saul's. She, too, had lost her family in the Chmielnicki massacres and in her escape had thrown in her lot with a band of gypsies, and somehow had covered the tortuous route to Salonika. Sabbatai had grown attached to her and now he felt he could trust her. He would take her aside on his farewell visit to the ghetto.

He set out right away. He did not want a street gathering. He thought it unpolitic. But he could not avoid it, for they had scent of his coming. He ushered them back into their hovels and went from door to door with his farewells. All the while, the woman did not leave his side. When all was done, she took him to her room where he stayed for a while. It was late when he stole out of the ghetto. He was carrying a small bag. He did not look back for he knew that one day he would return.

He left Salonika early the next morning, and took the stage for Athens. Near the port he found a hostelry. He booked quarters for one night, and paid immediately, saying that he had to leave at sunrise. He went to his room and immediately set to praying. He prayed for many things, but all his prayers were for his mother.

When the sun rose, a passer-by would have caught a glimpse of a young woman leaving the hostelry. She carried a small travelling bag and was walking in the direction of the port. But that passer-by would not have given her a second glance, for there was nothing untoward in her appearance at that early hour, for it was known that a boat sailed for Smyrna even as the cock crew.

As Sabbatai neared the harbour, the streets became alive with trade and people. He was surprised to find how easy it was to masquerade as a woman. He had no fear of moving amongst the crowds. His lean frame and clean-shaven face with its fragile look was more in tune with womanhood than with his own gender. His gait, too, seemed to have adjusted quite naturally. The small stride was dictated by the black hobble skirt, which neatly covered his own shoes. On his head he wore a long kerchief, and the ringlets of his creed peeped from its corners like eavesdroppers on his true faith. He joined the crowds at the harbour and was bold in his deceiving presence. Indeed, he almost revelled in his new person, and that delight disturbed him a little. When his turn came at the ticket-booth, he lifted his voice – a contralto was the most he could get away with – and he booked himself a first-class berth. The sailing to Smyrna could not be expected to take less than three or four days, given fair winds and weather. He needed his privacy. Above all for his prayers.

His room was small, neat and orderly, rather like a monk's cell. Sabbatai felt very much at home in it. It was a room designed for solitude, which attitude Sabbatai intended to pursue for the length of the journey. It would help avoid discovery, but principally it would allow him to study, meditate, perform his own rituals and to pray for his mother. Moveover, he would fast for most of the time. He knew his disguise was a sin for which he had to atone, but not for the breaking of the banishment order. It was a son's right to be at his mother's side. So he set to praying. Occasionally he took water from a jug that had been placed in his cell and which was renewed every morning. Otherwise he was undisturbed. He wore his disguise all the time, never taking it off even for the few hours of sleep that he granted himself. While praying, he would attune his swaying movements to the rolling of the sailing-ship and when the ship heaved, so would his prayer and its ardour. As long as he was praying for his mother he felt at peace. And as long as he crooked his arm on his back, he knew that she would stay alive.

So the days passed, as Sabbatai grew higher on hunger and prayer. He knew that they were nearing the end of their voyage because of the noise of heavy traffic that he heard from the deck. And the cheering and thanksgiving for safe arrival. He washed himself and straightened his woman's attire, then he joined the others on deck.

The harbour seemed to approach the ships, and on it were many people, a happy crowd, waving handkerchiefs and cheering. He wondered whether any of his followers were amongst them. He would walk through them as quickly as decency would allow, then he would take the long route over the sea-shore, where few people walked and where the silent roar of the sea would give him comfort. It was early morning, and a week-day, so that neither his father nor brothers would be at home. He would be alone with his mother, and his heart quickened with the joy of a lover. His steps, too, for he was anxious to be with her. His prayers never ceased. In rhythm with his footsteps he pleaded with God for her recovery. At the end of the shore-line, he was almost running. He climbed the dunes crouching, gripping the sand-grass for support. When he reached the road, he slowed his gait and made his way to his mother's house. He was surprised to find the streets crowded with people, many of whom he recognised. He tried not to notice their funeral dress, and when at last he had to acknowledge it, he refused to give it any special attention. After all, every day in Smyrna a Jew died. Nothing uncommon. But it was undeniable that they were taking the same route as he, and he prayed that at the next corner they would turn and direct their steps to a stranger's sorrow. They must turn, he prayed. They must. But they walked straight past that so-fervently-prayed-for corner, and it seemed that they were leading him, and he had no power to stop them. There were no more corners before his mother's house. He could only pray now that they would pass it. He lagged behind them to get a better view of their passage, of their non-stop, of their continuance. He would stand there and watch them until they were out of sight and then he would know it had all been a dream. His heart faltered as he saw the dragging of their steps, the signal that soon the walking must come to a stop. He stood there transfixed as he watched the crowd gather outside his mother's house and he cursed God aloud, using His very name, which was curse enough, but embellishing it with all manner of blasphemy. And he didn't even bother to match his voice with his skirt. He didn't care any more. 'I don't want to be your Messiah,' he wept. 'I shall suffer for myself, but no one person shall suffer because of me. I would sooner serve the Devil,' he shouted.

He was standing alone, the crowd having distanced itself. He started to walk, trembling. Once or twice he turned his head and shouted, 'I wish you to burn in hell,' as if he had left God behind him. His mother's house was a blur through his tears. He still hoped for a nightmare and that he would wake up in his cell on the ship. But his feet were moving. His tears were real and hot on his cheeks, and his mother's house was no vision, any more than that black crowd that stood outside it. He began to run, then suddenly his legs pulled him up and he landed still, quivering like a thrust arrow. For the door of the house had opened and that terrible box was lifted over the threshold. Behind it, his father, Joseph and Elijah, Nissim and Perla Arditti and a crowd of weeping women, and men who held back their tears. Sabbatai froze, too numb now even to curse the God he had left behind him. He watched as the procession turned into the street and painted it black with funeral. At last, he moved and

143

shadowed their snail's pace, keeping at a distance, not that he feared discovery, but out of a certain resentment that they, those strangers, seemed to assume more rights than he. He started to pray again, this time for forgiveness, and his fever waned.

It was a long way to the burial ground and the procession moved slowly. But as long as he was praying, the journey was timeless and when they reached the cemetery, it was as if he had been transported. The crowd gathered in the prayer-house, and Sabbatai, bound by his woman's skirts, stood at the open door. Though at the rear, his height gave him a full view of the family mourning. The coffin was covered with a black drape, on which was a white embroidery of the six-pronged Star of David. It rested on a carriage, its wooden wheels well-worn by its frequent Stygian ferrying. Alongside it stood his father and his brothers. There was room for him, in that space deliberately left for him, and where he should have been, but he would not mourn his mother as a woman. That gender in such circumstances shrieked discord. He was his mother's son, her first-born, and in her obsequies only that gender was harmonious.

Prayers were sung and tears were shed, then the Rabbis led the procession to the graveside. Although Rabbi Eskapa was among the mourners, he took no part in the ceremony, and Sabbatai was glad of it for his mother had doubtless died of the sentence he had laid on her son. He reached the grave as the final prayers were being intoned. His father lifted the first shovel of earth and his brothers followed. Then the others. Sabbatai waited. He was entitled to his portion of remembrance. He was the last to bid her farewell. Then he made his way alone, back to the sea-shore, and stayed there, praying on the sands till nightfall. He knew he should leave Smyrna quickly and take sail for Constantinople, but he wanted to take his father and brothers in his arms. He needed them to share his overwhelming sorrow. So he made his way to his mother's house.

Through the window he could see the mourning candle flickering in its glass, and three shadows in its flame. He opened the door and went inside. Elijah saw him first and stared, wide-eyed.

'Who are . . . Sabbatai!' he almost sang as he rushed towards him in embrace.

'Papa, Joseph,' Sabbatai said, and enfolded them too. None of them spoke. They stood there for a long while, holding each other. Then Sabbatai took off his kerchief for the first time since leaving Salonika, and in its place he donned a 'yarmulke' and was a man again. They sat around the table.

'How did Mama die?' Sabbatai asked.

'She was ill,' Mordecai said, with a finality that brooked no further questioning. She had died of an unmentionable word and if anyone should utter it, it would be as if she had died again.

'She talked about you all the time,' Elijah said. He felt deeply sorry for his brother that he had not been at their mother's side. He, Joseph and their father had sat with her, never at any time leaving her alone, and together they had guided her into her darkness. So now between them, they tried to share those hours with Sabbatai, detailing her every word and gesture, and her blessings especially for her exiled son. And they told him, too, of her silences that grew longer and more frequent as death drew near. And of the beauty and calm of her going. So, through the night, the four of them mourned together. None of them mentioned Sabbatai's disguise. They accepted it as a natural necessity for his return.

'What will you do?' his father said at last.

'I shall stay for the Shiva,' he said. 'I must not be seen or rumoured. I shall stay in my room till each nightfall, then we can be together.'

So for six more nights Sabbatai keened on a low stool, alone in his room, praying silently. There was peace and loving between them, and each hoped that it would hold

145

until the return to exile. But on the last night, when the mourning was over, and life was to resume its offensive normality, the peace that was between them was slowly eroded.

'I need all my sons by my side,' Mordecai said.

'But I am bound in exile, Papa.'

'Then give it up,' Mordecai raised his voice. What had been a seven-day whisper in prayer now broke into a scream. 'You are not the Redeemer!'

'Papa,' Joseph protested.

Sabbatai felt very alone. His mother's absence shuddered through the room. In spite of Joseph's mild protest, he felt cornered.

'It's what others say,' Sabbatai said. It was harder to brand a hundred lunatics than to certify one insane.

'You lead them on,' Elijah said.

'They beg me to lead them.' And there lay the catch. Unarguable.

Mordecai took Sabbatai's hand. Touch might help, he thought. A caress sometimes could offset the inevitable hurt. But Sabbatai would not be blackmailed by tenderness. He shook his father's hand away and Mordecai saw the traces of that son of his who was not whole. He was not surprised when Sabbatai addressed him then as 'Father'.

'You know, Father,' he said, 'you have never believed in me. You have been like the Rabbis. You and Elijah. From the Rabbis I expect persecution. They have more to fear from me. But from my own flesh and blood . . .' The sweat lay on his forehead. Minute drops, Mordecai noticed, and none of them threatened to fall. They were fixed there, hundreds of them, like pin-points in a cushion, and he stared at them, fascinated. If only one of them would burst, he thought, that default would humanise his son. But they were fixed, immutable.

Elijah came towards Sabbatai and put his arms around his shoulder. His touch was different. It came from a different source. It had never been sullied by expectation, sieved by disappointment; it was of itself alone. Fraternal. And Sabbatai could bear it, for it did not have the burden of his father's caress.

'It's only that we love you,' Elijah said, 'and our hearts are broken enough. Yours, too. Come home, Sabbatai,' he begged. 'Declare that you are a scholar and nothing more than that. The Messiah must never never come. For what then can we hope for?'

'We don't arrange these things,' Sabbatai said. 'I am of God's choosing.'

'Out,' Mordecai suddenly screamed. 'Out. Out of this house.' His anger was sublime, and he wished that it would curdle his love for his son, but he knew he used it as a cover. For in truth, that love was so intense, he was ashamed of it.

Sabbatai drew away. 'I'm leaving,' he said. He saw his father shrivel into a chair. He watched as he buried his face in his hands. He stared at his shoulders, shuddering with sobs. And for some reason, he was not moved. Then Elijah lunged towards him and struck him hard, surprised at his own strength, for when he took his hand from Sabbatai's face, he saw how it dripped with his brother's blood. He made no attempt at apology. The blow had been on behalf of his father's pain as well as his own. They stared at each other and knew of the space between. Joseph stood aside, silent. Even that time-honoured go-between, that gentle peace-maker, could find no bridge of truce. For what words were left for any of them, what gesture, what spleen, what tenderness? Only an abyss, unbridgeable.

But nevertheless, Mordecai tried to reach him, and he stretched out his arms over that chasm.

'Sabbatai,' he said softly. And that was all.

Then Sabbatai went to him. 'Papa,' he said.

And they were together again.

He stayed with them till the morning broke. They talked of Clara. They recalled her mothering and all the simple pleasures of their childhood. They even laughed sometimes with the memory of it all. They dwelt in the past, for that, however it had been lived, was safe. But no mention was made of Sabbatai's departure. That was the future and, for Mordecai, Elijah and even Joseph, unbearable.

Silently they accompanied him to the port. They insisted on it, and Sabbatai did not protest. At the port, their farewells were formal. In such a public place there was no room for a display of affection. They were all glad of it. In any case, all that was between them had already been laid bare, and neither the loathing nor the loving could stretch any further.

The ticket-booth was on the far side of the port. Once again, Sabbatai booked himself a private berth. Once again it was a cell, and he made himself at home there. Once out of port, he was free to reassume his normal dress. The boat was so crowded, no one would have remarked on his change. But for some reason, he was loth to discard his female attire. Over the past weeks, he had grown into it. His woman's gait was second nature. Even his occasional contralto was effected with ease. But more important than all, it seemed to him that the quality of his prayer had undergone a change that sometimes overwhelmed him. His dress had lent it a certain familiarity. Without losing its tone of worship and esteem, it had robbed his prayer of awe, and the result was comforting. He had never given much thought to the notion of pleasure. He reflected now that his life had been punctuated by punishment, most of it self-induced. Now he considered that he should use himself well, treat himself a little, and if that meant to sin, so be it. It was an untenable equation, and God had surely not conceived it. So to serve God well, he must please himself. He must taste those joys of the human flesh that worship denies. To this end, he straightened his kerchief, primped his ringlets, and took himself to the captain's table for lunch.

The smells were unfamiliar, but they smacked of sin. The sailing-ship was of a Greek line, and its cuisine likewise.

The hors d'oeuvres of fetta cheese, olives, houmus and aubergines would not have offended the palate of the most orthodox Jew. It was what came afterwards that was calumny. A kebab of pork, shamelessly rinsed in yoghurt, proclaimed two unpardonable dietary violations. The mixture of meat and milk was not to be forgiven, to say nothing of the meat itself which was quite beyond the pale. But Sabbatai indulged in it, relishing the mélange and the forbidden. And asked for more. He drank too. Apart from ceremonial wine, he rarely touched alcohol, but now he discovered a new pleasure and he resolved to indulge in it more often. The party grew more and more convivial. The gentleman on his right, a Greek trader from Athens, let his hands wander to Sabbatai's knee and linger there for a while, while Sabbatai savoured it and wished for more. When the table rose, the man suggested that Sabbatai visit his cabin. The temptation was overwhelming, but having succeeded thus far, Sabbatai did not wish to invite discovery. Besides, he was already chock-full with sin, enough to redeem him for a while. Moreover, his stomach grew uncomfortable. Pleasure, like sin, had to be habituated.

He slept for the rest of the day, another pursuit he was unused to, and in the evening took a stroll on the deck, avoiding the Greek trader. He viewed the moon and the stars with an exaltation he had never known, with an ecstasy almost, that had absolutely nothing to do with God. When night fell, he threw himself on his bed and didn't even bother to pray. There followed more than three days of indulgent debauch, stopping just short of discovery. During that time an orgy of forbidden foods passed his lips, but never once a prayer. Sabbatai Zvi disembarked at Constantinople a confirmed and exhilarated sinner.

8

A live sea scroll

It was early evening when he left the ship. The light was fading. Soon it would be the hour to stroll the streets and alleys as he had done on that first seductive visit to Constantinople. He had arranged for Aunt Sarah to put up at the same hostelry where he had previously stayed. But he would delay his arrival there. He longed to see Saul, but it was a longing that could be prolonged with pleasure. He made his way to the market-place for an appetizing recall. He heard the hum of haggling and trading long before he reached the square and, when he arrived, he found it thronged with people. But this time the wares were not slaves. They had a different smell altogether, a perfumed heaviness that, in the night air, was overpowering. He identified it with ease. Roses. Immediately he thought of his mother, and how, every year, at this time their courtyard in Smyrna was filled with the same overpowering scent. Wagon-loads of rose-petals would be delivered there, plucked from the fecund fields of Macedonia, and there the women would gather with their jars and cauldrons and, like benign witches, stir a brew of rose-petal jam. It was a fond memory yet caused him grief. Here there were no cauldrons nor stirrings. Just the petals and the traders filling the women's bags.

He stayed for a while, taking pleasure in a commerce that was far more benign than the one he had previously attended. He thought of Saul again, and longed for him, more intensely than ever before. He wondered whether his women's weeds had affected his heart as well as his soul.

He turned away from the square. He would walk back to the hostelry along the old route, through the alleys of the town, the underworld that drew him. Clusters of young women gathered on corners or strolled aimlessly along the narrow streets. There was no obvious touting for trade. There was time, and enough to go round for everybody. Besides, it was still early for play-hour. He walked unremarked amongst them. At the end of a lane, he noticed a woman standing alone. More than noticed her, for her appearance had a magnetic quality, and one could not help but move towards her, as if lured. As he approached, Sabbatai saw her features very clearly. The eyes claimed an unfair proportion of her face, but this did nothing to diminish her beauty. Indeed, it served to enhance it, to embellish her other features. Their ethereal look smudged her cheek, her nose and her chin. It seemed she was not part of the natural world, and certainly not of the alley where she lingered. Yet there was no doubt as to her trade. Her presence in the alley, loitering there, was proof enough of that. And her stance, too. One hand lay idly on her hip as she tossed an unruly mane of black hair. For her calling, unoriginal. It was clearly her own image of a harlot and so banal, it looked ridiculous. Sabbatai reached for his contralto and greeted her. She was cool in her response. She had no time for idle chatter.

'Are you hungry?' he asked her.

Her looked changed, and the great eyes threatened tears. She nodded her head, not trusting her voice.

'Then come with me,' he said. 'I'm hungry too. We can eat together, and I shall give you money for the time you lose.'

'But why?' she asked. 'What am I to you?'

'Company,' Sabbatai said. 'I know no one in this city. Just company,' he added, 'and perhaps a little conversation. Come.'

He led her through the alley and back into the square. All around there were tables where people were eating and drinking. He found an empty one and motioned her to sit down. She took her seat tentatively, still wary of his company. Her nostrils flared at the smell of food from a neighbouring table and her eyes misted over with hunger. Sabbatai attempted no conversation. He would wait until she had eaten.

A servant approached the table, the length of his arm covered with small dishes. One by one he put them on the table. Shortly he returned with pitta and lemonade, then left them to their choices. The girl stared at them for a long while, not knowing where to begin. So Sabbatai filled her plate and her glass and then his own.

'I'm hungry,' he said. 'Let's make a start.'

She waited for him to begin, then took her cue from his choices. Her eyes did not leave his face. She gazed at him, bewildered. But after a few mouthfuls, she concentrated on her food, savouring it with relish, yet with the utmost delicacy.

She paused and a smile grew around her eyes. 'They put me on sale in this market-place,' she said. 'But I ran away.' She laughed a little but more with despair than mirth.

'What's your name?' Sabbatai asked.

'Sarah. And yours?'

The question caught Sabbatai off his guard. He'd made no preparation for an answer. On the boat, the company had been so anonymous that no one had enquired of anybody's name. Fortunately he had a mouthful of food while the question was asked, and while swallowing, he had time to choose an identity. With little thought he replied, 'Clara.'

'That was my mother's name,' she said.

He'd almost expected it. It gave him a vague clue to his attraction to the girl. He wanted to reach out, and, without touching her, touch her spirit. For it was that, that spirit that shone in her eyes, that pulled him. He watched her eating and her glow of satisfaction. Perhaps now she might tell him her story.

'Where are you from?' he asked, as she sipped her lemonade.

She thought for a while as if trying to recollect information. As if it was someone else's provenance he had enquired after, as if she viewed herself in the third person. Sarah was not autobiographical. She was history, dependent on someone else's telling. But history sees her shrouded in mystery, surrounded by legend, rumour, fantasy. What is certain is that she herself was a pathological liar, so no self-account would be reliable. But sifting through the rumour and the legend, certain truths emerge.

Like many of her generation, she was orphaned in the Chmielnicki massacres. She was six years old when she was found wandering in a field and taken to a good Christian family who entrusted her to the care of nuns. She was reared like any Catholic orphan, in a convent. In the ten years she was its reluctant hostage, she fell in love with Christ as was her Catholic duty. But it wasn't the kind of love set down in the curriculum, and at the age of sixteen, she escaped to find that love, and to translate it into carnal knowledge. To this end, she wandered from city to city, looking for likely saviours. She is said to have arrived in Amsterdam where she had a brother whom she appraised of her search. Her brother, a menial tobacco-sorter, was unimpressed by her mission. Sensing his lack of co-operation, young Sarah took off from Amsterdam and after many wanderings, whoring from capital to capital, she settled in Leghorn. She had followed all the rumours of the Messiah's coming, and there were many around at the time. In Leghorn she heard of sightings in Smyrna and Salonika and then confirmation that he had been seen in those places. Then she heard that he was expected in Constantinople and she took her wretched witch-like beauty to the Turkish capital.

Sabbatai had heard nothing of her history, which was just as well, for he might, there and then, and in his hobble-skirt, have hamfistedly declared himself. He asked the question again. 'Where are you from?' he said.

'From everywhere.' Which indeed she was. 'I must go to work,' she said, suddenly.

'I'll walk with you,' Sabbatai said. He paid the waiter and walked her back to her corner.

'Shall we meet again?' she asked. 'I'm often hungry.'

'No, I'm going back to my village tomorrow,' Sabbatai said.

She shrugged her thin shoulders.

'Here, take this,' Sabbatai said. He gave her some money, more than enough to feed her hungry hours. She did not look at it, but stuffed it in a handkerchief between her breasts.

'If you were a man,' she said, 'you could have me for nothing.'

'Take care of yourself,' Sabbatai said, and meant it. He knew he had to see her again. He sensed that she would become part of him and he was glad that he would always know where to find her.

It was late when he reached the hostelry and his little family had retired. He went to his room and packed away his disguise. They would never know from him how he managed to attend his mother's funeral.

In the morning, their reunion was joyful. In his absence, Saul and David had been spreading Sabbatai's word, his theories of mysticism and restoration of the soul. They had gone into the ghettos of the city and given notice of Sabbatai's coming. The Rabbis, too, had had notice. As before, Sabbatai's reputation had preceded him, both as to his profound scholarship and strange eccentricities, but the learned men were willing to overlook the latter – indeed to find some sanctity in them – in favour of his renowned teachings. They had heard, too, of his treatment by the Rabbis of Smyrna and Salonika. Feeling themselves in any case superior to such provincial authority, they felt duty-bound to exercise far more tolerance of Sabbatai Zvi's little quirks.

Sabbatai went to their Council Chamber to introduce himself and to pay his respects. They were impressed by his saintly appearance of which they had heard much, and impressed too by his manner, which was polite and deferential. They could see no traces of eccentricity. At the time, Sabbatai was feverless, and had been since leaving Smyrna. But he knew that his sang-froid was only temporary, and that soon enough, when the Messianic craving was upon him, he would slide into exaltation. They asked him to deliver sermons at the main synagogue whenever he so wished. They would be honoured, they said. Sabbatai thanked them and returned to his quarters.

He lay low for a while, performing his rituals, and fasting. And he saw nobody. Occasionally at night, he went into the streets, and always found himself straying towards Sarah's corner. She was usually at her post, and he would stand, unnoticed, at a distance, and watch her ply her trade. She never made an approach. The invitation came from the clients. Some she refused. Others she led into an alleyway. Sabbatai waited and, after a while, saw her come out alone, stuffing her earnings into her bodice. Then he could be satisfied that she would eat that night.

After some weeks of comparative solitude, Sabbatai emerged and took to the streets. As was his wont, he went into the ghetto, where they were waiting for him and, without any declaration on his part, for he thought it better to lay low for a while, they called him the Redeemer. Word spread to the Rabbis of course, but they smiled benignly, marvelling at the naïveté of the poor. Sabbatai's preaching itinerary slowly stirred the fever inside him and sometimes he felt possessed by the Devil, who would escort him through the streets, deposit him on a ghetto corner, mock his God-sent messages, and singe the holy words with his own fire. At such meetings Sabbatai would break into a mindless stammer, and falter on each phrase, as if he himself did not understand the matter of his words. But this hesitation only served to reinforce the belief of the faithful who saw Sabbatai as but an unknowing vessel of transmitted divinity.

At one of these meetings, in the midst of prayer, there was a rustling in the murmuring crowd. A woman was making her way to the platform where Sabbatai stood. She waited for the prayer to be over, then looked up at him. Sabbatai could not help but see her, or rather feel her eyes upon him and, when he met them, he confirmed that it was Sarah. He wondered what she was doing there, yet he knew it was the only place for her to be.

'Do you not know me?' she whispered. She was panting with expectation. Her long journey through the capitals of Europe, through the wilderness of bordellos, alleys and kerbs, was now at its end. 'Do you not know me?' she pleaded again.

Sabbatai thought she recognised him from the hobble-skirt. He shook his head.

'But you *will* know me,' she said. 'I shall follow you and you will know me. When it is time, you will know. It is said, and it is written.' Then her face broke into a smile of such joy that it plainly displayed the pain that it had displaced. Then she turned, making her way through the crowd and no doubt back to the alleys whence she came.

After that meeting, she never failed to appear at his sermons and always with the same question. 'Do you not know me?' And each time Sabbatai would shake his head.

His disciples were growing in number and the Rabbis grew nervous. But they decided that as long as Sabbatai kept within the boundaries of Holy Law, they would tolerate him. It was as if Sabbatai had eavesdropped on their decision for, knowing their threshold, he was soon to overstep it.

One of his disciples was another learned Kabalist, Abraham Yakini. He was a preacher and the author of many works on the subject of Kabalistic interpretations of visions and dreams. He was mindful that the Messianic year was at hand, and he seriously considered Sabbatai as a possible candidate. Besides his knowledge of mysticism, Yakini had talents in other directions. He was a calligrapher of repute, and as such was often employed by Christian scholars as a copyist of ancient Hebrew manuscripts. Now calligraphy is an art that lends itself temptingly to abuse. In other words, calligraphy and copying are close, if reluctant, neighbours to forgery. And it was this aspect of Yakini's art that played a significant part in the growth of Sabbatai's Messianic career. Had Yakini been alive today, he would have made a pretty good if less than honourable living as an impresario. Not only would he set out to discover talent, but he would seek to promote his finds, for there is a certain kudos in discovery. There is no doubt that Yakini thought Sabbatai a possible Messiah. So why not make that possibility a certainty? Promotion is all. So he bought himself paper, inks, and dyes and with this bagful of cunning, he retired to his quarters and set to work.

At the time, Sabbatai was in a fever, and raging through the streets calling on all sinners to repent, to fast, to perform rituals and to purify themselves in preparation for the redemption. People paused, wondered, listened, then followed him, until they jammed the little streets with their worship. The Rabbis fidgeted, waiting to pounce. Then one day Sabbatai appeared in the market-place pushing a wheelbarrow, a spectacle strange enough in itself and even odder in view of the barrow's content. For inside, wrapped in a shawl, was a huge fish. Occasionally Sabbatai stopped and bent over to stroke it, while the crowd gathered and wondered. Some dared to ask its meaning. Sabbatai looked up from the fish, and saw amongst the crowd two thinly-disguised Rabbis from the Court. Dissatisfied with rumour and hearsay, they had come to see for themselves. And so that they would be in no doubt, Sabbatai stopped in his passage and directed his words at them.

'There was once, about two hundred years ago, a Jewish astronomer,' he said. He spoke with sober authority, for there was no fiction in his tale. 'In his reading of the stars and the charts of the skies, he prophesied that when the planets Jupiter and Saturn were in conjunction with the sign of Pisces, that is, the sign of the fish, the Messiah would be known.' Sabbatai paused to give weight to the conclusion of his tale. 'I am the fish and that time is now,' he said, slowly. The crowd gasped in wonder and Sabbatai saw how the two Rabbis threaded their way through the crowds and out into the streets, and he knew that they were on their way to the Council Chamber. He turned his barrow and walked once more, but this time they did not follow him. His near self-declaration had rooted them in awe. They stared after him, knowing that nothing would ever be the same again. Even Sarah, on the fringes of the crowd, did not dare to follow him. She knew now, with absolute certainty, that the man with the barrow was her predestined husband. She would not chase him any more. The time would come when he would send for her.

As the Rabbis did for Sabbatai. That very evening. When he walked into the Council Chamber, he was surprised by the presence of Rabbi Eskapa, his old teacher. It was unfortunate for Sabbatai that Eskapa happened to be in the capital at the time on a private visit to his sister, who lived there. Rabbi Eskapa had a glint in his eye, a gleam of 'I-told-you-so'. But it was not what was in his eye that disturbed Sabbatai. It was what the man held in his hand and was at no pains to hide. For in simple terms, it was a whip, a rehearsal, Sabbatai thought, for his crucifixion. A sense of martyrdom overcame him, and in a strange way, it was a relief, because suffering and pain were part of the Messiah's clothing. At the sight of the whip, he smiled faintly.

They were seated at a long table and Sabbatai was ordered to stand before them.

'Explain yourself,' their spokesman said.

161

'What should I explain?' Sabbatai asked. 'I am Sabbatai Avi, born in Smyrna on Tisha B'Av.' He stressed his birthdate, knowing that they knew of its significance.

But that only riled them further. 'Thousands of people are born on Tisha B'Av. All over the world,' one of them said.

Sabbatai could only smile, which they took as a sign of his contempt, and Rabbi Eskapa's whip quivered in his hand. Then the Chairman of the Council stood. It was sentence time. Undeniably.

'Your behaviour in this city does not please us,' he said. 'You have brought the Torah into disrepute. You have paraded it as a fish in the market-place. You consort with beggars. You are seen lurking in dark quarters.' In all innocence, he was Christ's biographer. 'You preach redemption through sin,' he concluded.

'But all that is in the Kabala,' Sabbatai said.

'Be that as it may,' the Chairman said. 'But the people are not ready for your Kabalistic exercises. We want you to leave this city.'

Sabbatai was expecting their banishment. It came almost as a relief. The Messianic role was an itinerant one, punctuated by exile and chastisement. Their judgment was right and proper. Not so right, and certainly not so proper, was the rider to their sentence.

'We have decided to teach you a lesson,' the Rabbi went on. 'Once and for all. You will be whipped. Your former master will teach you that lesson, and you may carry your scars back to Smyrna.'

'Smyrna?' Sabbatai asked.

'The ban is lifted,' Rabbi Eskapa said. 'Smyrna is your home. You will rest there and recover from your delusions. Your father and brothers will look after you. Your mother, God rest her soul, you sent to an early grave.'

Sabbatai's arm slipped automatically behind his back, cradling that infantile crater. And he held it there through-out the scourge, as Rabbi Eskapa stood trembling before him, striking him with the whip. It landed first on his thigh, then paused to allow the sting to burgeon. Then on the other thigh as the spasm echoed around the chamber. Sabbatai kept his hand on his back all the while, drumming with his fingers the score of his martyrdom. At twenty lashes, Rabbi Eskapa retired, exhausted. The sweat rose from his cheeks, crinkling his side-locks. His eyes watered with orgasm. Sabbatai looked at him with contempt. One day, he decided, he would kill Eskapa. It was no Messiah-like thought, but occasionally it was politic to be human.

Sabbatai limped his way back to the hostelry, where Saul and David dressed his wounds. Aunt Sarah too was allowed to care for him, and for a week he lay in his bed, in fever and pain, but in a state of exaltation. He sent a request for Yakini to visit him, but word came back that Yakini was in seclusion, hard at work at copying a Hebrew manuscript, that had been ordered by a Christian brotherhood in Frankfurt. In a week he would emerge and would welcome Sabbatai to his quarters.

It was a happy and undisturbed week for all his little family. Sabbatai was off the streets and all of them were glad to be going home. David most of all, for the continuous presence of Saul was beginning to unnerve him. He looked forward to spending his days and nights alone, without preaching, worshipping or jealousy. Not that his Messianic dream was in any way blurred, but that it was a vision more easily imagined in occasional solitude. He would never leave Sabbatai's wounded side but he needed a temporary distance from Sabbatai's fever and love for Saul.

Aunt Sarah too was anxious to see Smyrna again. She would go straight to her sister's grave, and only then would she find her death believable. On that same visit she would walk to where her mother lay, but on that burial ground, not a thousand headstones could convince her of her orphanhood. She would have to live in that place where they had lived together for so long. She would have to live there surrounded by her mother's absence, in the resounding echoes of her mother's anger and remorse, and finally and hopefully, in the whispers of her own forgiveness.

'I am not looking forward to our return. I will miss Clara who loved me, I think, on Sabbatai's behalf. Mordecai will be uneasy with me. No more than I am with myself. For I am weary of this life of mine, this stuttered repentance, which my passion overrides at every turn. I would be rid of my past, once and for all, for I can never come to terms with it. I would be rid of the Jew in me, that label that landed me in arrested boyhood. For years I have been running, but it is only back to that Polish field. There I was rooted, with their cries in my ears. Time froze me on that spot in all my fourteen years. Without future. With memories that I dare not recall, with hopes that I dare not hope for. I dream sometimes that I could invent myself a new past, and pretend that I have grown, in the simple course of nature, into a man. I dream that I leave that Polish field once and for all, without faith, without belief, without memory, and above all without history, thus anchored to no guilt-riddled past. But it is a dream. So I shall follow Sabbatai, that blotter of my guilt. I shall serve him and love him. But in the end, I know I shall betray him. Even as I betrayed my own father.'

In that week, while Sabbatai lay in bed recovering from his wounds, David and Sarah sat with him, joyfully anticipating their return. Saul kept himself apart, unable to share their loving excitement, but at night he crept into Sabbatai's bed and gave him a different kind of loving in that only area where his stunted manhood was immaterial.

At the end of the week, Sabbatai was sufficiently recovered to make preparations for their departure. He went first to the ghetto where they were overjoyed to see him, not just his person, but that person whole and healthy. For rumour had spread amongst them that Sabbatai had been whipped near to death and was crawling his way back to Smyrna. Their welcome was loud and idolatrous. He did not preach to them. He simply walked among them and said his farewells. But he promised to return. The time had come, he said, for redemption. The gates of the Holy City had been opened and soon they would return. They crowded about him, clinging to his coat. He looked amongst them, seeking that familiar face. But Sarah did not live in the ghetto. She lived in whatever street in whatever quarter provided a meal or a vision. He would seek her out before he left and invisibly say his farewells.

He left the ghetto and made his way to Yakini's quarters on the far side of the city. He announced himself outside his door. 'It's Sabbatai Zvi,' he shouted. 'I have come to say goodbye.' He heard a rustling inside and a scurrying of footsteps, as if something inside that room had to be quickly hidden. At last Yakini opened the door. On his face was a look of delighted conspiracy. He had news to impart.

'Come in,' he said, 'and welcome. I have something to show you. A discovery. It is for you and you alone. Are your wounds healed?' First things first. 'I heard about the whipping. They are frightened men. They don't understand you. So they fear you. You will be whipped again. But you will forgive. It is in your nature.'

'Tell me about your discovery,' Sabbatai said.

'I cannot tell you all,' Yakini said, 'for part of it is secret. It would betray the trust of another scholar.'

'What does the secret part refer to?' Sabbatai asked.

'That I cannot divulge,' Yakini said.

The air already smelt of perjury. Unmistakable. But Sabbatai feigned to ignore it. His instinct told him that what Yakini would reveal would be to his own Messianic advantage and that to question it at this stage would be to render it prematurely null and void. Yakini was relieved at his acceptance. Without a glance between them, for they avoided each other's eyes, and certainly without a single

165

word, an easy and confidential collusion was established between them so that everything that would follow would be, on all levels, acceptable.

'Sit down,' Yakini said, 'and listen to what I have to say. And it must go no further than these stone walls. Not at this time. Later, perhaps, when men are less blind, and their ears unstopped.' He took a seat and sat at Sabbatai's side, the better not to look him in the eye. Sabbatai was happy with such an arrangement. He, too, preferred to look at the graining on the oak table in front of him. Yakini's voice sank to a whisper.

'Some years ago,' he said, 'I was working in Gaza at a Rabbinical seminary. I was its copyist and calligrapher. One night a scholar came to my room. I had never met him before, but he was known to me as a Kabalist of some repute. At that time he was in his declining years and his strength was failing. He entrusted me with a manuscript for safe-keeping after his death and he told me how it came into his hands. Later on, I verified all his sources and found that its discovery was authentic enough. But of the manuscript itself there was no need for research, for it was clear to me that it was wholly genuine. In my profession,' Yakini confided, 'I encounter the sham often enough. But an expert is rarely fooled. The manuscript that that old scholar gave into my keeping was a miracle of discovery, and the greatest treasure a man could possess. I thanked that scholar and reassured him of my trust. I never saw him again, but I heard that he died shortly afterwards and that he is buried in Jerusalem.'

Such provenance as Yakini allowed himself to provide sounded authentic enough to Sabbatai's ear, and he dared to look Yakini in the eye. The latter did not flinch. They were partners. Then Yakini went to the far end of the room. The distance was narrow, for his room was almost a cell. On the floor stood an old oak chest, and this he unlocked, drawing the bolt slowly and softly out of its hinge. He opened the chest with both hands and leaned the lid against the wall. Then Sabbatai saw him bend, and with his hands he gently foraged its contents. Then slowly he withdrew a rolled parchment. He brought it to the table and held it there for a while. Then he looked directly at Sabbatai, and juggling their man-made truth between them, he said, 'This document concerns you. Of that I have no doubt. Which is why I give it into you hands.' Slowly he began to unroll it, spreading its age and authenticity across the table. Without reading the matter of it, Sabbatai observed the creases in the parchment, and the faded lettering, bleached with age.

'Read it,' Yakini said, and once again, 'It is for your eyes.'

The document was written in Aramaic, and he read the title aloud. *'The great wisdom of Solomon,'* he read. It could hardly have had a finer reference.

'Go on,' Yakini urged.

Sabbatai stood up. He felt the reading of such an ancient scroll called for some form of ceremony. He translated it slowly. *'I, Abraham Ascher,'* he read, *'was shut up for forty years in a cave in sore distress because the great monster that dwelleth in the river of Egypt still sat upon the throne. And I tried to solve the mystery why the age of miracles would not come, and lo, I heard the voice of my God saying, "In the year 5386, there shall be born to Mordecai Zvi, a son, and he shall call his name Sabbatai. And he shall overthrow the great dragon and kill the serpent. He shall be the Lord's anointed and shall sit upon My throne. His kingdom shall last for ever, and he and no other shall be the Saviour of my people, Israel."'*

He listened to the echo of his voice and it was thunderous although he could have sworn to have read the parchment in a whisper. He was trembling. He read it again to himself. It had faint overtones of a paraphrase of Isaiah, but that in no way touched on its authenticity. He believed every word of it. His feverish need for affirmation was overwhelming.

'Take it,' Yakini said. 'It's yours.'

Sabbatai touched it again and the parchment was fire in his fingers. It was not politic, he thought, to carry one's own credentials about one's person.

'You keep it,' Sabbatai said, 'and you will spread the word. My own person is proof of what I am.'

Yakini carefully re-rolled the parchment and returned it to the chest. The document was hot, and no amount of cold storage would cool it. But he was satisfied. Sabbatai had accepted his calling and had ordered him to let it be known.

They prayed for a while together, then said their farewells.

'We will meet in Jerusalem,' Yakini said. 'There you will be crowned.'

Sabbatai floated out of Yakini's dwelling. With the parchment in Yakini's deft hands, his future was secured. He would leave for Smyrna in the morning.

But first he had to say his final farewell. He walked in the direction of the market-place. He wanted to recapture their first meeting, to try to understand the nature of his attraction to Sarah. He knew that nature well, but feared to acknowledge it. For that nature dwelt in the gutter, an area which he had so often disguised as redemption through sin. The Kabala prescribed it. Sarah was simply its embodiment, and he knew that, even without his participation, she would inevitably become part of his life. He sat at the café where he had first fed her. A man sat at the table opposite him. He was relishing a large moussaka. Between mouthfuls, he savoured his mint tea. Sabbatai imagined that the smell of Sarah was still upon him, and that he was rounding off his pleasure with a hearty meal. And suddenly Sabbatai was jealous. It was a feeling that never before had assailed him and he was horrified at its power. For he wanted to go over to the man and choke him on his relish. He knew it was wholly irrational. It was possible that the man had never been near Sarah or any of her kind. But still the possibility existed that another's hand could touch her. He rose quickly from the table and made his way to the alley. She was not

168

on her corner and his stomach heaved. He hid himself out of view and he waited. He tried not to think of where she was and what she was doing, but he knew both, with total certainty. He tried to think of Saul by way of recompense, but that thought was elusive. So he clung to the image of the parchment, the only certainty of his future. He waited for a long while, his jealousy simmering. At last she returned to her corner, stuffing her earnings into her bodice as she walked. He watched her as she waited there, and prayed that no man would approach her, so that he could dwell awhile on her beauty. He stayed there for a long time, while she stood unencumbered by trade, her loveliness filling his eye. When at last a man approached her, Sabbatai for some reason was relieved. He watched her lead him to the end of the alley, then they both disappeared. For a while he stared at the emptiness she had left behind her, and the earth seemed to smoke where she had stood.

9

Home sweet home

'. . . To-day we walked along the sea-shore. We are leaving for Smyrna tomorrow. Sabbatai does not construe it as banishment. We are simply moving along the shore-line, he says. His home is bounded by the sea, wherever that sea may be. He was in a playful mood and we lay for a while in the sand. "They will be waiting in the streets of Smyrna to greet me," he said. "Let us plan some celebration."

I tried to caution him. I know about prophets in their own towns. But he was intent upon his welcome, and he expected it to be tumultuous. "We shall have a parade," he said, "and I shall stop and preach on the way. We will pass through the Armenian quarter, and then the streets of the Moslem poor. The Christian streets too, for everyone is Messiah-hungry. What shall I wear, Saul?" he asked.

He was like a child preparing for a party and I could have wept for him. We found a quiet beach and we bathed in the shallows. He lay on his back as the waves lapped around him. "I am in God's cradle," he said. "He rocks me like a mother rocks; He soothes me like a father; He conspires with me like a brother. And like a lover, He gives me His caress. There are stars in the daylight sky, and fish are flying through the clouds. He lights candles on my eyelids for His way is sometimes dark. There are torches in Smyrna, Saul. They are waiting." I knew that his fever was high, and I let it ride its hallucinated course. He will not sleep tonight, impatient for his homecoming.

173

I pray for him. I pray with all my heart that Smyrna will welcome him.

. . . for how can we blind ourselves to these empty streets? To all those people about their business, indifferent to our return. Who pass us by as if we are strangers?

"They are gathered outside my house," Sabbatai said. "Thousands of them. Let us go quickly."

I held him close. His fever drenched me. "They have forgotten us, Sabbatai," I said.

He pushed me away from him. Not with hate, but with fear and contempt. "I bought you as a brother," he said.'

Despite their earlier demands for Sabbatai's return, the people of Smyrna had forgotten him. Messiahs have to be on the spot, and all the time. A true Messiah is flesh and blood; the other kind exists only in man's imagination. Sabbatai had been away too long. Besides, all across Europe there was a sudden epidemic of Messiahs. They appeared amongst Christians in Germany, France and Poland. Even England contributed a claimant, a Quaker by the name of Jacob Naylor. Everyone was getting in on the act. In the Ottoman Empire itself, competition too close to home, in the small town of Ossa, a man calling himself Jesus Eli Messiah gave three positive nominal proofs of his Messianic qualifications.

But Sabbatai had his parchment. None of the others had such undeniable evidence. Yet it gave him little comfort, for his spirit was in its night-cycle. His desolation cast the whole house into mourning. Mordecai had welcomed his son's return; his arrival had lifted his heart. But he could not bear his melancholy. Every Sabbath he went to the synagogue and prayed for his recovery. At night, in privacy and solitude, he prayed for his son to be mad again, for at least in his madness Sabbatai found some joy. Then he asked God to forgive him for such a prayer.

A few weeks after Sabbatai's return, while he still lingered in his room, word came from Rabbi Eskapa's household that his old mentor lay on his death-bed and wished to see Sabbatai before he died. Mordecai first asked God's forgiveness, then he gave Him thanks. For surely such news, God forgive him, would bring joy to Sabbatai's heart. Aunt Sarah had told Mordecai the full story of the whipping and humiliation in Constantinople, so that even Mordecai would attend Eskapa's funeral with little sorrow. Word was conveyed to Sabbatai. At least the message got him out of his room. He had forgiven the Rabbi long since, accepting the scourge as part and parcel of his martyr's role.

He washed his body for the first time in many weeks, and the touch of water stirred longings in him for the sea. He walked through the house, wordless, and out of the door. Mordecai looked after him and dared to think that he looked a little better.

Sabbatai was shown into Rabbi Eskapa's bedroom and, on his entry, a nurse left the room. The old man lay propped up with pillows. His face was grey. Sabbatai had to fight down a distinct feeling of superiority, born out of his own upright position and health. He moved towards the bed.

'Don't speak, Rabbi,' he said, 'if it's a strain. Shall I read to you?' A Hebrew Bible lay on the bedside table, and Sabbatai reached out for it. The old man shook his head and motioned him to sit close. His voice was hoarse and Sabbatai had to lean towards him.

'There are three things I must tell you,' Rabbi Eskapa said. He was clearly conscious that he had little time left, and no doubt, in his dying mind, he had organised that time meticulously. His thinking was reduced to headings, for there was no time for ornamentation.

'First I ask for your forgiveness,' he said.

Sabbatai shook his head. 'There's no need,' he said. 'I forgave you even as you whipped me.'

Rabbi Eskapa curled his lip. Sabbatai's smug tone was distasteful and led him easily to his second heading.

'Secondly,' he said, 'I want you to know that you are not the Messiah. You are definitely not the Messiah.' His voice grew hoarse and angry. He'd clearly reserved his strength for this declaration. 'You are not, you are not, you are not,' he said. Then his head sank back on to the pillows and his breathing became heavy.

But he would not die yet. He had a third and final heading to deliver. Sabbatai touched his cold hands, and felt his own fever rising. And he revelled in it. He wondered what could follow that angry condemnation.

Rabbi Eskapa rested for a while. That which he had to say, he didn't understand himself. It had no logic. It simply expressed an instinctive need. And that need displeased him, for he knew he could not die in peace without having it satisfied. His fingers curled in nervousness.

'Sabbatai,' he said. 'I want you to bless me.'

As the words dropped from his lips, he heard the rudeness of his request. But it was politic too. In his state, he was in no position to offend either God or the Devil. He had to die with double indemnity.

Sabbatai wanted to laugh aloud, but he contained himself and stretched out his feverish hand to the old man's forehead. And silently he prayed. When it was done, Rabbi Eskapa muttered his thanks and motioned him to leave. Sabbatai nodded. He tried to think of something to say, but nothing seemed appropriate. In any case, there was a finality in his blessing. Besides, he was too full of joy, and whatever he said could not disguise it. He walked out of that room a conqueror, not because he was a survivor, but because he had been vindicated.

The light was fading in the sky, his favourite time. He made his way to the sea-shore, and felt that he was going home. Once there, he made himself naked, and plucked a handful of sharp sand-grass from the dunes, and scourged himself of all his doubts and uncertainties. There and then he decided to make preparations for his journey to Jerusalem. The time was ripe. In the Holy City, they would be waiting for him. He dived into the sea and swam to his rock. It had been so long since the sea-water had embraced him, that regenerative caress, which made him, in his own manic terms, whole. Even through the cold fondling, he felt his fever and revelled in it. He reached the rock, and clasped it, taking a deep breath. Then he dived into his silence. He opened his eyes and viewed the tiny fish that swam about him, and he marvelled at how, in their swift passage and turning, they managed to avoid his skin. He turned his body this way and that, yet still they skirted him. He wondered if they knew that he was the Messiah. With this thought he came up for air and looked at the stars that were gathering in the sky. He regarded them in his nakedness as his own personal backdrop, and the depths of the sea, his stage. He dived once more and listened to the silence which he broke with his own inward prayer, then he surfaced and returned to the sands. He dressed quickly and made his way home in a state of exaltation.

Mordecai did not doubt his fevered look, but he would not let it alarm him, for the joy on his son's face was sublime. Aunt Sarah too was infected by his happiness, and she busily prepared the evening meal. For the first time in many weeks the family would assemble at the table. She prepared a feast. Mordecai, Joseph, Elijah and Saul took their places with a shared sigh of relief. Sabbatai was the last to join them. Mordecai deferred to his eldest son the blessings on the bread and the wine, and when all was done, the sumptuous meal was served.

'He will die soon,' Sabbatai announced suddenly. 'Rabbi Eskapa will die.' Then he allowed a pause, long enough to omit the old man's first two headings. 'He asked me to bless him,' Sabbatai said.

They didn't know whether or not to believe him.

'Why should he ask *me* to bless him?' Sabbatai asked, then fell silent, leaving them to deal with the answers.

'He's lived to a good age,' Mordecai said, staying on neutral ground. 'I've known him for many years. He married your mother, God rest her, and me.'

'We shall all go to his funeral,' Sabbatai said, and he raised his glass as if in premature toast to his burial.

The others at the table did likewise, fearful of giving offence, though they thought it rather tasteless to bury the man while he still lingered. 'We shall go as a family,' Sabbatai went on, planning it like a festival, and Mordecai's stomach heaved at the thought of what production his son had in his sick mind.

They ate with frenzy, each one of them scratching in his mind for some neutral banality of conversation that would see them through the meal. Sabbatai helped them. He launched into a description of Rabbi Eskapa's bedroom, and the ample proportions of the nurse who attended him. Then he regaled them with stories of their sojourn in Constantinople, stories to which Saul and Aunt Sarah had not borne witness, so he was able to indulge in all his fantasies. And those at the table indulged him too, grateful for his conviviality, and all the time Mordecai prayed that Eskapa would live for ever.

But prayers rarely get answered and the following day word came to his ears that the revered Rabbi Eskapa, leading figure in the Smyrna community for so many years, had died in his sleep.

Sabbatai made frenzied preparations for the funeral. He asked Aunt Sarah to press his clothes and especially to clean the hem of his long kaftan. It was an ominous request. He brushed his hat himself, shined his shoes, and curled his side-locks, preening himself like a groom. Mordecai hoped at least that during the funeral ceremony the radiance of his features would be subdued. Both Elijah and Mordecai would have preferred to stay at home, but Saul sensed their fears and assured them that Sabbatai would be in his care, that nothing untoward would happen.

'He is not well,' Elijah said. 'He should be put away.'

'Never,' Mordecai shouted. He heard a small truth in Elijah's words, but never, never would he countenance it. 'Sabbatai is a man of God,' he said, and meant it, for whatever anybody said about his son, there was no doubting his piety.

The whole of Smyrna had turned out for Rabbi Eskapa's funeral. The gathering delighted Sabbatai for it provided him with a captive audience. In the funeral procession, he walked ahead of his family, assuming leadership. Mordecai, who walked behind him, noticed that his step was jaunty, skipping almost. Hardly the gait for a funeral. He dreaded the ceremony. He felt he should do something, say something to Sabbatai, but he did not want to pre-suppose trouble, and thus possibly cause it. It was best to be silent, but inside himself he was screaming. Screaming for his son's pain.

Elijah was walking by his side, and he held on to his arm firmly. A reliable alliance, but an uneasy one. Mordecai would have preferred to face Sabbatai alone. It was not fair to involve Elijah in his paternal sorrow. Elijah suffered the pain of brotherhood, and that was an anguish of another kind. But both were tinged with anger, and it was the anger rather than the pain that prompted the alliance. Joseph was different. Mordecai didn't altogether understand his second son. He had somehow grown unnoticed into manhood, straddling the first- and last-born like a fence of neutrality. When Sabbatai had taken his first confident steps into the Messianic wilderness, Joseph had tagged along. He had not made any positive choice; it just seemed the natural thing to do. He believed that Sabbatai was the true Messiah, but he didn't insist on it.

Aunt Sarah brought up the rear. She had joined the women, who tended to put a distance between themselves and the men in the procession. She stayed amongst them for her own protection, for along the route she had spotted Nahum, her old and constant love. She had not seen him for many years. Even now, on sight of him, her heart was a girl's. There was no sign of Lusi amongst the women. People rumoured that they were seldom seen together.

That Lusi rarely left the house. That she was in a state of constant depression and preferred the security of her own prison walls. Nahum was towards the end of the procession, and Aunt Sarah could see the back of him from where she walked. She knew that she would never recover from her love for him, and she knew too that his love for her was equally enduring. That their future lay in meetings at funeral processions, until one would follow the other's bier.

The burial ground was not far from Rabbi Eskapa's home, but it took some while before the tail of the cortège was assembled inside. There was no room for all of them in the little prayer-house. Aunt Sarah stood outside, but she distinctly heard Sabbatai's angelic voice rising above the rest, acknowledging the ways of the Lord. When the service came to an end, those outside stood aside, leaving a path for the movement of the trolley towards the grave, and immediately behind it, as if he were chief mourner, Sabbatai walked, his fever visible to every eye. Aunt Sarah trembled for him. She knew he was about to beg for his martyrdom.

Shortly behind him came Mordecai, Joseph and Elijah. They caught Aunt Sarah's eye and she smiled encouragement. And after them, Nahum. The smile was still on her face as he caught sight of her and, taking it for himself, he returned it. Both laughed shyly, then assumed a solemn mien befitting the occasion. It was an exchange that attested to a long and close familiarity, a loving that was beyond words. Sarah was ashamed of the happiness that stole over her. Ashamed because it was a girl's delight, and in any case, in this holy place, was ill-sited. But she didn't care. In many ways, here, amongst the head-stones and the mourning, was a right and proper place in which to renew life, to envisage a future. And she dared to do it. A future with Nahum. It was no longer so impossible.

There was not room for everybody at the graveside, and Sarah stood apart with the other women. They were within earshot of the prayers but they could see nothing of the paraphernalia of burial. The prayers sunk to a murmur, and Sarah presumed that the coffin was being lowered. Then she heard the silence broken only by the sound of wood against stone. Then a voice rang out. Bell-like, unassailable. Sabbatai's. 'I shall not resurrect you,' he pealed. 'Sabbatai Zvi will not resurrect Rabbi Eskapa.'

The crowd at the graveside fell back, unbelieving, and through the gaps they made, Sarah could see Sabbatai's lean body at the graveside, the echo of his words resounding from the open depths. She saw the soft sad hand of Mordecai touch his sleeve, and how Sabbatai brushed it off impatiently. And her happiness faded.

The crowd was returning from the grave, muttering its pity and horror. She stood watching until she was alone, the other women having joined their men-folk in their retreat. She looked back at the grave. Even the chief mourners had left, as if the tomb had been contaminated, leaving others to catch its sickness. There was just a small group around the grave. Sarah saw the faithful Ardittis comforting Mordecai on either side. Sabbatai stood alone and, from the hunch in his shoulders, she knew that his fever was high. David stood beside him, imitating his stance, a loyal disciple. Elijah, Joseph and Saul stood apart from each other, each harbouring thoughts that had absolutely nothing in common. But what riveted Sarah's eye was the figure that stood in front of Mordecai, and directly in her line of vision. Nahum. It was as if, in taking that stand, in showing that allegiance, he had appointed himself a member of the family. He just stood there, with no apparent function, neither comforting nor chastising. Just simply *being* in a place where he felt he belonged. Sarah's heart leapt with gratitude and loving and she went to stand by his side.

Around the grave not a word was spoken. All of them wanted to leave yet none would make the first move. They knew the dangers of leaving Sabbatai alone, yet not one of them dared touch him to urge him to go. At last Mordecai, from a safe distance, whispered, 'Sabbatai, it's time to go home.'

He turned around with surprising obedience. 'Yes,' he said, 'you're right, Father.'

Mordecai did not shrink from the word. From long use he knew that 'Father' went with fever and fever went occasionally with joy. He would settle for that. He watched his son as he went towards Aunt Sarah. He touched her on her wrist, and on Nahum's, too.

'But you I bless,' he said. 'Each one of you. And both.'

Sarah blushed with the inference. Sabbatai's blessing had prompted Nahum to take Sarah's hand and as if it was at a marriage ceremony, Sabbatai repeated, 'Both of you, I bless. Together.' Then he turned, and, walking alone, he led the family procession out of the burial ground.

The crowd stood outside the gates with the look of a lynch-mob. Nahum let go of Sarah's hand and rushed to Sabbatai's side. He had to give his move the appearance of company rather than protection, and immediately engaged Sabbatai in conversation.

'That was kind of you, that blessing. Thank you for it.' He shielded Sabbatai as they passed through the gates, and, with a look of steel, he dared the crowd to attack. Mordecai clung to his sons' sleeves like a child in terror, and Aunt Sarah followed closely behind. But the crowd would not touch the family. Their hands went out to them in pity, and Mordecai was glad that that pity was silent, for he could not have borne others' commiseration. Even Raphael the idiot, on the edge of the crowd, for once held his tongue as Sabbatai passed him by, but an 'I-told-you-so' look was clear on his face.

Once home, Sabbatai went straight to his room, where later Saul and Joseph joined him. Nahum, who had accompanied them all the way, now sat companionably with Mordecai, Elijah and Sarah. It was clearly time for a family debate but, when Nahum rose to leave, Mordecai detained him.

'You have known our family since you were a child,' he said. 'In many ways you are part of it. I want you to stay.'

Sarah went into the kitchen to make coffee, partly to ease the conversation that would ensue, but also to be alone for a while while her heart simmered. For at the graveside, after Sabbatai's blessing, her heart, a dormant volcano, had erupted, and all the loving that it had stored over the years found release in a measure of hope, and it was this last that she had to examine, understand, and finally put aside. Because of Lusi there was no future for them together, and this she would accept without despair, for the loving was confirmed and its storage had not been in vain. She brought the coffee to the table.

'What are we to do?' Mordecai said. He spoke for them all, but not posing a question. It was a simple statement of their own common helplessness.

'We must just be with him,' Nahum said. 'Support him. He's not always like this.'

'He does it on purpose,' Elijah said. His voice was like a child's. 'He does it to make us ashamed.'

'I don't care what people think,' Mordecai said. 'I care about Sabbatai, and so do you, Elijah.'

'He will go away again, I think,' Aunt Sarah said.

'Perhaps he should go to a seminary,' Nahum suggested, 'where he can live, study and sometimes preach. There are others like him, Mordecai,' he said gently. 'Part of their piety is frenzy.'

Mordecai seemed to find hope in that diagnosis. He did not want a unique son. It would be a relief to know that there were others like him. 'But where would he find such a place? There are none in Smyrna.'

'But there are many in Jerusalem,' Nahum said. 'Such a place might please him.'

There was a long silence between them. They used it to sip their coffee. All except Mordecai, who stared vacantly. Then suddenly, out of the silence, he cried, 'I want my son at home.'

They put their arms around him and let him sob. But Elijah could stand it no more. The sight of his father's sorrow drove him from the table and, in sublime anger, he shot like a thunderbolt into Sabbatai's room. He found the three of them at prayer, but, heedless of their sacred pursuit, he stayed Sabbatai's rocking motion with a firm hand.

'It can't go on like this,' he shouted. 'It's all madness. What are you going to do?'

Saul and Joseph stared at him, unnerved by his anger. But Sabbatai cooled them all.

'There is nothing for me here,' he said. 'I am going to Jerusalem.' He said it with such sadness, and with such despair, that Elijah was overcome with that loving of his, which, with all his efforts, he could never stifle. He went to his brother and held him close.

'Don't leave us, Sabbatai,' he said. 'We want you at home.'

'But I have to go,' Sabbatai said. He made no attempt to free himself from Elijah's embrace. 'Here nobody will listen to me. All over the world our people are running, running from the priests with their holy water, or from the Cossacks with their swords. The time is ripe for redemption. But first we must be pure. We must be clean. We must put all sins aside.' He freed himself from Elijah's hold, then held up his arms as if in a pulpit. 'We must prepare ourselves for the Redeemer. He is here. Believe me. I have proof. But our people are not ready. I must go out and prepare them. That is my given mission. Believe me, believe me,' he pleaded.

'But you could do all that here,' Elijah said. He knew it would bring shame on his own head, and that the family would be humiliated yet again. But he would put up with all that. His brother must not go away, because it would break his father's heart.

'I can do no more here,' Sabbatai said firmly. 'In Jerusalem, they will listen to me.' He turned and went on with his praying. Saul and Joseph, who had stood silently during the exchange, joined in the prayers, turning their backs on Elijah, who could do nothing now except leave the room.

Downstairs it was silent. They were clearly waiting for whatever report he would bring.

'He says he's going to Jerusalem,' Elijah said. Then, tonelessly, 'It was his own idea.'

'Alone?' Aunt Sarah said. This time she could not go with him. She had to nourish her own single love at home.

'He didn't say,' Elijah answered. 'But I think he means to go alone. Perhaps with Saul. I don't know.'

Mordecai said nothing. There were crumbs on the table-cloth, from the cake and bread that they had eaten. He sat and scooped them carefully into his hand. He concentrated on the task with studied diligence. He was intent on not leaving a single crumb behind. Over and over again he scooped the cloth, and when it was baldly clean, he clenched his crumb-filled fist.

'I'm hungry,' he almost shouted. 'You'll stay for supper, Nahum. I insist.'

It was a relief to them all. It gave Sarah escape to the kitchen, but above all, it freed them for a while from the haunting subject that rocked its prayers above them.

'Come,' Nahum said, 'let us take a turn in the garden before supper.' He wanted to get Mordecai out of the room, away from the insistent echoes of Sabbatai's manic piety. He took his arm and led him outside. 'The air will do us both good,' he said.

Elijah joined Sarah in the kitchen. She was glad of the company. She no longer needed to be alone, because she had absorbed and accepted what lay in her store.

'Will you go with him this time?' Elijah asked.

'No,' Aunt Sarah said. 'I have a life here in Smyrna. But I'm not like you, Elijah. Or your father. I believe in Sabbatai. I really do. As your mother believed in him. That's why I'm not sad. No harm will come to him. I know it.'

185

Elijah envied her her certainty. But the price she paid for it was for him too high, and not only high, but impossible. He would have to learn to live with his anguish. Through the window he could see the two figures in the garden silhouetted in the waning light. His father's hands were clasped behind his back, his body stooped, as he strolled in the manner of meditation. Nahum at his side was no taller, but his body was erect. His one arm was circled round Mordecai's shoulder, not touching it, but on watch there, as it were, for possible protection. They did not appear to be talking to each other but there was about them an air of undeniable togetherness. Sarah joined Elijah at the window.

'Nahum will be good for him,' she said. 'But you, Elijah,' she touched his arm, 'you carry everyone's pain. It's because you're the youngest.'

'It's my nature,' he said, and smiled for the first time that day. Aunt Sarah had so simply defined his caring, had given it a measure of logic, so that suddenly it became less burdensome. He looked at his father again and saw how his back had straightened, and how his arms now swung loosely at his side. Sarah called them into supper, and during the meal there was even laughter at the table, and the rocking upstairs went unheard.

10

In the footsteps of Hosea

Sabbatai was still reeling from his lack of acknowledgment in Smyrna. He could not risk an immediate plunge into the depths of Jerusalem. So he went paddling. First to Rhodes, where he stayed only a few months, and then on to Cairo. His sole companion was Saul.

'. . . we have in Cairo for almost half a year, and in all that time Sabbatai has been without fever. Our love is pure and utterly certain. It has no need of affirmation. We do not touch each other, yet our passion abides. We do not fast unless it is a holy day, and we do not scourge ourselves. We simply pray together and are at peace. Yet all the city knows that Sabbatai is here, and I hear his name whispered in the streets. I fear that he will listen to the whisperings and his fevers will come again. Especially I fear one of the whisperers, though I respect him, too, for he is a learned man, powerful and very rich. His name is Raphael Joseph and he is the Keeper of the Egyptian Treasury. We live in his house in the centre of the city. It is large and full of luxury. Yet Raphael himself is a simple-living man. He observes each and every ritual and under his rich robes it is said that he wears a sack-cloth next to his skin. He is completely under Sabbatai's spell. He will do anything for him. We leave this city tomorrow, and I am not sorry for it.'

Sabbatai gave a farewell sermon at the great Cairo synagogue. He took as his text the simple song of praise, the Ninety-sixth Psalm. In all its verses it contained not one syllable of the Good Shepherd, not one soupçon of Saviour, and the congregation accepted it as a show of sublime modesty. Moreover, the psalm lent itself to singing, and often during its telling he would veer into song, and his voice rose like a soaring eagle, heedless of prey, intent only on the beauty and the glory of the skies. With his voice Sabbatai led them into the neighbourhood of God, and they trembled. Sabbatai himself was transported in the acute joy of prayer, a clean joy without ecstasy and void of demonic threat. At such times he knew pure happiness, and a life's dedication to God, in obscure and humble dwelling, was more than he craved. During his song his eye fell on a member of the congregation whose face was familiar. She was staring at him out of her witch-eyed beauty, her bodice, even in that holy place, ajar for payment. She was waiting patiently for him to claim her, and she knew from the stir of expectation around her, that her time would soon come. But Sabbatai's eye barely lingered on her beauty. Somewhere and at some time he had seen her before and that was the sole blurred impression Sarah made on him. After the service, he made a general farewell. Raphael Joseph responded on behalf of the community. They regretted his departure and begged him to return. He himself would especially miss Sabbatai and the enrichment of their exchange.

In all his wanderings, Cairo was the only city which Sabbatai left of his own free will and the only city which rued his leave-taking.

That evening, as soon as the first star announced the end of the Sabbath, Sabbatai ushered it out with prayer and, together with Saul, set out on his journey to the Holy City. They stopped at Gaza. The prospect of setting foot in Jerusalem was an awesome one and Sabbatai felt the need to renew his spirit to prepare himself for that holy

190

ground. In Gaza they had heard of his coming, and they turned out to welcome him. Especially one amongst them. Nathan Ashkenazi, or, as he was known, Nathan of Gaza.

Nathan was a young man, not yet thirty, and still younger than Sabbatai. He already had a sound reputation as a prophet, with extraordinary powers of clairvoyance. He knew that Sabbatai would stop for a while in Gaza, even before Sabbatai had decided on it himself, and it was Nathan who led the Jews of Gaza into the streets to welcome him. Nathan himself had no Messianic cravings. His yearning was confined to the role of herald. A yearning as obsessive as Sabbatai's when in fever. Nathan's father travelled far afield to collect alms for the poor of Jerusalem and, in his letters to his son, he had often made mention of Sabbatai Zvi. Once he had shared the secret of that authentic scroll which Yakini had shown him in Constantinople. All the omens for the advent of the Messiah were set fair.

As Sabbatai and Saul entered the town of Gaza, Nathan went forward to meet them, and the crowd behind him cheered. Saul was apprehensive, but there was mercifully no sign of Sabbatai's fever. Nathan was possessed by his mission. His clairvoyance signalled that the Messiah was at hand. He had prepared a feast of welcome, and to it he had invited all the scholars and dignitaries of the city. He placed Sabbatai at the head of the table on a cushioned throne and he placed himself at his right side. Then, when the meal was done, he raised his glass in a toast to his guest. 'Blessed is he that cometh in the name of the Lord,' he said. 'Bless our king, Sabbatai Zvi.'

There was silence around the table. Saul, fearful of Sabbatai's response, placed a hand on his arm, and held it there while Sabbatai rose from his seat.

His voice was weary. 'It is not so,' he said, and slowly he left the table, his declaration faltering behind him. He went into the streets and walked awhile. Saul kept silent at his side.

191

'I was at peace,' Sabbatai said at last, 'and now they disturb my soul. Let us go soon to Jerusalem.'

'We shall leave tomorrow,' Saul said.

Later that night they went to Nathan's house. They found him cheerful and not in the least put out by Sabbatai's denial. Sabbatai could not help but warm towards him. His faith was so simple, so feverless.

'It's not the time, Nathan,' Sabbatai said.

'Perhaps not now,' Nathan said. 'But it will come. It has been prophesied. The people believe it.'

It seemed to Sabbatai that the longer he denied others' proclamations, the firmer their belief in his calling. But he shuddered at the thought of declaring himself. Sometimes he simply did not believe it. The role was a figment of others' imagination, a widespread wishful thinking. Besides, it terrified him. The burdensome onus of such a title and the martyrdom it would inevitably entail. He recalled those times when he had longed for it, when he had seriously believed himself to be what they so confidently assumed that he was. He recalled that, at those times, his spirit had not been as unruffled and as joyful as it was now.

Sabbatai reached out towards Nathan. 'Keep your faith,' he said, 'but don't centre it about me, and we shall not cease to be friends.'

Nathan wished that they spend their last evening at his home. They prayed and drank wine together, and at first light, Nathan's wife furnished them with rich provisions for the journey to Jerusalem.

On leaving Gaza, Sabbatai's spirits lifted, and Saul suggested they rode towards the sea-shore before turning inland to Jerusalem. As they neared the shore-line, their horses' nostrils flared with the scent of the sea. They broke into a gallop which they steadily maintained until they reached the sands.

The sun was rising towards early morning as they bared themselves on the beach, as Saul touched Sabbatai's body and knew that its heat was not fever. Here on this stretch of water, there was no Sabbatai's rock but he knew that the magic silence could be found even in the shallows. They cooled themselves for a while in the waves that lapped the shore. Then Sabbatai swam out into the deep and dived into that magic that had held him spellbound since childhood. He wanted to test himself. He wanted to discover whether his Redeemer-cravings had dogged him even to this place, to this distant sea that embraced the Holy City. He dived deep, holding his breath with ease. The silence he heard was as silent as he had heard before, under the rock at Smyrna. But here it had no divine echoes and when he rose to the surface, he felt that his demons had been exorcised once and for all. He was laughing as he swam to the shore, and his heart was full of unencumbered love for Saul. For his family, too, especially his father, realising how much he missed him.

They dressed in silence, then mounted their horses. Sabbatai took the lead and slowly, and with quiet joy, he sang his psalmed way to the Holy City.

Saul was nervous of their arrival. He fully expected Sabbatai to collapse at the sight of such sanctified ground. If God lived anywhere on earth, that place was in Jerusalem. It was a thought that would give anyone the shivers.

But Sabbatai's singing never faltered and his prayers were fervent but measured. On the fourth day they approached the outskirts of the city, and at the Western Wall they dismounted. Saul watched Sabbatai's face closely. He was looking for sweat on the forehead, a slight swelling of the temple vein, a blue tinge on his cheeks, all signs of the onset of fever. But all was clear.

He followed Sabbatai as he made his way to the Wailing Wall. And there they both prayed, their bodies rocking to the rhythm of other supplicants and their voices pealing to heaven.

After a while, Sabbatai rested his forehead against the cool stone, and thanked God for his wholeness.

In 1662, the year of Sabbatai's arrival in Jerusalem, the city was inhabited by 300 Jewish families. It was a poor community, eking a bare living off the land and in various artisan trades. The greater part of the male population was devoted to the pursuit of learning, the study of the Torah, the Talmud and the Kabala. For the year that Sabbatai spent in the city, he was undisturbed by manic illusion. During that period he often wrote letters to his family in Smyrna and all were addressed to Mordecai. They began with 'My dear Papa', and when Mordecai read that address, he breathed more easily, for he knew that Sabbatai still felt himself a son. He shared the frequent letters with the family and all marvelled and rejoiced at Sabbatai's miraculous cure.

'It's Jerusalem,' Aunt Sarah concluded. 'He has found his peace in the Holy City.'

And indeed it was peace that Sabbatai had found. The peace of undisturbed and unencumbered prayer. He wandered often and alone in the hills and caves of the Judean desert. He visited shrines and prayed at the graves of patriarchs. Occasionally Saul was by his side, but only as an echo of Sabbatai's supplications. For in the main, Sabbatai lived the life of a recluse with the immense presence of God for company. And so it would have continued. Until the end of his life perhaps, for, at the time, Sabbatai wished no other way. But then he was called. Ordered, in fact, to go on a mission. And he sensed the beginning of fever.

The poverty of the Jewish community was rendered more acute by the extortionate demands of the Ottoman government in the manner of taxation. Money was desperately needed. Now Sabbatai was deeply respected as a scholar and his aesthetic way of life impressed all who knew him. It was known too that he had influential contacts in Cairo, where Raphael Joseph, the Keeper of the Privy

Purse, was known to be a close friend. It was imperative to raise funds to stave off even greater poverty in the Holy City. They asked him to go begging to Cairo. It was a prestigious mission and for this very reason Sabbatai was reluctant to agree. Limelight did not please him unless he was in fever, and he feared, from experience, that one would bring about the other. Saul, ever on the alert, advised Sabbatai to refuse, but already the fever was soaring, and with it, the desperate hope for acknowledgment. And in a mixture of fear and ambition, Sabbatai accepted. He would go first to Hebron, he said, to visit and pray at the graves of Machpelah, to fortify himself.

He went alone, and on arrival, was already in a trance. On his way to the caves, the crowds gathered and followed him. On the route he sang psalms, and those who heard him swore to have heard the voice of angels. Those who stood near him were later to witness that to look at his face was like looking into a fire. For three days he stayed at the caves, fasting, praying and singing. Then he returned to Jerusalem. Once there, he refused to see Saul and made preparations for his journey. He decided he would write no more letters home.

'. . . He has gone, and without farewell. I fear no good will come of it. Who will hold his fevers in Cairo? I am in limbo here without him. Or indeed anywhere. My father lodges in my skull, nagging my spirit to atonement. Now is the time perhaps for the second treachery. But I love him. Enough to wait. To wait for the fevers to burn out of him. And for his calm, when he will return. I dawdle in the streets of Jerusalem. It is easy to make a living here. I lurk in the dark alleys with strangers and I move to the rhythm of Sabbatai's name . . . I heard today that four thousand lion's thalers from Cairo have found their way into Jerusalem's coffers. Sabbatai is the toast of the city. But news too I heard that Sabbatai will not return. He means to pursue his studies in Cairo . . . I scream his name in the alleys at night. I weep

his name as the dawn breaks. I must go to him. I cannot live without him . . .'

But it was not only the pursuit of scholarship that detained Sabbatai in Cairo. There was another reason, and, for Saul, a far more competitive one.

Once again in his fever, Sabbatai had taken to his nocturnal wanderings. His nose sniffed out the alleys of Cairo with the natural instinct of a hunter. And sniffed out the corner, too, where she stood. Night after night he returned to the same spot and, unseen, he watched her.

One night he sat at Raphael Joseph's table. They were alone together, sharing a rare meal. It was lavish and the wine flowed. Raphael was in good humour, as he always was with Sabbatai for company and, in their intimacy and slight inebriation, he dared to broach the subject of marriage.

'There is a woman in Cairo,' he began.

'There are thousands of women in Cairo,' Sabbatai laughed, sensing and fearing the direction of Raphael's exchange.

'This one is very special,' he said.

Sabbatai was silent. He refused to encourage further clarification. But Raphael persisted. 'She has been here for over a year. She arrived shortly before your first visit. My brother, who does much charitable work amongst the poor, found her sleeping with the beggars by the river. But she is not like the others, my brother says. She refuses charity, and she has a pride and beauty that is extraordinary. My brother was drawn to discover her story. She is vague about her background. It seemed that she was orphaned in the Polish massacres and brought up in a convent. She ran away when still a child and wandered all over Europe. She has visions, she says. She hears voices.'

Sabbatai had feigned a lack of interest but this last piece of information stirred his curiosity.

'What kind of visions?' he asked. 'What do the voices say?'

'They tell her she is destined to be the bride of the Messiah. So she seeks him and waits for him to call her.' Raphael watched Sabbatai's face very carefully for his reaction.

'What has it to do with me?' he asked. He felt the sweat on his brow, and he knew that Raphael could hardly mistake that symptom.

'Would you like to meet her?' Raphael asked.

'Where is she?'

'I know where she can be found. But first let me read to you a little.' He took down a Bible and opened it at the first chapter of Hosea. Then he read aloud, but leaning forward with a certain intimacy, as if the message he was about to deliver was for Sabbatai's ear alone.

'And the Lord said to Hosea,' he read, 'Go, take unto thee a wife of whoredoms, and children of whoredoms, for the land hath committed great whoredom departing from the Lord.'

Then Sabbatai knew who the woman was and that, in his heart, he had already called her.

Raphael rose from his seat. 'Come,' he said. 'It is dark. I shall take you to her.'

He led the way through the streets. Sabbatai followed, though he knew the way to her corner blindfold.

'Her name is Sarah,' Raphael called over his shoulder, but Sabbatai could have told him that too. Raphael was nervous of the narrow streets. He clearly was not at home in that quarter, and he motioned Sabbatai to walk at his side. They were approaching Sarah's hunting-ground, and Raphael chose Sabbatai's own spot for their invisible stand.

'I am ashamed here,' Raphael said. 'I am ashamed for my people.'

Sabbatai put his hand on his arm. 'Where is she?' he said, knowing full well, and noticing her empty corner.

'She will come soon,' Raphael said.

'Have you been here before?' Sabbatai asked.

'Once, with my brother. But I didn't talk to her. Neither must you. Just look at her. You will see that what he says is true. Here she comes.'

Sarah came out of a side-alley, stuffing the coins into her bodice.

'I weep for her,' Raphael said.

And so did Sabbatai, but his tears were of ecstacy. She had grown in beauty. Her eyes glistened with patience. 'I will not let her stand there,' Sabbatai said. 'I must go to her.'

'No. I will bring her to you. Tomorrow my brother will fetch her.'

He turned to go, but Sabbatai was loth to leave. Usually he would cling to his stand, and, with some vicarious pleasure, he would count and judge the measure of her clients. And as she sank lower in her degradation, so much more would he rejoice. Now she would bring that filth into his own house, and he would witness its supreme struggle for redemption.

Raphael tugged at his sleeve. 'Let us go,' he said.

That night Sabbatai could not sleep. He rose and dressed and went quietly from the house. He wanted to go back to where Sarah stood, but he feared he would be tempted to approach her. So he made his way to the river. He needed the sight of water. He needed to be soothed by its stillness. There was no one about on the river bank, and no signs of any shipping. He stared into the dark waters lit fitfully by a crescent moon. Without waves, sand or horizon, it still held for him that luring magic, its silence seducing him into long and fervent prayer, asking God for guidance, and feeling ashamed a little, for he had already decided on what he must do.

It was a week later that Raphael engineered their formal meeting. He chose one of the more intimate rooms in his large establishment and bade the servants prepare sweetmeats and wines. The room was candle-lit, throwing shadows on the damask walls and gold-embossed ceiling. Raphael's brother had been delighted to escort Sarah, who had been told of Sabbatai's bidding.

Raphael and Sabbatai sat waiting. Both were fasting, so no food or wine could help pass the time. Sabbatai fidgeted. He was excited at the prospect of meeting Sarah, of talking to her for the first time as a man. He vowed to himself never to divulge to her that once, long ago in Constantinople, he had fed her in the guise of a hobble-skirt. But he fidgeted too with indecision. He knew that, having bade this woman to come to him, he had accepted the Messiah role. The next step was to declare it himself, and not only to a few disciples, but to the people at large. With all his visions, with all his dreams, was he really the Chosen One? Or was he a fraud? He trembled at this last possibility and the question was undeniably connected with his fever, and that fever was now at this moment pulsating in his veins as he waited for the woman who would confirm his calling.

They heard noises at the outer door, and both men stood. Then a servant announced Isaac, Raphael's brother, but with no mention of the woman he escorted. And it seemed at first he had come alone, for he entered the room and stood at the portal for a while without gesture towards his brother. He simply stood still, orchestrating a silence as a fitting background for the entry of their guest.

Then she entered in the robes befitting the calling which she claimed. For she was dressed as a queen. Even to the extent of a small modest crown that balanced with an air of impudence on her black mane of hair. For a while they stared at each other, then Sabbatai called, 'Come,' and she came towards him, stopping a few feet away, then curtseying low. He gave her his hand and raised her, then studied her face for a while. She lowered her eyes, but that was affectation too, as she quenched the arrogance that was her natural mien. She would not look at him, so he was at liberty to examine her. The silks that fell about her body, the unaccustomed coverings around her neck,

199

and the pearls that fell over her chaste bodice in no way managed to disguise the harlot beneath, and that excited him even more, for the camouflage was an invitation to the thing itself. He asked her to sit and to tell him her name.

'My name is Sarah,' she said, 'and it is prophesied that I shall be your bride.'

'By whom is it prophesied?'

'By my voices and my visions.' For a moment she took her eyes off the floor but only to glance sideways at Isaac as if for his approval. He nodded. He had rehearsed her meticulously.

'Tell us your story,' Isaac said.

So Sarah looked at the floor again and began her recital. She told them about the Cossacks and her orphanhood. She hurried over her convent years, as if they might offend her audience, and she dwelt for a while on Amsterdam where she lived with her brother. It was there, she said, that she heard the first voices. They bade her go to Leghorn and seek the Messiah. From Leghorn they sent her to Frankfurt but again there was no sign of him. She began to think that the voices were teasing her and she decided to give them one last chance. When she heard the voices again, they were telling her to go to Constantinople. She felt him there, she said, though she did not see him. She began once again to believe in her voices, and when they ordered her at last to go to Cairo, she knew that she would find him. She paused a little, then, 'My voices were right,' she said. She raised her eyes and looked at Sabbatai, and a hint of the old arrogance returned. She was totally undeniable.

'It will be done,' Sabbatai said, hearing his words as if someone else had spoken them, and he wondered what he should do with them.

'I shall make all the arrangements,' Raphael said. 'This marriage will be a blessing on my house.' He rang a bell on the table beside him. A servant appeared with the wine and sweetmeats. Sarah was served and so was Isaac, but Raphael and Sabbatai refrained.

Sabbatai watched Sarah as she ate. Her table-manners, together with her misguided love for the saviour, were the only remnants of her convent days. She ate as shyly as a schoolgirl in adult company. As she put down her glass, she looked at Isaac for prompting. He nodded again, and she rose and took her leave on Isaac's arm.

When the room was empty of her, the two men savoured the vacancy for a while. Then Raphael said, 'It is done. It is the beginning of your ministry.'

The sweat burst from Sabbatai's brow, as the demons brushed his skin. He needed desperately to be on his own.

'I'm tired,' he said. 'I think I shall sleep.'

'Will you break your fast?' Raphael asked.

'Tomorrow,' Sabbatai said. 'At first light.' He made to leave, but was interrupted by a knock on the door. A servant entered with the message that there was a visitor for Sabbatai Zvi. Sabbatai was puzzled. It was late, and he could not imagine who would call upon him at this hour. When Saul appeared in the doorway, for a moment Sabbatai wondered who he was.

Saul, his purpose, his person, and his loving, had slipped entirely from his mind. He felt pleasure at seeing him again and wished to introduce him to Raphael. He hesitated as to the form of introduction. A friend? A brother? 'Lover' was out of the question. He settled for a 'follower'.

Saul's look questioned that label; the arrogance of it, the assumption. He didn't know himself what he was any more, but he suspected that it was a label most readily disposable.

'You will want to be alone,' Raphael said after greeting him. 'You are welcome, of course, as a guest in my house.'

They waited for Raphael to leave. Sabbatai sensed Saul's anger. He realised that he had made no effort to contact him since he had left Jerusalem, and that Saul had waited for a word that never came and had impulsively followed him to Cairo, propelled by rejection. And of course he *had* been rejected, and not only rejected, but replaced.

201

For what need had he of Saul now, when the depravity he craved would be on his own doorstep, and he himself would be absolved from participation? To be a witness was all that he wanted. Saul had been far more demanding. And as to the role Saul had played during his fevers, that too was now redundant. Now that Sabbatai had fully accepted the Messianic role, even to the extent of accepting a divinely chosen bride, he felt his fevers as his own true self. To exorcise them would be heresy. The demons inhabited him only as long as he refused his role.

As if reading his thoughts, Saul kept his distance. 'You are in fever, Sabbatai.'

'It's not fever,' Sabbatai said. 'It never was. We were always mistaken. It's the fire of God inside me. It's the branding of the Messiah.' He might as well tell Saul everything, he thought. 'It is different now for you and me,' he said. 'I have taken a bride. God has chosen her for me.'

Saul shivered. He felt suddenly faint with the agony of rejection. He wondered if he dared touch Sabbatai, and with a touch that perhaps would rekindle the old love between them. He had to try. He stumbled towards him and took him in his arms. But Sabbatai remained rigid in his embrace, and an air of disgust oozed out of him. He peeled Saul off his body, relieved at his own lack of response.

'You can still be my disciple,' he said. The word surprised him. Hitherto 'follower' had been enough. But now that label was too imprecise. It did not entail total devotion, and that was what Sabbatai would now demand from those who believed in him.

Saul stared at him with abject hatred. 'I'll follow you,' he shouted. 'I'll follow you to your rotten grave,' he said. 'And then I'll go before you and dig it myself.' He turned towards the door.

'Where will you go?' Sabbatai asked. His voice was toneless. In it was no concern, no residual affection. At most, a thin curiosity.

'To hell,' Saul said, 'where I shall prepare for your coming. Till then we shall never meet again.' He closed the door behind him quietly, without anger, in a manner that gave his parting shot a tone of warning. But Sabbatai had already looked upon Saul's visit as an interruption to his need for sleep and solitude. Only later in his life would he recall Saul's words, and their warnings would strike him with terror.

He sat for a while in Raphael's receiving room. The fire inside him blazed but caused him no discomfort. Whether the flames were from God's mouth or the Devil's didn't concern him. Both, after all, had had a hand in his redemption. Both were sponsors for his Messiah-hood. He was buoyant. He wanted to announce to the world that he had accepted God's crown. But first he must tell his family. Before retiring that night, he sat at the desk in his room, and after many months of silence, he wrote a letter to his father.

11

The proclamation

Each night before going to bed, Mordecai Zvi would say goodbye to his wardrobe, that sole relic of his childhood in Greece. The habit had started shortly after Clara had died, when he would often take long walks and look at trees. A fit enough pursuit for loneliness. Maples they were, mostly, and he had learned that some were over 600 years old. Trees were eternity. Maple was what his wardrobe was made of. So each night he said goodbye to it. To bid farewell to eternity seemed to be a fitting preparation for his own, and, at the age of sixty-five, he could expect it at any time. At night, after his prayers, he would fold himself into his bed, lifting one leg gently after the other on to the sheet. He would stroke the varicose veins of their long service, then he would cover them for their comfort. Then see to the rest of him. Slowly he would unfold his back and listen to the whispering of his bones. That settled, he would lay his head on the pillow, tucking it expertly behind his neck. His arms he would position last of all, crossing them loosely above his waist as he started to hum himself to sleep. But he would not close his eyes. Not until he had stared a while at his wardrobe and whispered his routine farewell. After all, one could never be too sure. Each night on retiring, he harboured a niggling doubt that he would wake the next morning. Whenever Mordecai woke, even if it was in the small hours, his waking came as a surprise. Surprise to find himself 'here' and not 'there', wherever 'there' was, and whatever it was made of. The waking sight of the wardrobe defined and confirmed the 'here'. So each night, just in case, he bade it farewell.

Not to the contents of it – they were unimportant – but to the container itself, that great mass of winking bird's eye maple. His eyes lingered on the whirligigs of the grain that curled in small and gnarled protest. He shivered at their randomness in the overall view but, on closer inspection, he had to acknowledge their compelling symmetry. He thought of the maples on his walks, and he understood without question that trees were serious. Perhaps that was why, approaching his closing years, the need to acknowledge his wardrobe was imperative. He would like a coffin in bird's-eye maple, he thought, a wood that would respect his mortality. But Jews didn't go in for smart coffins. A simple pine-box was all his faith entitled him to.

Mordecai closed his eyes, but he could not sleep, and he knew that night that sleep would not come easily. He pretended he didn't know what troubled him. It could be anything, he told himself. At sixty-five, simply the fear of waking into the 'there' would be enough. But something specific niggled him. He got up and eased his feet into the slippers under the bed. Clara's slippers, the backs trodden flat to adjust to his larger feet. Getting up and going to bed when one wished was the only bonus of widowhood. Even so, out of habit, he eased the indentation of the bed as he rose, and tip-toed stealthily out of the room, looking back to make sure that he had not disturbed that vacancy at his side. He stopped outside Joseph's and Elijah's doors and listened to their sleeping, then at Aunt Sarah's whose door was open, her sleeping visible to any passer-by. He padded softly into the kitchen.

Sabbatai's letter lay on the table, held in place by his reading-glasses. When the letter had come that morning, the mere fact of its arrival had been surprise enough. There had not been a letter from Sabbatai for many months. He had read it but not fully taken in its contents.

Aunt Sarah had made the only comment. 'Not a word about Saul,' she had said. He picked up the letter and looked at it, and forced himself to read it once more, word by terrible word. He could not keep the words inside himself, so he read them aloud, as if, with their release, they would trouble him no more.

'*Dear Father*,' he read. That word, that fever word, a million miles from 'papa', from a son who was sometimes whole. He read it again and louder this time, hearing the echo of its insult and wishing to be rid of it once and for all. '*I have accepted the Crown*,' Sabbatai wrote. '*For many years I have turned away from the terrible burden of kingship, but the hand of God has placed the crown upon my head. And sent me a wife for a queen.*'

Mordecai paused in his reading. Such news should have made him rejoice, but he knew his son's nature, and he knew too, that that nature was unchangeable. Sabbatai's taking of a bride was an act of cunning, and the following sentence served to confirm his opinion.

'*I have walked in the steps of Hosea*,' he read, '*and as God commanded him, I shall take to wife a harlot.*'

Mordecai trembled and read the following words quickly, sweeping them into the air like particles of filthy dust.

'*She comes from everywhere*,' he read. '*From every capital, out of every alley, from all sewers that run below the cities, and from all corners that punctuate their course. She is a thing of the most perfect beauty, and rotten to her very core. I send my greetings to you, Father, my brothers Joseph and Elijah, and to Aunt Sarah. I entreat you all to follow me, for I will lead you into Paradise. You will hear of me and know where I am. Your loving son, and every man's, Sabbatai Zvi.*'

'Zvi?' Mordecai questioned. Was there another Sabbatai? One who was whole? He had had such a son once, from time to time, in feverless days. Perhaps that son would come again, but he doubted that he would live to receive him. He picked up the letter and tore it across, once, twice and three times. He took the pieces and scrambled them into a ball. This he placed carefully on the dying embers of the fire. He sat for a while watching until it was mere ash, with the sad sense of witnessing his son's funeral pyre. Then he went upstairs again, tip-toeing into his room, creeping into his bed, and settling himself once more. Again he looked at his wardrobe and bade it farewell.

Sabbatai's wedding ceremony took place in Raphael Joseph's house. The Chief Rabbi of Egypt was honoured to officiate and all the dignitaries of the town were in attendance. Most of them were in government service and most of them were not Jews. But they sensed the significance of the occasion. They acknowledged Sabbatai's crown without any resentment or sense that they had been pipped at the post. For Messiah-craving was not the monopoly of the Jews. They were simply in a greater hurry, so it was natural that they should produce one of their own. In any case, this Sabbatai fellow looked the part, and they said that his reputation for scholarship was world-wide. A Messiah, even a false one, put people in the mood for reform, and there was nothing wrong with that.

The wedding ceremony took place in the garden, under a gold-embroidered canopy. In the ordinary course of events, a Polish bride of an orthodox Jew would be expected to shave her head before marriage and to don the traditional wig or 'scheitel'. But this event was not ordinary, and when the question of losing her locks was proposed to Sarah, she refused on the grounds that the bride of the Messiah was above such ruling, and nobody dared deny her. For Sarah had no intention of forfeiting her wonderful hair, a great commercial advantage in her trade. And she certainly had no intention of retiring, though in the future that trade would have to be plied indoors and with a better class of person. Such were her thoughts as she stood under the canopy beside her groom as her divine destiny was being fulfilled. Sabbatai's thoughts too, dwelt in the same area.

He assumed that Sarah would not change. She clearly had a talent for courtesanship, and it would be unfair to nip that gift in the bud, or, as in Sarah's case, in full bloom. He himself had no intention of laying a finger on her. Never. He had no interest in woman's flesh. Indeed, it repulsed him. Besides, his touch might cleanse her a little, and he wanted none of that. He wanted her as he had first set eyes on her, corner-clinging, alley-driven, her filthy bodice ajar. No amount of gold trappings, silks and jewels could disguise her rotten core.

After the ceremony, the guests adjourned to the house where the hospitality was lavish. The men sang and danced in circles, while the women, embargoed on both, stiffened their legs and swallowed their melodies. The festivities went on till daybreak, but Sabbatai and his bride were permitted to leave at nightfall and to repair by carriage to a villa on the banks of the Nile, a wedding-present from an anonymous disciple. The coachman noted the full moon and the star-studded sky and saw that it was divinely appropriate to the occasion. He noted, too, the utter silence from his passengers, and he generously ascribed it to shyness. But in truth, back on the velvet upholstered seats, Sabbatai and Sarah had nothing to say to each other. For both of them, the marriage had been a triumphant achievement. Nothing more had to be done, and no comment was necessary.

It was a long drive to the villa and the coachman noted the silence all the way. It disturbed him a little. Even extreme coyness was able to find some mode of expression. A giggle, perhaps, a sigh, or a burst of suppressed laughter. But his passengers might just as well have been dead. He began to worry, and without slowing his horses, he turned and took an illicit peep through the curtains that separated him from his fare. The groom was hunched into the angle of his seat. The bride sat likewise. He was appalled at their separateness. Again, in his generosity he surmised that such a special pair were probably subject to special rules, a period of separation and silence being one of them. Yet

211

it unnerved him, he was relieved when he turned the horses into the long drive and stopped outside the villa.

He got down from his seat and opened the carriage door. Should he help her out, he wondered? If the groom could not touch her, dare he, a simple coachman, take her hand? But Sarah's hand was already outstretched towards him, and had there been an alley close by, she surely would have led him in that direction. For habits, good and bad, die hard. She waited for Sabbatai at the doors of the villa, and the coachman withdrew, relieved. He chivvied his horses into a trot and by the time he reached the end of the drive, he was already in mid-song, for something had to break the oppressive silence he had endured. Someone had to applaud the full moon and the stars and, once on the open road, he lifted his voice in freedom and joy, and gave not a thought to those he had left behind.

The villa was littered with servants, one of whom led the couple to their bed-chamber. Sabbatai was nervous. He'd been through it all before. Two dress-rehearsals in fact, but practice had not improved his performance. They climbed a wide and graceful staircase, side by side. Sarah's gold-embroidered train carpeted the stairs and its tail still covered the lowest rise as she reached the landing. Another servant manoeuvred it up the stairs, as if it were something appended to nothing, as separate indeed as the pair he followed. On reaching their room, Sarah waited for her train to arrive, then she picked it up and hauled it like a piece of luggage through the door. Sabbatai followed and closed the door behind him. With relish he noted that he was in a suite that contained two very positive and separate bedrooms. The door between them was ajar, but that presented no problem. He began to rehearse what he should say to her. He tried to remember the rubbish he'd doled out to his previous and nameless wives, but he didn't try too hard, knowing how futile those words had turned out to be. Sarah rescued him. She went to the adjoining door and opened it wide. She smiled at him and gave him her first words of the day.

'I wish you goodnight,' she said, and she motioned him to enter the room. 'Sleep well,' she whispered when he was safely inside, then she shut the door firmly against intrusion.

Such was the nature of their marriage. But after some months, Sabbatai grew restless. Sometimes he looked at Sarah and wondered what on earth had possessed him to marry her. He presumed it was the promptings of his demons which had returned to him with a vengeance. But this time they brought with them no ecstasy, no illumination. Only darkness and nightmare in which they sieved his spirit. He continued to pray, to fast, and to subject his body to self-mortification and most of the time he was alone.

Sarah found nothing untoward in his behaviour. Whatever her cunning and shrewdness, her belief in him as the Messiah was genuinely sincere, and she ascribed his sullen moods to the enormity of his burden. She did not even try to comfort him, for solace might have been blasphemy. She spent her days reverting to the skills she had learned in the convent, that of tapestry and the playing of the rebeck. Sometimes she hankered after her alley-nights, and occasionally she found her discreet pleasure with a passing stranger.

'. . . I watch her sometimes in the streets. I know it is she, because I loiter outside their house and I see her emerge in her disguise. I follow her into the market-place where she always takes up the same stand. And waits. But never for long. Sometimes she plies her trade the whole day through. Yesterday I watched her until sunset. Then I followed her home and stood outside. Soon there was candlelight in her window, and her shadow crossed the curtains. Sabbatai's too . . . oh, my heart . . . they stood together for a long while. They were talking to each other. Or rather, it was she who* *spoke. Then after a while, Sabbatai neared her, and without touching her body, he sniffed at her. Sniffed and sniffed. Like a dog. All over her. I could smell his fever from where I stood. I turned away. I could not bear it. But I was bound to him. Bound, too, against my will, to her he had chosen in my stead. I cannot help but follow them. They will leave Cairo soon. I am sure of it.'*

The Sabbatai movement was still in its infancy. All over Europe there were pockets of intense Messianic belief with Sabbatai Zvi as its core, but the movement had not yet achieved universal drive and acceptance. This was partly due to Sabbatai's own inconsistency. His occasional self-declaration was often followed by a complete withdrawal. The notion of himself as Saviour at times appeared to him to be of the utmost logic and credibility; and at times, sometimes even at the same moment, to be utterly ridiculous. These moments of indecision were terrible for him, for they forced him to doubt his own sanity, and he would withdraw into solitude as he did now, intensifying all the paraphernalia of his piety as if that ritual would hold him back from the brink of madness.

He stared out of his window on to the murky waters of the Nile, and he longed for the sea. For the first time in many months he thought of Saul and yearned for him. He stood by the window until it grew dark, and the full moon asserted itself over the water. Its reflection bounced off the river and on to the glass and mirrored his face in utter clarity. He stared at it, examining each feature very closely. He was looking for madness, though he didn't know its signs or even whether such signs were visible. But he was desperate to find some rogue feature, for to certify himself insane would have been a relief. It would account for everything and he would live with it and make what he could of it, and no one could blame him for the hurt and unhappiness he had wrought in other people's lives. Inevitably he thought of his father. If only he could, with some conviction, some proof even, write to his father and declare his lunacy, then his father would forgive him. 'I am mad,' he said to the glass, trying it out on himself. But he was not entirely convinced for he could not rid himself of that residual Messiah-craving that clung to him like a burr. He stared at his reflection and it seemed to him that it was slowly fading, and after a while, he was gazing at an empty pane of glass, and fear struck him and his knees melted in terror, for now he knew he had no face at all and that the lack of a mirror-image condemned him to Bedlam.

If Sarah had not been so fast asleep, she might have heard him scream, and when the scream subsided, she would have heard his sobbing; and she would have known that there was nothing she could do to help him.

But Sarah knew that he certainly needed help of a kind, and that that help had to come from outside. From her convent education, she knew a thing or two about Messiahs. The salient message was that no Messiah could get off the ground without an impresario. And she wasn't thinking of levitation. Without Paul afterwards, or John the Baptist before, Christ would have sunk into the Sea of Galilee without trace. Her Sabbatai needed a publicist, an apostle with drive, one who was prepared to devote his heart and soul to the propagation of Sabbatai's claim.

Sabbatai had told her about those who truly believed in him. In a tender moment he had even confided to her the existence of Yakini's scroll. But all those followers were armchair disciples. After the initial fiery enthusiasm, their ardour had cooled. Sabbatai needed more enduring devotion, such as would overlook his occasional trance, his spasmodic eccentricities. He needed someone whose state of Messianic ecstasy was permanent. Such a man she knew lived in Gaza. Not only had Sabbatai spoken of him, but others, too. Learned men all of them. It seemed to Sarah that as Sabbatai was a born Messiah, so Nathan of Gaza was his born prophet. She decided that she would approach Sabbatai with the suggestion that they travel to Gaza.

When morning came, Sabbatai appeared, his eyes swollen with fatigue and sorrow.

'I need the sea,' he said simply. In his mind he thought that somewhere along the shore-line he would find Saul.

'We shall go to Gaza,' Sarah said. 'We shall go and see Nathan.'

As they made their preparations, her decision was confirmed by an outside agency. It came from Gaza itself in the form of a letter from Nathan. The letter was not addressed to Sabbatai, but to his friend Raphael Joseph who, that morning, hurried to Sabbatai's house with Nathan's missive. It told of his ecstatic vision, one that had lasted a whole day. Raphael had never met Nathan, but he knew of his scholarship and his power of clairvoyance, his periods of divine illumination. Unlike Sabbatai Zvi, Nathan of Gaza was stable, and a vision from that quarter was to be taken seriously. It seemed that after prolonged fasting and penitential prayer, Nathan had perceived the sphere of divine lights and the sundry manifestations of God. And he heard a voice which told him that his Saviour Sabbatai Zvi would come. And in no uncertain terms, for the voice repeated the prophecy three times. Moreover, this Messiah would be different from all others. No miracles would be expected of him, and all the world would follow him without proof of his mission. The vision, as Nathan reported it, left no loopholes for failure. It was all very tidy. Nathan added that his letter to Raphael Joseph was his only personal one for he knew of his proximity to and friendship with Sabbatai Zvi. All other letters had been circular ones, he wrote, addressed to the 'Brethren of Israel', and they were sent to all quarters of the Jewish world. A copy of this circular was enclosed for Raphael Joseph's perusal and left no doubt as to the authenticity of the Lord's choice. Thus Jews in Salonika, Venice, Frankfurt, Constantinople, Amsterdam and even in London heard of the coming of the Messiah. A Messiah who was identified by name and origin and who was hailed by a source whose authenticity could not be denied.

This revelation in the year 1665 marked the serious beginning of the Sabbataian movement.

When Sabbatai and Sarah were appraised of the news and advised to repair to the place of the prophet, Sabbatai saw the connection with his sudden desire for the sea. For in that element he would find both God and his own prophet. At last somebody had spoken for him, and proclaimed him, and in a voice that would not suffer itself to be drowned in its own echo, but would reverberate forever throughout the Jewish world. His fears suddenly evaporated, his nightmarish faceless night was quickly forgotten, some sureness of himself refuelled him. He returned to his room to pray for strength to fulfil his mission. As he did so, he felt his fever rising, and he was glad of it for he knew that the fever was part of his Messiah's clothing, and as such, it was easily portable.

Raphael was as excited as Sabbatai and he gave him a purse of 4000 thalers to distribute to the poor of Jerusalem. 'Let them cease work for a day,' he told him, 'so that they may repent and be in fit state for redemption.' He wanted to organise a grand caravan for their journey to Gaza, with many attendant servants as befitting the role that Sabbatai was called upon to play, but Sabbatai insisted on a simple retinue, for in his eyes a humble passage was more appropriate. But he allowed Sarah a maid, for the journey was long and tiring.

Yet even without trappings, they attracted much attention, for rumour had already spread of his coming. At each settlement on their route, they were greeted with ceremony, and gifts were thrust on Sarah, which Sabbatai bade her refuse. Sometimes, where there were gatherings, he would stop and preach and sing psalms, and all his listeners were overcome. Some of them followed him on his way, and gradually a small procession of travellers wound over the hills, swelling in numbers as he neared Gaza. By the time they arrived in that city, the Sabbatai show was undeniably on the road.

Nathan came out to greet them. Sarah was astonished at his youth – he was a good ten years younger than Sabbatai – and also by his beauty. She had a nose for godliness, and had no doubt that Nathan was genuine. A slight alley-urge overcame her when she looked at him, but she curbed it, knowing not to mix business with pleasure. Nathan addressed the crowd and urged them to pitch their tents, to fast and to pray and to make their souls pure. 'Soon,' he promised them, 'we shall travel to Jerusalem.'

Nathan welcomed Sabbatai into his house. They were pleased to see each other again. Especially Sabbatai who felt Nathan was a man to be trusted. Above all, he was happy with his style of promotion. It was undemanding; it called for no evidence, no proof of godhead. It might even find some loophole against the final martyrdom. Because although Sabbatai knew that suffering was part of the Messiah's clothing, he could not pretend to enjoy it. When he thought of Eskapa's whipping, he still felt the sting on his flesh. With Nathan of Gaza he felt safe.

'I hope I shall be worthy of you,' Nathan was saying, and Sabbatai was honest enough to wonder whether the Messiah would be worthy of his prophet.

Nathan had prepared a bandwagon of publicity and promotion. The seemingly commercial trappings of the production in no way reflected a lack of seriousness on Nathan's part, or indeed Sabbatai's. Nathan was a born evangelist, and a talent for promotion is a natural part of that pursuit. His intense belief nurtured that talent. Like Sabbatai, he was often manic; he had visions, he fell into trances. But unlike Sabbatai, he was never withdrawn, never depressed and never melancholy. His mania was constant and stable. He was an admirable foil for Sabbatai's unreliability, and Sabbatai had the wit to recognise the difference between them.

* * *

Nathan's opening promotional gambit was the acquisition of a pure white stallion with flowing mane. The sort of horse that is seen on distant mountain peaks carrying a legendary rider, who, according to history, was well and truly killed in battle but who, in the eyes of his followers, is immortal. Such a mythical throne was deemed appropriate enough for a Messiah, and Sabbatai willingly mounted it, his long white robe – also part of the production – draping the horse's flanks. His mission was to ride around the city and to appoint twelve apostles, each one a representative of the tribes of Israel.

It was an authoritative move and marked the beginning of Sabbatai's ministry.

Sabbatai was not unused to this method of travel and on horseback he acquitted himself fairly enough. But to mount a tall white stallion, his cloak matching its silky hide, and to be surrounded by hundreds of silent worshippers, was enough to give any man ideas above his station. If that man be the Messiah, there are not too many stations to go. In fact, there is one only, and that is the godhead, and it was in this persona that Sabbatai Zvi rode out of Nathan's courtyard and into a state of divine hallucination. His love of God had now become a self-love and he could rely on his fever to feed it. The crowd stared after him, wary of following, for he looked as if he was on the way to heaven. In the city itself there were crowds enough and each male face amongst them looked a suitable apostle. Sabbatai chose at random, for all had equal faith. But only eleven. Eleven good men and true. The twelfth place he would reserve for Saul. Somewhere along the shore or in the streets of Jerusalem he would find him.

He stayed for a while in Gaza, spreading his Messianic word, while Nathan spread it by letter and report across Europe. Nathan had timed their departure from Gaza so that the sacred caravan would arrive in the Holy City at Passover, when Jerusalem would be full of pilgrims from all over the world. Pilgrims who would return to their homes with stories of the new Messiah, his white robes matching his stallion, and of the eleven apostles. And they would surmise on the patent shortfall and ascribe it to some divine sanction.

The procession made its way out of Gaza on the morning of Palm Sunday, but it was not until the evening that its tail shed the city. Gaza was left a ghost town. Only old men, some women and young children remained. All others had caught the Messiah-fever and taken off to the Promised Land. On the way, others joined them, and their singing and their laughter and their prayers were heard and rumoured in the Holy City long before their arrival, giving time for the Rabbis to assemble and consider their strategy. Because it was not only the time-honoured trouble-maker Sabbatai Zvi they would have to deal with, but eleven so-called apostles and a multitude of a following. Moreover, though none mentioned it, all were uneasy about the white stallion. And as usual, the Rabbis were divided. As a result, they could decide on no positive strategy to deal with his arrival, and to confuse matters even further, when the head of Sabbatai's train made its entry into the city, more than half the Rabbis left the assembly to join the worshipping throng.

Sabbatai's entry into Jerusalem was triumphant. He came as much a conqueror as a Redeemer, and those Christian pilgrims on their way to Bethlehem and all the Easter shrines could not help but wonder at the procession and marvel at its timing. They went their own and separate ways, confused and bewildered. Some of them were angered by this Jewish intrusion into their holy days, but each one of them was armed with a story to carry home.

The day after their arrival was Good Friday, and Sabbatai ordered his followers to spend the day in prayer and repentance. On Easter Sunday he went out alone, forbidding the crowds to follow, and he mounted his horse and circled the Holy City seven times. Amongst those who saw him, those hundreds on their way to worship, he made an even greater impression than he had when accompanied by his apostles. Indeed, alone, he seemed to shed a light of greater authority, of undeniable self-assertion. He did not look at them, and his horse, without guidance, seemed to know its way. Its rider's eyes were fixed on the horizon, and only he knew what he saw. All the time his lips trembled in prayer and his fever was high.

As he prayed, it occured to him that his prayers were outdated. The world was about to change. His people would no longer be a nation in exile, a nation that obeyed the exile laws. Now new laws were required to overturn the restrictions of the Diaspora. Dietary laws for example, those made by the Rabbis for a people in exile, for a nation in its wanderings. Now that nation was coming home and the laws must change accordingly. He pondered on these questions while his stallion circled the city, and by its seventh turning, Sabbatai had created a new catechism.

In the eyes of Nathan, Sabbatai's apostles, and all his followers, their leader could do no wrong. In others' eyes, he was nothing but a trouble-maker. But more than trouble. Chaos. Over the next few days, orders went out from Sabbatai's court proclaiming the new laws for the new repentant, redeemable nation. Permission was given for the consumption of all foods. No longer did a fish need scales. Neither did an animal need a cloven foot, or to chew the cud, or to suckle its young. Thus the meat of the pig was no longer taboo. Meat could be eaten together with milk, if one relished it so. Moreover, feasts were to be abolished except for purposes of mortification of the flesh. His followers heard his words with wonder but without question and with total and absolute faith. Because no argument on earth can overcome the sheer and craven will to believe.

The Rabbis, on the other hand, had apoplexy. They called Sabbatai to the courthouse to give an account of himself. But Sabbatai sent back word with one willing apostle that he had to account to nobody, least of all those who had so long denied him. So they called Nathan of Gaza, and he, too, by the same apostle, refused. So they sent word that Sabbatai would be banished. Back went a message from Nathan, and by the same apostle, by this time rather weary of his comings and goings, that, should they banish Sabbatai, then the Messiah would choose Gaza as his headquarters rather than the Holy City. It was this latter threat that struck the hard core. For supposing Sabbatai *was* the Messiah, and thousands across the world believed that he was, thousands that included the most learned Rabbis and scholars, then the withdrawal of Jerusalem from his favours would be too heavy a burden for the Rabbis to shoulder. They seethed in their anger.

They held their tongues till the Passover, which fell late in that year, long after the Christians had gone back home with their stories, and left the Promised Land to its inheritors. Would Sabbatai Zvi forbid that feast? Would he order the eating of bread instead of the unleavened matzoth? Such a thought was unthinkable. But Sabbatai did not interfere with the Passover. It was a commemoration, he said, a homage to history, and in the light of their new deliverance, should be celebrated with even greater fervour.

It was during this feast that Sabbatai chose to distribute Raphael Joseph's bounty to the poor of Jerusalem. Again the Rabbis were affronted. It was their job to apportion alms, and they spread rumours that Sabbatai was giving disproportionate amounts to his own followers. But theirs was a losing battle. They had to sit tight until Sabbatai Zvi went away, and as far as they were concerned, his departure could be none too soon.

After the Passover, Sabbatai announced his plan of campaign. He would travel to Aleppo, he said, and thence to other places on the way, but the goal of that journey would be that place whence he came, that place where he had been born on the Ninth of Av. No accidental timing that, and people had better believe it. He was going to that place that had both honoured and spurned him. All places en route were but stop-overs to Smyrna. This he announced with pride in the streets of Jerusalem.

'I am bound for my birthplace,' he said. But to himself, even in his fevered state, 'I am going to embrace my father.'

For the few days prior to his departure, Sabbatai went alone, on foot, and in simple black kaftan, and scoured the streets of Jerusalem for Saul.

But there was no sign of him. So absent was he, that he feared at moments that he might be dead. In his despair, he enquired of passers-by, and when they asked for details of his person, he was loth to give them public airing. Only his name he gave them. 'Saul,' he kept saying. 'He's called Saul.' He couldn't give a surname, for he was sure that Saul was no longer using Zvi.

'What does he look like?' they kept asking him.

But Sabbatai held his tongue. For Saul's person had become Sabbatai's own secret, Saul's body and spirit his own intimacy, and to divulge either would have been to lose him entirely.

'His name's Saul,' he kept saying angrily. 'Isn't that enough for you?'

And he called his name aloud, hearing its echoes in the narrow alleys where he walked, calling it again and again, so that the whole of Jerusalem would resonate his plea. Before he went home, he made his way to the Wailing Wall. He did not hope to find Saul there, but he would leave a message in one of the cracks in the wall. He knew that this was blasphemous, that those cracks were reserved for pleas to God to cure a loved one, or give strength to endure a legitimate grief, whereas Sabbatai's plea was for his own self-gratification, for the pursuance of a love which, in God's eyes, was calumny. Nevertheless he would plead. He found pen and paper and wrote his message. '*He knows of my love for him*,' he wrote. '*Tell him to return.*' He did not write Saul's name. God would know. He had heard it from his own lustful soul often enough. He folded the paper and placed it carefully in a crack in the wall. Then he prayed before it, and made his way home.

His spirits were low, and when Sarah offered him comfort, he accepted it with some relief, as one would the comfort of strangers. For Sarah was alien to him. She was but a live-in symbol of his own depravity. No more, no less. Yet as a symbol she could coaccide him. Shortly after their wedding, he had told her of Saul, how he had loved him and rejected him. Now he told her that he loved him still. She could see his grief, but she didn't understand him. She had no knowledge of the pain or joy of loving, for she herself had never experienced either. She had heard about loving, in her varied travels, but that condition seemed not to apply to her. She had loved symbols in her time, and those bodies that encased them had been mere packaging. Her appetites were carnal, impulsive, passionate, but with never an aftermath. She envied Sabbatai his heart that could so grieve. She offered to seek Saul herself. As a one-time nomad of long standing, she had a nose for the hide-outs of the displaced and rejected. She asked Sabbatai to describe Saul to her, and suddenly he found it easy to share him. And almost pleasurable. He told her in detail of his stature, his colouring, his gait, the contours of his body and, as he relished them, his tears flowed.

'I'll find him for you,' Sarah said.

The following day she stole out of he house wrapped in a simple black shawl that covered her forehead, so that she could pass as a simple Arab woman about her domestic business. She had left Sabbatai at prayer and she had no doubt as to what he was praying for. She held out little hope for her mission. She had forgotten Saul's description, for she knew there was no point in remembering it. All men looked the same to her, and were equal instruments of instantly forgettable pleasure. But she called his name in the market-place, and those who heard her thought she was looking for her lost child. She repeated it over and over again like a mantra, until she no longer remembered what business she was about. Her nature drew her to the alleys of the Holy City, and she was surprised to find her true sisters there, plying their trade with the nonchalance that she knew, seemingly unaware that they were sinning in the very eye of God and in His very house. For a moment she was tempted to join them, and would have resisted it had she not been accosted by an old man whose poor clothing was clearly a cover for his little folly. For he was well-spoken and his good manners were undisguisable.

'Saul?' she whispered. You could never tell. One had to be careful. There was no response, so she led him into an alley that she found with ease, and with all her old instincts, and with utter and abandoned pleasure, she serviced him. He paid her well for she had pleased him, and promised to see her again and again. And happily would she have obliged him, had it not been her last day in the city. For a while she whispered 'Saul' around its walls, then returned home, empty-handed but for her earnings. Sabbatai had no expectations of her search, but he blessed her for her understanding.

'. . . and I have reached out to him. In my own tormented way, I have touched him. Tonight she was crying "Saul" in the streets . . . I approached her. "Saul?" she whispered. I shook my head. Then we went into an alley close by the Jaffa gate. There I stamped my print on her. The print of my body and its flavour. Its smell of love and longing. And of treachery too. And he will sniff at it, and know that I have reached him.'

Their departure from Jerusalem was engineered by Nathan as a masterpiece of *mise-en-scéne*. It seemed that no one would be left in the Holy City, so great was the procession. Nathan had ensured that Aleppo had advance notice of their coming, and all the stopping-places en route. As they assembled at the city gates for departure, Nathan chose that moment to reveal Yakini's live sea scroll, which somehow or other, probably through his father, had come into his hands. As he declaimed it, he knew that it was but the confirmation of what the followers already believed. Their cheers echoed around the city walls, and those reluctant Rabbis, hidden in their council chamber, trembled.

Once again the show was on the road, led by Sabbatai on his white stallion, his queen mounted at his side. And far, far distant, at the rear of the procession, Nathan rode alone, orchestrating the hundreds of followers into repentance and joy. And thus they travelled the long route to Smyrna.

12

Burdened with Saviour

During the course of that journey, Sabbatai slowly sank into a mood of deep depression. As often as possible he insisted on travelling close to the sea-shore. He had not given up hope of finding Saul, and he was obsessed with the notion that he lingered somewhere by the sea. Nathan, understanding his moods, though ignorant of their present cause, covered up for him, and saw that in their stopping-places he camped alone. Sabbatai cheered a little when they reached Aleppo, uplifted by the welcome he received. But the adulation and almost hysterical worship could not sustain his pleasure, and on leaving the city he grew sombre once more. And in that melancholy state, he began to dread his arrival in Smyrna. On the way he called for many stops, and one morning, as they neared his birthplace, he froze on his bed in terror. No one could persuade him to rise. He had offered up fantastic prayers that as they moved towards Smyrna, it would move further and further away. But the city loomed like a nightmarish threat.

He prayed fervently, but his intense love of God in no way softened his sadness. He knew that for some reason God was rejecting him. In his days of solitude, when he wandered alone in his prayers, he knew that God was with him and returned his love. Now he could only surmise that God was offended by his entourage and the vulgar razzmatazz of his Messianic parade. In a sudden shaft of offensive clarity, he saw Nathan, his prophet, as a sham; Yakini, with his scroll, a simple forger; even Raphael Joseph and all those learned men who sponsored his calling as scholarly pimps. Yet he was trapped in the tinsel paraphernalia of promotion. The price he was being asked to pay for public acceptance was too high for his true nature, which was one that favoured solitude and uninterrupted devotion. He thought of Saul and of the sinful diversion of that love, and though he missed him profoundly, he knew that that love was as nothing compared to his simple adoration of his Maker, and in loving that Only One, he could blissfully spend the rest of his days. Besides, it was a love that would earn his father's embrace, Elijah's comfort, and a peaceful touching between them all. He despaired now that he would ever find an escape route to that solitude, that in all of his folly and nudging ambition he had willingly entered the net that Nathan and the others had cast, and that only death could now free him. He dared to long for that too, and hoped that with such a monstrous wish God would give him some sign, some reproach, some comfort. Some vision to repair his spirit. But all was darkness, and he trembled in the blind and silent night.

On the last lap of their journey, Nathan and Sarah had to drag him on to his horse.

It's possible that, had Smyrna ignored his arrival, turned a deaf ear to all the rumours of his coming, to all the reported signs, to all the authentication that Nathan had devised; if Smyrna had simply turned its indifferent back, it is more than possible that Sabbatai would have dropped the whole Messiah business. And with a great sigh of relief. But he was not to be given that reprieve. For Smyrna went wild in its welcome.

The Zvi family lay in siege. On all sides of the house the worshippers had gathered. Though the crowd was huge, there was little noise except for the murmur of intense prayer. Those for whom there was no room had gathered at the gates of the city to welcome the Messiah. Inside the house was a muted excitement, but one that was not without fear.

It was seven years since Mordecai had last seen his son. In that time there had been letters of loving, 'Papa' letters, that had melted his heart. But there had been 'Father' letters too, and they, for some painful reason, had done the same. He recalled the 'normal' times he had spent with his first-born and, because they were so few, they were memorable. Most belonged to Sabbatai's childhood. A game on the sands, a race over the dunes, a walk in the park. Small pickings and scarcely enough to feed his hunger for a natural son, for other memories intervened, those of 'Father' and of fever.

For the last weeks Mordecai had rarely left the house, fearing the crowd's excitement. Sightings of the Messiah's procession spread from village to village, and for months the gates of Smyrna had never been without sentry or the tricklings of an impatient crowd. The progress of the procession was monitored daily, and as the estimated time of arrival approached, the crowds at the gate grew denser. Work came practically to a standstill. Fishermen left their nets and craftsmen their tools. Even the merchants suspended their profits for greater gains to come. Students' attendances at the Jewish seminaries dropped considerably, for what purpose now in study when redemption was just around the corner? The Rabbis sulked in their empty classrooms, their powers diluted now by the overwhelming numbers of Sabbatai's followers.

On the day that the procession was sighted at the city gates, the ram's horn was taken from the synagogue and blown in the streets of Smyrna. It was a rallying cry, and left no one indoors, except for those in siege in the Zvi household. For many days they had talked of Sabbatai's impending arrival. But only in general terms. They had avoided the particulars of his welcome. But now, in the echo of the ram's horn, it was imperative that they decide which members of the family should go to the gates to meet him. David Arditti was already there, together with the band of Sabbatai's long-term disciples, waiting for glorious vindication. But they were not family. Joseph was the obvious choice but he refused to go alone. His single presence at the gates would only serve to underline the absence of the rest of the family and point to their fear and lack of faith.

'Why can't we all go?' he said.

'Someone must be here to welcome him,' Mordecai said. He was wary of going to the gates. He longed to see Sabbatai but it was a father's longing, and he was not sure that Sabbatai was returning as his son. Indeed, in the echo of the ram's horn, that filial figure dissolved into a stranger. He could not bear a rejection at the gates. Though he cared little for public opinion, he knew that the pain of a possible rejection was made more acute by public humiliation.

'You can go to the gates if you like. I'll stay here to welcome him,' Aunt Sarah quickly volunteered, glad of an excuse to stay at home. For Nahum would be there, and in his shadow, Lusi, who of late had emerged from her retreat in the name of the Messiah who had come to her in a dream, so Nahum had said, and had guaranteed her personal salvation. 'I think she's going mad,' Nahum had said, and then in a whisper, 'Perhaps I have driven her to it.'

'Messiah madness,' Mordecai had commiserated with him. 'We are not responsible. We bear the burden of witness.'

From the sound of the tumult outside the house it seemed that few had escaped that lunacy.

'The house cannot be left,' Elijah said, 'or they will invade.' He spoke with authority. 'You will both go to the gates,' he said. 'I shall stay here with Papa.' His voice had the ring of the last word.

Joseph took Aunt Sarah's arm and he shielded her out of the house. As he approached the gates, he was recognised and a respectful way was made for him and those about him were silent. At the gates he joined David and the disciples. Aunt Sarah followed him.

'I think that Saul is not with him,' she said suddenly.

'That will be a bad omen,' Joseph said, but did not know why he said it and now regretted that he had given voice to it at all. And it so preyed on his mind that when the procession came into view, his eyes searched only for Saul, whose absence would pierce the ram's horn like a cracked passing-bell. And as if to underline his fear, that great familiar bellow punctured the pious air, and the crowd made way for Raphael, the holy fool, and his perennial, unchanging message. So unchanging that people were tempted to chant it with him in mocking chorus but, in fear of his wrath, refrained.

'Beware of false prophets,' he thundered, and for the first time Joseph heard in his cry a fearful ring of truth.

He scanned the head of the procession for Saul, for that's where he should have been. But there was no sign of him. Instead, a woman, on a chestnut horse, riding by his brother's side. Her face held him for a while, so rare was its beauty, then dragging his eyes from her strange loveliness, he looked upon his brother and it seemed to him that he was bathed in light. As it must have seemed to many others, for a sudden silence fell upon the crowd and some of them swooned or crumbled into a trance.

Nathan, who now was riding at Sabbatai's side, called the procession to a halt to give the crowds space to recover. Over their months of journeying from Jerusalem, Nathan had become even more expert in promotion. There had been many dress-rehearsals for this final arrival, and he had learned the value of a pause. How a short delay in the procession, a delay superbly timed, could heighten the excitement of the crowd. Nathan was well-pleased with this home-coming. He had been nervous of Smyrna, with a nervousness that had been prompted by Sabbatai's deep despondency, his unwillingness each morning to tear himself from prayer, to mount his horse and get the show on the road. Only yesterday, within earshot of Smyrna's cheering, Sabbatai had feigned sickness and almost refused to rise from his bed, though it was clear to Nathan that he had only just rested there having spent the whole night rocking on his feet in prayer. Most of the day he rode with his head bowed, his body a-shiver. Towards evening, when the noise from Smyrna grew louder and singing could be heard, Nathan saw how Sabbatai's head slowly raised itself and how a small smile stole over his features. It was when the ram's horn was heard, faint but unmistakable, that that light had begun to filter through Sabbatai's eyes and to sieve his hair through a rainbow. A light that had brightened with each step towards Smyrna. Sabbatai was in a trance. Those seductive sounds of welcome had swept away his despair.

Now he was impatient to arrive. Smyrna was his vindication. Not because it was his birthplace; it held far more alluring charms. In its bordering sea, his rock of God held dominion and the divine silence beneath. It was the town where he had wrought a miracle, forbidding his grandmother to die. It was where a fearful Rabbi Eskapa, time-honoured enemy of his Messianic claim, had nevertheless, on his death-bed, asked for his blessing. In its cemetery he had sanctified Aunt Sarah's marriage. Above all, Smyrna was the holy site of his mother's grave. But to his father, he gave no thought at all.

Joseph went towards him. He had no difficulty in claiming kinship. He could embrace his brother and fully expect his embrace in return. Sabbatai was overjoyed to see him, and with Joseph's lead, all the disciples, those who had followed Sabbatai from their early youth and who had laboured to promote him in his absence, now gathered around their leader and spearheaded the procession through the streets. Nathan rode up alongside.

'I shall tell the crowds to disperse,' he said, 'and we shall meet later in the synagogue.' The welcome had been overwhelming, and if prolonged he knew it might become unruly, for enthusiasm must be given pause, else it leads to riot. He urged the crowds to go back to their homes and to allow Sabbatai Zvi to rest a while. Most of them followed Sabbatai to his house, but once there, they dispersed silently.

Some returned to the gates where Sabbatai's procession was still entering the city. It would be nightfall before the last of them reached the gates, by which time even the craving zealots would be subdued. The redeemable city of Smyrna would be slumbering, so that no one would welcome the last of the stragglers who had prayed the route from Jerusalem.

But had a witness remained at the gates out of sheer curiosity, or simply for the want of something better to do, he would have seen a solitary figure on a game but weary horse, riding towards the city. He rode alone. On his face was a look of studied patience, the look of a man who, with utter confidence, was biding his time. He had spoken to nobody in the course of his long journey, keeping himself to himself. Sometimes at night, he had loitered around Sabbatai's tent and eavesdropped on his fever or despair. Once he had been tempted to reveal himself, but the pain of that sudden rejection in Cairo was still with him and he dared not risk a further dismissal. Since that time he had brooded in various cities, earning his living as Sarah had done, but unlike Sarah hating every human contact. He had grown lean with hatred, his body consumed by his survivor's guilt. His father's ghost haunted his every alley, and the cries of his mother and sisters wailed their sad descant from the walls. For a while, Sabbatai's love for him had kept those sounds to a bearable murmur, but his rejection had unleashed them into thunder. Now his sole purpose in life was to translate his monumental hatred into one final and monstrous gesture, which was why he had followed Sabbatai to Smyrna. So had any witness remained at the gates, he could not have helped but notice the doomed figure of Saul adopted Zvi on his measured and patient way to his revenge and final peace.

Inside Sabbatai's house, Mordecai and Elijah waited. They could hear the crowd as it approached and above all the shuffling footsteps rang the voice of Sabbatai as he psalm-sung his way home. Elijah urged his father to go to the door but, wary of the welcome, Mordecai would not risk public display. He sat himself by the window so that his son might see him and know that he was waiting.

235

As Sabbatai approached the house, that window-shadow was his first reminder of his father. He turned to Sarah. 'This is my mother's house,' he said.

At the door, they dismounted, and Sabbatai led Sarah inside.

'Father,' he called.

Mordecai heard him and knew from that appellation how his son would dictate the tenor of their meeting. It would call for the formality of strangers and for a wounding politeness and courtesy. Sabbatai appeared at the living-room door.

'This is my wife,' he said. 'This is Sarah.' Thus he delegated another to take the brunt of the first greeting, hoping that his father might exhaust at least some of his welcome on his daughter-in-law.

What struck Mordecai in the greeting was, that of all of his short-lived daughters-in-law, only this one seemed to have a name, at least a name that his son could utter. He derived a small hope from the introduction and thought that it augured well for a marriage. So desperate was he for his son's happiness that even this tiniest token of communication was enough to raise his hopes far beyond any logical expectation. And in a mood that, within the space of seconds, had become euphoric, he welcomed Sarah with exaggerated embrace. This woman, whatever they said of her, had saved his son, had made him whole once more, had made him his 'Papa's' son, for she was the only one whom he had been able to call by name.

Sabbatai's gaze lingered on Elijah. Though his younger brother was no disciple, and indeed had, at times, painfully thwarted his ambitions, Sabbatai held a special love for him that neither Joseph nor even Saul could claim. He respected his resistance, his outsiderness, characteristics which he knew he himself owned but to vastly different purpose. He went towards him and embraced him tenderly. As a brother with only a fraternal claim. And Elijah responded in like manner. Between them, for the time being, there was forgiveness.

Then he embraced Aunt Sarah, recalling with fondness how she had dressed his whipping-wounds in Constantinople, her love for Nahum and how, over his enemy's grave, he had joined them together. He looked around the room. This was his family. This was the gathering he had yearned for in countless Jerusalem nights, sleepless with longing, reliving their love and abrasion, for his spirit called out for both. Yes, this was his family. But was that *all* it was? Was it all so much in his heart that finally it might as well have been nothing? For God was his family. Only God in Whom dwelt more love and certainly more abrasion than any human being could consume.

Suddenly he had an overwhelming need to be alone. Sarah was happily in conversation with his father. He could rely on her discretion, although he knew that whatever she divulged, his father would forgive her. He wished he could love her as he loved Saul, and would continue to love him, he knew, for the rest of his life.

'I shall go to my room,' he told them.

They were all glad to let him go. The close presence of a proclaimed Messiah was oppressive. Such a figure belonged on a pedestal, untouched by human hand. Only an outright cynic would risk proximity. Non-believers as they were, Mordecai and Elijah were kin, a condition that precludes cynicism, that embraces only loving and despair and both sentiments were wary of expression. They watched him climb the stairway. From the back of him he might have been an old man. Unhorsed, his dignified bearing had melted into a slouch. Mordecai's eyes were fixed on his son's heels. They had slipped out of the sandals and were treading helplessly on the back supports. Their colour intrigued him; their brilliant and deathly whiteness blending with the sheen of his kingly kaftan. And without a single wrinkle, not even as they sloped in the ascent. Smooth as alabaster, Mordecai thought. Feet of clay. He has started to die, my son, he imagined. Death will creep upon his limbs like scaling gangrene and consume him entire. He hoped his son was not going to sleep, for in Death's grasp, the state of sleep is easy pickings.

But Mordecai need not have worried. Sleep was far beyond the reach of Sabbatai's intent. For he was high in fever and exaltation. Awareness was all. He sat upright on his bed, and though he had no need for comfort or nostalgia, he slipped his arm over his shoulder and cradled that chasm of longing. 'Mama,' he whispered. 'It is as you always said it would be. I am your son, the Redeemer.' And with the declaration came the familiar stab of fear. But it no longer troubled him. He knew that fear was part of the Messiah's clothing, an ornamental trimming, like the fringes on his prayer-shawl. Besides, his fever was too high to admit to any doubts or uncertainties. Rather it engendered an arrogant assertiveness. 'I must make an earth-shattering statement,' he decided, 'one that will confirm my undisputed authority.' The matter of that statement needed little consideration. A week hence would mark the most solemn day in the Jewish calendar. There was no doubt in Sabbatai's mind that Nathan had timed their arrival in Smyrna to herald the great Day of Atonement. The New Year of 5426 had just begun, a joyful celebration, but was cut short soon afterwards by a reminder that all pleasure was sin. Sabbatai wondered why the Day of Atonement could not mark the end of the Jewish year instead of its beginning, so that the suffering might be well and truly over before joy was permissible. But Jewish timing tended to be perverse in the extreme. The act of circumcision at the age of eight days, and the initiation into manhood in the thirteenth year, were instances of such sophistry. But he would turn all that around, Sabbatai decided. It was too late to back-date the great fast of expiation, but he would turn the Day of Atonement into one of feast instead of fast, of joy instead of breast-beating, a day of no pious resolution, in short, a day devoted simply to the pursuit of pleasure, in which all things were permissible.

He would announce the changes that very evening in the synagogue. He could not help but giggle at the thought of the rabbinical apoplexy that would ensue, and he relished it, for their waning powers could no longer touch him. Besides, if he had a mind to, he could even be generous and offer them an explanation. Now that the Messiah had come, the Laws of the Exile were no longer valid. Expiation was an anachronism in the presence of the Redeemer. He saw their ageing mouths drop open, both with astonishment and salivation and the sight of such holy helplessness warmed the cockles of his heart. He peeled his signalling arm from off his back, donned his prayer-shawl, and rocking his spirit into God's embrace, he prayed until it grew dark.

Downstairs they listened to the rhythm of his prayer. The creaking floor-boards translated his frenzy as if, on their joists, a pair of lovers were plighting their troth. Which indeed they were. Sabbatai and his God, an incestuous love perhaps, but one so intense, it could threaten the floor-boards of heaven.

He came downstairs when darkness fell. His first and most intimate band of disciples were there to greet him and together they left the house for the synagogue. Sabbatai turned at the door. 'Will you come, Father?' he asked. 'Sarah will bring you. Elijah too. There will be a surprise,' he said. He smiled. Not a smile of pleasure, not even one of contempt. But Mordecai knew its sub-titles. Had known them since Sabbatai's birth. His blackmailing smiles as an infant, as a boy chicken-herd in their poverty days; as the barmitzvah boy with David behind the side-board; as the young twice-tried groom in the flush of Saul. Oh yes, he knew the sub-titles of that smile, and they had nothing to do with joy or pain. They were simply evidence of power unassailable. So Mordecai did not bother to smile back at his son as he stood on the threshold.

'You will enjoy it, Father,' Sabbatai smiled his words.

Mordecai waited for them to leave, then he offered Sarah his arm. He felt safe with her, even to the extent of granting Elijah his wish to stay at home. Elijah had always been his protector, and he was glad now to relieve him of such a burden. But Aunt Sarah would not be done out of any surprises and, though she would risk meeting Lusi in Nahum's shadow, her love for Sabbatai overcame the possible pain she would endure. Mordecai gave Aunt Sarah his other arm. As they left the house, his step was almost jaunty. Elijah had no doubt that his father was skipping to the gallows.

The streets were empty. Ominously so. The Jewish life and soul of Smyrna had long been ensconced in the synagogue awaiting the final and definitive call. From where he walked, still some distance from the house of prayer, Mordecai heard its preamble in the roar of the congregation as Sabbatai made his way down the aisle. Mordecai slowed his steps to a standstill. The old fear had suddenly invaded him. Fear of others' expectations and cravings and terror at his son's desperate gullibility. Suddenly he began to hurry as if he would be in time to save him.

When they reached the synagogue, the first surprise greeted him. Men and women were not separated. In the main body of the hall, couples crowded, and the erstwhile ladies' gallery had likewise opened its protective doors to invaders. He was shocked at such flagrant and perilous law-breaking. Slowly he made his way down the aisle. The congregation was standing, singing the Hallelujah. His son stood on the platform, a willing recipient of their prayer. Mordecai could not deny the light that framed him. Wishful thinking could not have created that light, nor craven belief, for he was prone to neither. But it was there. Simply there. Out of his clear and faithless eye, Mordecai could see it, symmetrical as a halo around his son's head. He fought down a panic moment of belief. A halo was not enough for him. No divine illumination, no miracle, no vision, would ever convince him of his son's godhead. He could not *afford* a Messiah in his house. His heart was not fashioned to such siring. And never had been. It was a simple father's heart he

240

had, mundane, pedestrian, boring even, but pulsating with unfettered and uncontrollable love.

The halo persisted on the retina as Nathan of Gaza joined Sabbatai on the platform and the prophet bathed in its reflection. Both men were undeniably beautiful. Mordecai had to admit that their beauty was of a special kind, unearthly, elite, forbidding. Again he suffered a spasm of belief. He looked around at the congregation and saw how their faces sweated with frenzied faith. 'I am the only sane one amongst you,' he thought, but as he looked once more at his haloed son, the thought crossed his mind that, amongst all those who worshipped around him, he was the only one who was not whole. He shuddered and longed for Elijah's protection.

Nathan raised his hands over the congregation. 'Friends,' he said. His voice was a whisper yet it rang like a bell throughout the hall. 'Friends,' he repeated, 'our Redeemer is come.'

A cosmic sigh heaved with holiness across the congregation in communally-throated awe and wonder. No more words need ever have been uttered. No more cries of pain. No more murmurings of despair. For all were annulled once and for all by his coming. Mordecai heard a sigh from his own throat. But it was not of the congregation. It was a discord in their holy harmony. A protest sigh. 'Save my son from your greedy cravings,' he pleaded. 'How is it,' he wondered, 'that your hearts are mended, while mine, by the same source, is broken?' He turned his ears away. Deafness was solace. So was blindness, he considered. So he shut his eyes to the congregation.

Thus he did not see their surprise nor hear their gasps of astonishment. It was only afterwards that he heard how his son had repealed atonement, and in its place, promoted hedonism. But no sigh came from his throat, for nothing now could surprise him. The world had turned; the natural order had soured. His son, his eldest, his most beloved, had curdled it, and though others looked at him and envied what should have been his pride as a father, he shrank within his own shame and, blind to all those around him, he looked only at Sarah, hoping to find in her expression some hint of disbelief. In her he would have understood it, for she loved his son as he did, and pathetically he hoped that that love need not include agreement. But her eyes were bright with faith and confirmation. He could stand it no more.

'I'm not well,' he whispered to Aunt Sarah. 'I need air.' Quickly he shuffled past them and made his way out of the hall. Nobody noticed him, for all their senses were fixed on the platform. I feel well enough, Mordecai thought as he reached the threshold of the synagogue, and breathed deeply of what he hoped was still God's clean air. Mordecai never thought about his health, but suddenly he was aware of feeling very fit. In view of his broken spirit, his body's health appalled him. It was not natural that his limbs did not translate his despair and crumple around and beneath him, retreating from the life his heart could no longer endure. His health offended him, as it had so acutely when Clara lay dying, and now he wished with all his strength that he could join her, for he could not bear to go on living in the chill of his son's cold heart and under the barbed wire of his tongue. He made for home and Elijah and their small oasis of sanity.

In the synagogue, the roof-beams heaved with Halle-lujahs and still Sarah had not noticed the gap at her side. Not even Aunt Sarah, whose eyes, if they roamed at all from the platform, looked furtively at Nahum and his Lusi shadow. But one there was who had noticed Mordecai's leaving. He had felt it rather than seen it, for his bones shivered at the affront. He had seen the broken snub of his father's back as it turned away from his prophecies, and the weary disgust of his gait as he shuffled from the house of prayer. His father's constant rejection of his Messianic calling had, until that moment, filled him with anger and disdain. Now he felt no rage. Only sadness at his lack of acceptance. He knew that Mordecai would never change. That father of his would go to his grave convinced that the Messiah was but the divine idea of redemption, an idea that must never assume flesh and blood. He sought out Joseph's face in the congregation, that only kin of his who truly followed him. And he thought of Saul and longed for him again.

When the Hallelujahs were done, Sabbatai urged his listeners into their final repentance. Not to prepare for death, but for life itself. Redemption was no longer at hand. It was here before their very eyes. It was no longer a promise. It was a present fulfilment. After the Day of Atonement, they must prepare themselves to go home, home to the Promised Land. They must put an end to exile, for the Kingdom of God was upon the earth.

Beside him, he heard Nathan sigh, not in awe or wonderment, but as if in warning. The call to return to the Promised Land had not been part of Nathan's promotion. At least, not yet. That call had been premature. Whilst the Sultan of the Ottoman Empire ruled Palestine, it would be folly for the Jews to assume territorial rights, to take possession of a land that belonged to them only by Biblical charter. Such a charter would hold little sway with Ottoman power. He was uneasy with the timing of Sabbatai's proposal. With it, he had precipitated the final move which the people would be within their rights to demand of their saviour. Nathan knew that Sabbatai was by no means ready to take that gigantic leap into power. For if it failed, then no one would believe in him anymore.

But would Sabbatai *ever* be ready for such a move? It called for cunning, courage and conviction. In courage and cunning Sabbatai was not lacking. His unsteady and spasmodic rise to the throne had shown both. His only impediment was lack of conviction. A lack of belief in himself. If his Messianic claim was rejected, he would grow angry, and if acknowledged, he would be afraid. Messiahhood came not out of anger or fear, but out of a simple assertion of self-belief, and Sabbatai's was unreliable. Nathan loved and knew him well, seeing in Sabbatai the

243

seeds of madness that he himself had known but which he had nurtured into visions and miracles well within his own control. Sabbatai's seeds were rampant, ubiquitous, unbridled, beyond restraint. And Nathan knew that in that respect, Sabbatai could never change. Nathan had no doubts that Sabbatai was the true and the divine Messiah, but sometimes he thought that God, God forgive him, had made a misguided choice. With Sabbatai's proposal that night in the synagogue, Nathan's promotional plans had careered off course. Now he knew that the final move was inevitable. He must pray not only for the people's deliverance, but for that of their Messiah as well.

The people of Smyrna lost no time in making their preparations. And not only in Smyrna. Word had spread to all the capitals of Europe. In France the Jews packed the tools of their trade or, without baggage, their portable talents, and made their way to Marseilles. In Poland, Lithuania, Latvia, Russia, Germany, and fearful Spain, they trekked overland to their nearest ports. In Smyrna itself, trade came to a halt. Fishermen folded their nets, farmers sold their stock, fruit rotted unpicked and tailors covered their machines. Teachers closed their schools. Only the Rabbis went about their daily business, but now they talked only to each other for everyone else was too busy packing to listen to their words which, in any case, now sounded pathetically outdated. Even their time-honoured ally, Raphael the idiot, was packing too. His ordained place was at the side of any false Messiah, wherever they might be, especially on God's doorstep. His warning cry would be simmering on his lips.

The non-Jewish population of Smyrna grew restive and trouble was in the air. Nathan smelt it and feared a pogrom. The move out of Smyrna grew daily more imperative. The thought of thousands of Jews thronging the ports of Europe was terrifying, but it was too late to call a halt. Sabbatai must be prepared and schooled for the final move.

In his room, Sabbatai prayed. He knew the whirlwind he had sown and he prayed for guidance. For he knew what was expected of him. Indeed what would be demanded of him. And that there was no way in which he could refuse. He trembled with fear.

'Am I, am I, am I?' he cried. 'Out of every Jew in this world, am I the Chosen One?' he pleaded. 'For God's sake,' he shouted, 'give me a sign.' He heard a plaintive knock on his door.

'Sabbatai. It's Papa. Can I come in?' Mordecai wanted to make it clear that he would not enter as 'Father'. Under that label, he had nothing to give his son. Only tears, too proud to fall. It was Sabbatai's choice to grant or deny him entry.

Sabbatai heard his father's call as a sign, that sign he had asked God to show him and, heedless of interrupted prayer, he rushed to the door. He expected his father to be bathed in light, to hold in his hand a sword perhaps, to lead his crusade, or even a bare outstretched palm of surrender. But Mordecai came empty-handed, both hands clasped tensely on his chest, as if he locked in his pain in fear of its fatal release. Sabbatai saw in front of him the undeniable figure of 'Papa', that figure he could so rarely accommodate, but whom he needed to love more than anyone on earth. He raised his shield. 'What is it you want, Father?' he said.

Mordecai hesitated. 'To see you. That's all,' he said. 'To talk with you. It's been such a long time.'

Still Sabbatai did not ask him inside.

'I like . . . I like your wife,' Mordecai pleaded, 'very much.' He offered it as a visa for entry, and out of sheer pity, Sabbatai let him in.

Mordecai sat himself on the bed. Sabbatai watched him, waiting. Waiting for the words that he wanted to give him. 'I missed you,' Mordecai said. 'Every day. So very much. Tell me about your travels.'

'Wherever I went, Father . . . .'

Mordecai shivered, but if there was to be conversation, both men knew that 'Father' was part of the deal. 'Papa' needs no utterance, just touch and embrace, but between them at that moment lay continents. 'Wherever I went,' Sabbatai said again, 'the word spread. News of my travels must surely have reached Smyrna.'

'Oh yes,' Mordecai agreed. The town buzzed with information. But how many mouths had it passed through before it reached Smyrna? And each mouth had its own version, adding a little here, taking there. 'Truth does not travel reliably,' he said. 'I want to hear it from your own lips.'

He paused for a while before his next question, a question he knew Sabbatai was bound to answer.

'Where is Saul?' he said.

He saw how Sabbatai trembled and he feared for his adopted son. 'Is he alive?' he asked. 'Tell me the truth,' he almost shouted.

'He must be alive,' Sabbatai said. His voice broke. How could anyone on earth suggest otherwise? 'Of course he's alive,' he said. 'We quarrelled. He left me in Cairo.' He would go no further.

'When you got married?' Mordecai said.

'That had nothing to do with it.'

But Mordecai had had his answer. 'As long as he's alive,' he said. He unclasped his hands. He was relieved that no harm had come to Saul, for despite the sewer he had shared with his son, his heart was moved by his orphanhood.

'Now tell me about you,' he said. 'Tell me how you met Sarah.' He felt that with Sarah the ground was safe. Other more perilous questions could come later. But Sabbatai's answer was a minefield.

'In a whorehouse,' he said. 'Where else?'

Mordecai clasped his hands again. He was determined not to break. 'Were you preaching there?' he asked.

'In a fashion,' Sabbatai said.

246

Mordecai took care not to look at his son's face for he knew that it was smiling.

'The only way to preach amongst whores,' Sabbatai said, 'is to join them.'

He is slowly and quite deliberately digging my grave, Mordecai thought. He stood, his hands unclasped, his tearless pain released.

'I will die in God's good time, Sabbatai,' he said. He turned to leave the room, and when he reached the door, he felt Sabbatai's hand on his shoulder.

'Papa,' he heard.

He turned, his heart melting.

'Papa,' he said again, 'they will ask terrible things of me. They will want *everything* from me. Even perhaps my life.' He put his hand on his father's cheek. 'Papa,' he said, and his voice was like a child's. 'I need you to believe in me.'

Mordecai dared to take his hand. 'I believe in you as my son, Sabbatai. I believe in you as a good, a loving and a pious man.' He could not pretend to believe more than that.

'Is there no more?' Sabbatai asked. 'I *need* your faith in me.' He was almost weeping. 'I need you, your voice more than any other, to call me the Redeemer.'

'I cannot lie to you,' Mordecai said, and swiftly left the room.

Sabbatai stared after him. His father's denial was final. He had risked his son's love to utter it. But it was irrevocable. Sabbatai knew it and knew too that his father's visit was the sign for which he had prayed and his fever subsided with relief.

'I am not he,' he whispered. 'I am not he.'

He lay on his bed cradling his arm along his spine. 'I am not he,' he lullabied, and even during sleep he sang his mantra still. Outside his window a small crowd had gathered serenading his sleep with a 'Hallelujah'. But Sabbatai was deaf to everything except his own lullaby.

But no matter how long he lulled himself, nor how confirmed his Messiah-abdication, the thousands of his followers would brook no recantation. Decisions regarding their future were no longer in Sabbatai's hands. In the morning, he woke to their persistent Hallelujah. He recalled his abdication and longed to sleep again. For waking was a nightmare.

13

Reluctant journeys

Sabbatai listened to the song of praise outside his window and he felt trapped. For a moment he was tempted to open the window wide and to announce in his broken voice his irrevocable renunciation of the throne. But he knew it was futile. Not one of them would believe him. Not even Nathan who knew of his doubts before. For Nathan believed in him as did the thousands of others. That was enough. Their blind belief. What Sabbatai said was almost irrelevant. Even where he was and what he did. For he was now simply a symbol, a cypher for others' worship.

In fear he rose from his bed, and for the first time, he broke the habit of his manhood. He reached out for his phylacteries, touched them, and recoiled as if they were fire. He would not don them, he decided. He would not pray that morning. Nor any other morning. Ever again. If all those outside would not take his abdication seriously, then he would make sure that at least God got his message. He would not be communicating with Him any more. In resigning from His court, he forfeited all privileges of kinship. He was no longer of His family.

He wrapped the phylacteries and his prayer-shawl and he wondered where he could hide his past from himself. But he knew there was no point in hiding it. He would never wish to seek it again, nor care if anyone else found it. He would erase it as if it had never been. He secured that holy parcel and opened the window wide. He did not hurl it in rage, but dropped it gently below with the slow sadness of burial. He did not look outside, but he heard their communal gasp, a gasp that melted into a sigh of awe.

Then a voice cried, 'It is his gift to us. It is his bond. The Redeemer has promised us.'

Now Sabbatai knew that all was lost. He was chained to them by their craven need to trust in him. He heard footsteps outside. They lacked the hesitancy of his father's tread. They were confident, urgent and business-like. He knew it would be Nathan with the programme of the day. He opened the door to him.

'We must talk,' Nathan said. 'When your prayers are done.'

'They're done,' Sabbatai lied. 'And now I want to eat.' He wanted Nathan to go away. He wanted to sit with his family at breakfast. He wanted to lead a normal life, to eat, to sleep, to laugh and to care. Somehow or other, he would deal with his fevers.

'Shall I come to you later?' Nathan asked.

Sabbatai wished never to lay eyes on Nathan again, but he knew that his so-called prophet was part of the nightmare of waking, as were those crowds that now gathered outside the house. That he could no more be rid of them than reality itself.

'I need to spend time with my family,' he said. He realised how rarely he used that word, and how easily, without impediment, it had fallen from his lips. In that moment he recalled his childhood, the family picnics, the gatherings for rose-petal jam, sweet memories that his Messianic cravings would never allow. He would dwell on them, he decided, and make them green again. He stretched to his full height.

'I wish to visit my mother's grave,' he said. 'Simply with the family.' Again that word. 'I want no followers.'

'Of course,' Nathan said. 'I shall arrange it.' He was a little unnerved by Sabbatai's sudden assertiveness. He did not want Sabbatai in an argumentative mood. For in the decisions that had to be made that day, he needed him docile, pliant, and full of faith. He hoped that a visit to his mother's grave would temper his assertiveness a little.

'I would like to go myself,' Nathan said. 'Later. With followers.'

He should have felt honoured, Sabbatai knew. Whoever visited his mother's grave, prolonged her memory. And an acknowledgement by her son's prophet and his followers would have eased and pleased her rest in the shadows. Yet he didn't want Nathan to go. He and the followers would only serve to negate his abdication. His mother was his private grief. He wanted no public falsehoods on her grave. Yet he could not deny Nathan. Nor his followers. His mother was as captive to their trust as he himself.

'I stood amongst the crowd outside the house, that house where my years accumulated but forever bypassed manhood. That room where we loved, that window where we worshipped. My exiled home in exile. Sabbatai was inside with his fevers and there was no one at hand to hold them. For none of them feel their heat, their frenzy, their unutterable fear. None but Mordecai and Elijah and they can only turn their faces to the wall . . . Nathan came out of the house. Bewildered. Helpless. Without words. Yet he has to say something, or the crowd will stone his silence. Soon we will set out for Jerusalem, he told them. They cheered. Do they not know that Jerusalem belongs to the Sultan? How can we dwell in a land that is not ours? I dared to ask that question. The crowd were uneasy. "He's right," one of them said. "The land belongs to the Sultan." "Even the Sultan is subject to the Messiah," Nathan said. The crowd was satisfied. It is simple to send a symbol to its death.'

Nathan walked alone. He had to debate with himself the manner of his approach to Sabbatai. He needed him docile. Or even in a state of mania which would be conducive to the final assault of the crusade. Nathan could deal with that. But the Sabbatai he had seen that morning was a stranger to him. He had voiced the despairing logic of normalcy. Nathan prayed that it was just a passing phase.

And Nathan's prayers were answered. It took very little, a single word, the smallest gesture, to catapult Sabbatai back into his time-honoured fantasy. A throne is not easily forfeit. Neither are visions or voices. And without divine intervention, how can they be explained? As he sat down to breakfast amongst his family, he was acutely aware of their astonishment. It takes two to be normal. Acceptance is part of change. But there was no acceptance around the table. Simply the silence of stupefaction.

'Why are you staring at me?' Sabbatai shouted, and already the fever grew upon him.

Nobody spoke. Words were dangerous. Any words. So they all hid in a trench of silence. Sabbatai was the first to fire, softly and without aim, for he addressed the table in general, and so randomly that it was clear he was talking to himself.

'It's too late,' he said. 'It's all too late.'

'What's too late?' Aunt Sarah dared.

'It's too late for change,' Sabbatai said. 'I have been driven. Driven outside this table.'

'Not by us,' Mordecai pleaded. 'Stay, stay; this is your home.'

'It doesn't matter who drives me,' Sabbatai said helplessly. 'I am driven.' He looked from one face to another. 'I love you all,' he said, trembling, 'but I cannot help myself.'

He rose. 'I shall fast,' he said. He needed to pray and he rushed to his room. Then he remembered how he had dispensed with his tools of prayer and he panicked. He stood on the landing. Joseph's bedroom door was open. So was Elijah's. He hesitated. He knew that Joseph's prayer-shawl and phylacteries would throb with the same vibrations as his own. But Elijah's shawl was different. It throbbed of exile still, and he longed to have it embrace him, to experience those promptings that he had never known. But he feared that such a shawl would infect him once more with abdication, and he knew that, as much as he wished for it, it was against God's will. Joseph's prayer-shawl was safer. He took it from his room and returned to his own. Quickly he donned the phylacteries. He prayed in his fever, but he had no idea on earth where his heart was. In or out of the prayer, he knew not. He stood outside himself and watched as he wound the leather thongs about his arms. That man who is praying is the Messiah, he thought to himself, and it was in that man that his heart lay, for his own body was as cold as death itself.

Thus he prayed for the rest of the morning, whilst downstairs they listened to his rocking.

In the afternoon they went to the cemetery. It was a silent pilgrimage and no one disturbed them. Not only out of respect for Sabbatai's privacy, but because they were too busy elsewhere. And not, as Sabbatai feared, with their preparations for departure. On their retreat from Sabbatai's house, his followers had met with some opposition. Not from the Rabbis. They had the sense to keep themselves indoors. The protest came from one Chaim Pagna, a rich merchant of Smyrna. A widower with beautiful twin daughters. Pagna had long been an opponent of Sabbatai's Messianic claims, but as long as the Rabbis manned the opposition fort, he contented himself with voicing his private disapproval. Now the Rabbis' cowardly retreat incensed him, and he was driven to declare his hostility in public. Only a fool would have dared the streets that day had he not been one of Sabbatai's followers. A fool, or a man of enormous courage. And since both traits often dwell in the same body, Pagna had his share of each.

He lived in a villa in the centre of the town, a main thoroughfare which led either way to all quarters of the city. So it was natural that the crowds of Sabbatai's followers should pass his door on their way to their preparations for departure. He heard the stampeding of their footsteps, and the crescendo of their march inflamed his rage. He bade his daughters retire to the rear of the house. Knowing his temper, they begged him to come with them.

'Go to your rooms,' he shouted at them, and they obeyed, fearful. But they went upstairs to a front room of the house, from where, by carefully raising the curtain, they would have a perfect sight of the brawl that they feared. As the crowds approached the villa, having no need to stop before it, intent on their own business, Pagna's daughters saw how their father stepped out into the road, stationing himself in front of them and raising one hand. They trembled. The crowd, bewildered but obedient, came to a standstill.

'What is it, Mr Pagna?' one of them said.

'You are fools,' he shouted. 'He's leading you to your own destruction, Sabbatai Zvi. He is not the Messiah. He is a fool and a charlatan. Or perhaps he is mad. But whatever he is, he is false. You are deceived, all of you. He is a curse on Judaism. He should be poisoned.'

The girls at the window had no difficulty in hearing his words for they were swollen with his anger and indignation. Neither did they miss the shocked and offended silence that followed. The word 'poisoned' was whispered down the line, until it roared with fury. Then one of the crowd, yelling, picked up a stone. It was a cry of havoc, for all followed suit. Pagna's daughters shrunk behind the curtains as they watched their father dodge the fall of stones and rush for safety behind his own front door. They heard his call. 'Come,' he shouted.

They ran downstairs and stole out into the garden in terror. Then through the side-gate and into the alley, where they crouched in fear.

'Enough,' someone shouted. Then the same voice thundered, 'We shall come back for you, Pagna.'

They listened as the footsteps gathered and the march continued, but even after its long silence, they were still loth to return to the house.

'I will go to the Rabbis,' Pagna said. 'They simply must do something, or we are all destroyed.'

256

'Be careful, Papa,' they said together.

He kissed them and left. But they stayed in the alley a long time before they risked re-entering their marked dwelling.

Word soon spread around Smyrna, mainly through the mouths of the rioters themselves, and any Jew in whose heart dwelt a lingering doubt of Sabbatai's Messianic crown kept himself indoors, his windows and lips firmly sealed. So the stoning stopped, for there was no declared target. Sabbatai reigned fearful and supreme. But though there were no more stones, there was something far more sinister. The stone-throwing had released an energy that was akin to ecstasy. The memory of such joyful power was not easily forfeit, and without specific target it had to find outlet otherwise.

Over the next few weeks in Smyrna, and while Nathan was planning the final assault of the campaign, the town was gripped in frenzy. The passion of stone-throwing translated itself, with the utmost ease, into hysteria. Miracles proliferated. One man swore he saw the moon in flames, and on this pronouncement all those around him saw it too. A pillar of fire in the middle of a field was another's vision, and a star rising from the sea another's. Some performed their ritual ablutions in the ocean, and though it was mid-winter, they declared the water warmed by the Divine Spirit. New-born babies were heard to utter the name of Sabbatai while first at their mother's breasts, and grown men and women fell in the streets into fits of religious ecstasy. Hysteria is eminently contagious, and even the twin daughters of Chaim Pagna were infected. For when the merchant came home one day from yet another secret meeting with the Rabbis, he found his children writhing on the floor and foaming at the mouth, swearing that they had seen Sabbatai Zvi on a throne in the keyhole of heaven. Whereupon Pagna himself gave up his struggle and joined the ranks of the believers.

One outcome of hysteria is impatience, and the people grew restive. They were prepared. They had packed their belongings. They were in a state of grace. Why were they waiting? Although it was only a matter of three frenzied weeks since Sabbatai had arrived in Smyrna in all his glory, their feet itched for the Holy Land. Even Raphael the idiot yearned for another site for his protest, and though he continued to warn in the market-place that they should beware of false prophets, he added a new plea for the next inevitable move.

There was now no point in further delay, and no excuse for procrastination. The people in their frenzy would not be mollified. The final move was obvious to everybody. And though it was earth-shattering, no one feared it more than Sabbatai. And so terrified was he that he dared not even voice the nature of the final stage of his campaign. But the people had to be told. They were already gathered in the synagogue where they assembled each night, impatient for the climactic move. Sabbatai begged Nathan to make the announcement on his behalf. He himself would stay in his room and ask God for guidance, for never in his life had he felt such an urgent need for prayer.

'Remember, Nathan, remember to tell them that we will give the Sultan a chance. We must give him a chance.' He was panting with fear. 'Tell them that. We will first give him a chance.'

'Don't worry,' Nathan said. 'I shall tell them.'

When Nathan left and Sabbatai was alone, he still felt unsafe and afraid, and he crouched in the corner of his room, his prayer-shawl covering his head, his eyes tightly shut, as if his own blindness would render him invisible to all. Downstairs, they heard the floorboards creak, and noticed the absence of ecstasy. Mordecai recalled Sabbatai's helplessness. 'It's all too late,' he had said, and he was not surprised to hear him sobbing.

The crowds in the synagogue fell silent when Nathan entered. They were curious as to Sabbatai's absence and, in fear of yet another postponement, they started to chant his name and in their communal voice Nathan heard a strain of anger. So as he walked down the aisle, he stretched out his arms, and gradually they grew silent. He mounted the podium.

'Friends,' he said, 'our Saviour is at earnest prayer. He asks for guidance, for he has been commended by the Holy One to fulfil the last act of our crusade.'

Heedless of the sanctified ground on which they stood, the crowd cheered and went wild with joy. Once again Nathan of Gaza raised his arms and soon they were silent.

'Sabbatai Zvi will travel with a few followers to Constantinople.' Again there was a sudden cheer, for they knew the inference of that capital connection. When silence returned, Nathan made the bald statement, 'There, with myself and his disciples,' he said, 'Sabbatai Zvi will seek an audience with the great Sultan. First he will offer him the chance of conversion so that, as a good and pious Jew, he may continue to hold sway over Jerusalem. Our Redeemer in his virtue insists that this choice be given him.'

The congregation sighed. The notion of a Jewish Sultan was beyond their imagination.

Nathan paused to give weight to the enormous burden of the Sultan's expected refusal. 'If the Sultan turns his back on conversion, then Sabbatai Zvi, in all his might and holiness, will surely depose him.' This time there were no cheers. The magnitude of the final move had at last come. Their silence was awesome. 'Now go,' Nathan told them, 'and learn patience. Go back to your work, unfold your nets, uncover your machines and set up your stalls in the market-place. News of our progress will reach Smyrna by messengers whom we will send. Let your prayers go with Sabbatai Zvi on this great journey. Hallelujah.'

Slowly and in orderly fashion the congregation left the synagogue. Once in the street they started to sing, and though there were hundreds of them, their voices were muted. It was the Twenty-first Psalm that they chose, that psalm that prefaced all their services. 'The King shall joy in Thy strength, O Lord.' Sabbatai Zvi's chosen song, and had Sabbatai's ears not been shrouded in his prayer-shawl or his soul wrecked with sobbing, he might have heard it and melted in fear.

Aunt Sarah walked alone. She was troubled. Of all the congregation, she was one of the few who envisaged the possibility of failure. She feared for Sabbatai and knew that he feared as well. Like Mordecai, she too recalled his helpless plea, 'It's all too late, I am driven.' She felt a touch on her shoulder. Turning, she saw Nahum. Automatically she looked around him, but no Lusi stood in his shadow.

'I am alone,' he said.

They walked along silently for a while. The crowd passed them by and their psalm dwindled to a distant echo.

'Will you go to Jerusalem?' Aunt Sarah said at last.

'Lusi is going. I cannot stop her. And I cannot let her go alone.'

'But do you believe?' Aunt Sarah asked.

'No,' he said. A silence again. 'But she will be lost without me.'

'She is lost in any case,' Aunt Sarah said, only half-knowing what she meant.

Nahum put his arms about her and faced her squarely. 'Beloved,' he said. 'We are all lost.'

He kissed her and held her for a long time. 'Will you come too?' he said softly.

She held his hand and they walked closely together. 'How can I leave Mordecai?' she said.

Nahum's warning that all were lost struck terror in her heart. Not only for Sabbatai but for those who would survive, whether they believed in him or not.

'Elijah will look after him.' He held her once more almost hurting her in his grip. 'We cannot live without love, Sarah,' he said. 'The love of God is simply not enough. Besides,

Clara left Sabbatai in your care. What's more, you believe in him.'

'Take me home,' she said. 'We must tell Mordecai what Sabbatai is going to do. He will know it. He has always known it. And he knows that it is all too late. But we will go and comfort him.'

He took her arm once more and then seemed to hurry as if he himself could hold Sabbatai back from the brink. But as he reached the house, he slowed his pace. He knew, as all knew, those who truly loved Sabbatai, not as a god-head but as a man, that time had overtaken him and that he could do nothing but follow in its shadow.

After the congregation had dispersed, Nathan had stayed in the synagogue. Despite all his sublime faith both in God and in Sabbatai, the terror of possible failure haunted him. He prayed fervently, begging and pleading with God to ease their path. And he grew angry too, for surely God of all people knew the hideous consequences of failure? So his begging and his pleading became more and more urgent and later turned to outright demand. Even threats he hurled on God's name, warning Him that He Himself would be the greatest loser. Then he prayed for forgiveness for his effrontery and himself joined in the singing of the Twenty-first Psalm, the echoes of which he heard in the distance. When it was done, he kissed the fringes of his shawl and folded it into its velvet wrapper. Then slowly he made his way down the aisle. As he reached the door he heard the sound of prayer. A muffled sound, muted more by weeping than entreaty. He peered in the darkness and discerned a shape at the back of the hall. Its head was covered with a prayer-shawl which shivered spasmodically with sobbing. Nathan paused. He knew that his announcement from the pulpit had given as much reason to mourn as to rejoice, and he wondered whether he should offer some comfort. But there was about the praying figure, so crouched in desolation, an air of untouchability.

261

Inconsolable. Nathan passed by, even more troubled than before. On his way to his lodgings he passed by Sabbatai's house. An unusual silence surrounded it, the silence of mourning and helplessness. He lingered there for a while, then went on his way, praying.

Saul stayed in the synagogue till dawn, and all the time he crouched, wrapped in his holy covering. But he was not sobbing, as Nathan had surmised, for the possible failure of Sabbatai's mission, nor for the precarious future of Jews under Ottoman rule. He cared neither for failure nor future. Indeed, for the first, he had no thought, for he himself would ensure the failure of Sabbatai's mission. And as to the future, either for the Jews in general or for himself in particular, he was totally indifferent. As a boy, he had ruled out the possibility of a future, running for his life in some Polish field, the sole and guilty survivor of his whole family. Since that time he had merely lived out his allotted days and longed for their termination. Occasionally, when Sabbatai had loved him, he had envisaged the possibility of a future, and so bright was its light and so joyful its prospect that when it dimmed on that Cairo journey the blackness that ensued was darker than ever before. Now he would follow Sabbatai to the capital and settle his account once and for all. Until that time he would keep Sabbatai at a distance, for the sight of his beauty might threaten his resolve.

At morning light he wrapped his prayer-shawl and slunk out of the synagogue. Like Sabbatai he craved invisibility and he longed to get back to his lodgings to hide himself from his own treachery.

That day it seemed as if the town of Smyrna had returned to normal. The shore-line was strewn with fishing-nets and black with boats. The market-place was alive again, whirring with machines, scissors and lathes. But rumour had spread. Those non-Jews of Smyrna heard it and laughed.

The notion of a Jew going to the capital and deposing the great Sultan was hardly to be taken seriously. But for the Rabbis of Smyrna it was no laughing matter. They feared for their lives. So did other Jews, those who had never believed in Sabbatai but had been too fearful to voice their opposition. So again there was a fever of packing, not for the Promised Land, but for those countries well beyond Ottoman powers. But they did it secretly, and over the next few days they stole furtively out of Smyrna and left the unholy city to reap the whirlwind it had sown. Most of them settled in Germany, thus condemning their lineage to a future whirlwind of another kind.

But they were not missed in Smyrna. For many years now the Rabbinate had ceased to be the official authority. Sabbatai's followers viewed them with contempt. When Sabbatai heard of their disappearance, his fears were compounded. For although he was in complete disagreement with their exile-logic, indeed had hated them at times, their sudden absence was a new kind of peril. Now he was completely alone, with all Smyrna in agreement, with no loop-hole for recantation.

For three days after Nathan's announcement, Sabbatai kept to his room. Fasting and praying. Every day Nathan visited him and outlined the plans for their departure. Occasionally Sarah came to him and offered him comfort.

'How is my father?' he kept asking her.

'He will understand in time,' she told him.

'He understands already,' Sabbatai said. 'Understanding is no comfort.' He paused before his next question, loth to ask for it would uncover his frailty.

'Does he want to see me?' he asked.

'He won't come unless you call him,' Sarah said. 'Shall I call him for you?' she asked after a while.

Sabbatai shook his head. 'He would have no words for me,' he said.

'You're proud,' she told him.

'No,' Sabbatai said. 'I'm afraid.'

263

She wanted to hold him close but she feared he would bristle under her touch. She laid her hand on his covered arm. 'What can I do for you?' she said.

'Keep faith with my father,' he said.

'But my faith is all in you.'

He shook his arm from her hand. 'You're like all of them,' he shouted. 'Is there no one at all to comfort my father?'

'There's Elijah,' Sarah said.

'It's too heavy a burden for one. In time, he will turn against me. Even as a brother.' Sabbatai knew how well Elijah loved him, and knew too the sometimes unbearable pain of that love. To kill the thing one loves is a way of easing that pain, even though that which replaces it can barely be borne.

'Do you want to see Elijah?' Sarah tried again.

Sabbatai shook his head. He was more fearful of Elijah than of his father. Neither would have words for him, but Elijah's silence would pierce him like a sword.

'Go now,' he told Sarah, 'and bring me a little to eat to break my fast.'

She was glad to do such a service for him, for he had not eaten for three days. Downstairs she announced his request for food, and they almost shouted for joy. Mordecai laughed aloud. At least his son would live. For he had surmised that Sabbatai, driven as he was, and so helpless in face of others' propulsion, had decided to mourn himself to death.

'Make him a feast, Aunt Sarah,' Elijah said.

'No,' Mordecai counselled them. 'Just a little. Some small thing to relish. He has only just begun to live again. I shall take it to him,' Mordecai said.

Sarah was nervous of his offer, but she could not refuse him. In the kitchen Aunt Sarah prepared a tray. She was relieved that Sabbatai would break his long fast and she would feed him to make him strong, but not strong enough, she prayed, for him to travel to Constantinople. She recalled

264

Nahum's words. 'We are all lost,' he had said. She worried that the Rabbis had fled, and that certain families she knew of, rich enough to flee, had, like animals sensing the onset of an earthquake, run for cover. Since leaving Nahum, she had felt her faith on the wane, and she was offended by it, considering its dilution as an act of betrayal. Sabbatai was alone. Even in his crusade he was alone. She didn't know how she could help him.

Mordecai took the tray. His spirits were high, and he almost sang his way to Sabbatai's room. He called his name and waited for the door to open. He tried not to notice how long he had to wait. He hummed quietly to himself, shifting his weight from one foot to another in rhythm with his song. Inside the room Sabbatai heard him, and punished himself with his father's patience. Then he could bear it no longer. He rushed to the door and opened it wide.

'I've brought your food,' Mordecai said. I'm glad you will eat again.'

'Why are you glad, Father?' Sabbatai asked, and Mordecai wished himself downstairs again, out of the line of 'Father'-fire. He was angry. 'Because I want you to live,' he screamed at him. He put down the tray and stared into his son's gaunt features.

'To live for what, Papa?' Sabbatai whispered. 'To be led to my failure?'

'Then stay,' Mordecai pleaded.

'It's too late,' Sabbatai said again. 'It's too late. I am driven.'

'But you can refuse. Say you are ill.' Mordecai was clutching at straws.

'They will wait for me to get better.' He put his head in his hands. 'I am lost, Papa,' he said.

Mordecai dared to hold him, and Sabbatai gratefully stooped into his embrace. Mordecai held him for a long while, aware that, despite the calamity that threatened them all, with his boy in his arms, he had never in his life been so happy.

'You know Papa,' Sabbatai was saying, 'the Sultan will punish all the Jews of Smyrna. Of Turkey. Of the whole Ottoman Empire. He will destroy us.'

Mordecai held him close. 'You must not go, Sabbatai. You must not lead your people to their destruction.'

'It is they who lead me,' Sabbatai said.

Mordecai cradled him like a child. In all of Sabbatai's growing, he had feared his fevers and the manic 'Father' rage that attended them. He had longed for his peace. Now, in his arms, his son was cool and mended, a 'Papa' child, yet full of despair and fear. For a moment he wished the fevers to come again, even if it meant 'Father' and mania, but at least his son would be wreathed in joy. All he could do now was to hold him.

'Eat,' he said, 'then sleep a little. It's a way of forgetting.' He sat close to him and watched him eat without appetite. Then he took the tray away and guided him to his bed. He even undressed him like a child, nurturing his son's regression into his infancy, and on putting him to bed, he even placed an arm along his back, confirming his mother's memory and her love. He crept from the room. He had no right to the joy in his heart, that 'Papa' joy that was so rare. But Sabbatai was right. It was all too late.

He said nothing when he went downstairs except to tell them that Sabbatai was sleeping. As they left the table, Mordecai called Elijah to his side. 'Stay with me a little, Elijahle,' he said.

Elijah knew that his father wanted to talk about Sabbatai and their future. He knew of his father's fears, and he shared them. In the streets of Smyrna he had heard of the families who had fled. Some he knew and respected. All had left behind their dire warnings, reported to Elijah by Sabbatai's followers. Reported in jest. But Elijah pitied those followers for their short-sightedness, and his anger at his brother grew to monstrous proportions at the thought that one single man, that man of his own torn heart, could lead them all to damnation. So he was not surprised when his father divulged the matter of his conversation with his eldest son. But his father was not angry. Nor even resigned. His manner puzzled him, for despite the dire consequences of his son's crusade, of which Mordecai was well aware, his father seemed undisturbed. Indeed, there was a certain euphoria about him which Elijah could not understand, and which he found unnerving, for it seemed to him that his father was losing his mind. Then his own anger against his brother became unbearable.

'I am so tired,' his father said at last. 'Let us sleep. Tomorrow the sun will shine.'

Elijah could have wept for his father's frailty. He could not sleep that night. His anger itched at every turn. In the morning it was still upon him, sharpened now by his fatigue.

'I will take Sabbatai his breakfast,' he announced.

Aunt Sarah prepared the tray and he took it upstairs. He did not knock on Sabbatai's door. He kicked it open with fury. The sight of his brother crouched in his prayer-shawl in the corner of the room broke his step, and his knees threatened to melt. He put down the tray and sat on the bed. He watched his brother and the anger drained out of him, and in its place flooded a compassion that was equally unbearable.

'Sabbatai,' he whispered. 'I've brought you your breakfast.'

The figure did not stir. Elijah went towards it and clasped it in his arms. He helped Sabbatai to his feet. He seemed very weak. Elijah hoped it was only the hunger.

'You must eat, Sabbatai,' he said.

He helped him to a chair, unwrapped him of his shawl and set the tray before him. 'I'm going to watch you,' he forced a laugh. 'I'm going to see that you eat everything. The sun is shining today,' he said. He didn't know why he said it. It wasn't even true. He was simply echoing his father's hopes in Sabbatai's future. Sabbatai stared at the tray.

'Eat,' Elijah said.

267

Then Sabbatai raised his eyes to him with a look of such paralysed helplessness, that his brother had to turn away. Gaunt that look, death-wishing, and unbearable to view. Elijah picked up the fork, scooped some food and put it gently into Sabbatai's mouth. Like a child, he opened it and fed. So they sat for a while, saying nothing, while Elijah fed his elder brother, the Messiah of God's choosing. He would wait until Sabbatai was finished then he would try to talk to him. 'Are you enjoying it?' he asked.

Sabbatai nodded with a hint of a genuine smile. When he had finished, Elijah asked if he wanted more.

'Later,' he said. 'I shall eat again. My appetite returns.'

He put his hand over Elijah's. It was cold, but the love in its touch was undisguisable. Elijah let it lie there, recalling his father's strange euphoria, and in sharing it, he began to understand. He took the tray away.

'What will you do?' he said.

'I shall be led to Constantinople. There is no other way. You know it.'

'But you have rights,' Elijah said. 'You are their leader.'

'Not any more,' Sabbatai said. 'The swell of the followers has almost drowned me. They keep me afloat as a symbol.'

'You must not let them,' Elijah said. 'You just must not let them.' He was almost weeping.

'It's too late,' Sabbatai said. The phrase was becoming an obligatory chorus.

'You keep saying that,' Elijah said, grasping a reason for anger, for anger was far easier to deal with than tears. 'What's going to happen? You will go to Constantinople and destroy us all.'

'Even you, Elijah,' Sabbatai said. 'You, who have never believed in me.'

'Yes, me,' Elijah shouted. 'Papa, too. We neither of us believe in you.'

'You are blind, both of you.'

Elijah stared at him. He saw how he straightened his body out of its slouch. He saw, too, a light in his eye, a hint of that old Messianic claim. He knew without touching him, that he was in fever. He grew angry at his own helplessness. Sabbatai was a battle not to be fought. He had tried often enough, he and his father. Sabbatai's fevers were deliberate. Punitive. He looked at him with contempt.

'D'you believe in yourself any more?' he asked. 'Tell me the truth if you can.'

The question was enough to make the fever rise, and with the fever, the self-assertion, the bliss of self-belief.

'I am the Messiah,' he shouted. 'I, Sabbatai Zvi, born on Tisha B'Av. If my people are destroyed, it is because God wills it. I am the mere tool of that destruction.'

It was too much for Elijah and he made to leave the room. On his way, his eye fell on the fork on Sabbatai's breakfast tray. He picked it up simply because it was there. And then, looking at it in his hand, its purpose was abundantly clear. He rushed at Sabbatai, grabbed his shoulder and held the fork at his throat. The prongs shivered on the adam's apple, and Elijah's hand trembled. It seemed to him that his brother's throat volunteered to the prongs as if in plea for the martyrdom of fratricide. Elijah dropped the fork and his whole body trembled.

'I didn't do anything,' he whispered. He would not look at his brother because he knew that there would be forgiveness in his eye. He had done nothing that called for pardon. He stumbled out of the room. On the landing he paused, panting for breath. He was sweating. He sniffed at himself. Whatever he had done or not done, or had or had not meant to do, he smelt like a killer, and he knew that Cain-like, he would carry that smell to his grave. He went to his room and locked himself inside. He could not bear to be seen by anybody.

Downstairs, they heard the prayer-rocking once more. Joseph was relieved. His brother, whatever his doubts and uncertainties, was at one with his God. Aunt Sarah heard the sound with little reaction, for the decision to stay with Mordecai, to let Nahum go forever, still tortured her. As for Mordecai, he still bathed in the love and the trust his son had shown him. It was a love that would last out the length of his days.

All that day, Sabbatai's close disciples called on him. Nathan came and went, and came again with the air of one who was about his business. The final move was in the air. At nightfall Elijah emerged from his room. He wanted to embrace his father but he felt unclean. Mordecai saw how wretched he looked and he himself took him in his arms.

'We have done all we can,' he said. 'Whatever we have done, we have done out of love. Sabbatai knows it. What he says is true. He cannot help himself. And so we cannot blame him. We can only love him.' He paused. 'I think he is going tonight,' he said. 'We will go with him to the shore. The sea is a good place for farewells,' he said, 'because it is also a place of return. Our love will bring him home. Believe me,' he said.

'Is Joseph going?' Elijah asked. He prayed that he would stay.

'Joseph will follow him,' Mordecai said, 'when he is called. But Sarah his wife will go. Her place is by Sabbatai's side.'

When night fell, Sabbatai left his room. Sarah was with him. As they descended the stairs, he laid his hand on her arm, like a king escorting his consort. The Messiah-light was once again firm in his eye, and the ring of fire that crowned his head was, even to the most heathen, undeniable.

'Will you come with us to the shore?' he asked.

Wordless, they followed him. Aunt Sarah, Joseph, Elijah and Mordecai. In his hands Mordecai clasped a velvet bag. The streets were deserted. The time of their departure had been kept a secret. Very softly Sabbatai started to sing a psalm. 'The King trusteth in the Lord, and through the memory of the most High, he shall not be moved.' No one joined in his song in fear of discord, for his voice haunted the air like an angel's. Over and over he sang his psalm until they reached the shore-line. Fishing-boats lay at anchor, rocking as if in prayer. But one amongst them was fully sailed, and Mordecai could discern the figure of Nathan amongst others on the boat. And David Arditti too. As they approached, Nathan was seen to wave. Sabbatai stopped and turned to his family. 'I love you all,' he said. 'Papa, Joseph, Elijah, Aunt Sarah. I want no farewells,' he said. 'We shall all meet again in Jerusalem.' Then he kissed them, one by one. First Aunt Sarah. 'Take care of my family,' he said. And to Joseph,'Look after them all.' To Elijah, 'I love you even more than you can imagine,' and finally to his father, whom he was loth to release from his embrace. 'I love you, Papa. Always remember that,' he said.

Mordecai handed him the velvet bag. 'It's my "tallis",' he said. 'I want you to have it. It was your grandfather's. He gave it to me when I left Patras. A prayer-shawl carries a blessing, Sabbatai, and that I give to you.'

Sabbatai held it and kissed it. Then he turned, taking Sarah's arm. They watched him as he helped her into the small caique, then turning, he waved, and Mordecai saw about his son the halo of light that would guide his passage to the Sultan's throne. They stood there until the boat rounded the bend of the shore-line, and they watched the still and empty sea for a long time thereafter. Then they turned and silently made for home.

Had a witness passed by who, unable to sleep, sought the solace of the still waters, he would have noticed how one of the fishing-boats rocked with a sudden acceleration. And how a figure, seemingly a fisherman, stood erect in its prow, gazing along the shore-line. And after a while, how he put out to sea, a small lantern guiding his way. The witness would have watched his passage awhile, and then continued on his somnambulant way, seeing nothing extraordinary in the sight, for fisherman were known to put out their boats occasionally at night to set their lobster-pots along the rocky coast. But lobster-potting was not on that fisherman's mind, for he was a fisherman only in the oil-skins that he wore. His goal was Constantinople, as was that of the boat that had preceded him. He would follow it like a sleuth, shadow its every tack and turn, and finally overcome it with his treachery.

Once out of sight of the shore-line, Saul hoisted his sail. His, like Sabbatai's, was a reluctant journey, but one which neither of them could forgo.

14

The arrest

'Poor Sabbatai. He is being led like a lamb to the slaughter. Do they care, I wonder, those disciples of his? Do they love him as I do? They love but the spirit of him. The symbol of him. The sweat of his fevers, the fire of his eye. But they do not know the flesh and the blood of him. They cannot know, for symbols have no flesh or blood. I am tempted so often to look upon him. Today I went to the synagogue. But Nathan came in his stead. I wanted to save him. But he is beyond my loving. I think Sabbatai is beyond himself. Sadness, sadness.'

Sabbatai set sail from Smyrna on December 30th, 1665. He was thirty-nine years old. The seas were heavy and the journey was slow. Sabbatai's caique was not conspicuous. It was one of many that plied the Aegean, mercantile crafts on their way to the Bosphorus. Most clung to the shore-line for shelter from the high winds. Amongst them, Saul's fishing-craft. He kept well behind Sabbatai's craft, but he held it always in his eyeline, day after day of their journey. At night the boats pulled ashore and their crews made for the ports' taverns for refreshments and provisions. As for Sabbatai, he stayed aboard, often alone, and prayed for a miracle. He felt utterly lost. Each night Nathan brought him news picked up from the ports' gossips. The Jews of Constantinople awaited his arrival with joy in their hearts. Already they were lining the quayside for a sight of his sail.

And like the Jews of Smyrna, they were prepared for their journey to Jerusalem. Nathan brought him, too, tales of miracles and voices and visions in the Ottoman capital. And how the prophet Elijah was seen wandering in the market-place. All this Nathan was told, and all this he believed, and he urged Sabbatai to believe it too. He did not give account of other stories he had heard. These he would leave to David Arditti, that loyal friend and disciple who, despite Nathan's warnings, would keep no secrets from his friend. David told of miracles too, and of the joy of the people, but he tempered that joy with stories of the fear and antagonism of his enemies. And not only of the Gentiles, but of Jews. Rabbis, infected by rumour from their brethren in Smyrna, fearful of their authority, had sent a deputation to the Grand Vizier and warned him of Sabbatai's intent. And more than that. They had demanded his death as a traitor. Even now the Vizier's guards were patrolling the coast-line for a sight of their craft.

'They will not dare to touch you,' Nathan said.

'Nathan is right. God will stay their hand,' David added.

They huddled together under the canvas. They were silent. All were afraid. But none more than Sabbatai. He tried to reason with himself. If he were truly the Messiah, then God would protect him. He welcomed the fever that was growing upon him, for it signalled the onset of self-assurance. 'I *am* the Messiah,' he said to himself. 'I have to be, or my life is worth nothing.' So he recapped on all his qualifications, dwelling on them at length, not just the facts of them, but their matter.

He hummed his psalm, 'The king trusteth in the Lord', then he slept.

In the morning light Sarah crept back into the boat, her arms full of provisions and her bodice ajar with her earnings. She covered him gently and lay by his side for she knew he loved the smell of strangers upon her.

Day after day they sailed, sheltering when the sea was too rough. When they took cover, Saul did likewise. At a distance. He longed to reach the capital and get his mission over and done with. He was not afraid that the passing of time would engender a change of heart. He was resolved and nothing would shake him. Not even the profound love that drew him to the man he would betray. Because betrayal was the prime factor, and no love on earth could satisfy that primal need. For he had betrayed his father, and in surviving had found a happiness of sorts. His survival itself was rude enough, but his happiness was unpardonable. He would betray that man who had given him joy and settle accounts with his father. And when it was all done, he would join his lost family. Sometimes, when the winds favoured his direction and the seas were calm, they would carry the sound of Sabbatai's psalm. Saul would listen with love and nostalgia, and he would join with him in distant descant. Across the sea he could hear the sound of the psalm from other boats echoing across the water, Sabbatai's followers from all the coastal towns where Nathan and David had called. Few could resist the compulsion to follow him, and as they neared the Sea of Marmara, the waters were studded with an Armada of faith, crooning its way to redemption.

The capital buzzed with expectation. And unease. Ahmed Köprülü, the Vizier, had taken heed of the Rabbis' warnings. In the absence of Sultan Mehmed IV, who was at the war-front in Crete, he had the sole responsibility of dealing with the trouble-maker. His spies in Smyrna had sent a description of Sabbatai's craft, but since it was a boat like any other, and there were so many of them on the high seas, it could hardly lead to his apprehension. But he sent his armed boats into the Marmara Sea, and his patrols to the shore-line. He had no idea what he would do once Sabbatai was captured, and he half-hoped that he would manage to give his men the slip.

And for the first few days, Sabbatai did just that. It was not difficult. There were so many boats in the area and he could have been on any one of them. He actually watched one of the patrol boats passing by, and he heard an officer call his name into the blue, demanding his surrender. But he was not afraid. He was the Messiah. Untouchable. When night came, the patrol-boats dropped anchor. Nathan suggested they sail onwards. The sea was calm and they were unlikely to be heard. In the daytime they would take cover. Thereafter, until they reached the capital they would sail only by night.

For the next few days this was the procedure. They used the daytime for hiding and sleeping in the coves. During this time Saul never lost sight of them. He, too, rested when they did, and sailed with them through the night. Then one morning they reached Lapseki, a small port on the west bank of the Marmara, lying on its most narrow stretch. On the other side of the bank, almost opposite, lay the port of Gallipoli. Early that morning, as light was beginning to break, Saul saw how Sabbatai's boat crawled into a cove. He lowered his sail and lingered in its shadow. He saw the figures of Nathan and David step ashore, as they did nightly, making their way to the inland village for news. Then shortly afterwards he watched Sarah climb from the boat with her basket for provisions and her cloak for her pleasure. And suddenly he was overcome with such longing and such a hunger for his love. He tried to contain it, to wrap its fever inside the raging ghosts of his father, his mother and his sisters, but all shadows of them melted in his hungry fire. He set sail for the cove. He moored alongside and stepped softly on to Sabbatai's craft.

'Sabbatai,' he whispered. That name, forever hanging on his lips, now exploded like a tear-drop. 'Sabbatai,' he called, again and again, while his heart wept with joy.

Wrapped in his prayer-shawl, Sabbatai listened, and wondered that his name had entered his prayers. God had called him yet again. Saul knelt by his side and touched him. Sabbatai, long-acquainted with the finger of God, knew that this was no divine touch. But a touch he knew as even more beautiful. He dropped the prayer-shawl from his face and looked at that face that in its years-long absence had never left him.

'Saul,' he whispered. Then he folded him into his shawl and lay him on the deck. Then covering his body with his own, he impaled him on his divine sword and together they cried their joy to heaven. Then Sabbatai kissed him gently.

'Go. Wait for me in Constantinople,' he said, 'and together we shall go to Jerusalem.'

Saul stood and lifted Sabbatai to his feet. 'I love you,' he said. 'Beyond all loving.' Then he held his face in his hands and planted his lips on his. As he kissed him his lips cooled, as slowly his father's ghost assumed dominion. He shivered and squeezed Sabbatai's hand and with no word of parting he boarded his own craft.

As he sailed out of the cove, under its perfect cover of overhanging rock, he heard the approach of the patrol-boat. But it was a distant sound and he had sailed well past the cove before it came into sight. He heard the officer call Sabbatai's name. Then Saul started to sing his victim's psalm. He sang it until he reached their boat, then, drawing up alongside, he shouted, 'I can take you to where he is.'

'Who are you?' one of them asked.

The lingering print of Sabbatai's mouth now bled on Saul's lips.

'I am my brother's keeper,' he said.

'Show us then.'

Saul turned his sail and they followed him. In time he reached their hiding-place. Then, pointing in its direction, he sailed past it, turned once more, and made his way to the capital. As he passed the hiding-place on his return, he heard many voices, and above them all, the angelic plea of the one who proclaimed himself King.

Sabbatai offered no resistance. In many ways he welcomed the arrest. He regarded it as a natural station on his crusade. He refused Nathan's offer to accompany him, bidding him go to Constantinople and preach on his behalf.

'We are in sight of Jerusalem,' he said.

The soldiers put him in chains. That, too, he relished. For the first time he felt physically equipped for his role. His spirit was high, as was his fever. He practically led his captors into their boat.

They took him across the narrow strait to Gallipoli and, without ceremony, threw him in the dungeons. With this last splendid humiliation, Sabbatai's conviction reached its peak.

'I am the true one,' he said to himself. 'Inviolate.'

He did not know how many days he lay there. Neither did he care. He was high on prayer and fasting. They brought him food at regular intervals, but he left the plates untouched. His guards thought he might be bent on a slow suicide, and after a week they reported the matter to the Office of the Vizier.

Sabbatai Zvi and his Messianic claims had become a thorn in the Vizier's flesh. The capital was restive. Trade and merchandising, in which Jews played a major part, had come to a standstill. An hysteria of faith had emptied the market-place and lined the quayside with expectation. And then there were the Rabbis who hammered at his office urging him to take radical steps against the impostor. But the Vizier knew better than to make a martyr of Sabbatai Zvi. He ordered his chains to be removed, and his transfer to private quarters in the prison. A decent bed, and food of his choice. He was to be treated as an honoured visitor. He prayed that his prisoner would accept his generosity.

The guards entered the dungeons with a sudden air of deference. When they attempted to unlock Sabbatai's chains, he brushed them aside.

'It is part of my role,' he told them.

But when they informed him that on the orders of the Vizier he was to be removed from the dungeons and treated as an honoured guest, Sabbatai relented and thanked God for answer to his prayers. For such treatment could only be accorded to one whose mission would be received with respect and honour. In time he knew he would meet with the Sultan, who would joyfully join him in his crusade.

But the Vizier would save the Sultan from such a meeting. He himself would deal with the renegade.

News spread around the city of Sabbatai's luxurious quartering. The disciples rejoiced, and the Rabbis were stunned. Many of them prepared to leave the capital and to look elsewhere for reinforcements. Meanwhile, Nathan's boat docked in the harbour, and with it a flotilla of followers. News was brought to him of Sabbatai's state and immediately he sought to visit him. But he was refused. Even Sarah was turned away by the guards.

So the prophet went about his master's business in the streets of the capital. He acquired three white horses and bade Sarah dress as a queen. She rode between himself and David Arditti and their sheer silent presence on the streets sent their followers into states of trance. There was singing from the crowd – the Twenty-first Psalm was their Saviour's song – and with it they confirmed his leadership and their own worship. Word came back to the Vizier. Now he regretted his move. Whether martyred or not, Sabbatai Zvi was a profound disturbance. He decided to summon him to his presence.

Sabbatai was called in the middle of prayer. He dismissed the guards, upbraiding them for their interruption. Bewildered, the guards withdrew. The man had some authority in his voice and, though Moslem, they suddenly understood his following. They waited outside his room in silence. Eventually he called them. They told him he was summoned to the Vizier. To this end, he put on his white kaftan. One of the guards swore he saw a halo of light around his head. He fell to his knees.

'What they say is true,' he said.

'What do they say?' Sabbatai asked.

'That you are the Chosen One.'

'Then follow me,' Sabbatai said, 'and you will be redeemed.'

He took it as a good omen. If the Vizier's guard believed in him, it was but a short step to the Sultan. He practically floated into the Vizier's chamber.

He made no obeisance. He simply wished him a good day, and hoped that he was well in health. Then he took a seat, and waited for the conversation to begin.

The Vizier was disarmed by his innocence. And puzzled, too. Was it possible that this man did not know that his intentions in the capital were punishable by death?

'Sabbatai Zvi,' he began, 'your fame has spread abroad. What is your mission in Constantinople?'

'I am to offer the great Sultan conversion to the faith of Judaism,' he said.

The Vizier tried to hide a smile. The man's outspokenness was part and parcel of his innocence.

'To what purpose?' he asked.

'So that the land of Palestine and its holy capital of Jerusalem shall belong to the Jews.'

The Vizier took care not to ask of Sabbatai his alternative, should the Sultan refuse conversion. He knew the answer and he did not want this man, in all his naïveté, to admit to sedition and condemn himself out of his own mouth. Besides, Sabbatai fascinated him. His fluent Arabic was impressive along with his compelling beauty and his innocent faith.

'What proof have you that you are the true Messiah?' he asked.

'The scrolls that have been discovered in my name do not call for proof. God sends me visions and voices which tell me what to do.'

'What are they like, these voices? What is their sound?'

'They have no sound. They are vibrations.'

'And your visions? What do they look like?'

'They are not anything you see. They are something you feel. A deaf man could hear my voices, and a blind one see my visions.'

'But why you? Why Sabbatai Zvi above all others?'

Sabbatai trembled. The man was stealing his very own self-questioning. His hesitation was not lost on Köprülü.

'Do you have doubts sometimes?'

'Of course I have doubts.' Sabbatai raised his voice. 'All holy men have doubts. They have to. Otherwise their piety would be arrogance.' He would make a virtue of doubting. It was the only way to deal with it.

Köprülü allowed a silence between them. Then after a while, 'Do you favour martyrdom?' he asked.

'All religions have their martyrs,' Sabbatai said.

'But you personally? You, Sabbatai Zvi?'

'If God willed it so,' Sabbatai said.

'Are you prepared?'

Sabbatai trembled again. He did not like this man. 'I hope God will help me,' he said.

'You may well have to call upon Him.' Köprülü smiled to offset the threat of his remark. He rose, signalling that the meeting was at an end. Sabbatai did not trust his feet. He trembled so. 'May I see my wife?' he dared to ask.

'Of course. I will arrange it.'

Sabbatai rose slowly. He did not want this man to see him weakening. With a supreme effort, he affected his Messianic gait and walked to the door. He felt Köprülü's gaze burning into his back. Once outside the door, he crumpled. The guard who had knelt before him helped him to his feet. This sign of human frailty in the face of earthly power only served to increase his credulity. He escorted him to his quarters and suggested that he sleep a while. Sabbatai recalled his father's words: 'Sleep is a way of forgetting.' But it was difficult to rest easy in the shadow of the gallows. He tried to stop himself trembling. He longed for Saul and solace. Lately, he noticed, Saul had never been out of his thoughts. He knew that somehow Saul was trying to reach him. There was no doubt in his mind that the whole world knew where the Messiah languished and he wondered why Saul did not seek him out. He lay on his bed and induced visions to heighten his fever. For if his fever were high enough, it would cancel out fear. But he felt no visions, and throbbed with no voices. He rose and for the first time he opened the velvet bag that his father had given him and he wrapped the prayer-shawl around his body. He crouched in the corner, covering his head.

'I am not he. I am not he,' he whispered to himself. His father was right. His prayer-shawl confirmed it with its warmth. He slipped his arm on to his back in mourning lullaby, and he rocked himself back into his infancy.

The Vizier was pleased with the interview. He knew that Sabbatai had been shaken. But the man had impressed him with his innocence. He preferred to think that his crusade to convert the Sultan was but a metaphor for his own fantasies. The man was harmless.

Yet he had to temper the mob's enthusiasm. So he put it out that, in the course of time, Sabbatai Zvi would stand trial for sedition. They would know that such a charge, if proven, carried the death penalty. That should cool their zealous heels a little. At the same time, he would allow his prisoner visitors. In the mob's view, that would heighten the perils of their leader's situation. And the lush apartments too. They could regard it all as a last fling. On the whole, Köprülü was mightily pleased with himself and his manoeuvrings.

When news was conveyed to Nathan, he took to the streets to cheer the people. He told them that he would see their leader and asked for a message that he could take from his followers. Their response was a mixture of wails and rejoicing.

'God is with him,' they shouted. 'No harm will come to him.'

Armed with this reassurance, Nathan made his way to the Vizier's palace, together with Sarah and David. He would have preferred to go alone. He had no idea of Sabbatai's state of mind, but whether high or low, he knew that he was the only one who could handle him. For they were both so alike. In front of Sarah and David, Sabbatai might hold his tongue or, like a madman, give vent to his torment. But they had insisted on coming.

'I wish Saul were here,' Sarah had said, for whatever Nathan's influence, she knew that only Saul could touch Sabbatai's heart. It was not logic he needed. Nor argument. Nor even solace. He wanted love, and only Saul could give him that. David had taken her aside, out of Nathan's hearing.

'But don't you understand,' he said to her, 'that I love him too?'

'So do I,' Sarah said. 'But it's Saul he pines for.' David's confession saddened her. She felt very close to him.

'God is not enough!' David said.

For the first time she heard anger in his voice.

'For some it has to be enough,' she said. 'For people like you and me. For followers, for disciples. For people who cannot bear to know themselves. Who can only bear the reflection of others. That's how it has been for me all my life. They taught me in that convent that I was nothing. But that I could reflect the glory of another. That other was Christ, they told me. So I went looking for the Messiah. And now I live in his shadow. As you do. It has to be enough for us.'

'It wasn't enough for Saul!'

'Saul was not a true disciple,' Sarah said. 'He was looking for his own way, and he was lost.'

'Then he is dead, I think,' David said. 'Death was the only way he could find himself.'

'You must not speak of him to Sabbatai,' Sarah said. 'Sabbatai lives in hope.'

'I think Sabbatai will speak of him himself,' David said.

David was right. 'Saul' was the first word to drop from Sabbatai's lips. 'Saul?' he queried, as he heard his door open.

They found him crouched in the corner, his body wrapped in his father's 'tallis'. He did not look at them, nor even turn his head, but he knew from the pulse of them that, whoever they were, none of them was Saul.

'It's Nathan.' The prophet was first to introduce himself. 'Sarah is with me,' he said. 'And David.' Nathan was appalled by his master's despair. He knew that posture well. Sabbatai's life had become a veil between himself and reality. The shroud of 'tallis' confirmed it. His spirit was breaking and he was desperately trying to hold the pieces of it intact in the wrapping of his father's prayer-shawl. Nathan could have wept for him.

'The multitude send their worship to you,' he said. 'God will protect you. You will come to no harm.'

'Where is Saul?' Sabbatai pleaded.

No one of them answered. For it was not a question. Sabbatai was talking to himself. Slowly he uncovered his face and looked at them, though he did not budge from his cowering place.

'Lately I have had many visions,' he said.

Nathan allowed himself a little hope. If the visions had returned, so had his Messianic belief in himself.

'Visions of Saul,' Sabbatai added.

Then Nathan knew that they were no divine visions. They were fantasies of love-sickness, day-dreams of wishful thinking. The kind of 'visions' that can be induced by the most ordinary of men. Nevertheless, Sabbatai had given him an opening for conversation.

'What kind of visions?' Nathan asked. 'Describe them to us.'

Sabbatai stirred and straightened himself a little, and Nathan noticed the known and loved rays of fever in his eye. 'I stood on a rock,' Sabbatai began. 'Always the same rock. Overlooking the sea. Not far away there is another rock, and standing on its peak there is a figure. I stare at it and, without doubt, it is I. It is I as a young boy. He looks at me in horror at what I have become. And I look at him, ashamed.'

Nathan went towards him and dared to put his hand on his shoulder. But Sabbatai quickly brushed it off.

'The vision is not ended,' he said. 'The figure of the boy slowly changes. It is Saul. As I first saw him. Up for sale on the rock. And I know that he has always been there. He *is* the boy I was. He is the man I have become. He is me and I am him. And then the figure changes yet again. Back into the young boy. He looks at me and I at him, over the great divide of years, over the chasm of pain and loneliness, filled to the brim with God, and we smile a little at each other, for we know that neither of us is to blame.' He paused, then looked directly at them, into each face, pointedly and with infinite patience. 'Where is Saul, d'you think?' he said.

'He will come,' Sarah said. 'He will hear where you are. He will come to you. I know it.' But the more she confirmed it, the less her confidence in its truth. Saul had betrayed him. That was his role. And Sabbatai knew it as well as she herself. She crouched beside him and touched his arm. He did not rebuff her.

David approached and crouched on Sabbatai's other side. He put his arms about him and Sabbatai buried his head in his lap.

Nathan looked at them, that unholy trinity, and he felt an outsider. He said nothing but sat apart. He rubbed his hand against the satin covering of the chair's arm, for the first time noticing the luxury of Sabbatai's quarters. The floor was of white marble, scattered with Persian rugs of deep and rich pile. The bed was canopied in silk and the tables and chairs inlaid with ornate marquetry. Yet in all this luxury, Sabbatai Zvi, his leader, the people's Saviour, the Redeemer of the whole world, crouched like a black cockroach in the corner on the floor. He would say nothing about that to the people. Instead, he would tell them of Sabbatai's apartment, and he memorised every detail of its luxury, the more to authenticate his tale. But he was sick at

287

heart, for he knew that Sabbatai's faith was on the wane, in himself as well as in God, and that he was not strong enough to endure a trial and certainly not its possible consequences. He prayed fervently for Sabbatai's renewal of faith.

They sat for a long while in silence, broken only by Sabbatai's sighs. Then he said, 'Go now. I want to be alone. I need to pray.'

It was a hopeful sign, Nathan thought, and encouraged him to ask of Sabbatai if he had any messages for his followers.

'Tell them to pray for me,' he said.

But Nathan would not tell them that. Such a message smacked of helplessness and abdication. It was a begging message, unfit for a Messiah to relay. 'Is there more?' Nathan asked.

'Find Saul for me,' Sabbatai begged. 'I am naked without him.'

'. . . so I betrayed him, Judas-like. Out of sheer love. Even as Judas did. I felt no euphoria of revenge. That was not my intent. For how can I, an obscene survivor, entertain thoughts of revenge? I wanted him taken. I wanted to force his mission. I wanted to see him crowned, even if it be with thorns. Then I can cease my witnessing. I watched him enter the boat with his captors. I sailed as near as I dared. He accepted his arrest with gladness, as if it had been a gift. I should have sailed on. My work was done. But his work? His fulfilment furled my sails. I idled there for a while. Then I followed him to the shore. Dear God, when will my witnessing be done?'

15

A death in season

Ever since Sabbatai had left Smyrna, the harbour had been lined with followers awaiting his return. Even when news came through of his arrest, they waited there still, or took turns with their vigil. Those men who worked during the day took the night-watch; the daylight hours were the sentry-shift for women and children. Over the weeks the town of Smyrna assumed an air of normality. Trading returned to its brisk pace. Fish were brought out of the sea and crops harvested from the land. The market-place buzzed as of old. But in every Jewish household, a bag was packed ready for departure. Except in the house of Sabbatai Zvi.

In Aunt Sarah's room an empty valise lay open on the floor, a reflection of her own tormented indecision. She knew that Nahum and Lusi were prepared for their departure. The news of Sabbatai's arrest had come as no surprise to Nahum. But it had driven Lusi to further frenetic packing. Joseph was taken prisoner in Egypt, she had said, yet he emerged victorious. And how can we hope to see our Messiah free, unless he is first in chains? Nahum could not deal with her logic. Only with tenderness. His wife was as mad as her Saviour.

'Supposing he is in prison for years and years?' he suggested.

'We will go in any case,' Lusi said. 'We will prepare for his coming.'

Her intentions were shared by most of the Jews in Smyrna.

No iron bars would delay their passage. They would wait for the trial to be over and done with, and then, whatever its outcome, they would make sail.

'But supposing he is put to death?' Nahum had insisted.

Lusi shivered. 'He will return again,' she said. 'He is the Messiah.'

So he let it lie, and stroked her hand as she parcelled their future.

Meanwhile, Aunt Sarah's case lay open and empty. Her dilemma did not lie in whether or not she should follow Sabbatai. She believed in him out of love rather than faith. She loved him for the miracle of her mother, and for his acknowledgment of her time-honoured love. Her faith did not stretch to rationalising his incarceration. She could not accept the logistics of martyrdom. No. Her dilemma lay in whether or not she should follow Nahum, and the open and empty suitcase said it all.

In Joseph's room, the travelling chest was strapped down. He, like Lusi, in whatever circumstances, would travel. But in Elijah's room, and in Mordecai's, there was no sign of departure. Since Sabbatai's leave-taking, Mordecai had changed and with a change that bewildered his family. For the first time Elijah could remember, except for isolated incidents in his childhood, he saw his father in a state of permanent and constant happiness. He seemed not to worry about Sabbatai's future. Even the news of his arrest had only for a moment fazed him. Then he seemed almost grateful, as if he had expected it. He did not worry about Sabbatai. His father's prayer-shawl would succour him even as it had led himself into survival. In that category of faith Mordecai was not lacking, in that faith in continuity and a respect for the past. Since Sabbatai's departure he had understood that continuity was guaranteed less by faith than by love: the love his son had shown him before his final mission. That love would make the past forgivable, and would sustain him for the rest of his days. Which was why Mordecai dwelt in near-euphoria. Though it pleased

Elijah to witness his father's happiness, he feared it too, for it seemed to presage withdrawal. During these days he watched him very carefully.

Their daily life followed its erstwhile routine. Mordecai and Elijah would go together into the city into the business of merchandising and transaction. En route they would often pass through the market-place, and would bear witness to Raphael the idiot, his travelling bag under his arm, on call for salvation, yet roaring his ominous prophecy. 'Beware of false prophets,' he called, stopping at each stall in repetition, then having covered the alley, he would retrace his steps, bellowing with the consequences of such false faith. 'Which come to you in sheep's clothing, but inwardly they are ravening wolves.' After one round he would pause, accept a coin from a passer-by, or even a sweetmeat, and occasionally he would suffer a pat on the head, knowing that for most people he was only bearable if viewed as a child. Mordecai and Elijah passed on, both heartily agreeing with him, yet keeping their mouths firmly closed.

'What news of Sabbatai Zvi?' people called after them.

'We know only what you know,' Mordecai told them, and smiled as if they had congratulated him. For all he thought of now was Sabbatai's declared love and that was triumph worthy of congratulation.

'They keep talking about Sabbatai's arrest,' Mordecai said to Elijah. 'If they truly believe in him, they should rejoice. At some time or another he must be captured. All Messiah stories have their chapter on arrest.'

'But does it not worry you?' Elijah asked.

'I am not worried for Sabbatai,' Mordecai said. 'He will survive. But for me perhaps. I am worried about me. Not worried exactly. But it will mean a change.'

'What does that mean?' Elijah tried to hide his alarm.

'I don't understand it myself,' Mordecai said. 'I just feel it.'

They walked on through the market-place.

'Are you not well, Papa?' Elijah asked.

'You mustn't worry, Elijahle,' his father said.

But Elijah was worried, and when they reached their offices, he took his father's coat, and held him at arm's length and studied him. He looked well enough. His colour was good. Even a bloom of youth had touched his cheeks. And his stance. Erect. Energy-brimming.

'Let's get to work,' Mordecai said. He lifted a huge pile of ledgers from the floor and when Elijah went to help him, he brushed him aside. 'I'm not an old man yet,' he laughed. Nor ever will be, he thought to himself, for old age was not what he had in mind. His health, or rather lack of it, was on his side. What Elijah had taken for the bloom of youth on his father's cheeks was in reality one of the symptoms of a rapid pulse and Mordecai knew that he should take the utmost care, do nothing that would exert his strength and, above all, that he should rest daily. These were precautions easily ignored, and Mordecai sought every opportunity to infringe them. He would tire himself out lifting, bending, running even and then give himself no pause for rest. He took infinite enjoyment in the constant risk. He was not even daring Death. He was inviting it. And for a very simple reason. He wanted to die before love soured, that filial love that Sabbatai had so simply declared. He feared for his son. He feared for his very life. He did not think that he would have the courage to endure Sabbatai's ignominy. He would sooner die a coward, but sure and steadfast in the love of his son. So he exerted himself as much as he could and cared not for the consequences. He did not know when Sabbatai would be brought to judgment, but he intended to do his very best to die before the trial.

Whilst Elijah was content to assume that life had returned to normal, Joseph found it difficult to return to the work routine. Every day he would go down to the harbour hoping for a message with the latest news of Sabbatai. Often he thought of making sail for Gallipoli. It was for his own sake and comfort that he wanted to go. But he feared for his father. Unlike Elijah, he was not fooled by his father's flushed cheeks. He knew they presaged peril. He knew, too, of his father's fears for Sabbatai and of his terror of confronting the dangers he was in. Often he wondered whether he should interfere and insist on his father's retirement. But should Sabbatai fail, and die as a result, the vision of his father's pain was unbearable. It was his father's life and indeed his death, to do with them what he willed. So he stood aside and watched helplessly as his father went about his dying.

Then something ominous happened. A sign of deep foreboding. The Rabbis returned to Smyrna. They had travelled to Constantinople, and through various channels had won the ear of the Vizier, warning him of the threat to the great Sultan's throne. Most of the Rabbis of the capital had given them their support, fearing not only the Sultan's overthrow, but the massacres that would ensue. Now, having ensured Sabbatai's imprisonment, and in the knowledge of his impending trial, the outcome of which was his sure and certain death, they had slunk back to Smyrna in all their smugness, and waited for the moment when they could chorus, 'I told you so.'

They went back to the synagogues to conduct services, but their congregations were sparse, and many of those who attended were simply spies from Sabbatai's camp. Raphael the idiot was a regular attendant, and although he was on the Rabbis' side, he volunteered as an informer. For it was important to keep the fires burning. Without the threat of Sabbatai's crusade, his prophetic warnings were irrelevant. So he played his part in kindling the flames of discord even to the point of invention.

As the day of the trial approached, Sabbatai's followers, no doubt frightened by rumours of its dire result, grew panicky and set out to silence all those who spoke against their Saviour. To this end they lined up outside the synagogues before each service, and chanted abuse at all those who entered. The abuse led to stone-throwing, so that even Raphael the idiot, their effective double-agent, refused to cross the line. The Rabbis ended up praying to each other. But it was a dubious victory. It did nothing to lessen the fears of the followers.

News came across the waters that the trial had been delayed. It gave them a breathing space, but no more. For the reasons for the deferment were ominous. The trial would await the return of the Sultan from his wars with Crete. His required presence rendered Sabbatai's judgment a show-trial. There could be only one outcome, and that tragedy would serve as a warning to anyone who sought, for whatever purpose, to threaten the throne.

Across Europe, baggage lay strewn on the port-sides where thousands of Jews waited. Some had heard the news of the delay, others were ignorant even of the trial, but all were burning with a hope fuelled by their craving to believe. Even some Rabbis were amongst them, having given up the battle, or offered themselves for genuine conversion. And there was a sprinkling of Raphaels too, for every movement had its prophets of doom.

The Passover was approaching and the advent of that festival gave cause for a little cheer. For did it not celebrate the release from exile and the subsequent journey to the Promised Land? Sabbatai's followers ignored the Rabbis and held services in their own homes. That key-note of the 'Haggadah' had never been more pertinent. 'In every generation each man must regard himself as if he himself had gone forth from Egypt.' Never before in their history had that injunction rung a more congruous bell. And 'next year in Jerusalem' was no longer a wish, a hope or a dream. Now it was a certainty. So they gave thanks as never before and ate of forbidden fruits in their celebrations, as Sabbatai had ordered them to do. But despite their celebrations, despite their faith that seemed not to waver, the shadow of Sabbatai's approaching trial darkened their souls.

The Jews of Smyrna were more privy than most to the latest developments in Gallipoli, for Nathan's spies and messengers were everywhere. But even the most fervent of them could find few loopholes for optimism. There were no baggage-laden pilgrims to be found on the Smyrna harbour, only those spying out the sea and waiting for boats that carried the latest news. Amongst them, Joseph. Occasionally Elijah accompanied him, but they avoided all talk of their father. And in avoiding that topic, it was easy not to talk of Sabbatai. So they exchanged childhood reminiscences, avoiding those events in which Sabbatai had played a role. Thus they spoke of their years together in the Hebrew school, when Sabbatai was already in the Seminar. They spoke of their mother too, and grandmother, and speculated on the past and future of Aunt Sarah. They marvelled at how easy it was to talk together without reference to Sabbatai who had seemingly dominated every moment of their lives. Slowly the whole issue of their elder brother assumed a smaller significance. It was as if they were preparing for a future without him. Over the next few weeks, while Sabbatai languished in his so-called prison, the two brothers grew close together for the very first time in their lives. But still not close enough to talk about their father. For both, with or without reason, were terrified of losing him.

One evening, when Joseph and Elijah were walking along the quay-side, a boat sailed into harbour carrying one of Nathan's emissaries. He seemed in haste to come ashore. He clearly had fresh tidings. The brothers ran to secure the boat and help the messenger to the quay-side.

'There is news,' he told them. 'Neither good nor bad. The trial has been postponed yet again. The Vizier has been called to join the Sultan in the wars on Crete. Before his departure, he ordered that Sabbatai be transferred to the fortress of Gallipoli, a prison reserved for political prisoners. The treatment is harsh there, I am told. I tell this to you because you are his brothers,' the man said, 'but it is better, Nathan believes, that it should not be widely known.'

A crowd had begun to gather and the man drew the brothers aside. 'Let us meet somewhere, where we will not be disturbed,' he said.

'There is nowhere,' Joseph said, 'where we will not be followed. Tell them that you have returned to Smyrna for family reasons. They will go away, then we can walk along the shore for a while. What's your name?'

'Emmanuel,' the man replied. 'I have followed the Saviour from Gaza.'

He turned to address the crowd and told them that there was no news.

'But have you seen him?' the people insisted.

'Not I,' he said. 'Nathan the prophet sees him. And Sarah, our queen. He is well in spirit. He asks you to be patient, and sends his blessings.'

It had to be enough for them, and most of them straggled to their homes. Emmanuel and the brothers turned in the opposite direction and walked along the quay-side. They were silent for a while. Then Emmanuel stopped and faced them.

'You must forgive me,' he said. 'But I must ask you a question. I have known about and believed in your brother for many years. Whatever happens to him, I shall remain his disciple. I love him as you must do. But there are some things I do not understand, so forgive me please, but I must ask you a question.'

'What is it?' Elijah said, sensing full well the nature of the man's unease.

Emmanuel paused, then looked at them both directly. 'Is there . . . is there . . . anything . . . wrong with your brother? Your brother Sabbatai Zvi?'

'Wrong?' Elijah asked. He did not think Joseph was able to handle the questioning.

'He seemed to be in a strange state of mind,' Emmanuel said. It was as far as he dared go. Elijah would have let it lie, but for Joseph it was not enough.

'What exactly do you mean?' he persisted.

298

Then Emmanuel threw all politic to the winds. 'He may be mad,' he said.

'You are no disciple,' Joseph said. 'You do not understand that Sabbatai is divinely inspired. Few mortal men, very few,' he insisted, 'stand in direct communication with God, and when they do, they respond in a manner which to us ordinary people would seem unnatural. Insane, even. But my brother dwells on a different dimension. The norms are different there.'

Elijah stared at his brother in astonishment. He had accepted Joseph as a blind and loyal believer. He had not expected him to have formulated a rationale for his belief. Now he understood why Sabbatai's lunacy did not pain him.

'I will follow him,' Emmanuel said, 'to the ends of the earth. But at times he behaves in a way that I cannot understand. Now you have helped to explain it all. I have been blind. I have expected of him as I have expected of other men. But as you say, he is not like other men.' Emmanuel appeared to be satisfied, but Elijah's curiosity was aroused.

'What did he do that was so strange?' he asked.

'Do you want to know?' Emmanuel's question was directed at Joseph.

'Only if you need to tell me,' Joseph replied.

Emmanuel put his hand on Joseph's arm. 'Brother,' he said, 'I need to speak. It is *my* need. You are right.'

'Then tell us,' Joseph said.

'I confess that I have seen him,' Emmanuel said. 'I was with him when news came through of the transfer. Nathan was there too. And David and Sarah. Sabbatai Zvi was crouching in the corner. He had been sitting like that, Nathan told me, for many days. He said one phrase, over and over again. "I am not entire. I am not entire." That was all. Crouched in the corner. Shrouded in his "tallis".'

'Is that what you mean by "wrong"?' Joseph asked.

'That's only the beginning,' Emmanuel said. 'After a while, a messenger came into the room. He approached Sabbatai and addressed him in a whisper. It was a long message that none of us, apart from Sabbatai, could hear. But we watched him as he uncovered his head and slowly rose, stretching himself to his full height. His face glowed with a wondrous light. I noticed particularly that he was sweating. Beads of perspiration prickled his forehead. But they didn't burst. They were static, like a rash. He dismissed the messenger with what sounded like a polite greeting. When he had gone, Sabbatai turned to us and spoke. His voice was human enough and that surprised me, for it seemed at odds with his god-like appearance. Yet he spoke with the tongues of men and of angels. "They are taking me to the fortress at Gallipoli," he said. "There is much work to do. Tomorrow is the Passover," he said. "You must bring me a lamb." "But how?" I asked. "You are a prisoner." He gave me money to bribe the guard and to buy all that was necessary for the sacrifice. I was worried. Our scriptures forbid any sacrifice outside the city of Jerusalem. But I remembered Sabbatai's order to do that which is forbidden. That evening, we accompanied him to the fortress. There were crowds of thousands. The sacrifice was made and Sabbatai went alone into the dungeons.'

He paused and looked at the brothers in bewilderment.

'But what do you mean by "wrong"?' Joseph insisted.

Emmanuel looked down at his feet. What he had to say was not easily conveyable. But it had to be said, if only for his own hearing. 'I think God is too much with your brother,' he said. 'I think God has driven him mad.'

Joseph put his hand on Emmanuel's arm. 'Sabbatai is different,' he said. 'I tell you again. He is not like other men. What appears madness in your eye is simply a divine illumination.'

'Yet I fear for him,' Emmanuel said.

'So do we all.'

There were other messengers besides Emmanuel, unofficial ones, those from the enemy camp, with news dire enough to set Raphael the idiot bellowing once more. They brought news of the dungeons into which Sabbatai Zvi had been thrown. And brought it with relish. The Rabbis were delighted. Sabbatai Zvi's violent downfall was now only a matter of time. They didn't need the synagogue for preaching, they decided. They would follow the example of Sabbatai Zvi and take their 'I-told-you-sos' into the streets.

They went in numbers for their own protection. One could not help but admire their courage. Their slogan was simple. 'We have returned to the laws of the Exile. Sabbatai Zvi was a false Messiah.' At first the disciples decided to ignore them, to bypass their oratory in the streets. Only Raphael the idiot came to listen, his baggage still arrogantly tucked under his arm.

'Put your bags away,' they told him. 'The laws of the Exile have returned.'

But they were uneasy. And humiliated. It was shameful to preach on street-corners with only a lunatic as audience, especially since that lunatic would go hot-foot to the enemy camp to report the Rabbis' singular lack of progress in their campaign. But still they persisted in the market-place and on the corners of the streets. Sabbatai's followers took to jeering at them while passing by, so that they became a public laughing-stock. This was more than the Rabbis could tolerate. They withdrew to revise their tactics.

The disciples called a meeting. In Sabbatai's absence they regarded Joseph as their leader. They found it difficult to ignore the Rabbis' jibes. They needed a boost to the faith. But Joseph prescribed caution. Sabbatai's imprisonment was a temporary state. As to his suffering, his brother accepted it was part of his role. The torture that was meted out to him only served to confirm his god-head.

'We must pray for him,' he told them, 'and keep his name forever on our lips. As to the Rabbis, they will tire. They will retreat to their empty classrooms and synagogues. They are the losers, and know it well.'

But Joseph was wrong. The Rabbis indeed retreated, but only to revise their strategy. As Joseph had said, they acknowledged a losing battle, and this acceptance only served to fuel their anger, and it was this overwhelming rage that dictated the nature of their subsequent attack. It was to be a campaign of slander, insult and vilification. *That* would make Sabbatai's sheep bleat a little. They took to the streets once more. They gathered in the market-place early on a Friday. It was crowded with shoppers preparing for the Sabbath. A captive audience. And with a monstrous curse on Sabbatai Zvi and his followers, they opened their account. At first the audience couldn't believe it, and they had perforce to listen hard to be sure of what they were hearing. Then when the message was quite clear, there was a silence which the Rabbis allowed to ensure that the curses had exploded and it was then, after the silence, that the first stone was thrown. It was aimed at the Rabbis' feet, and issued simply as a warning. And it worked. The worthy men took to their heels and ran, the air still echoing with their curses and then drowned by the laughter of their pursuers.

But the Rabbis were not deterred. They knew that curses on the name of Sabbatai Zvi could only incense his followers. They had already tasted their anger. And anger was better than indifference. It could possibly lead to dialogue and an eventual return to the proper faith. So they recruited bodyguards. No Jew would attend them, of whatever persuasion, so they enlisted a group of thieving vagabonds who were wont to haunt the market-place with knives and hammers. On the Rabbis' next sortie to the market-place on the following Friday, they could hardly be seen for the posse of hooligans that surrounded them.

But the followers were prepared. Joseph was with them, and he had instructed them to feign total indifference. To go about their business as if nothing untoward was happening, as if no terrible curses sounded in their ears, nor the unspeakable slandering of their Redeemer. An unconcerned neutrality was their most powerful weapon.

The Rabbis took up their position on a corner where their imprecations could be heard on all sides. 'We have come to

302

lay a curse on Sabbatai Zvi,' they shouted together, because there was safety in chorus. 'Cursed be he who seeks to destroy his people.'

The marketers went about their business though their ears were cocked for every slander. Then one of the Rabbis held up a piece of paper. 'I have a letter here from the Rabbis of Constantinople,' he declared. 'Listen, my friends, for it affects us all.' He held the letter high and the shoppers forbore to look, turning their backs on him, though listening all the while. 'The man Sabbatai Zvi,' they heard, 'against whose innovations we are protesting, must be regarded as an unbeliever, and any man who kills him will be received by God as though he had won a large number of souls. The hand that is raised to kill Sabbatai Zvi will be blessed by God and man.'

The Rabbis waited. They expected and almost hoped for a violent response. Surrounded by their loutish protectors, they felt secure. But their audience, though so sorely provoked, maintained their calm. So the missive was read again, thus doubling the threat. Another Rabbi read it this time, his voice louder and more menacing. Still there was no response, though the temptation was acute. This time the bodyguards became restless. Their natural role was one of provocation rather than protection, and their palms itched for a showdown. One of them picked up a stone and hurled it into the crowd. Of all the people in the market-place, it was Joseph, prominently placed in its centre and clearly the director of the proceedings, who was the obvious target. The stone caught him square on the jaw. It was a cue for the shoppers to drop the mask of indifference, to shed it with relief and to replace it with an outburst of rage. Their anger was sublime. They rushed to Joseph. The blood spurted from his cheek. They were horrified. Then the mob took the offensive and, behind the backs of their protectors, the Rabbis fled for their lives. They left behind them a raging battle.

A man in the crowd tore off his shirt and with it he dressed

Joseph's wound. Then with others, he helped him back to his house.

Only Aunt Sarah was at home. Mordecai and Elijah were in the city, ignorant of the clash in the market-place. Aunt Sarah was nurse once more as she had been to Sabbatai after Rabbi Eskapa's whipping. Joseph's wound looked unsightly, and Aunt Sarah feared that Mordecai, at the sight of it, would finally cast off that mask of contentment that he had worn ever since Sabbatai's departure. She dressed the wound carefully and tried to hide its ugliness. She asked him no questions. Just comforted him. Then went to prepare the Sabbath meal.

Mordecai and Elijah returned earlier than was usual. Word had come to their offices of the battle in the market-place, and for the first time in many months, Elijah noted a tinge of anger that further flushed his father's cheek. They made for home. Joseph had refused to lie down. He wanted to trivialise the incident in order to diminish the anger he expected from his father. But the wound was painful and made him giddy, and he was forced to take to his bed. Which was where his father found him on his return. And exploded.

'What happened?' he roared. Had he not already given one son to this madness? Of all Sabbatai's followers, was not he himself, he who did not believe, its greatest martyr? He took Joseph in his arms, that middle son of his, that innocent, and he let fall tears that had nothing to do with Joseph's wound, nor even with Sabbatai's imprisonment, nor yet for Elijah's painful filial loyalty, but for all the many years of loving that the three of them had engendered. He wept for the past, for his some-time neglect of that love. Now he would willingly drown in it. There was no smoother path to one's grave. And echoing the prophet Elijah's plea, 'It is enough, O Lord,' he cried. 'It is enough.'

They comforted him, and later he asked Joseph to tell him in detail of the events in the market-place. This Joseph was glad to do, because words between them lessened the pain of silence. When it was told, Aunt Sarah called them to supper. Ritual, like words, diminished the pain. They gathered together and said the blessing over the bread and wine, and in subdued piety they welcomed the Sabbath. After supper, they sat around the table for a while. It was memory time, in the safety and sadness of the past. As they recollected their childhood, Mordecai noticed how close the brothers had lately become, those two eclipsed siblings, and it pleased him. Yet the absence of Sabbatai's name in all their youthful recall hovered like a ghost over the table. It was as if he had been deliberately excluded. He had to bring it out. He had to say his name. He had to invite him to their Sabbath.

'Sabbatai is in the dungeons,' he said. 'And where is Saul?'

Thus it was out, uncovering the camouflage of all his pain. There was a silence round the table.

'I think Saul is dead,' Mordecai said.

'We will not mourn him yet,' Joseph said. It sounded like an order. In the absence of Sabbatai, he was suddenly in charge.

That night Mordecai did not sleep. He clung frantically to Sabbatai's last declaration of love. 'I love you, Papa,' he had said. He had heard it in his ears ever since, but of late its echo had waned. The passing of time does not change the *fact* of it, he told himself. But he needed the *sound*. The sound made it real. It was as if Sabbatai was still by his side. He cupped his ears, limiting the space for the words' exit, and by that means perhaps to sharpen their pitch, but they were faint, laden with murmur, as if they echoed from the very dungeons where Sabbatai slept. The thought of his present dwelling did little to lessen Mordecai's despair. He no longer wondered what would be the outcome of it all. He knew, and he knew too that he would not have the strength to endure it. Which was why he murmured, Elijah-like, that it was enough. He wanted to die before the sound of Sabbatai's words was drowned, if not by time, then by his own fading credulity. Over his prayers he slept, woke, prayed and slept again.

For many weeks now, Mordecai had refrained from going to the synagogue for the Sabbath service. He had not wanted to cross the line, for although he didn't believe in Sabbatai the Saviour, he had a desperate faith in Sabbatai as his son, and to cross the line would have seemed to him a betrayal of that faith, of that love. So he had conducted his own service with his family at home. But that morning, he felt a need for the synagogue. He longed for the Ark of the Covenant, the Scrolls of the Law. Joseph was feeling unwell, and Aunt Sarah insisted he kept to his bed. Elijah offered to accompany his father.

When they reached the synagogue, no protestors barred their way. They knew that the congregation was, in any case, sparse, and opposition was not worth their while. And they were right, for there was only a handful of worshippers inside. Mordecai would have wished for a crowded hall. Prayer was strengthened by community. It was sanctioned by crowd, its safe passage assured.

As he moved into the family pew, Mordecai was happy to recall their early days, when, all together, they went every Sabbath to pray. He looked up at the ladies' gallery, now totally empty, and thought he saw Clara there, with Grandma Beki. Indeed, he spent the whole service hardly heeding the Rabbi's prayers, recapturing those times when this venue had recorded the turning-points in all their lives. He knew that such recall would be painful. But he would not cheat on it. He would start at the very beginning and give each episode its right though anguished due. He saw Clara as a bride as he waited for her under the canopy. She walked down the aisle on her father's arm. Next to him stood Grandma Beki and Aunt Sarah. So young, all of them, with no trace in their faces of the pain that would follow. Clara stood by his side and he heard Rabbi Eskapa sing the blessings. Then he heard his own voice, 'Behold I am wedded to you according to the Laws of Moses and Israel.' Then the breaking of the glass under his foot, and the lifting of the veil and the kiss to seal his love. Not painful that episode, and Mordecai was emboldened to recall further. In the same pew with his friend Nissim Arditti by his side. The morning of Tisha B'Av. He recalled the great beam of light that streaked the Ark, his panicked return to the chicken-coops and his first sight of his son. He remembered his joy and he steeled himself to its aftermath. Yet he felt no sadness. Rather he felt at peace, his soul purged.

When the service was over, he hurried out of the synagogue. He did not wish for conversation, and certainly not for the greetings of the Rabbis who, although he believed as they did, did not cease to persecute his son. Elijah followed him, taking his restless arm. He was glad to see the flush on his father's cheek once more.

That evening when the Sabbath was over, the Rabbis came to visit. A group of them, shame-faced, repentant. Mordecai was polite though it was an effort for him. He welcomed them and invited them to partake of some sweetmeats. They readily accepted, hoping that a communal pursuit would ease the tension.

'Where is Joseph?' they asked. 'And how is he? We were sad to hear of his mischance.'

Elijah laughed. He knew that his father would not speak his mind, but somebody had to vent his anger on his behalf.

'My brother is in bed. He is not well,' he said. 'And it was no mischance.' He raised his voice.

'We are sorry,' one of the Rabbis said. 'But it was an accident. An unfortunate accident.'

'How can you be so smug?' Elijah shouted. 'You're cowards, all of you. My brother Sabbatai is a threat to you. He threatens your living. He threatens your power. That's why you hate him. Not, as you insist, because he threatens Judaism and the Jewish people. He threatens *you*, the whole rotten lot of you.'

During this outburst Mordecai said nothing. His silence sanctioned it. Occasionally Aunt Sarah gave a little cry, for although she hated the Rabbis, she harboured a residual respect for their calling, mindful of Jewish tradition. But even she made no move to stop Elijah. Their silence was collusion and it was not lost on the Rabbis.

'Your brother brought it on himself,' one of them said. 'There will be many more accidents. Deaths even, and all can be laid at Sabbatai's door. For years now he has been deceiving the people. Calling himself the Messiah. And why?' he shouted. 'Because of his lust for power. Because of his arrogance, his conceit. He has lied, he has forged, he has espoused corruption, filth and decadence. He has . . .' He stopped suddenly. Not because he had run out of abuse. Indeed his mouth was still chock-a-block full of vilification, but that he saw Mordecai rise slowly to his feet. The look on his face, of such overpowering rage, silenced him.

'Rabbi,' Mordecai began. His voice was a whisper, a deliberate choice, for he knew that what he had to say would end in a scream. 'Rabbi,' he said again, 'I am Sabbatai's father. I love him as a son. In that way I have always loved him. Like you, I do not believe he is the Saviour. But unlike you, I am not afraid of him. Listen to me. You are all learned men. You know the Law as you know your mother-tongue. You know all the rules. You know all the transgressions. But do you know about dreams? Do you know about visions? Do you know about the glory of the imagination? And if you do not know about these things, can you not accept them in one who is as learned and devout as yourselves? Must you not pause for a while in view of Sabbatai's scholarship? And wonder?' He gathered his breath. Elijah stared at him, glad to see the beginnings of a flush on his cheeks. His anger was making him well again.

'No,' Mordecai went on, and his voice gathered strength, 'there is no room in minds like yours for thoughts that have no cause or reason. You dwell in the sole and banal dimension of logic. You have no visions, for your eyes are not open. You read the Law, but you do not divine the space between the words. You hear the sound of the shofar, but you hear no harmonies, no discord, no descant. It is you who are corrupt in your blindness, it is you who are deaf to the voices from heaven.' He was almost shouting now, and his face glowed with a flush of rage. 'My son *is* a god of a kind,' he screamed.

Then he faltered and clasped the table for support. Elijah rushed to him, and Aunt Sarah, but he brushed them aside. He needed no touch. No proximity. For out of his screaming, his ears were unstopped, and he heard Sabbatai's voice, loud and clear. No longer was there an echo. No murmur was there of dungeons. But ringing in his soul, and now-breaking heart, he heard its song. 'I love you, Papa'. It is enough, he thought. It is time. The song has endured to my end. He fell forward on to the table. Elijah held him in his arms. Aunt Sarah looked at his still and beautiful face, and screamed. Upstairs Joseph heard it, and he ran. He reached the room as the scream found its echo. He looked at his father. Then at the Rabbis.

'Murderers!' he screamed at them. 'Assassins!'

They cowered, but even fear could not still their tasteless tongues. 'Could we not say a blessing?' one of them whispered. It was a daring move, and might have cost him his life, had not Elijah restrained his brother, who was intent on their extermination.

'Blessings, curses?' Joseph spat at them. 'Out of your mouths, both are filth.'

It was Aunt Sarah who took control. She walked to where the Rabbis stood and ushered them towards the door. She was polite, with that hangover of Jewish respect for the ministry. 'You must go now,' she said.

'A long life,' they said to her. 'A long life to you all.' Automatically they uttered the traditional Jewish greeting to the bereaved. As they left, she whispered after them.

309

'Joseph was right,' she said. 'You killed Mordecai, as you meant to kill Sabbatai.'

Then she shut the door.

Now they were free to mourn. They caressed Mordecai's body in silent grief.

'It was his time,' Joseph said, 'He chose it. It was what he wished.'

Mordecai Zvi was buried on the following day. Only one Rabbi braved the funeral. He made it as far as the house, then seeing the crowds gathered outside, he had second thoughts and, guilt-laden, he slunk home. There was much weeping and wailing in the streets of Smyrna that day, and for many days afterwards. The father of their Saviour had been laid to rest, and it was for Sabbatai Zvi's heart-break that they grieved.

After the seven days of mourning, Elijah and Joseph Zvi set sail for Gallipoli, to break the news to their brother.

16

The Judas

'Why do I postpone my quietus? Is not my treachery enough? But I have an unseemly desire to witness it, to eavesdrop on the rumour of the ruin I have wrought. I stand outside his prison with the hundreds of worshippers from all over the lands. I am a voyeur. That seems to be my present role. A pursuit that promotes survival. I hear he is not in discomfort and that lightens my heart. Sometimes as I linger here, I see her in her disguise, searching amongst the worshippers. I hear her calling my name. I bite temptation in its tongue. He longs for me, I know. As I long for him. But my father's longing is stronger. God help us both . . . today I saw Joseph and Elijah disembark at the quay-side. Their faces are grief-laden, as if they carry a deep sorrow.'

The brothers' journey through the Aegean was calm and storm-free, and contrasted oddly with the turbulence of their spirits, and the heavy load they bore. But when after some days they approached the Dardanelles, their pace slowed. Sea-traffic was almost at a standstill. The straits were packed with hundreds of boats, their passengers bent on paying homage to their Saviour. Overnight Gallipoli had become a centre of prosperity and, as such, lent itself to all manner of corruption and exploitation. Out of nowhere a tax materialised on every boat that wished to sail the straits. On arrival at Gallipoli there was a long queue, and escalating prices for moorings, and tax-touts did a roaring black-market trade. The winding road to the fortress was littered with stalls selling all manner of gifts that the Saviour was rumoured to find pleasure in. Ornate carpets from Persia, wall hangings, brass ornaments, and stalls selling sweetmeats known to be to the Saviour's taste. As one neared the fortress, there was a separate enclave of shops specialising in relics. As far as their owners were concerned, the Redeemer was already dead, or certainly as good as, so it was appropriate, if tasteless, to put up for sale all manner of the Saviour's person. Fringes from his prayer-shawl, locks from his hair, parings of finger and toe-nails, all packaged in holy tissues and ribbons. The road to the fortress had become a veritable Via Dolorosa, with all its crude exploitation of pain. The people trod the cobble-stones in their thousands. Day after day, pilgrims from Germany, Poland, Italy and Holland, and even as far away as Africa, came to pay homage to the prisoner. Word had spread world-wide of his incarceration, due in the main to letters sent by Nathan to the Jewish communities of the Exile. They in their turn, sent delegations to express their faith and trust in the Redeemer.

The whole of Europe was affected by the Messianic turn of events. In Holland the Jews were optimistic, seeing the imprisonment as a natural phase in the crusade, and from its ports a hundred and twenty-five boats set sail direct to the Promised Land. In Italy, new-born boys were named Sabbatai to herald the new Messianic age. In Spain and Portugal, there were more Marranos than there were Jews, hushed converts to survival, and the coming of Sabbatai Zvi was a sublime opportunity at last to shuffle off their time-honoured Christian disguise.

The Jews of Poland, with their legacy of massacre, were natural followers of one who would redeem all their sufferings, but even the non-oppressed communities of Amsterdam, Leghorn and Salonika, in which latter city, at that time, was concentrated the largest Jewish community in the world; even in these places Sabbataiism had taken

314

firm root. In general, the non-Jewish populations of these countries were tolerant of the crusade and some even supported it. Except, unsurprisingly enough, in Germany. Because those Jewish families who were leaving, and there were four hundred from Frankfurt alone, were collecting the debts that were owed to them, and their creditors were not pleased. From time immemorial, if a German has a Jew in his sights, there is inevitably a stone in his itching palm, and sporadic antisemitic riots broke out in German cities.

For whatever reason, the time was ripe for migration. European Jewry was on the move. Amongst them many Rabbis, for not all were like their brethren in Smyrna. Foremost amongst these was one Nehemiah HaCohen who hailed from Poland. If there is a Judas in the story of Sabbatai Zvi, Nehemiah HaCohen would surely qualify. When Saul had divulged Sabbatai's hiding-place, it was less an act of betrayal than a prelude to his own salvation. But HaCohen's betrayal was of the worst kind. Not even for money, but simply to save his own pious skin.

His journey over land and sea from Poland took three months. He was travelling in response to Sabbatai's own personal invitation. For while he languished in the Citadel, Sabbatai had taken on the role of host. His rumoured dungeons, through the gifts of his disciples, together with bribes and pay-offs, had become a dwelling of the most flesh-pot kind, its numerous apartments equipped for family, guests and visiting dignitaries. Sabbatai himself held court in a hall hung with tapestries and appointed in all manner of luxury. In it he held levées, receptions and lengthy discussions on the Kabala. And all the time he was attended by Nathan, David and Sarah. The stream of visitors did not cease. Many came to question him or simply to renew their faith, and all left satisfied. During this period, Sabbatai celebrated his fortieth birthday. It was Tisha B'Av, that day of traditional mourning. The day was worth a celebration. So Sabbatai declared that, from that time, Tisha B'Av should no longer be a

315

day of fasting, but should be devoted to feasting and revelry.

At the time Sabbatai was in a state of illumination, a state fed by the people's idolatry. Occasionally he became manic, and he would dance about his apartments like one possessed. Nathan watched from the side-lines, and waited for the inevitable desolation that would follow. But fed by the faith of his followers, he maintained his ecstasy, and by the time a travel-weary Nehemiah HaCohen was ushered into the apartments, Sabbatai Zvi was coasting in the regions of Nirvana. He received the Rabbi with what little decorum his manic state allowed. He had to be reminded who this visitor was, and why he had been sent for. Nathan took him aside and, in a whisper, he told him that Rabbi HaCohen was the most scholarly expert on the Kabala and that he, Sabbatai, had wished to converse with him. This information seemed to sober Sabbatai a little, and he welcomed his guest and bade him feed and rest for a while. Then he issued orders that over the next few days no visitors were to be permitted. Only his close entourage could attend the discussions.

Rabbi HaCohen had travelled with an open mind. But he was a very different man from Sabbatai Zvi. Sabbatai was above all else a visionary; HaCohen was a scholar to whom imagination was foreign, tainted even, for it allowed for no evidence or proof. He knew the Kabala word for holy word, and to every one of them he gave a literal interpretation. He believed that Sabbatai Zvi was the true Messiah and during his long and wearisome journey he was comforted by the fact that he would soon be close to his Redeemer. But one look at Sabbatai's lavish apartments sowed doubts in his heart. Sabbatai himself was richly robed in the purple of emperors; his table was heavy with foods and wines. It was not the way he'd expected a Saviour to live. He decided to voice his doubts in their discussions.

While he was resting after his journey, Sabbatai was urged to rest too, but he preferred to spend his time alone in prayer. Nathan worried about the outcome of their discussions. In similar encounters, when cornered, Sabbatai would always resort to the language of the visionary and usually he was able to get away with it. But Rabbi HaCohen would brook no loose talk of visions and voices. He would want chapter and verse for every one of Sabbatai's Messianic claims. With those, he would travel back to Poland and sanction the crusade. Without them, he would expose Sabbatai as a fraud. At such moments Nathan had doubts that they would live to see the fulfilment of their dreams. But never did he doubt Sabbatai. For Sabbatai's visions were his own sights, and Sabbatai's voices his own language.

The following day the apartments were cleared of all visitors, sightseers and sycophants, and the ominous discussions began. On Nathan's suggestion, Sabbatai wore a simple black kaftan. He extended a formal and rather exaggerated welcome to his guest. Nehemiah HaCohen then posed his first question. Or rather, stated his first impression.

'I am honoured to be in your presence,' he began, 'but I have to confess that I am troubled by the manner in which you live. These luxurious surroundings do not conform in my mind to the life-style of a Saviour.' He waited politely for an explanation.

But Sabbatai was ready for him. 'Rabbi,' he said, 'you have followed news of my wanderings over many years. You have heard of my sufferings, of my deprivations. You have heard how I have been whipped and humiliated. Yet I have clung to my faith, that faith that you yourself espouse. As to my present surroundings, they are the work of others. It would be hurtful to refuse such gifts, much as I urge my followers towards simplicity.'

Sarah nodded from the side-lines. She thought her husband had acquitted himself rather well. But Nehemiah

317

HaCohen was not satisfied. He cast his eye about the apartments, and even without the revelling visitors it retained an air of frivolity. And the sight of Sarah's beauty unnerved him. For it was not the beauty of a virtuous woman. He wished she would go away.

'I believe in you, Sabbatai Zvi,' Nehemiah went on, 'but because of some doubts, I must play the Devil's advocate. You have never in your whole life been poor, dogged by the poverty that one associates with the bringer of redemption.'

'Poverty is not measured solely in terms of money,' Sabbatai countered. 'Poverty can be defined in lack of recognition, in ridicule, and in both of these things I have been poor indeed. Moreover, I have suffered the greatest poverty of all. My own self-doubts. To these I freely admit. There is no pain greater than uncertainty.'

For a whole day and night they argued on this theme. Nehemiah quoted verbatim long tracts from the Kabala and Sabbatai countered with his own. Over the hours that passed they tested each other's scholarship, and in friendly fashion, so that the original matter of their argument was soon lost in their exchange of learning.

On the second day, Nehemiah proposed another topic, one, he said, which concerned him deeply and which raised serious doubts in his mind. 'It is the question of the forerunner of the Messiah,' he said. 'It is ordained that the Messiah of the House of Joseph has to appear before the advent of the true Messiah of the House of David. Where is he from the House of Joseph?' he asked. 'Where is that first martyr of the crusade? For without his prior appearance, anyone who calls himself the Messiah from the House of David is an impostor.'

Sabbatai was ready for that argument. He had encountered it before, and he gave the same answer that had satisfied so many of HaCohen's predecessors.

'Why,' he said, ' he has already appeared. His story has been told to me by various sources. There's no doubting their authenticity. He was an unknown scholar who was murdered for his faith in your own country, in Poland during the Chmielnicki massacres.'

'There were thousands who died for their faith in those massacres. And most of them unknown,' Nehemiah said.

'But around this unknown there have grown legends,' Sabbatai said. 'In his own single anonymity this unknown embodied the symbol of the sacrifice that was to precede the true Messiah. And I am he.'

'But I know your name,' Nehemiah said. 'You are known as Sabbatai Zvi. But what name can I give this man? This so-called forerunner of the Messiah?' The scorn was evident in his voice.

'Did any of the thirty-six Just Men have a name?' Sabbatai whispered. 'The unknown from Poland was simply one of the Just, not even known unto himself.'

This latter statement was unarguable. The thirty-six Just Men of Jewish legend were regarded with awe and were never, never questioned. But Nehemiah was not satisfied. And not only dissatisfied, but angry. Suddenly a rage overcame him that seemed not to be merited by the argument.

'But whoever he was,' he shouted, 'he was not the Messiah of the tribe of Joseph.'

Some historians have suggested that HaCohen's rage was due to jealousy, for he himself had illusions of being the Messiah of the House of Joseph. And out of that rage, he cursed Sabbatai as an impostor, a pretender and a fraud, and vowed that he would spread the word abroad and demolish his bogus ministry for ever.

He turned to leave without formality. But in his turning he shivered, for he felt around him a burning hatred and an enmity that made his every step towards the door possibly his last. He froze as hostility seethed around him. For in every pious mind in Sabbatai's prison apartment dwelt the thought that Nehemiah HaCohen must not leave the fortress alive. Nehemiah heard them whispering, then he felt a movement towards him. And he ran, his knees melting with fear. Those in the corridors, waiting to see their Saviour, sensed something amiss, and they too pursued him, echoing the curses that had come from Sabbatai's quarters. The poor man had barely reached the street when he was confronted by more fanatics camped in the square in front of the fortress. But amongst them there were Ottoman guards, curious bystanders of the pilgrimage. In a rare moment of inspiration, which had nothing to do with chapter and verse, but was prompted by a desperate need to save his skin, he threw off his fur hat and ran to the nearest guard, took his turban off his head, and clamped it on his own.

'Allah,' he proclaimed. 'There is no God but Allah.'

The disciples shrunk from him in horror as if he bore the pestilence and his words were of the plague.

'Your Messiah is a charlatan,' he thundered. 'He is a fraud and a deceiver. Go back to your homes and seek shelter there. Renounce him for your own safety. I shall go to the Sultan's palace and condemn him for his deception.'

He was seen to have a word with the guard. Other guards began to group around him and, after a while, he was escorted to an army wagon and driven away. The respect accorded to him by the Turks was not lost on the eye-witnesses and they trembled. But heedless of his advice, they held their stand. Nothing he could say could shake their hungry faith. They started to sing Sabbatai's psalm and it echoed like an ominous passing-bell.

News was quickly brought to Sabbatai's quarters of Nehemiah HaCohen's betrayal. Sabbatai ordered everybody from his chamber. He wanted to be alone. The Polish Rabbi had fed his own self-doubts. When he had called him a deceiver and a fraud, he had for a moment inwardly agreed with him. He was relieved to see him go, and all the others too, for he wanted no witnesses to his own uncertainties. The familiar melancholy, that inevitably followed his spasms of ecstasy, now seeped through his bones. His desolation seemed to invoke physical pain, and he rose with difficulty from his seat, his legs cramping, and he made his way into his familiar corner and crouched there. After a while a vision came to him, without prompting or provocation, and it was accompanied by a violent pain in his side. He endured it without touching himself for solace, for he knew that the pain and the vision were one. He saw his father approaching and by his side was God. It was clear in the vision that God was by his father's side. For his father loomed large, with God a mere appendix. Then it seemed that his father stood behind God and placed his arms on God's shoulders, absorbing him entirely. For a long while it seemed, his father stared at him, then slowly his face broke into a smile. Sabbatai gave a cry. It seemed that his body was shrinking under his skin, and that soon only his packaging would remain. He watched as his father faded, part by part of him, but the smile lingered for a long time. Then he knew that his father was gone.

He unfolded himself from the floor and went to his cupboard. Out of it he took the blue velvet bag that held his father's 'tallis'. He draped it around his shoulders, then resumed his crouch on the floor. Then, holding it in his trembling fingers, he began to plait the fringes of his father's prayer-shawl. One over two, three over one, two over three, one over two, three over one, two over three, and so on till he had plaited them all. 'I am not he, I am not he,' he whispered the while. Then he unplaited the strands and started all over again, chanting the prayers for the dead, punctuating them with the doleful cry, 'I am not he, I am not he.'

In this manner he chanted through the whole night till the sun rose, and it was thus that his brothers, weary after their long journey, found him.

They knelt by his side, putting their arms about his shoulders. They were silent for a while, then Sabbatai raised his eyes. 'How did Papa die?' he asked.

These were the first words between them.

'How did you know?' Elijah whispered.

'I had a vision.'

'He died in peace,' Joseph said. 'He had willed it.'

They sat by his side and told him.

When it was over, Sabbatai lifted the shawl and spread it around their shoulders, thus sharing their grief with their father's spirit. In this manner they sat for seven days in traditional mourning.

News leaked out of the apartments of Sabbatai's bereavement. The arresting officers sent by the Sultan's delegate were obliged to cool their heels outside the fortress until the mourning was at an end. They had arrived a few days previously, equipped with chains. They had been sent on account of Nehemiah HaCohen's denunciation. That newly-minted Muslim, his turban planted firmly on his head, his side-locks hastily clipped in transit, had, at his own request, been taken to the Sultan's palace. And there, to a body of the Sultanate, he had denounced Sabbatai Zvi as a charlatan, a hoaxer, and one who was bent on usurping the Sultan's throne and appropriating it to himself.

'If you have any feeling in your heart for the Jewish nation,' he said, 'and for its survival, I urge you to arrest this man. He is guilty of treason and should go to the gallows. Then we will all be saved. All of us.'

The Sultanate listened attentively, salivating. Enough complaints had come to their notice. Many noteworthy Jews had begged for Sabbatai's silence. But this one was different. This one had taken the turban. They were speaking to one of their own. So they ordered the guards to the fortress, with instructions to put the prisoner in chains and to transfer him to the prison of Adrianopoli, nowadays called Edirne, some 150 miles from Gallipoli.

Contradictory reports surround the fate of Nehemiah HaCohen, but most agree that he eventually returned to Poland, abandoning the turban en route. That he repented sorely of his betrayal and that he promoted Sabbatai Zvi as the veritable Messiah. Eventually his conscience drove him into madness.

The guards entered the fortress. There were four of them. They had been chosen carefully, both for their unshakable loyalty to the Sultan and their strict observance of Islam. All had been privy to the discussions concerning Sabbatai's fate. Opinions differed as to what to do with their prisoner. Some favoured killing him forthwith, and without any formalities of trial. The ambassador from the Hapsburg empire to Constantinople strongly advised against such a measure in the opinion that Sabbatai Zvi would become a martyr and a saint, and, dead, would be more trouble to the Ottoman authorities than he had been when alive.

The officers entered Sabbatai's room without ceremony. Most of Sabbatai's entourage was present at the time, with the addition of his two brothers who stood on either side of him. At the entry of the guards, Nathan, David and Sarah rushed to Sabbatai's side.

'Sabbatai Zvi,' one of the guards shouted. 'You are to come with us. We are ordered to take you to the prison at Adrianopoli, where you will be held until your trial.'

'He will not go with you,' Nathan said. He tried to inject some authority into his voice, but it sounded weak and helpless.

'We will use force if we must,' another officer said.

'We will come with you. All of us,' Sarah said.

'He comes alone. And he comes in chains. That is the order,' the officer said.

Elijah stepped forward. 'Let us go with him,' he pleaded. 'We are his brothers. We have just mourned the death of our father.'

'I am sorry for your grief,' the officer said. 'But he comes alone.'

'Don't worry, Elijah,' Sarah said. 'We will all follow him. I will pack for you, Sabbatai,' she said.

'He brings nothing,' the officers said. 'He comes in what he stands.'

Sabbatai clutched his father's prayer-shawl around him. He wanted nothing else. Nothing else in the world mattered to him any more, except that one holy bond with his father.

'I am ready,' he said.

They locked the chains gently on his ankles and they led him out of the chamber.

His entourage followed him, stunned. The crowds had gathered outside the fortress. It was clear from the presence of the carriage and the guards that something was afoot. And they had seen the chains which the guards had taken no pains to hide. They waited, angry and afraid. When Sabbatai emerged, they let out a cry.

'How can you save us when you yourself are in chains?'

'Was not Joseph a prisoner in Egypt?' Sabbatai answered them.

Then he was led to the carriage. They clustered around him as near as the guards would allow, then they stared at the dust that followed the carriage, and there they waited, dumbfounded, and there they stayed long after the sound of the wheels had died away.

Overnight Gallipoli became a ghost city. The followers decamped and, their faith only slightly shaken, began the weary trek inland in the steps of their leader. Stalls shut up shop, souvenirs were redundant, since no more would come to Gallipoli to remember. But the relics of Sabbatai Zvi were stored for the future, for there was no doubt in the stall-holders' minds that that future was fast approaching. Within a few days, the straits of the Dardanelles offered traffic-free passage, and moorings could be had for two-a-piastre. But the city had made its pile and was satisfied.

Sabbatai gave his guards no trouble. He fasted and prayed for the soul of his father. His escort looked upon him with growing respect. One of them thought he saw a light around Sabbatai's head, but he refrained from mentioning it to his companions in fear of their derision. But the others had noticed it too, and for similar reasons each refrained from comment.

'Tell us about your father,' one of them said. 'You must have loved him very much.'

Sabbatai did not respond for a while. Never in his life had he talked to anybody about his father. It would have been like divulging a secret. A secret that had been told to him, and that he himself had not understood, and because of that, a secret that he feared. He recalled his many cruelties to his father, and he shivered with shame and remorse. Yet he had loved him. Was it now too late, he wondered, to forgive himself for the hurt he had caused? It would be a relief to speak about him to strangers.

'He was a very simple man,' he said, and as he spoke his father's face appeared to him in utmost clarity, as if urging him to define every feature. 'His forehead is high,' he said, his eyes glued to the vision, 'and the cheek-bones too, though they are partially covered with his side-locks. He has a long black beard, growing grey now, and he trims it daily. His nose is very straight – I take after him in that respect – and his eyes are set wide apart. My brother Elijah has his eyes. Mine are like my mother's.' He would not look at the guards as he spoke, for he knew that only a constant gaze would keep the image clear. He was aware of a strange feeling of relief and even contentment, as he displayed, in front of these strangers, his captors, the detailed features of the man he had loved above any other, and whom, at this late moment, he was beginning to know. 'I think I loved him more than anyone on earth,' Sabbatai said. 'Though he didn't believe in me.'

He looked at the guards for the first time. He wondered at their astonishment. 'Do you find that strange?' he asked.

'How can one *not* believe in you?' one of the guards said. He still saw the light above Sabbatai's head. He knelt at his feet and unlocked the chains. The others joined him on the floor of the wagon.

'Forgive us,' they said. They urged Sabbatai to eat a little, and to tell them tales of his childhood. They wanted his history, his recall, his retreat into the safety of his past. They wanted that for his own comfort, for they feared that they were escorting him to the gallows.

After Sabbatai had been taken from the fortress, his entourage prepared to leave. Although most of them would have been willing to leave everything behind, Sarah insisted on taking all the trappings: the carpets, the hangings, the silver and silks. 'He is the King of Israel,' she kept saying. Hers was the only voice with any confidence. 'A sign will come,' she said.

Nathan was the first to leave the apartments. Outside he addressed the crowd of the faithful. 'Do not lose heart,' he told them. 'It is only Sabbatai Zvi's body that is in chains. The spirit of the Messiah is amongst you. Our prayers will set his body free, and he will lead us to Jerusalem. Some of us already wait at the gates of the Holy City. Join them with your families. The redemption has come.'

Then they sang Sabbatai's psalm, and Nathan went amongst them in their singing, and led them out of the gates of Gallipoli. Shortly afterwards the wagons were loaded, and Sabbatai's retinue set off for Adrianopoli. Joseph and Elijah travelled together in the first wagon.

'What will become of him?' Elijah said. Then, trembling, 'Will he die?'

'Sabbatai can never die,' Joseph said.

Elijah held Joseph's hand. 'He can, Joseph,' he said softly. 'Our brother is only flesh and blood. His spirit will live perhaps. But his spirit is not enough for me. I want to hold him,' Elijah pleaded, 'like I'm holding you.'

'There will be a sign,' Joseph said.

'There was no sign for Christ,' Elijah raised his voice in anger. 'He rotted on the cross.'

'There will be a sign for Sabbatai,' Joseph said calmly.

Elijah marvelled at his brother's blind faith. 'We must do something to save him,' he said helplessly.

'He will be saved,' was all Joseph could reply.

They travelled all day and night, stopping only to change the horses and to buy provisions. After a few days, Sabbatai's carriage came within their sight, and thereafter they timed their journey according to its rhythm. It was a relief to be in view of his carriage, as if he were again under their protection.

But they could have been no better protectors than the arresting officers themselves, who were by now, each of them, in thrall to Sabbatai. Even to the extent of diverting their route to save him from the Sultan's condemnation. When they tentatively put this suggestion to Sabbatai himself, he thanked them for their consideration. But he refused their help.

'It is part of my crusade,' he told them. 'To be spared, to be condemned, to die even. Otherwise I am not the true Messiah.'

'Master,' one of them said after a while, 'do you ever have doubts?'

Sabbatai put his hand on the man's arm. 'Of course,' he said. 'But not when people deny me. Nor even when they follow in my path. My doubts have nothing to do with anyone except myself. Sometimes I think perhaps I am mad. That my visions and my voices are loose strands in my brain. Lunatics have visions too, you know. It may be that Jesus was mad as well, or that he ate excessively of magic mushrooms. In Judaism,' he told them, 'there are thirty-six Just Men who, unknowingly, carry the torch of our faith. God puts them on earth for this purpose. Perhaps in the same way, and in every generation, He plants a lunatic, and occasionally that madman assumes the role of the Messiah. For God needs a Messiah as ardently as a Messiah needs God.'

'If you die,' one of them asked, 'will you come again?'

'For every Messiah there is a second coming. There must be, to sustain people's belief. Your own Imam lies hidden in a cave. He *must* return, if you believe.'

They noticed that he was sweating and that, for the first time, he was smiling.

'Are you all right?' one of them asked.

'I have no need of mushrooms,' Sabbatai said. 'My visions and my voices come without bidding, with no bait, no witchery. They come to my third eye, and into my third ear, those with which God has provided me. I will pray now,' he said. He draped his father's 'tallis' around his shoulders and he plaited and unplaited his way to Adrianopoli.

As they neared the city, Nathan's wagon overtook the prisoner's, in order to spy out the land before his arrival. He was astonished at what they found. Gallipoli was a quiet Sunday by comparison. The streets were crowded with Sabbatai's followers and a throng of curious onlookers who had heard of the Messiah's coming. Rumours had spread around the city that, on arrival, Sabbatai Zvi would relieve the Sultan of his crown and place it upon his own head. The street leading to the Sultan's palace was carpeted its whole length and strewn with flower petals. The crowd, though excited, were orderly. Many fell into a gentle trance; some danced in ecstasy; and as the prisoner's carriage came into view, they chanted Sabbatai's psalm.

He was not chained when they led him out of the carriage. Indeed, in his mien, it seemed that he was escorting the arresting officers who, with respect and in awe, walked in his shadow. As he neared the carpet, he stopped and faced the crowd. The mere sight of him was sufficient to command silence. Even the trances were suspended as his voice rang out over the square.

'God has taken away my chains,' he said. 'I come to lead you to the Holy Land. I have no need of mushrooms.' Then he turned and beckoned the officers to follow him.

The people did not understand his words, but he was the Messiah and he spoke in the language of God. Untroubled, they psalmed his way into the Palace. When the doors closed behind him, they stayed and kept vigil. And remained there for three whole days and nights, their faith fuelled by community of prayer. Nathan led them in their supplications. The end of the Exile was at hand.

17

The first and last martyr

'I follow them, a sheep amongst sheep. They whisper his name with every step. The whisper of worship. I whisper it too, but with love. Day after day we travel. Sometimes on carts which make room for us. But more often on foot. Whispering all the while. And though they speak with many tongues, the name Sabbatai Zvi is heard amongst them all.'

By the time Sabbatai arrived in Adrianopoli, his fever was high indeed. He entered the grounds of the Sultan's palace in a state of manic delusion. He was convinced that the Sultan had called him to the palace for the express purpose of handing over his crown.

He was not led directly to the royal quarters as he expected, but was given rooms in the seraglio, there to cool his heels and his fiery spirit at the Sultan's pleasure. He asked that his wife and brothers and some of his followers attend him and the officers were happy to fulfil his request. So Sarah was brought to the seraglio, together with Joseph, Elijah and David. Nathan accompanied them, and three Rabbis. Whatever was to happen at the Palace, Nathan sensed that some debate would be necessary. And support too. For Nathan knew that Sabbatai could often crumble in his lack of self-belief.

But when he saw Sabbatai, he knew that he was beyond debate or discussion of any kind, and certainly indifferent to support. For he was high on self-esteem, to the point of arrogance.

'What shall I wear, Nathan, to accept the crown?' was his first question on greeting them. Then without waiting for a reply he said, 'I shall put on my white kaftan, with my serpent ring on my hand. Proofs of my god-head. And Papa's "tallis",' he added. 'I must wear that. What more proof is needed?' Then he embraced Sarah and his brothers and announced that he would fast until his audience with the Sultan.

Elijah was desolate. He looked tenderly at his brother. Of all the company, he was the only one who saw death around him. And if not death, annihilation of a kind. He went towards him, and held him in close embrace. 'Come home, Sabbatai,' he said, helplessly. 'Come home with me,' he pleaded. 'I don't want to lose you.'

Sabbatai distanced himself from the embrace. 'Why are you crying, Elijah?' he said. 'We are going home. All of us. I shall lead you to the Holy City. We shall go as the holy family.'

Then Joseph embraced him, and Sarah and David, but distantly, as true disciples.

'Let us make merry,' Sarah said. 'I have brought wine and food. Why must you fast, Sabbatai? This is a day of rejoicing. Begin your fast tomorrow.'

He would not deny her. She was infected by his state of ecstasy. As were the others. All of them, except for Elijah.

'You look at me in mourning, Elijah,' Sabbatai said.

'I fear for you. I fear for all of us. Come home. I beg of you.'

'Our home is not Smyrna any more,' Sabbatai said. 'Our home is Jerusalem.'

'Home is Smyrna where our parents are buried,' Elijah said.

But this reminder of his orphanhood in no way dented Sabbatai's frenzy. 'We shall return to Smyrna for the sole purpose of bringing their bones to the Holy Land.' He began to finger the shawl again, coaxing its soft texture, as if he would breathe life into his father. 'Come,' he said. 'We shall do as Sarah says. We shall celebrate the night through. We shall dance and sing psalms and drink ourselves into divine glory.'

Sarah made the preparations. The arresting officers who guarded the door were invited to join in their festivities. Willing initiates, they brought their own sweetmeats, and, at their own terrible risk, smuggled in the favourites of the harem, young girls and boys. Without doubt it was an undeclared preparation for an orgy. Its calling card was loud and clear. 'Rejoice in the Lord, and do that which is forbidden, for only from the basest depth can one rise to the kiss of the divine.' God occasionally comes in handy.

Throughout the night they danced and sang, and came close enough for comfort. All the while Sarah coupled and uncoupled them, clothed and naked. Sabbatai danced all night, singing and praying and denuding himself the while, and by the morning, he could be found naked in the arms of an equally naked young boy, both of them bound together by the plaited fringes of his father's prayer-shawl. And the night long, Elijah sat on the side-lines, and turned his face to the wall.

Thus in the morning were they found by the Sultan's messenger. It was not a good beginning. On his entry, Sabbatai disentangled himself from his lover, and standing erect, naked and unashamed, and with great presence of his unbalanced mind, he announced, 'I am somebody else.'

It was a brave try. But there was no mistaking Sabbatai. Even in his nakedness, surrounded by the nakedness of others, a condition in which all men look the same, he was discernible, for he was clutching the plaited fringes of his father's 'tallis' in his hand.

The messenger stared about him. He was young and unused to such sights. He turned his back and waited. He hoped he was giving them time to clothe themselves. He heard a frantic scrambling behind him and he was satisfied. He would wait. Then someone touched him on the shoulder. Out of the corner of his eye he saw the sleeve of a jacket. Whoever touched him was clothed.

'It's all part of a religious ritual,' he heard the whisper in his ear. 'It is sanctioned by the Lord. Believe me.' Elijah walked around him so that they were face to face. 'But it is a secret ritual,' he added. 'It should never be seen by one who is not of our faith. You must report it to nobody.'

The young boy shook his head vigorously.

'You didn't see it,' Elijah said. 'You saw nothing. When I tell you, you will turn around and that which you see is that which you shall report.'

The boy nodded with the same vigour. Elijah remained standing in front of him, looking over his shoulder, viewing the frantic and clumsy change into decency. He waited till all was done, then signalled the messenger to turn round.

The boy trembled. What met his eyes was a blanket of funereal sober black. Muted in utter silence. He began to believe he had been seeing things, so wholly contrasting was the transformation. He would be happy to think it so. He opened his mouth to speak. But it was dry. Moreover, he had forgotten his words, so carefully rehearsed in the corridors leading to the seraglio. He knew that they were of a formal nature. Some of the phrases he hadn't even understood, but he'd learned them by rote and they sounded full of authority. But he remembered the gist of the message, which was a summons to the palace and the Chamber of the Privy Council. He licked his lips and tried once more.

'You've . . . you've got to go . . .' he stammered. 'You've got to go to the Privy Council.' Slowly the phraseology returned. 'You are summoned,' he said. 'You are summoned into the Presence. I am sent to escort you.' He smiled a little then, pleased with his recital.

'I am ready,' Sabbatai said.

He was not dressed in the ceremonial manner he'd proposed. But that did not trouble him. He wore his simple black kaftan draped with his father's shawl. His fever was still upon him, fuelled by the aftermath of coupling, and he knew that the halo of light shone around his head. That light in itself was enough to claim the crown. He turned to his followers. 'I shall not be long,' he said. He did not expect that the transfer of power would be an elaborate drawn-out affair. Only protocol could prolong it. He would allow the Sultan that. After all, a whole kingdom is not donated without some little ceremony.

'Not too long,' he added. 'When I return, we shall all fast together.'

They watched him go. Of them all, only Elijah saw no halo of light above his brother's head. He winced at the manic step, sensing it an unseemly gait for the gallows, and he thanked God that his brother didn't know what he was doing.

Neither did Sultan Mehmed IV. Ever since Sabbatai had been transferred from the fortress he had debated with his Vizier, Köprülü, as to what should be done with him. For something had to be done. The Sultan was not unmindful of how his crown was challenged. He could not blind himself to the sight of thousands of believers waiting in the streets outside the palace. Nor could he ignore those thousands of disciples and delegates reported to have travelled to Gallipoli from Germany, Italy, Greece and Egypt. Unnamed, peaceful, patient. It was their silence above all that unnerved him. The silence of utter confidence. He had to be very careful with the treatment he meted out to Sabbatai Zvi. Such treatment had to be carefully debated, for if it was mistaken, it could cause a cosmic upheaval.

They decided that a charge of treason was out of the question, and that any form of punishment would sow the seeds of martyrdom. There was only one alternative that would save him from penalty, but that was so far-fetched and so seemingly impossible, that not one of the

Council dared suggest it for fear of derision. Except for the Sultan's physician, one Mustapha Hayatizadé, himself an apostate Jew. Those who convert, to whatever religion, tend painfully towards proselytising. To convert others may be a way of assuaging their own guilts, or merely as a punitive measure, for they are rarely able to forgive themselves. Hayatizadé fell into both categories. As a result of his conversion, he had been appointed the Sultan's physician, a position he would never have attained in the guise of a Jew. And his conversion was of such an extreme nature that it had bred in him more than a trace of antisemitism. Of all the counsellors in that chamber, he it was who hated Sabbatai most. The Sultan had only to glance in his direction to prompt him to offer his suggestion.

'There is only one choice,' he said, and with a tone of authority which suggested he would take full responsibility should such an alternative fail. 'Sabbatai Zvi must be offered the turban as an alternative to death.'

The Sultan withdrew to a gallery, and from behind a latticed screen, he saw and heard the proceedings.

When Sabbatai came into the chamber, the Sultan was immediately aware of a presence. His clothes were sombre black, yet there was a flamboyance about him, a light in his eyes that almost pierced the gallery where he stood. In that first moment Sultan Mehmed understood the man's tumultuous following, and he himself felt drawn by a Messianic magnetism. And was that a light above the man's head, or simply the rays of the sun falling through the lattice window? The Sultan trembled. This man, patient, unarmed and silent, was an enemy indeed.

Sabbatai looked among the group of Councillors, but he couldn't recognise one as the Presence. 'Where is the Sultan?' he demanded. 'I speak to no one except the Sultan.'

'The Sultan hears you,' Köprülü said. 'He is here but he

does not show himself. That is our Law.'

'Then where is his crown?' Sabbatai asked.

There was a gasp from the assembly. They had not expected such effrontery.

'I come for the crown,' Sabbatai said. There was no anger in his voice. Just a threatening patience.

'The crown is on the Sultan's head,' Köprülü said, with equal patience.

'On his head,' Hayatizadé echoed, 'where it shall stay.'

'What is all this about?' Sabbatai asked, advancing towards the table.

Köprülü drew in a chair. 'Sit down, Sabbatai Zvi,' he said. He noticed the sweat on his forehead. From where he stood, he felt irradiated by Sabbatai's fever. Perhaps the man was the Messiah after all. He remembered his first meeting with him, and recalled those same feelings. He was aware of dealing with a landmine.

'There is no need to sit down,' Sabbatai was saying. 'I have little time. I must begin my fast.'

Hayatizadé stood to his full height. 'Sit down,' he thundered. 'You have not come to us. We have summoned you. You are here to answer our questions. You are here to give an account of yourself.'

'I will gladly answer your questions,' Sabbatai said. 'If I can. There are many things I don't know about myself. Those things that only God knows. Such questions I cannot answer. But I will do my best,' he said.

Köprülü once more handed him the chair and Sabbatai sat down. Carefully he wrapped his father's shawl around his shoulders, and began his manual mantra of plaiting. It was not a movement calculated to put his interrogators at ease, and some were tempted to pull the shawl from his hands, but amongst them there was a niggling nudge of belief that made his apparel, as well as his person, untouchable. Sabbatai plaited and unplaited away, murmuring the 'Kaddish' awhile, for the peace of his father's soul. They listened to him, afraid to interrupt. Besides, they grew more and

339

more uncomfortable. They sensed they had little right to question this holy man.

From his balcony, the Sultan listened to the silence below, and it worried him. He had no doubt of what was holding their tongues. He grew angry and was tempted to cough, to remind them of the authority that eavesdropped on their examination. But he refrained. It would be sorely lacking in protocol to announce his presence to Sabbatai Zvi. He waited, his patience frayed.

Even Hayatizadé was silent. His physician was holding his tongue, but not out of any nudging nostalgia. He could not afford to believe in Sabbatai Zvi, and he turned his mind firmly away from such a thought. He was silent because it was not his place to start the ball rolling. It was Köprülü who must be the first interrogator.

At last the Grand Vizier spoke. 'What is your first question, gentlemen?' He addressed the assembly. He was passing the responsibility to others, for even he, loyal as a brother to the Sultan, was afraid of offending a possible Divine.

Silence fell again while the Sultan seethed with anger. At last, one of them spoke. Selim Kemal, the Keeper of the Sultan's purse. He stood up and it was clear that he was trembling. 'I cannot question this man,' he said. 'I believe he is the son of God.' He distanced himself from the table, nodded his head to the assembled company and quietly left the room.

Sabbatai did not look after him, neither did he interrupt his prayer. He simply continued his plaiting. The silence that followed Kemal's exit was of a different kind. The men were tempted to look at the gallery for guidance, but such a glance was strictly forbidden. Kemal's pronouncement, its every syllable blazoning treachery, had frightened them. They did not want to be assumed part of it. Now they would fall over themselves with questions to the impostor.

'What was your purpose in coming to the capital?' Köprülü opened his account.

'I have already told you,' Sabbatai said. 'I told you at Gallipoli. I come here to take the Sultan's crown, and thus return Jerusalem to my people.'

'But that is sedition, punishable by death,' Köprülü said.

'And so it would be,' Sabbatai said, 'if it were simple sedition. But in my case it is different.'

They waited for him to clarify, but he went on plaiting.

'In which way is your case different?' The questioner was Mehmed Vani Effendi, the Sultan's chief preacher, who now had the courage to open his mouth.

'I am the son of God,' Sabbatai said. Of the hundreds of beads of sweat that stood on his forehead, one fell. He watched it fall on the prayer-shawl. He took it as God's sanction. 'I am the Messiah,' he said, in case he had not made himself abundantly clear.

'What proof have you that you are the Messiah?' This question from Kuru Mustapha Pasha, the deputy of Adrianopoli.

'I am weary of such questions,' Sabbatai said. 'I see visions. I hear voices. They come from God. These are proofs. I have no other. I ask you to believe in me.'

'This Chamber needs more tangible proofs than your voices and visions,' the Sheikh al-Islam put in his piastre's worth.

'I have no means of giving you any,' Sabbatai said simply.

Now was the moment for the kill.

'May we suggest one?' Mustapha Pasha asked.

'If you wish,' Sabbatai said. 'I have no fear.' And indeed he had not, for his fever was at its highest. They all looked at Köprülü. It was his move. Undeniably. He coughed, hoping to draw Sabbatai's attention away from his eternal plaiting. But Sabbatai was absorbed in his mantra.

'We have a suggestion,' Köprülü said. 'We have long discussed this matter and we have decided that there is a way in which you can prove your god-head.'

Sabbatai continued plaiting. 'Tell me about it,' he said. His tone was almost insolent, so sublime at that moment was his self-belief.

Köprülü spoke slowly. He wanted to make himself very clear. From the balcony the Sultan nursed a measure of hope. 'We have stationed four expert bowmen in the courtyard,' Köprülü said. He waited for some reaction, but nothing was forthcoming. The simple undoing of yet another plait was Sabbatai's sole comment.

'They are the most expert bowmen in the country.' Köprülü drove his point home. 'You will be taken to the courtyard, and you will stand in front of them. In other words, your body will be their target.'

Another plait. And yet another.

Köprülü raised his voice. 'They have poisonous arrows. You will not move. Those arrows will be aimed directly at your heart. If you are, as you say, the son of God, then those arrows will glance off your body like feathers and do you no harm. But if you are deluded,' he emphasised the word, for he preferred to accuse Sabbatai of sickness rather than mendacity, 'then you will forfeit your life for your arrogant assumption.'

He paused, while Sabbatai went on plaiting. 'Sabbatai Zvi,' he said, after a while. 'Do you agree?'

At last a reaction was visible. Sabbatai finished the plait he was working on, took off his father's shawl, and folded it with infinite care. Then he rose.

'Of course,' he said. 'I am ready. Lead me to your courtyard.'

The Privy Council trembled. There was no courtyard. There were no bowmen, aces or otherwise. Only the echo they had hoped for from the walls outside. 'God, my God, why hast Thou forsaken me?' Sabbatai's innocent willingness for martyrdom had thrown them all. During their debates, no one had envisaged this astonishing reaction, and they were by no means geared for its follow-up. They had expected the so-called Messiah to crumble on hearing their proposition, to make quick confession of his bogus claims and to get down on his knees and beg for

342

mercy. Yet here he stood, erect and unafraid, offering himself to proof of his god-head, ignorant of the empty courtyard and its mythical bowmen.

Hayatizadé felt suddenly redundant. His practised oratory on the virtues of apostasy was now irrelevant. Nobody was sure of the next move. It was Köprülü who salvaged what was left of their deliberations.

'We were testing you, Sabbatai Zvi,' he said. 'You have satisfied us as to the integrity of your own conviction. We will now adjourn to debate the next stage of our proceedings. You will return to the seraglio and remain there until you are summoned.'

The escort led him away, though Sabbatai needed no guidance. He floated back to his quarters where his retinue were anxiously waiting. They crowded about him, but they did not touch him, for they recognised the familiar signs of divine fever. He was at the height of his ecstasy, but only Nathan recognised it, and knew that his rapid descent into hell was now imminent. He hurried to catch him on his crest, so that he could report what had happened.

'What did they say, Master? Tell us now,' he said. 'And from the beginning.'

Sabbatai lost no time. His tale did not lack chronology nor any detail. In his mind he had reproduced every feature of the Chamber and of its many Councillors. His ear had recorded every syllable of argument. This he presented to them like a huge and highly defined picture with his own vibrant commentary. At the end of it he said, 'I shall fast now, and pray, and will continue to do so until they come for me again.' He wrapped the shawl about him and retreated to his corner. There he crouched as the beads of sweat on his forehead slowly burst and he steeled himself for his painful decline.

Around him his followers were silent. Then after a while, Nathan said, 'He called their bluff. The Almighty guided him. It is now only a matter of time before we all leave for Jerusalem.'

Sarah agreed with him. So did David and Joseph. The others thanked God for Sabbatai's fever and thought that he had simply been lucky. Elijah thanked God for his brother's life. For his brother's reprieve. For that was how he viewed it. He had already begun to mourn him.

'What will happen now?' he asked Joseph. 'What will happen at the next summons?'

'The Sultan will hand over his crown,' Joseph said.

Elijah put his hand on his arm. Joseph was as innocent as Sabbatai.

For the next few days in the seraglio, Sarah tended her husband's meagre needs, and watched as desolation overcame him. He kept the shawl around him at all times, though a heavy lethargy had stilled his plaiting fingers. They prayed with him, Nathan leading the prayers, for Sabbatai was in a liturgy all of his own. And they waited for the next summons.

In the palace there was an uproar. The Sultan was less concerned with their next move than with the outright treachery of the Keeper of his Purse. His withdrawal from the Chamber, his refusal to question the prisoner, had sparked off Sabbatai Zvi's confident arrogance and his willingness to offer himself to their offensive proof. Kemal must be severely punished. The Council debated for a while, and with little imagination, or heed of its consequences, they unanimously condemned the unfortunate Kemal to death on the gallows, the sentence to be executed forthwith.

The gallows was erected in the public square and was never dismantled because of its constant use. All hangings were public and a source of regular entertainment for the citizens of Adrianopoli. Exact timings of shows – they were usually in the morning – were publicised by the town-crier, together with the reason for the punishment. At the time, all squares and open spaces in the city were already crowded with Sabbatai's followers. Mostly they were silent, in a silence broken occasionally with the singing

344

of psalms. So Selim Kemal's hanging would find a captive audience.

When they heard the announcement, they attached little significance to it. They regretted his untimely death, and whoever he was, they would, between their Sabbatai prayers, pray for the wretch's soul. But when they heard the nature of the crime for which the man would be despatched, that ominous charge of sedition rang a familiar bell. For was not that the word that had been coupled with the name of their leader? Their prayers now were racked with fervour and fear.

Inside the seraglio, they heard the tumult in the streets, and the town-crier's announcement, over and over again. Nathan immediately grasped the implications, and knowing the full story of Kemal's so-called sedition, he knew he had to tell it to Sabbatai's followers as graphically as their leader had told it himself. He instructed David and Joseph to follow him and in haste they took to the streets.

Within hours the story of Selim Kemal's defection spread around the city of Adrianopoli. It was clear now that Kemal's would not be just another hanging. The following day would mark the despatch of the very first martyr of the Sabbataian movement. The fact that he was not even a Jew was not only irrelevant, it added strength to their crusade. The gallows now appeared as a fiery beacon of faith, a symbol that even their leader himself could not have devised. They would mourn Kemal as they would a Jew, they would find his grave and honour it, and at the gates of Jerusalem, within sight of the Temple, they would build him an eternal memorial. And they would call him Solomon.

Thus the hanging, which the Sultan and his advisors had considered just and appropriate, and of no more consequence than any other just and appropriate hanging in the public square, now turned into a mighty arm of the Sabbataian crusade. Selim Solomon Kemal had already been taken in chains to the square, before the Privy Council realised how grossly their decision had backfired. They did not even have the time to stop his mouth, for as he mounted the gallows, he turned to look at his last audience and as they placed the noose around his neck, he stayed the rope with his one hand. Then he held the other high.

'Friends,' he shouted. 'The Messiah is in our midst. Sabbatai Zvi is come to Adrianopoli. I know that my Redeemer liveth.' These were his last words. The hangman tore the man's hand from the noose, and tightened its knot and viciously kicked open the trap-door. Selim Solomon Kemal swung there while the echo of his mighty words still rang over the square. If there were any doubts in the souls of any one of the crowd that day, his plaintive cry from the gallows put an end to them once and for all.

Of all the documents and scrolls proving Sabbatai's god-head, forged and genuine, of all the miracles that he had performed, rumoured and real, there had never been a greater boost to the Messianic crusade. The Sultan might as well have given Sabbatai his crown.

The crowds began to murmur the prayers for the dead. However virtuous a man Selim Kemal had been in his earth-bound days, nothing in his life could have become him like the leaving of it.

From the palace balcony, the Sultan and his Councillors viewed the pious crowd and heard their prayers. The name 'Solomon' echoed with threatening frequency. Each of them knew that a ghastly mistake had been made, but since it had been a unanimous decision, there was no one whom they could blame. This heightened their frustration, and when they reconvened their Council to decide on Sabbatai's fate, their mood was angry and thwarted, and smacked of defeat. They cursed Sabbatai Zvi and wished the worst for him, but they had learned the futile lesson of martyrdom. Something far more devastating must be devised. So they debated with black looks and hatred in their hearts.

Sabbatai still crouched in his corner. It was the fifth day of his fast. Only water had passed his lips, and he had never ceased from prayer. As high as he had been in the Sultan's presence, so now was he low. He talked to no one, and seemed to be deaf to their solace and entreaties. So that, when Nathan brought him the news from outside, he was impervious to the information. Nothing on earth could hearten him. Nathan feared that he wished to die and that if the Sultan saw fit at this moment to sentence the trouble-maker to death, Sabbatai's first smile would be for the gallows. His soul and his spirit was anaesthetised with prayer.

It was thus that the Sultan's.messenger found him when he came for a second time to summon him to the Royal Presence. It was with the greatest difficulty that Sabbatai was able to rise from his corner. When he understood what was being asked of him, he trembled like a child. 'Can Nathan come with me?' he asked.

The messenger returned to the Council and reported Sabbatai's request. He did not omit to report also on Sabbatai's condition. The Councillors took heart. The so-called Messiah in a state of dejection would be easy enough prey. So they were generous.

'Let him bring his whole retinue,' they offered.

'All but his wife,' Köprülü added. 'She has no right in this Chamber.'

The messenger carried back their offer. Sabbatai had returned to his crouched corner. His followers welcomed the general invitation. They thought that, in view of the patent turn of events, the Sultan, his back to the wall, might well offer a compromise and one that had to be discussed amongst them all. This they tried to convey to Sabbatai, but he was deaf with lethargy. Eventually they persuaded him to rise and to interrupt his prayers for the duration of the interview.

Nathan was worried. For although Sabbatai was desolate, his mind was abundantly clear. It was a mind that would sniff danger and threat. It was not a mind that would volunteer to expert bowmen. It was a mind that would

347

accept anything for the sake of peace. Anything in return for being left alone. Nathan knew that this interview was crucial, and he feared its outcome.

They were welcomed profusely on their arrival in the Chamber. Wine and sweetmeats had been prepared for them. Köprülü insisted that they ate and drank before the discussions began. This time the Sultan was present in the Chamber, and though he sat at a distance, attended by two slaves, he was patently visible to all the invitees. Even Sabbatai noted him, but found no interest in his presence. Sabbatai shook his head when food was offered him and Nathan explained that their leader was fasting.

'Has he lost his tongue then?' one of them asked jocularly.

'He is very tired,' Nathan said. Then regretted it, for he had confirmed that which they had already surmised, that Sabbatai could easily be taken advantage of.

The sweetmeats were taken away and Sabbatai was ordered to stand before the table. The others were relegated to the back of the Chamber. All except Nathan who was allowed to stand by Sabbatai's side. Elijah sat in Sabbatai's direct line of vision. He noticed how his brother suddenly crooked his arm behind his back and began rocking himself in its cradle.

It was Köprülü who opened the proceedings. 'Sabbatai Zvi,' he began. 'There are two charges against you. One, that the purpose of your visit to the capital was to dethrone the great Sultan. The punishment for that crime is death and death of the most cruel and tormenting kind. Second, that you claim to be the Messiah and have, with such a claim, deceived the people and wrought untold tragedy in their lives. For this crime, the punishment is also death though of a gentler kind.'

Sabbatai was heard to mumble.

'What is it, Master?' Nathan put his ear close to Sabbatai's mouth.

'I am not he. I am not he.' Despite his melancholy, he had no appetite for death, even a gentle one. Like any

348

man, he was afraid of dying. Surely that fear proved his ordinariness in mankind? Let Nathan tell them that, for he didn't have the courage to confront such authority. 'Papa,' he whispered into the shawl. 'I am in the presence of the Sultan and I don't know what I'm doing here.'

Nathan deciphered it with horror, and decided that it was untranslatable. Yet he had to say something.

'Sabbatai Zvi declares that he is honoured to be in your company.' That was non-committal. It was a declaration that could offend nobody.

'We thank him for that compliment,' Köprülü said. 'Does it mean that he has recognised at last that he is lesser than the Sultan?'

'He is the Messiah,' Nathan said quickly. 'Of that there is no doubt.'

Köprülü exploded. 'Only a few days ago, the Keeper of the Sultan's Purse went to the gallows. He was hanged with your exact words in his throat. Take care that your master does not go the same way.'

Köprülü was in a dilemma. Although he knew the danger of martyrdom, its temptation was overwhelming. It was now clearly time to introduce Hayatizadé, whose mission had been thwarted at their last meeting. His hopes now rested on that man. Köprülü did not like Hayatizadé. Nor did he trust him, a feeling shared by most of the Privy Council. An apostate is rarely welcome amongst those in power. And seldom trusted. Even though, in an evangelical faith, to effect a conversion is considered a triumph, there lingers a residue of suspicion. And above all, of contempt. Hayatizadé was a friendless man, shunned by those Jews who had once been his friends and bypassed by those whose friendship he would cultivate. In his isolation he had grown to hate everybody, and most of all, himself. It was this self-hatred that he was about to unleash on Sabbatai Zvi.

He waited to be introduced by Köprülü, who gave him out simply as the Sultan's physician. There was no mention of his own apostasy. Hayatizadé rose. He was aware of how they all depended on him, and that power pleased him. But he was equally aware that, if he failed, their wrath might well turn upon him and strip him of all those bonuses that he had acquired through his conversion. He prayed that he would succeed. And he prayed quietly to his own natural God, to Yahweh, because, despite his apostasy, he could never really trust the Other One. Even as he prayed, he realised how futile was such a prayer, for how could Sabbatai Zvi's God encourage his so-called son to turn away? So he added a quick postscript to Allah, and hoped for the best.

'Sabbatai Zvi,' he said. 'We are not here to discuss your guilt or your innocence. We know that you are guilty, simply because you have already told us so. You have confessed to the purpose of your journey to the capital. You have admitted that your purpose is to usurp the Sultan's throne. In other words, you have openly, and if I may add, proudly confessed to the sin of treason. In all our history there has been but one punishment for such a crime. Death. No more. No less.' He paused, and was pleased to hear a terrible sigh from the back of the Chamber. He waited for the sigh to subside. He knew the value of a pause. Then he leaned forward, with an air of friendly intimacy and confidence. 'Let me tell you a little about the forms such death can take.' He embarked upon his gruesome tale as if it was a fairy story. 'If the offender is a common man, illiterate, ignorant, we donate no ceremony to his death. Or, as in the case of the traitor, Selim Kemal, if we are anxious for a quick despatch, we cut him down with the contempt that he deserves. A rope around his neck, and a trap-door. Such a man is lucky, my friend. His death is quick and painless. Let me tell you now of some of our other methods of despatch. We have time, I think.' He smiled, then looked around at his fellow-ministers and transferred the smile to them.

They all saw how Sabbatai Zvi trembled.

'There is what we call the horse treatment,' Hayatizadé went on. 'This we use when our hangman is on holiday. The poor victim is attached to a frisky horse – we train them especially for this purpose. The victim is naked, and the horse drags him at a gallop. Sometimes he stops, and the victim thinks it's all over. But not for long,' Hayatizadé laughed. 'He's off again. At a canter maybe. It's a slow death, that. Slow and infinitely painful.' He paused again. 'But this week,' he laughed, 'the horses have gone to stud. And our hangman's on holiday. So what do we have for you, Sabbatai Zvi?' Another pause. 'Something very special. Because you, Sabbatai Zvi, are a very special person. You are, after all, or so you say you are, the Messiah. Your followers say there is a light about you. A divine illumination. Alas, we poor mortals in this Chamber cannot see it. So we will make our own lights. Poor by comparison, of course. We will have to make do with burning torches.' He had to pause then because Sabbatai crumbled. He cried out in pain, as if his flesh was already afire. But Hayatizadé chose to press on.

'We shall tie a burning torch to each of your limbs, and wait for the divine illumination to put out the fires. But . . .' he shouted.

Sabbatai raised his head. Was there a hope in that 'but'? Did that 'but' presage a choice? For anything, anything on earth was better than the fire.

Hayatizadé was now taking his time. He had won, he knew. The rest was pure pleasure. He leaned forward, almost touching his victim's face. 'I was a Jew like you. Once,' he said. 'But I was shown the light. My kind of light. My kind of truth. The only truth. I took the turban, and I was saved. Not from death. But from a life of darkness.'

He crossed over and stood by Sabbatai's side. 'We are offering you your life,' he said. 'And something else. And both offers are indivisible. We offer you the truth of Islam. If you want to live, you must cease publicly and privately to be a Jew.' He turned and went back to his seat. He looked towards the Sultan who gave him an almost imperceptible nod of approval.

Sabbatai opened his mouth to speak and Nathan feared the words that he would utter.

'May we have a little time together? Privately?' Nathan asked.

Köprülü spoke. 'You may retire to the back of the Chamber,' he said. 'But we will not wait long. A decision must be made within the hour.'

Sabbatai was loth to leave his interrogators. As far as he was concerned, he was prepared to snatch the nearest turban, shout 'Allah' three times, and take himself off to the biggest mosque and pray there for ever. Nathan had practically to drag him to the back of the hall.

They huddled together. Nathan was the first to speak or rather to whisper, not wishing to be overheard.

'It's impossible,' he said. 'Conversion is out of the question.'

'D'you want me to go the fire?' Sabbatai's voice was raised. Suddenly his spirits had risen too. With the prospect of reprieve, his melancholy had lifted, and already he began to programme his life as a Moslem. 'Conversion is God's bidding,' he said.

'You are mistaken, Master,' Nathan said. 'To bow to the turban would mark the end of the Sabbataian movement. Martyrdom is the only answer. And afterwards you are assured of a place on the right hand of God.'

'But first there is the fire,' Sabbatai said.

'He must convert. There's no alternative,' Elijah had stepped forward. 'I forbid his martyrdom. Do you hear me?' he shouted at Nathan.

'You are not a follower,' Nathan said. 'You have no say in this matter.'

'He must convert.' Now it was Joseph's turn. 'And I shall follow him.'

'So will we all,' the Rabbis said.

But David Arditti stood on one side, and said nothing.

Nathan was outnumbered. 'Then I shall go into the wilderness, Sabbatai,' he said, 'and I shall try to carry your torch.'

At the mention of torches, Sabbatai turned to face the Council. Slowly he walked towards the assembly. They marvelled at the change in him. His gait was upright, and though they would fain shut their eyes to it, there was an undoubted light around his head. Even the Sultan could see it. We have converted the Messiah to Islam, he thought, and his crown trembled once more. Sabbatai took the skull-cap from his head, and laid it on the table. Then he spoke. His voice was firm and bright as an angel's.

'I ask for the turban,' he said.

A white turban was ready, set on a silk cushion, and alongside it, the Koran. These they placed before him. Then two attendants brought a white kaftan. They helped Sabbatai discard his Jewish gaberdine, and they draped the cape around his shoulders. But first they took away his father's prayer-shawl. Sabbatai's heart turned over as the shawl that sealed the Jew in him was peeled from his soul. This was true apostasy. One of the attendants folded it gently and returned it to him.

'Let it be a memento of your past,' a Council member said. 'A memory of a life of misled worship. Soon you will unfold it and find it as ill-fitting and as alien as a woman's robe.'

There were sighs from the back of the Chamber, both of relief and wonderment. Then a small procession towards the table.

'We follow Sabbatai Zvi,' Joseph said. He was followed by the three Rabbis. Elijah remained at the back of the hall, and by his side, David Arditti. Somewhere aloof, in terrible limbo, stood Nathan of Gaza. It would seem to all three that the movement was at an end. To Elijah, all that mattered was that his brother would live. Nathan speculated on his own future. But David Arditti did not speculate. He knew.

The Sultan now made his presence felt. 'You have done well, Sabbatai Zvi,' he said. 'Henceforth you will be known as Mehmed Effendi, and I offer you the post of Chamberlain to the seraglio.'

Sabbatai felt the beginnings of fever. He was glad of it, because he knew that in fever, anything was possible. Even a God by any other name.

They returned to their quarters in the seraglio where Sabbatai broke the news to Sarah. She accepted it with gratitude and announced her intention to take the Muslim veil. 'We must celebrate,' Sarah said. 'It is a new life for all of us.' And so they caroused into the night. Those who heard them in the seraglio, the Sultan's men, turned a tolerant and deaf ear, considering it a last fling. The celebrations inside Sabbatai's apartment were loud and desperate, so loud and so desperate that nobody noticed that David Arditti was gone.

Not even Sabbatai, who held himself in a corner, aloof from the celebrations. For it was not their joy he would celebrate, but his own. His fever steamed inside him. He looked at the Koran in his hand. Did it not exude on his palm the same Old Testament sweat? He touched his turban and felt on his fevered forehead that same divine stamp that so lately his phylacteries had imprinted. And when tonight he would sleep with God, as his fever bade him, it would be so simple, in their loving and steamy embrace, to call Him Allah.

'There is a terrible silence outside the palace. The silence of news repressed. I saw David Arditti making his way through the crowds. I was tempted to approach him but I could see that he was in no mood to speak. Something has happened inside the palace and I am afraid . . . I do not believe it. I cannot believe it. It is only a rumour after all. I make for the market-place. There the money-changers will know. They must know. Their trade depends on it . . . They are dancing in the market-place. I fear what they celebrate. So afraid am

I that I stifle enquiry. They are singing too, and I cannot help but hear their song.

> *The traitor has taken the turban,*
> *Allah forgives, Allah forgives . . .*

I turned away. The time has come to end my witnessing, that handmaid to survival. I want to witness no more. Tomorrow I shall make my way to the capital, and there hire me a sail.'

18

After the fall

After their celebrations, their last Judaic fling, Sabbatai
asked the revellers to leave him for a while. He needed to
be alone. During the night in his sweated fever, he'd had
a vision of Saul, but it was blurred, teasing and undefined.
In his fertile fever, that vision had sown the seeds of
melancholy, and he knew he would have to dwell on it
alone. He crouched on the floor, and in the ebbing of his
fever a vision appeared. He waited patiently, confident
that it would find its own defined shape and spell out its
undeniable message. He saw himself. As he was. In this
time and space. Crouched too, but in his own prayer-shawl.
He watched the shawl swell slowly with the presence of
another figure facing him in the shawl's embrace. Saul.
The outline of his face was pure in its clarity, its features
shadowed in black. Inconsolable. For a while it stayed
there, its body swelling the contours of the shawl. Sabbatai
watched and waited in terror, for he feared that no prayer-
shawl on earth, no pallium, no surplice, was large enough to
contain the passion between them. He waited, trembling for
its shattering. But almost at breaking point it paused. Then
slowly, very slowly, deflated. Then Sabbatai's terror was
greater, for the passion had not been enough. Not enough
to sustain his wholeness. In abject horror he watched his
sundered identity as the shawl deflated like a grounded
balloon, wrinkled, lifeless and empty by his side. 'I am
gone,' he whispered to himself. 'Saul has taken the greater

part of me.' He whispered Saul's name into the shell of the shawl, and it reverberated with the sounds of the sea.

After he had left Adrianopoli, Saul had made his way to the capital. There he hired a boat and sailed through the narrow strait that led to the Black Sea. He was one of a flotilla of boats brimful of bereaved disciples whose redemption had been so treacherously withdrawn. He sailed on, hugging the coast-line through the strait. The banks were visible on both sides, far too narrow a passage, he decided, in which to give up his ghost. For in such a place his quietus would be visible, investigated, tracked down. They would forage for his provenance and his name. No, he needed the wide open sea, a limitless horizon, a spatial anonymity, in order to pierce a raging hole into the ocean floor. A shoreless grave, marked for a moment with a banal bubble or two, then covered with sublimely indifferent calm.

Towards the end of the strait he had glimpses of that vast Black Sea infinity and he sailed towards it in final preparation. He took himself back to his birthplace at Homel. Into the house where he had been born. Early morning. He remembered that it was dark and a drizzle of rain coated the windows. He would relive each second of that day. He would recall his past, item by item, though he was in no danger of repeating it, for he had no threat of future. He sat each member of the family around the table, his father at its head. He examined his beard minutely, hair by hair almost, as he watched it curl over the white collar capping his chin. Then his side-locks and bush of black hair. He saw its ensemble as a frame of a holy picture. His blue eyes, forever twinkling, even in anger. For it was with anger that he ruled the table that morning. He would not speak of it in front of the children. But they knew. They knew of the killings in the villages. They knew of the firings in the synagogues. They knew the name of Chmielnicki. It was a silent table.

At the other end, his mother. She was serving the oatmeal, ladling the thick stew into each dish. She smiled at them. It was the only comfort left to them. As he conjured her image, he saw for the first time her beauty and he wondered why he had never been struck by it before. But a boy's eye takes a mother's beauty for granted. Now he saw each feature of her face, her black almost almond-shaped eyes, the pointed chin and the tiny mole on her cheek which he was seeing now for the first time. He turned away from her, her beauty unbearable.

Then to Miriam by his side. His little sister. The spoilt one, whom at times he had resented, sulking at the favours lavished on her. His dying would be worth her forgiveness alone.

Then Esther, the middle one, the limbo-child, the loner. Now he saw in her eye the look of prophecy, for she seemed to hear the din of destruction even before its echo. He saw her rise from the table. 'We must hide, Papa,' she said.

They heard the rumblings in the streets and the roaring of the fires.

'Come as you are,' his father had said, 'and follow me.' But before he left the table, Saul remembered how he said the blessing after the meal and the indecent but pardonable haste with which it was bestowed. They'd followed him. Miriam clung to her mother's skirt and nibbled at what was left of her bread. He himself joined his father while Esther walked alone. Their target was clear. The synagogue. As it was clear to hundreds of others who ran in panic towards the temple. When they saw his father they crowded around him, as if the proximity of a Rabbi would afford them shelter. He led them into the synagogue praying all the while, and murmuring the 'Shema', that prayer that would do for life as well as death. They crowded inside, and when they attempted to bar the doors, he remembered how his father forbade them.

'The house of God is always open,' he had said.

And as it turned out, it was open to Chmielnicki and his armed ragged following. Saul remembered one of them, a young boy, his finger trembling on the trigger, his soft lips drooling with the foretaste of quarry. Chmielnicki's voice had pierced the sudden silence of fear.

'Turn to Christ and you will be spared.'

Then his father walked slowly to the platform and turned to face the congregation. He was smiling.

'Let us remember those who have already died for our faith,' he said. 'And let us pray.'

It was enough for them. Those who had prayer-shawls covered themselves and their families as if they were shrouds. The 'Shema' was heard across the hall. And the shooting began.

Saul stood upright in his boat and loosened the sail. He did not want to remember what followed. But he knew that without total recall, his death would be a fraud. Even as he stood, he felt a tugging at his trousers. Little Miriam, seeking his protection. And roughly he had loosened her hand, and crawled through the seats, over the bodies of those who had already fallen, making his way to that door that his father had forbidden them to close. The house of God is open for those who will enter, but also for those who would leave. Once again, he saw the empty street, silent, sealed witness to the massacre. And he had run. Run for his young life. Stopping his ears from the screams that pierced his heels with terror. And he ran and ran. Into the fields, across the ditches. And still he heard the screaming.

Now, in the midst of a calm sea, his sails furled, he heard those screams again, and he was glad of it, for they were fitting orchestration to his own welcome if tardy martyrdom. He was glad the sea was calm. He wanted no storms to signify accident. He was taking his life with utmost deliberation. And by drowning. For by that method there was no way that he could save himself. Then he thought of Sabbatai who had teased him often enough for his inability to swim. But he did not want Sabbatai to be his last thought.

He lowered himself over the side of the boat and he began the 'Shema'. With that prayer, he was shipped right back into the synagogue and the bullet-riddled bosom of his family. As the water covered his head, he made no effort to rise. He did not thrash his arms or curl his legs. He straightened his body to facilitate the descent. He felt no pain, and though his ears were deaf to life, he heard the screaming still. And then it faded, and Saul was at peace.

In his crouched prison, Sabbatai uttered a cry of pain. A cry in labour, as if he were giving reluctant birth to his soul. 'Saul is dead,' he whispered to himself, 'and has taken my very spirit.' He wrapped his father's shawl around his body. Now it was too large for him. He could have wrapped it round his soulless frame a thousand times. Even a simple handkerchief would have been too large to package his shrunken spirit. He crouched in his corner and mourned his own demise.

When David Arditti left the seraglio, he was recognised by the crowd outside as one of their Saviour's chief disciples.

'What news? What news?' they asked him.

But he was silent. He would tell them nothing. He could not, for he himself could not believe it. Yet he had seen Sabbatai take the Koran in his hand; he had seen the turban placed on his head. But he willed them both to be his own deluded vision. All that he was certain of was the 'tallis' around Sabbatai's shoulders. He would blind himself to any other image.

'No news, no news,' he managed to say, and he threaded his way through the multitudes and felt deeply sorry for them. He felt alien, isolated. He was not one of those followers any more. He wanted to walk amongst those who had always been strangers and thus find amongst them a common alienation. He found his way to the Bedestin, the covered bazaar on the outskirts of the town. There he wandered from stall to stall, hearing the language of the invader, of that intruder into his faith. Of that coloniser, he had to admit to himself, of that conqueror. But he, David

Arditti, would not be colonised. He would go underground, and like Nathan, carry Sabbatai's torch into the wilderness.

But what was breaking his heart was the thought that Sabbatai's mission was now barely worth a candle, for its light, no matter how dim, could only illuminate a monstrous betrayal, and on such a vast scale, it was barely imaginable. Once again he saw the turban and the Koran, but now the prayer-shawl had faded and he knew it was because it could not sustain the competition. Though he knew that Sabbatai's apostasy would wreak havoc in the world-wide Jewish community, though he knew that a thousand hearts would break, he thought only of the personal betrayal. Sabbatai had rejected him once, and that had been painful enough. He considered this last rejection unbearable. For infidelity of the flesh, with all its anguish, can eventually be understood. And even forgiven. But to commit adultery with the spirit is unpardonable. He had nothing in his life any more; no faith, no love and no future to believe in.

He found himself on the banks of the river Maritsa, and although he didn't know the city, and had never come to this spot before, he knew that he had nosed it out with a martyr's desperate need. He would in no way prepare. In his mind was no preamble of nostalgia. He steeled his heart against any recall. For he knew his past to be inexpressibly futile. A fleeting thought of his now mercifully dead parents aroused a sickening pity, so grievous that it only served to quicken his steps to the water's edge.

The river ran swiftly that day, and promised depth and quick oblivion. He moved easily into its current and lay in the perilous cradle. As it rocked him downstream, and finally turned its offended and unnatural cargo, David thought he saw Saul coming to greet him.

That voluntary exit of David Arditti was the first of hundreds that followed Sabbatai's apostasy. The Turks were quick to spread the news of the conversion. It was their coup after all. Those close to Sabbatai tried to keep it quiet, or at most to claim that it was a vicious rumour. The bombshell took its time to detonate, and to disperse its lethal load throughout Europe. It allowed time for myth and legend to generate, and all kinds of rationale to validate the catastrophic event. Most of Sabbatai's followers had, over the past years, fashioned their whole lives to a future of redemption. They could not easily forfeit such a future. Besides, there was no replacement. They *had* to believe that Sabbatai Zvi was their Messiah, else their whole past was entirely negated.

Some fashioned a mystical reason for the apostasy. It was not Sabbatai Zvi who wore the turban. It was his shadow. He himself had ascended to heaven, there to wait a while until his people had truly repented. Then he would return. But those followers who could not accept this explanation returned to the bosoms of the old Rabbis with sickness in their hearts. However they sought or did not seek to explain it, in the very depth of their beings they knew that the apostasy was the end.

For a while Sabbatai kept to his apartments in the seraglio and bade everyone to call him by his Muslim name. But when he heard it, he shivered. In private he prayed with the Koran in one hand and the Torah in the other. Sometimes with the phylacteries on his forehead, and always with his father's 'tallis' wrapped about him. But when his followers joined him in the seraglio he put his Jewish trappings aside.

Nathan had left with the intent of travelling around Europe promoting the god-head of Sabbatai Zvi. For him the promotion itself was now the crusade. Elijah returned to Smyrna. He could not help thinking that, of all of them, he, who had never believed, was the only true Jew amongst them.

There are many versions of Sabbatai's life after the apostasy and each account relies heavily on its own rationale. Most agree that he took another wife in accordance with Moslem law, and no doubt Sarah schooled her in the art of non-expectation. He is said to have travelled often to Constantinople, ostensibly to convert his people to the Crescent. To this end he preached in synagogues, but behind those holy doors he discarded the Koran. Rumour spread of his deception and he was finally arrested and banished with his followers. His palace of exile was Dulcigno, nowadays known as Ulcinj, on the southernmost tip of Yugoslavia.

After his fall from other people's grace, Sabbatai was much alone. In his fevers which, since the turban, had become more and more frequent, he was convinced of his god-head and shouted it aloud. But in the chasms of melancholy that followed, he hugged his father's shawl around him, and realised with horror the obscene depth of his betrayal. He recalled the early years of his mission and the adulation and faith of his followers. Now in his exile and treachery, he choked with solitude. All the time Joseph was at his side, unsurprised as always by his brother's fevers and visions, and holding him in their black aftermath.

'You are a saint, Joseph,' Sabbatai said to him one day.

'Jews have no saints,' Joseph laughed.

'But everything is different now,' Sabbatai said, and began to plait the fringes of the shawl.

In the summer of 1675, Sabbatai, in fever, asked Joseph to send for Elijah.

'I have had a vision,' he said. 'God came to me in a blinding light and promised that He would take me into His kingdom on the Day of Atonement. He is allowing the time for Elijah to come to me.'

Joseph at once sent letters to Smyrna. When, years before, the news of Sabbatai's apostasy was filtering through the Jewish world, the town of Smyrna, like a parent, was the last to hear. Like a parent, it refused to believe. Then it rationalised with a cunning above all the rest. And, like a parent, it remained loyal for ever. The Ardittis had mercifully died before the apostasy. Like Mordecai perhaps, they had chosen their proper season so that they would be beyond the pain of their son's mourning. But Elijah had heard of David's death, and for him it was the sole and saddest proof of Sabbatai's betrayal. And he mourned David Arditti as he would a brother.

When Elijah received Sabbatai's summons, he knew it to be a bidding to his death-bed. Although he had never believed in Sabbatai's god-head, he had been impressed at times by his instinctive sense of prophecy. He made immediate arrangements to travel to his brother's exile. But first he broke the news to Aunt Sarah. She had aged well, her years fuelled by Nahum's love. Lusi had died shortly after her Saviour's fall. She would accept no reason for his apostasy. No myth, no legend. Sabbatai Zvi had personally betrayed her. She would never forgive herself for the trust she had placed in him. One day, shortly after she heard the news, she had lain on her bed and died of sheer disappointment and blighted hope. When Nahum held her body in his arms, he felt its life-time emptiness, its frozen, soured heart, and in her starved features, he saw the face of utter deprivation. He would let no one touch her. He himself carried out the ritual washing, although it was against the Law. Then he held her in his arms again and would not let her go. It was Aunt Sarah who gently prised her rival from his embrace. Thereafter he had mourned at Aunt Sarah's house, and accepted her solace and her love which slowly he had learned to return again.

When Aunt Sarah and Nahum heard of Sabbatai's summons, they, like Elijah, knew that it was to his death-bed. There were two months left to heed God's bidding, but before he left Smyrna, Elijah went to visit his parents' graves. He did not expect a revelation of any kind. He was a devout Jew who did not believe in any cloud-cuckoo-land hereafter. He did not expect voices from the graves. The dead were dead. He believed in that finality. So he could not account for the euphoria that overwhelmed him as he entered the cemetery, nor the joy in his heart as he stood by their graves. He crouched beside them, strewing pebbles over their stones. 'Sabbatai will soon be with you,' he said. He knew that his joy came from inside himself, prompted by his acceptance of the certain death of the brother he had loved all his life and beyond reason. At last there would be an end to Sabbatai's pain. An end to the fevers and inconsolable uncertainties, an end to his desolate doubts. God had been cruel to his brother, Elijah thought. His only kindness would be to put an end to his pain.

When he left Smyrna, a multitude of his brother's disciples gathered on the quay-side to wish him well. They had heard of the summons, and they too had understood that the end was near. Many of them were relieved, for however credible the rationale, death was more acceptable than apostasy. So they wished him well, singing Sabbatai's psalm, as his ship sailed out of harbour. Elijah heard its echo long after the shore-line had slipped his sight and he realised, perhaps for the first time, how thoroughly his brother had convulsed the Jewish spirit.

The sailing took two weeks. At first Elijah was grateful for the time allowed to him for preparation to meet his brother's end. But then, towards the end of the journey, as the ship skirted Dubrovnik, he grew impatient and fearful that he would not be in time. The last sea-miles were endless, and he stood on the deck throughout the night and day, willing harbour. At last Dulcigno came in sight and he started shouting his brother's name. 'Wait for me, wait for me, Sabbatai,' he pleaded. 'I need you by my side.'

He fretted by the rail, inching the ship into port. When it arrived, he leapt down, impatient of the gangway, and made his frantic way through the streets of his brother's exile.

It was early morning and the light was dim. He heard a cock crow in the distance. He had no idea of the day for his wakeful nights had blurred his calendar. He had his brother's address, but he trusted no stranger to direct him. He passed a synagogue. Its doors were open and he

knew that whoever was inside would safely direct him
to his brother's house. He went inside. A lone figure
stood on the platform. Its back was towards him, bent
over the lectern, and shivering in prayer. Elijah had the
impression that whoever it was had been there for ever.
He watched for a while and listened, and shortly deciphered
the prayer for the New Year. Then he knew that he had
but nine days' grace until the Day of Atonement. He
listened, and the voice soared. His brother's voice, without
a doubt, ringing oddly like a boy's out of the body of an old
man.

He did not trust himself to go to him. His heart stuttered
its sadness. He watched, containing himself until the prayer
was over. Then Sabbatai turned, as if sensing someone
behind him, and from where he stood, Elijah could see
the beads of sweat, full yet stock-still, on his brother's
brow. They looked at one another for a moment, then
magnetically moved, neared, and reached out for touch.

'The prophet Elijah has come for me,' Sabbatai said.

Then they held each other close and the heat of Sabbatai's
body almost burned his brother's flesh.

'The sun is inside me', Sabbatai said. 'I am already
half-way to heaven.'

They looked at each other and saw the leap of ten years'
absence. And both wished that they had been there to see
the creases fold on the face, to watch daily, yet unseeing,
how time would reap its irresistible harvest. They forgave
the years and embraced.

'You arrive for the New Year, Elijah,' Sabbatai said.

'Do you celebrate our New Year still? Ours, that was
once yours?'

'It has never ceased to be mine,' Sabbatai said. He was
calm suddenly. 'I have never ceased to be a Jew.'

Elijah was astonished. Although at the time, ten years
before, he had insisted on his brother's conversion, it had
been for the sole purpose of saving his life. But he had never
believed that that was Sabbatai's purpose. His brother's

Messianic fever was so intense, that it could have sweated from the brow of any god-head, Allah included.

'Listen to me,' Sabbatai said. 'There are many ways of reaching Jerusalem. The turban is only a detour, an extra station on our crusade. For me, the apostasy was God's bidding. He ordered that I enter the world of Islam in order to convert it wholesale to Judaism. The turban is fancy-dress. Temporal, trivial. Beneath it I can still weave my Messianic return. Do you doubt me still, Elijah?'

'I have never not believed in you as my brother,' Elijah said.

'Then you must wear the turban. I keep it by me,' Sabbatai said. He drew it out from under his kaftan. 'It keeps at bay the evil spirits,' he said. 'For it itself is evil.' Then he laughed, handing the turban to his brother. 'Wear it for me,' he said. 'Even as Saul would take my fever. Where is Saul?' he asked. 'And where is David? Did they marry in their treachery? Come,' he said. 'Let us go home. Not to Smyrna, but to my exile. God has made your brother a Turk,' he said, 'and I have left my visions under my pillow.'

Elijah held his arm. 'Let it not be long,' he prayed. 'Let God take him soon in his mania while the fever is still upon him. Let him rise to his own heaven in his sweated joy, and never know that there is nothing more but darkness for ever.'

Sabbatai practically skipped along the street, waving his turban with contempt. Elijah was glad that only the odd passer-by could see him. Again a cock crew, and Sabbatai took up the cry. 'They are all calling me,' he said.

The house was on the sea's edge. He had come full circle.

'You never swam with me, Elijah,' Sabbatai said.

'Once. When Grandma Beki was ill. D'you remember? The day of the miracle.' Elijah would give him that.

'It was not my first miracle you know,' Sabbatai said. 'I resurrected Saul. In Constantinople. In the market-place.'

How painfully Saul's memory must haunt him, Elijah thought.

'Will you come into the sea with me?' Sabbatai asked. 'It still holds the warmth of summer.'

Elijah would refuse him nothing, and together they stripped on the sands. It was not just his brow that was in fever, Elijah noticed. His brother's body was pin-pricked all over with sweat and he felt his relief as he watched him wallow in the waves. Elijah followed him, his simple pious body, with no divine protection, shivering on the water's edge.

'Let us swim to the rocks,' Sabbatai shouted.

Elijah plunged and followed his brother. Both in their silent and separate strokes were recalling their quarrelsome and loving Smyrna childhood. For both it was a preparation for the Day of Atonement, the final forgiveness of each other, so that the grief of bereavement is not prolonged by guilt. When they reached the rocks, they submerged, each to their own silence. Then, holding that silence, they swam back to the shore. They dressed and did not speak until they reached the house.

'Joseph will be happy to see you,' Sabbatai said, as he opened the door.

Elijah saw that it was a simple dwelling, not unlike their first home in Smyrna. Bare of everything but what was necessary, and smelling of the warmth and anguish of family. Joseph looked drawn and tired, and Elijah knew that he had already begun to mourn. They embraced. Their loving would help them endure. Sarah and Sabbatai's second wife, who seemed like his first two futile brides not to have a name, twittered like sisters in joy of Elijah's coming.

'Come, let us make a feast,' Sarah said.

'I shall not eat again,' Sabbatai announced, 'until the eve of the Day of Atonement. Then I shall break my fast to gather strength for my last journey. I want you all to come with me to the edge of the night. Then you shall bury my body where the Jews lay, with Jewish prayers, and out of hearing of the muezzin, and out of sight of the mosque.'

When he spoke, the beads of sweat inflated, and heat shone from his eyes. Joseph saw the circle of light around his head. And so did Sarah and the other one. But not Elijah.

Over the next few days, Sabbatai kept to his room. Occasionally he asked for water but no food passed his lips. They heard him praying and the constant creak of the floor-boards as he rocked his path to God's ear. On the fifth day, he went into the streets. On his head he wore a turban, but his phylacteries were bound about his arm and forehead. His father's prayer-shawl was wrapped around his white kaftan, and in his hand he carried the Koran.

'Remember the Second Coming,' he shouted. 'Soon I shall take my leave, so that I may come again. For I am the Messiah, Sabbatai Zvi, I shall return when your penance is done.'

Joseph and Elijah followed him all the way, as he took his cry through the crowded streets of Dulcigno and into the teeming market-place. Elijah feared he would be arrested, despite the turban on his head, and the Koran in his hand. For his message was treason. People stopped and listened, but shrugging, let him pass. They made gangways for him, and some actually patted his turbaned head with pity. He had become Raphael the idiot of Dulcigno.

Elijah's heart turned. He had always known his brother was not whole. He and his father had shared that painful certainty. But to have it publicly acknowledged, with gestures of pity and benign tolerance, only increased that pain, and he wanted to slap those hands of compassion and bid them leave his brother's madness inside the bosom of his own family.

They followed him as he made his way towards the sea. At the water's edge he stood and raised his arms. They saw him trembling and they rushed to his side. His eyes were brighter than the sun and they were filled with tears. But like the beads of sweat on his forehead, they did not break, but stood on the rim of his eye for a while, before properly going back to where they came from. It was the first time in his life that Elijah had seen his brother close to weeping. Then Sabbatai opened his mouth to speak, holding it ajar for a while. The sound that came out was blotted by the roll of the waves but it persisted in crescendo until it would have out-sung a roll of thunder. Just one single word. One loaded syllable of grief. One harrowing cry of pain. 'Saul!'

And in its cry, the waves broke, astonished.

They held him, his two whole brothers, and led him home. 'In two more days, I shall begin my return,' he said. Elijah kept his eye on the beads of sweat on Sabbatai's forehead. Still solid and inexplodable. He was relieved. His brother's manic illusion was assured. It would light his way to heaven.

Once home, Sabbatai retired to his room and his prayers. No one of them persuaded him to break his fast, for food was known to trim the edges of his light, and lead to the darkness of melancholy. They heard him praying, and his voice was strong, and his rocking a lunatic's lullaby. Thus he prayed through the night until the dawn of the Day of Atonement. 'Now go to the synagogue and pray for me,' he told them. 'Tell them all to prepare for the Second Coming. That they should fast on the day of my death, and rejoice on the day of my birth, for on that day I shall come again.'

When they had gone, Sabbatai went down to the sea for the last time. There, naked on the sands, he scourged himself, whipping his body over the edges of pain. He plunged into the sea, his fever higher than ever before, heightened by his cleansing. Then he made his joyful and psalmed way home.

When the brothers returned, Sabbatai was still at prayer. Elijah watched him and marvelled at his strength and endurance. There was no reason why his brother should die of natural causes. Yet he knew that he would die before night came. He was willing his own death, even as their father had chosen his own season.

'Soon I shall break my fast,' Sabbatai said. 'But first you must wash my body and shroud me.'

This his brothers did, praying all the while. Then they laid him on his bed and held his hands, not to lead him into his darkness, but to share his peace. Sabbatai called for Sarah and the other one. They came, bringing sweetmeats, but he pushed them aside. 'Bring me the turban,' he said. 'And a knife and a plate.' They wondered at his request, but did not question it. When it was brought, he took the knife and cut the turban slowly and meticulously into small pieces. The procedure took some time and was carried out in silence. They all watched him, appalled. When it was done, he heaped the pieces on to the plate, then looked about him, satisfied.

'I shall break my fast on the turban,' he said. 'With it, I shall put away all my transgressions, all my sins. It has done what God ordered it to do. Now it must be consumed.'

He picked up his first slice of turban and, without a prayer, for it merited no blessing, he put it in his mouth. 'Thus I consume Islam,' he said.

He chewed a while, then swallowed and took water to aid its digestion. Thus, piece by piece, and over many hours, he devoured that trap of faith that had been set to waylay him, and when it was done, he was cleansed once more.

'Now bring me Papa's "tallis",' he said.

Joseph and Elijah wrapped it about him. Then Sabbatai unplaited its fringes, those metronomes of his pain, and smoothed them out gently. Then he turned on his side and crooked his arm on his back, into that infantile crater, that milk caress.

'Return every man to his home,' he said. 'How long will you hold fast to me?'

Those were his last hopeless words. Elijah grasped Joseph's hand as they looked at their dead brother. They watched the myriad beads of sweat on his brow, and saw how at last they burst and washed his face with those tears he had rarely been able to shed. He lay there in the truth of his father's unplaited prayer-shawl, and in the loving of his mother's embrace. At last he had offered amnesty to them both.

The final fragment of Saul's parchments was found amongst Sabbatai's papers after his death.

'. . . and so my beloved so-more-than-brother Sabbatai. We are as one. Married in our separate treacheries. You have become as I myself. Once I was your mirror-image. Now you are mine, and I cannot bear the reflection. So I go to my end. Without witness. Let my spectacle make of nobody a survivor. I go to Kingdom Come, where my father is waiting.'

GO TELL THE
LEMMING

Bernice Rubens

'Dear Angela. I can't stand it any more, so I'm going to put my head in the gas oven . . .'

For Angela Morrow the death of her marriage is the ultimate in rejection. She debates whether to address her suicide note to her parents, to her son or to David, her defecting husband – and ends up writing it to herself. In fact, Angela writes to Angela rather a lot.

But David, a successful film producer, is beginning to prefer Angela's unpredictability to the vacuous calm of his mistress. he invites her to work on locations in his new film. So Angela postpones killing herself and goes instead to Rome . . .

Also by Bernice Rubens in Abacus:

KINGDOM COME
MATE IN THREE
SET ON EDGE
BROTHERS
MR WAKEFIELD'S CRUSADE
OUR FATHER
BIRDS OF PASSAGE
I SENT A LETTER TO MY LOVE
SUNDAY BEST
PONSONBY POST
THE ELECTED MEMBER
FIVE YEAR SENTENCE
MADAME SOUSATZKA
SPRING SONATA

0 349 10147 7
ABACUS FICTION

☐	MATE IN THREE	BERNICE RUBENS	£4.99
☐	SET ON EDGE	BERNICE RUBENS	£4.99
☐	BROTHERS	BERNICE RUBENS	£5.99
☐	MR WAKEFIELD'S CRUSADE	BERNICE RUBENS	£4.99
☐	OUR FATHER	BERNICE RUBENS	£4.99
☐	BIRDS OF PASSAGE	BERNICE RUBENS	£4.99
☐	SUNDAY BEST	BERNICE RUBENS	£4.99
☐	PONSONBY POST	BERNICE RUBENS	£4.99
☐	ELECTED MEMBER	BERNICE RUBENS	£4.99
☐	SPRING SONATA	BERNICE RUBENS	£4.99
☐	FIVE YEAR SENTENCE	BERNICE RUBENS	£4.99
☐	MADAME SOUSATZKA	BERNICE RUBENS	£4.99

Abacus now offers an exciting range of quality titles by both established and new authors. All of the books in this series are available from:
Sphere Books, Cash Sales Department,
P.O. Box 11,
Falmouth,
Cornwall TR10 9EN

Alternatively you may fax your order to the above address. Fax No. 0326 376423.

Payments can be made as follows: Cheque, postal order (payable to Macdonald & Co (Publishers) Ltd) or by credit cards, Visa/Access. Do not send cash or currency. UK customers and B.F.P.O.: please send a cheque or postal order (no currency) and allow £1.00 for postage and packing for the first book, plus 50p for the second book, plus 30p for each additional book up to a maximum charge of £3.00 (7 books plus).

Overseas customers including Ireland, please allow £2.00 for postage and packing for the first book, plus £1.00 for the second book, plus 50p for each additional book.

NAME (Block Letters) ....

ADDRESS ....

....

☐ I enclose my remittance for   _____

☐ I wish to pay by Access/Visa Card

Number ☐☐☐☐☐☐☐☐☐☐☐☐☐☐☐☐☐☐

Card Expiry Date ☐☐☐☐